A Casual Temptation

by

Stephen Barrett

For permission requests, please contact:
stephen.barrett@gmx.net

ISBN: 978-3-9826188-1-4

Find out more about the author and upcoming books at Facebook: stephen.barrett.author, or Instagram: stephenbarrett_writer

Produced in United Kingdom.

About the Author

Stephen Barrett has spent more than thirty-five years working in the financial services industry in the UK, Germany and across Europe. Writing has been his passion for many years, and *A Casual Temptation* is his first novel based on the many diverse experiences gained in his long career.

Stephen lives in Düsseldorf and spends as much time as possible in Worthing, which despite the many years he´s been away, is still very much his home.

Dedication

I dedicate this book to my wife, Anja, my family and
close friends – you know who you are – for their love
and support in making

A Casual Temptation

come true.

Author's Note

If financial crime is measured in dollars, euros and pounds, it's probably the biggest industry in the world.

The perpetrators of financial crime never sleep. And their creativity never slackens.

Between 1994 and 1999, German entrepreneur Manfred Schmider initiated one of the biggest fraud schemes ever created. He founded FlowTex, a company that developed horizontal drilling machines for laying cables and pipelines. At first, the company aimed to develop a sound business model before Schmider and several other perpetrators developed a fraud scheme selling non-existent machines to a consortium of banks. For this, they organised on-site demonstrations, moving the same equipment from one site to the other and wildly exaggerating the number of machines they could produce and sell. They manipulated documents and identification plates (serial numbers) to achieve this. The banks were only too willing to fund the operations, resulting in a staggering EUR 3.7 billion worth of damages. This inspired the fraud described in part one of this book.

Invoice fraud is one of the biggest areas of fraud today. The total volume of damages resulting from invoice fraud was estimated to amount to a staggering USD 12 billion in 2022.

The manipulation of software described in this book is based on a true event. The targeted bank preferred to keep quiet about the manipulation due to the possible impact on reputation and a loss of trust in their customer base. These days, cyber-attacks, focusing on hijacking IT systems and forcing companies to pay ransoms, are a new and more successful trend. According to a recent survey, damage resulting from cyber-attacks amounted to more than EUR 200 billion in the European Union in 2022.

As so often in life, truth is stranger than fiction.

Part One

1

I stand in front of the bathroom mirror. The face looking back at me is ashen with dark rings under the eyes. God, I'll never get the job, looking like this, anguish rising like bile. My thoughts return to the night – I'd given up on sleep at 3 a.m. Just too nervous. Tossing and turning, running through the interview in my mind: potential angles of questions, possible answers that will convince Willem that I'm the best candidate. Why do you think you are the man for this job? I was exhausted after twelve rounds in the ring with this question. Adding to my nervousness, I have been asked to come in for an interview with Willem de Vries, CEO of Hamlays. This surprised me as I'd gone through the motions with Kevin Sunderland, the boss of the Key Account Team and HR. Why the CEO wants to interview me for this position is beyond me.

I hear the coffee percolator burbling away in the kitchen. The familiar scent drifts through from the kitchen and makes me relax just that little bit. I'd chucked in an extra spoonful of coffee and I know the coffee will be too strong, but I need to get awake. I showered, letting the hot water run over me for a few comforting minutes before turning the hot water tap off and gasping under the ice-cold water. I shaved carefully, making sure I didn't cut myself. Applying thick cream, I check for razor burn. Looking good, I think, trying an engaging smile as I mentally grasp Willem's hand.

"Neil Wilson," I say to my reflection, "so good to see you."

I look in on Emma; she's still fast asleep. Curled up under her duvet, all I see is her blonde hair. I made sure not to disturb her as I climbed out of bed, but she sleeps like a rock anyway. I walk across to the kitchen where I'd laid out my new suit, shirt and tie. My new cap-toe Oxfords stand gleaming by the kitchen chair. I dress, sipping coffee as I complete each step of the process. I want to get everything just right. It takes me three attempts to get the knot on my tie right, perfectly aligned with the glossy black belt of my trousers. I tick off the checklist in my head. I take up position in front of the mirror in the hallway. Perfect. Again, I try the smile: confident, not arrogant – the right dose of self-assuredness. First impressions are so vital. A memory flashes up in my head. My mum watching *An Officer and Gentleman* with Richard Gere. "Oh, look at him in that smart white uniform," she'd exclaimed. Yes, I feel a bit like that. In corporate finance, the suit is the uniform.

I go through the motions of making toast, which I know I won't be able to eat. I try but my stomach refuses to accommodate it. Sitting at the kitchen table, sipping the last of my second mug of coffee, I play through the interview once more in my mind: the likely questions and the most convincing answers. I'm nervous as hell despite telling myself again and again to relax. But it's not just any job interview. For me, this is the big thing. This is the job

I've wanted all along. A big step up from ordinary sales guy to key account manager. From First Division to Premier League. I feel so excited, exhilarated even, at the prospect of leaving the ranks and becoming…what? An officer and a gentleman? I raise my coffee cup to toast Mum. She'd just love that.

As I sit munching little bites of my toast, memories of family and home pop into my head. Dad, always the patriarch, sitting at the head of the table at mealtime, dispensing his worldview. Stiff, unloving, an engineer with a strong right arm when it came to dealing out justice and instilling discipline. Always grumpy, at least in my memory. The most expensive three minutes of fun, he'd said to me once, blaming me for the botched-up vasectomy that should have ensured me never being born. Mum, a kind, patient and permanently worn-out housewife. I can see her in the kitchen, making endless towers of marmite on toast or apple crumble with custard or tackling mountains of ironing, engulfed in steam from the iron with the big water tank. Images of my brothers come into my mind, making me smile. Me, the youngest of four lads, snotty-nosed and always bruised from the heavy play three older brothers inflicted. I wonder what my dad would say to me if he could see me. Long dead now, stricken down by a premature heart attack.

"Yes, what would you say, Dad?" I ask the ghost of his memory, my voice suddenly loud in the quiet of the morning.

I have trouble conjuring up a face by now. He's been gone too long. But the memories of our fights still linger. I loved him; I hated him. I think he didn't bother *seeing* me. Our biggest fight still riles me. That episode is so vivid in my mind to this day.

3

Admittedly, I was a lazy sod at university. "A business degree?" he'd asked when I told him my plans. "Fine with me," he'd said. My other brothers had made him proud. I was the last in line to get myself sorted and leave the house.

The thing was, I'd never been ambitious. I was too busy leading a life of partying, socialising and getting to know the female students. University was a cesspool of sin and alcohol, and I nearly screwed it all up. I got a girl pregnant, or so I thought, and failed too many exams as a result. Before that, I'd been coasting through and fairly relaxed about it all. No worries, a comfortable lower second would be mine at this rate.

I can still see my dad standing in the kitchen, looking at me or, better said, screaming at me through his eyes. His face is red and contorted; never had I seen him so enraged. At first, no words came out, but then, like storm clouds out to sea, the thunderstorm rose like an anvil, readying itself to unleash its energy. The hammer that came crashing down was meant to smash me. He threatened, and he almost became physically violent at my show of indifference to his rage. Of course, I was petrified underneath, but I was determined not to show it. He had the upper hand – he was funding my university course – but being young and stupid, I gave him the mental up yours. He'd shown little interest in me so far, and to this day I'm not sure whether his outrage was greater at my getting this girl into trouble or whether it was about me becoming a potential uni dropout. For my dad, appearances were paramount, even if we were middle-class nobodies. My dad had his peculiar moral compass. Getting a girl pregnant didn't rank as high as having a son who might become a uni dropout.

It was my Uncle George who came to the rescue. He took Dad and me down to Shoreham for a weekend's sailing on his yacht. He'd recently bought her. A second-hand Beneteau Oceanis 320, a 32-foot sloop. He called her *Florence* and spent hours looking after her. Uncle George took us out into the Channel. The wind was good and he made us work the sails, forcing us to work together as a team. Reluctantly at first, but Dad and I gelled after a while and performed well together, trimming the sails just perfect. The wind increased; we had a force five by midday. The leaning angle increased and Uncle George got us sweating. We were sliding around in the cockpit, the salty sea spray showering us every time we hit a wave. "Wet sailing" Uncle George called it, and he loved it. Finally, we returned to the marina, physically exhausted but mentally refreshed. After dinner, Uncle George coached Dad and me through our unresolved fight. I remember well the way he did it, and I am still impressed. He guided and cajoled us, never forcing a solution on us but letting us work out the solution for ourselves. He had it all sorted of course. It taught me a valuable lesson, and I have tried to use his technique in many a business scenario with clients or colleagues.

Fortunately, the girl hadn't been pregnant after all, and now it was down to getting university sorted. We made a deal that night, sitting in the cockpit of his yacht in the Lady Bee Marina in Shoreham, drinking beer and wine and, later on, rum, which I hate. We made the deal that saw me become studious and antisocial. My drinking buddies and party pals soon gave up on me as I forced myself to focus on accounting, controlling and corporate finance. My only social life was working behind the bar in the local pub, earning extra income to lessen my dependence on my dad's funding. "Just get that degree" was the deal I'd made with my dad. Uncle George put in his bit, promising he could fix me up with a bank called Hamlays. I applied myself to the task and quite unexpectedly, I got interested in the mechanics of corporate finance, the creativity and the innovative products available to those who understood their benefit. I discovered ambition and drive within myself. I never knew I had it in me.

And now, here I am, five years down the line. I'd got my degree, Uncle George let his connections play and I started work as a junior sales representative for Hamlays Asset Finance Ltd. I'd performed well in those five years, had been successful in generating more and more new business and proven my loyalty. My track record was impeccable and when the position as key account manager came up, I'd told my boss I was applying.

"Go for it, lad," he'd said.

Emma comes into the kitchen, dressed in her oversized pyjamas. Bleary-eyed, still half asleep, she gives me a peck and slumps down in the other chair. I pour her some coffee. It will take a while for Emma to get going. Over the rim of my cup, I look at her – thick blonde hair, light blue eyes and whiter-than-white skin. She never gets brown on holiday, which riles her. She was a cracker when I first met her. Fun to be with, gregarious, always the party girl. She's still a cracker in that she has a nice figure and keeps herself fit. Her hair is shoulder-length now, way too short for my liking, but she says she needs a functional haircut for her work at the charity. But the rest? Well, the gel that has held us together over the years has gone. Emma and I, we're on different wavelengths these days.

"You good?" she mumbles.

"Yep. Fine. Ready."

She raises a questioning eyebrow.

We sit sipping coffee and I study her some more whilst she yawns. I used to love that cute sleepy look of hers. But now, her and me, we're in a terminal phase. We both know it but we're not able to admit it. Our relationship was founded on a strong physical attraction. Like strong magnets, we had been drawn to each other. Nowadays, it's as if the magnets have been turned around and we're bouncing off each other. Once the physical attraction wore off, the friendship that was supposed to follow didn't materialise. It boils down to one simple issue: she wants a family – the white picket fence dream of a house, garden, kids and a devoted, loving husband. I don't. Simple as that. Once the facts were clear, the disappointment and frustration grew. We argued and fought. She calls me selfish, and it's true. I always was and will probably stay so. It's not that I have big dreams of what I want to achieve; I'm more inclined to coast along. I guess one could say I want independence more than anything else. And I want success – a career, money, yes, all these material things. But mostly independence and the freedom to live my life. At this point in our relationship, it's clear we won't be running the course together. Partly because of this realisation and perhaps as a way of letting me feel her disappointment, Emma despises the line of work I'm in. Corporate finance is abhorrent to her, on the same level as selling insurance. "It's all about greed and personal gain," she always says.

"'Bout time," I say, checking my watch. "Better get going."

We rise, and she follows me out into the hallway. I put on my coat.

"Take a scarf," she says. "It's March and it's still cold out." I grab a scarf and wrap it around my head. She laughs. "You plonker…" She gives me an appraising look. "Looking good, Mr Wilson." A quick hug and a peck on the cheek.

"You gonna wish me luck?"

She smiles at me, but her look conveys her unspoken words: if that's what you want.

2

The Central Line tube hurtles along its tracks. The train sways and rumbles through its tunnel. The smells of oil, steel and musty fabric fill the carriage. I feel the force of its steely velocity quite differently than ever before. I'm carried along, a vibrant body with a purposeful mind in its enclosed steel belly. Usually, I feel like an animal in a herd, like dull cattle being transported to a dull destination. But not today. I'm fully aware of every motion the train makes. I feel its energy charging through me, energising me like a mobile phone on its mains charger. I glance once more at myself in the reflection of the window opposite. I see a young man, not quite thirty, on a mission. I grin at my reflection, much to the annoyance of the guy sitting opposite. I wonder what he sees, looking at me, looking back at him. He probably thinks I'm high on drugs, another overpaid stockbroker or whatever job titles are given to young professional finance artists who flock into the city daily.

The tube slows and pulls into St. Paul's, and I jump up from my seat. "Have a great day," I call to him as I dash out of the carriage. I see him through the window, shaking his head as I stride along the platform, passing the carriage.

From St. Paul's, it's a brief walk to King Edward Street, the corporate head office of Hamlays Bank plc. This is where the gods reside. The top brass, with the privileged positions and unlimited expense accounts. The rest of us

– the common workers – are based in Richmond in a drab seventies office complex. Not quite so salubrious.

I enter the glass and steel building, the reception area all golden marble and leather. It smells of money. I announce myself at the desk and am told to sit and wait. Nothing unusual in that; gods like you to sit and wait. I sit, my feet tapping away. Too full of jittery energy.

The lift doors open and a young woman strides out. She's Premier League as far as personal assistants go – professional haughtiness, tight, long pencil skirt and white blouse. She radiates efficiency and no-nonsense as she strides towards me with fast, energetic and ridiculously small steps, her skirt too tight. I almost snigger.

"Mr Wilson." It's not a question but a statement. "Please follow me." I rise and do as I'm told. I follow. It's nice to follow her, though; her sway is great and the curves are something to behold.

We travel up to the top floor and the doors open onto a wide-open reception area. Ahead is another reception desk, behind which two more hard-faced young women gatekeepers are guarding the entrance. Behind them, a floor-to-ceiling glass wall, like a glass wall you'd expect in a zoo, and beyond an open area where I see plenty of desks and computer terminals manned by young professionals in too-expensive suits just like myself. Some are staring at me, hungry, looking like hyenas. My stomach lurches; I feel like I might be their lunch.

My guide marches out of the lift cabin, turning to the left. Again, I follow. We come to a frosted glass door. A keycard swipe on the terminal and the door opens inward. Automatically, of course, no strained pushing here. A long corridor, glass-walled offices to the left and right. Glass and burnished steel, it's all glass and steel, I think. Three or four staff per office and further along we go, the offices become the homes of single occupants. We're rising up the corporate hierarchy now, I think, and before long, we'll reach another keycard-protected door. Again, a determined swipe and as we enter, I see this is the inner sanctum. The contrast is striking. Here the burnished metal, hard marble floor and cold, harsh lighting has transformed into soft carpet, highly polished wood and subdued lighting. The walls are still glass but what was stark and utilitarian outside is elegant and classy here. Another wide reception but this time, an elegant, middle-aged woman sits tapping away at a computer terminal. She looks up and her smile is almost genuine.

"Mr Wilson," she says in an unexpectedly warm voice. A stark contrast to the robots down at ground level. "Welcome. I hope you've had a good trip in. Willem will see you shortly. Please take a seat." She gestures to a leather sofa. "Would you like some coffee? Tea? Or water?" A smile follows that reduces my pulse considerably.

"Water will be fine, thanks." I smile back.

Again, I sit. Upright. After a minute, I realise too stiffly. I need to show confidence, so I lean back, trying to demonstrate nonchalant self-assuredness.

My tight-skirted guide appears at my side, a glass of water on a burnished silver mirror tray. She sets it down on the coffee table to my side. She gives me a look and manages a smile. I wait. Every so often, I take a sip and covertly survey the inner sanctum. The silence is absolute. Sounds are absorbed here. No shrill phones, no hammering on keyboards, no loud booming voices. Peace and quiet. Power comes silently here. After an hour, I start thinking they've forgotten me, but Tight Skirt reappears before I get too nervous.

"Willem will see you now," she says.

I stop myself from jumping up to attention, but I rise swiftly. After all, this is the CEO with whom I have an interview; one doesn't keep divinities waiting. With a smart about-turn, Tight Skirt moves off and once more, I follow meekly. We circle the reception area and walk along a wide, curved corridor. At the end, a heavy wooden floor-to-ceiling door stands ajar. Tight Skirt gives a small knock, the heavy wood totally absorbing the sound. She opens the door wide and lets me enter.

As I walk into Willem's office, I just barely suppress a "fuck me, look at that". Fortunately, I check myself just in time. I am literally gobsmacked and have to forcibly close my gaping jaw. The sight is amazing. An office larger than my flat. A desk bigger than an altar. Floor-to-ceiling windows with a view across London. You could have a ball in here with more than fifty people. The carpet was thick and soft, there were original paintings on the walls, two massive sofas facing each other on one side, and a massive, glass-topped, oval coffee table between the two sofas. A smell of leather and cigar smoke slowly manifests itself the further I walk into the office. And behind the desk, a smartly dressed, tall George Clooney-type rises and comes around, the most charming smile in place. Showing perfect white teeth, he stretches out his hand like greeting an old friend.

"Neil," he cries, "so good of you to come." As if I were making an inconvenient but special effort to see the CEO of one of the largest financial institutes in the world. He shakes my hand, a tight but not unpleasant grip. He shows me to the sofa with the view out across London and sinks into the opposite-facing one with his back to the view. I guess you get bored of being able to see London from the top floor every day.

"Something to drink? Coffee? Tea? Water?" His accent has a very slight foreign twang. I know him to be Dutch.

"Water," I say. There is no way I am going to risk spilling coffee or tea here.

"Water for Neil, please, Maggie." Then after a moment's thought he adds, "And a latte for me, thanks."

So Tight Skirt has a name, Maggie. Cute, actually it suits her.

"So," he says, "so good of you to come." He smiles at me.

"Well, thank you for finding the time to see me, er…Willem." At this level, we're apparently on first-name terms.

"Yes." He settles into professional mode, picking up a slim file. "We have an opportunity in our Key Account Team, and I'm very happy to see you applied for it."

"Oh, absolutely," I say, trying on my part to settle into professional mode, which doesn't come too easily for me. My nerves are shot and my hands are sweating like a river. I desperately fight the urge to wipe them dry on my two-thousand-pound merino suit trousers. I'm still wondering why this particular applicant merits a personal grilling by the CEO, but I'm determined to give it my best.

"I read your CV," he starts, opening the file, and I pray he won't start ripping it apart. "You've been with us five years now. So, tell me, what makes you think you're the right man for this job?"

3

We take the A24 out of Horsham, travelling south. Kevin Sunderland, my new boss, is driving. He's enjoying the drive, the six-cylinder BMW 5 Series purring sweetly at 70 mph. I can see he's itching to go faster. He has a big grin on his long, slim face. He's crept up to 70 mph, pushing the accelerator that little bit more the further south we've driven. I'm just waiting for him to flick the lever into manual shift so that he can knock it down a gear. He does so with a boyish grin, just coming off the roundabout at the golf course. Normally, juniors are given the task of driving, but Kevin insisted. As he unlocked the 5 Series, I knew why. I don't own a car, relying totally on public transport to get around. Sitting in this powerful BMW, with its saddle-brown leather seats and solid road feel, is an experience.

The real big experience today, however, is the first meeting with Alexis Theophilou, aka William Holden, and his management team at Holden Industrial's complex south of Horsham. I had grown frustrated by all the training and courses I'd had to complete since my appointment and I'd said as much to Kevin, who'd reminded me to stay calm and be patient. Weeks had flown by, and I was itching to get started. Although excited at meeting my first major account, I'm half as nervous as when I went for the interview with Willem. I feel quite comfortable that I'll be able to hold my own. I just pray that I won't spill coffee or otherwise make a fool of myself.

In the last weeks, I have discussed the account in detail with Kevin. My predecessor left the company in a hurry, no one knowing why, and the file he left behind is sketchy. Important details are missing and I have wondered about that. Kevin and I sat down in one of the meeting rooms in the Richmond offices and went through the details and our strategy for the meeting. As he wasn't too familiar with the account either, he'd asked me to prepare a presentation as a basis for our talk, and I'd worked days putting it all together. He sat back, his long frame sprawled in the chair, sipping his coffee from the vending machine, listening to my pitch.

I started with the history. "Holden Industrial, referred to internally as H.I., was founded roughly one hundred years ago as a small metal workshop maintaining and repairing agricultural machines for local farmers." I presented a slide with a timeline, having put in the salient points of development. "The company expanded into tooling and established its range of products for the agricultural and machining sector. The big turning point for the company came after the war. The owner-manager at the time, a Terence – later Sir Terence – Holden, ex-army ordnance officer, won a contract to scrap or remarket surplus military equipment. This included all types of vehicles, jeeps, lorries and a significant number of tracked carriers. Loosely referred to as "Bren Gun Carriers", these were small vehicles used in a general purpose capacity for transporting material and also for towing trailers or even weapons." I had included some photos showing the vehicles in their various forms. "The main point here is that these carriers inspired Terence

Holden to develop a machine for drilling horizontally, which he fitted onto the carrier. Apparently, he'd watched Telecom engineers digging up trenches in order to lay cables. He asked himself, why dig up streets if you can drill underneath and pull the cables through? The main benefit being saving on time and cost. The vehicle could be positioned anywhere and the machine would drill underneath tarmac or walls for any required length. Once through, the cables could be pulled. A fantastic idea."

I glanced at Kevin to see whether he was following. He nodded.

"As far as I can tell from the information we have, Sir Terence was unable to develop a marketable machine, so sold his idea and a couple of prototypes to a friend of his – also ex-army – who was working in the oil and gas sector in the USA. In turn, he acquired the distribution rights for the UK and Western Europe. And that's when the business took off. The Americans had the capital to invest and the engineering know-how to develop marketable machines in all sizes and for all purposes. Holden Industrial would act as their distributor in Europe. It was a win–win situation if it hadn't been because H.I. was under-capitalised and couldn't keep up with the investment required. The company went into receivership, and that's when Mr Theophilou appears on the scene."

"When was that?" Kevin asked.

I checked the notes I'd made. "Roughly fifteen years ago."

I waited to see if Kevin had any more questions, but he asked me to continue.

"Okay, this is where it gets interesting," I continued. "Alexis Theophilou seems quite a character. A Greek Cypriot with a portfolio of operative companies and

16

investments throughout the world. He poured capital into H.I. and developed the company. Today, H.I. is an established player in the market, with its main base in Horsham. Machines are imported from the US and assembled in Horsham for their specific purpose and destination. There's a wide scope of applications with bespoke drilling gear depending on requirements." I showed some photos of H.I.'s various machine types to illustrate the range of machines.

"Wasn't there some controversy with Mr Theophilou? I remember reading something about it," Kevin asked.

"Yes, that's what I meant with 'quite a character'." I had copied some clippings from newspaper reports and included them in the presentation. I flicked forward to the appropriate slides. "Mr Theophilou became a subject of much ridicule when he came forward with a claim that he was related to the Holden family. He was supported in this by the widow of Sir Terence Holden, who at this point was well into her eighties and suffering from advanced dementia. It was a ridiculous claim and he was the laughing stock for some time. It didn't stop him from going through with it and presenting a family tree that supposedly underpinned his claim. He changed his name to William Terence Holding. Rumour has it that he did this to get a knighthood. The ridicule and backlash were so severe that 'Sir William', as he is often referred to jokingly, withdrew largely from the public eye. Shortly after this farce, he appointed a new general manager, a guy called David Willoughby, who has been the managing director ever since. But interestingly, our main contact is a certain Michalis Likidis, who has no official function but acts as finance director. I can't find any notes in our file of direct dealings with Mr Willoughby or Mr Theophilou, aka 'Sir William'."

"Very strange," Kevin agreed. "So where is Mr Theophilou, then?"

"Oh, he's very much still there. But tends to keep behind the scenes."

Kevin shrugged. "Okay, and what's the nature of Hamlays' relationship with H.I.?"

I brought up the slides showing our business with H.I. "We don't have much exposure from the asset finance side of things. Although the machines are ideal for us. H.I. have a substantial rental fleet of machines. Most customers don't buy but prefer to rent. They bundle these and expect the banks to finance these en bloc rather than machine by machine. According to some older call reports – strangely, the file was far from complete – our pricing has been too expensive. And, on top, our credit department has always shied away from the risks of block-funding. They say the risks are too concentrated if we do block financing. We have substantial exposure in the corporate banking sector, mainly cash management solutions and other products. I saw that Willem de Vries has put in some direct support for some projects and appeared to be very supportive in the past."

"Yes, I have heard that he knows Alexis Theophilou personally," Kevin said, then grinned at me. "And so, Neil, what would be your pitch?"

"Well, I think we ought to pitch aggressively for the funding of their rental fleet. It would get us a foot in the door and we can build on that. I appreciate block-funding is low margin, but better low margins than no margins." If you're not in, you're not earning. That was how I saw it. "Willem might want to support us," I concluded.

He just smiled at me. "That's down to you, son, to make that a real possibility."

I liked the "son". He wasn't that much older than me.

Lost to my thoughts and enjoying the countryside flashing past, Kevin rudely interrupts my reverie by making a seatbelt jerking brake and a sharp left turn into a minor road. He doesn't believe in using his sat nav and spotted the sign for Holden Industrial at the last moment. We coast along the road for a bit, passing a monstrosity of a house on the right-hand side. From this point of view, the house is staggeringly ugly and not what one expects in such a typical English rural landscape. It appears to be constructed solely of concrete slabs and glass walls. Three floors are visible from our limited vantage point in the BMW, a bit like three matchboxes stacked on each other. We crane our necks, but high hedges and trees obstruct our view as we follow the road around a bend.

"That's the infamous Holden mansion," Kevin says. "The design was stolen from some famous Spanish place, apparently."

"Mind-blowingly ugly," I say, still recovering from my surprise at such a house in the middle of rural Sussex.

"According to the tales, it's a lot better from the other side. There's a massive patio and garden, a swimming pool, an outdoor sauna, an annex with guest rooms, a games room, etc. Apparently, the Holden parties are quite notorious, not that I've ever been invited," he adds.

The bend in the road continues, and I'm almost convinced we've done a complete circle when suddenly the road widens and we drive onto a large tarmacked yard. To our right is an expanse of manicured lawn and pruned trees, and I can see the rear of the gardens that must belong to the house we have just driven past. To our left

19

stands a two-level office complex and, next to that, a parking lot, in which we draw up.

"Here goes," Kevin says as he parks the car and switches off the engine. "Ready?" he asks, looking at me.

"Ready," I say and get out of the car.

Standing next to the BMW, I survey the setup of Holden Industrial's operations. The office block has been built fairly recently. Functional but not unrepresentative. Behind the office is an open expanse of tarmacked yard, large enough for a lorry plus trailer to do a full circle, and several large concrete workshops. I count six and they are of identical design. All have big foldaway or sliding doors, like hangars. They have the look of units erected in the seventies or early eighties. An articulated lorry stands in front of one of the units and I can see workers preparing to unload tracked undercarriages. I catch a glimpse of some more drilling machines lined up in one of the units with the doors pushed wide open. They are a lot bigger than I had expected.

Presenting ourselves at the reception desk, we are escorted by a young man up to the first floor and into a meeting room. The meeting room, situated at the rear of the office complex, overlooks the workshops and the expanse of tarmacked yard where the lorry stands. We stand at the window, looking out across the yard. We can see more activity in the workshops and in the yard below. Workmen in blue overalls are manhandling machines around the yard. Some are self-propelled and others, on what look like low-wheeled trolleys, are being pushed by forklift trucks into a unit further down and are partially obscured by the lorry with its trailer. In the workshop opposite, we can see workmen on a machine, using a crane mounted on rails under the roof to lower the drilling apparatus onto the carriage below. It's fascinating watching.

"Good afternoon, gentlemen," a voice like sandpaper on rough wood from behind.

We turn to see a gaunt, middle-aged man with salt-and-pepper hair standing in the doorway. He smiles, showing a chain-smoker's yellow teeth. He comes over to us, hand outstretched in greeting. We shake hands and standing by the window, he looks down into the yard and workshops.

"What you see here is the heart of H.I.'s activities. Here, we receive the carriages that come over from the US. As you know, we are distributors for the UK and Western Europe. We assemble the machines, mount the drill and add the bits that are needed for the various applications. And then we package them up and send them to the countries to be sold or to be rented out."

"Looks very impressive," I say, raising Kevin's brow. Kevin is relaxed and easy-going in the company of colleagues, but he has a keen sense of professionalism when it comes to interaction with clients. That much I have learnt in the short period of time I have been in his team. To him, it's not the kind of comment a professional banker is supposed to make. It's too much like a kid staring at a massive model railway or Scalextric setup. I feel my face redden, wondering what I should have said instead.

Michalis gestures for us to sit. Arranged on the conference table are Thermos flasks with coffee, tea, water and some digestive biscuits. I feel my stomach rumble. Seated, Michalis hands us his business card, and we do likewise. His is modest in comparison to our flashy gold-lettered ones. He scrutinises our business cards, and the thought crosses my mind that he's already thinking our rates will be too high just in order to afford the expensive printers. He looks up at me and gives a smile. He probably can read thoughts, too.

We wait, expecting Alexis Theophilou or the MD, David Willoughby, to join us, but no one else appears. Michalis does not explain; he just looks at us expectantly. Kevin gives me a brief look and then takes the lead, which is fine with me. He's good too. He has a polished confidence, a professional air about him that's quite different from his laid-back approach in the meetings I have attended so far. Kevin is tall and thin, almost gaunt. His boyish looks are deceptive; he says he comes across as too young. He's thirty-five yet looks twenty-one – a fact he tries to cover up by sporting an unshaven look and by dressing well. He gives a brief verbal presentation of Hamlays and the financial solutions we have on offer for corporate customers. He finishes by introducing me as the new key account manager and hands over so I can introduce myself. I have prepared for this and give Michalis a summary of my career so far at Hamlays, ending on how keen I am to develop the relationship further and that I'd do anything to help H.I. grow their business and satisfy their needs. Michalis gives me a long look, and I wonder if he is weighing up how much I mean what I have just said. I feel his eyes boring into me – a very unsettling experience.

Michalis reciprocates by summarising H.I.'s current performance, which is incredibly positive. Sales are up, profits are up, and there is a strong demand for the products. He hands us a dossier showing the current profit and loss statements, balance sheet and outlook. I notice the data and forecasts have been prepared by an external company, Charlton Hudson, who are seemingly H.I.'s accountants.

"What we need," he concludes after he has taken us through the data, "is funding for our rental fleet. We have about one hundred machines in our UK rental fleet and many more in our European entities. Our customers prefer to rent rather than buy, which strains our balance sheet. As you can see, our capital base is very good but limits our business growth. We have a short-term requirement to fund another hundred machines in the UK and Ireland and a lot more in Europe."

"What would be the total amount of finance required?" I ask, the mental calculator poised.

"Roughly twenty-five million sterling for the UK, more in Europe if you can provide finance for these countries," Michalis says.

"We don't have operations in Europe," Kevin says, "but we have a network of partners and I'm sure we can arrange an introduction." Michalis just shrugs. "But for the UK, we can certainly find a solution."

A figure like that is powerfully appealing if you are a young, inexperienced, sales-driven guy like me. In my mind, I'm trying to work out the commission from a twenty-five million deal. Once more, I feel Michalis's eyes on me, but I don't really know why. It feels like he's trying to get into my mind. I stay expressionless, but I assume he must have felt my nerves tingling at the prospect of landing such a deal.

Kevin is studying the dossier, and from his posture, I gather that he, too, is weighing up the probability of successfully submitting a deal of this size with our credit department.

"What kind of structure are you envisaging?" he asks, barely looking up.

"Well, the machines come in parts and are assembled here. With our other banks and financing partners, we use a sale-and-lease-back scheme with the right to sublet to our customers. Unless you want to fund the bits and pieces, we would expect to implement the same scheme."

Kevin nods at this; simplicity in the handling is always a priority. No way do we want to finance bits and pieces. I make a note to ask him about the sale-and-lease-back with the right to sublet on the return journey. At this point, I don't know what it implies.

"Please, take the dossier, discuss it internally and if you feel it's doable, let me know. And now, if you like, I will show you around." He rises, ready to take us on a company tour. I grab a couple of digestives on the way out, vowing to myself never to attend a client meeting on an empty stomach again.

4

Kevin and I meet Hamilton, the senior credit analyst, in one of the austere meeting rooms in our Richmond offices. Devoid of décor and smelling of old microwaved meals, we sit down. Mentally I'm prepared for it to be ripped to pieces but determined to sell my pitch.

"Let's see your proposal," Hamilton says in a condescending tone.

I feel the heat rising within me, but Kevin smiles. He's used to it. Hamilton reads my application, and we let him do so without saying a word. Whilst he's reading, I study him. He's a small man, thin, with old acne scars on his face. Kevin says he's a relic. According to him, he's been with Hamlays forever. I find it difficult to judge his age. He could be fifty or sixty. "He's experienced," Kevin had said when it became clear that Hamilton would be handling my application from the credit perspective. "Whatever happens, keep your cool," Kevin warned me just before the meeting. That's a tough assignment, as I want to jump in every time he mumbles a disparaging comment or noise.

Reaching the end of my credit application, he looks up. "Well, not bad, Neil." He says it in such an insincere way I want to hit him. "But why a sale-and-lease-back with sublet?"

I'm about to answer when Kevin gets in first. He obviously doesn't trust me to keep cool and worries about the answer I was likely to give. He'd told me ahead of our meeting that Hamilton is a smiling two-faced bastard who will use any unsubstantiated answer as an excuse to chuck the application out of the window.

"The machines come over from the US and are assembled in Horsham. Before they are assembled, all we have is bits and pieces. A chassis, and separate from that, a drill head plus the nuts and bolts. We want the assembled machine, not its components, on our books. Also, this is not the type of equipment that a customer buys. It's rented. We finance the rental fleet. We have title to every single machine in the package."

"Mmm." Hamilton's body language shows he's not keen to finance packages. "The risk of a sale-and-lease-back is that we can't validate the underlying values," he says.

"But we can," Kevin replies. "The documentation shows the price paid for the chassis and the price of the drilling head separately. They are not looking for us to finance a mark-up or any other margin."

"Mmm...and I suppose there's no way out of the sublet? Can't we finance the rental contracts directly with the end customers?"

"Not really," Kevin states. "H.I. are keen to keep the rental contracts between themselves and the end customers. Why? Apart from keeping the face-to-face relationship with their customer, plenty of administration goes into the rental and service portion of the contract. We wouldn't be able to handle the administration aspects. Plus, this is not a high-margin business. It would cost us too much time and effort lowering our margins."

"I see," Hamilton says.

"A sale-and-lease-back is the only way we can structure this," Kevin says in an authoritative tone. "H.I. is a long-established company, and we can fully trust their capabilities. The financial statements are sound. They have a good capital base and generate sound profits, which they use to bolster their capital."

"Yes, the financial data is very good," Hamilton concedes. "A lot better than I would have expected. I would endorse the application secured by a corporate guarantee from H.I." He looks at us with a benevolent smile.

"Won't work," Kevin says. "We can't expect a corporate guarantee just because we don't like the structure. A sale-and-lease-back is reasonable and the sublet is acceptable too. H.I. has sufficient credit status to justify the risk."

"Then you'll have to argue that in front of the credit committee," Hamilton says with a hint of stubbornness in his voice. "I agree the financial status is good and I think they have sufficient creditworthiness, but, as you know, it's Hamlays policy to underpin these structures with a guarantee."

We sit looking at each other. There's nothing more to add: case discussed and opinions voiced. Hamilton gathers up his papers, looks at Kevin and me in turn and, with a curt nod, gets up and leaves the room. As the door closes, I look at Kevin, eagerly awaiting his assessment of the meeting.

"I didn't mean to exclude you, Neil, but one has to be careful with Hamilton. He'll use any little excuse to withhold his endorsement. As you saw."

"Yes," I agree. It's the first time I've experienced such a discussion. "It boils down to trust, I assume. H.I. seems trustworthy enough to me."

"Quite. Old farts like Hamilton are naturally suspicious. It's why they become credit managers. They wouldn't survive doing anything else." He laughs. "He's all right, really. Just prefers to always take the easy option. Corporate guarantee, my arse."

But I can see that Kevin is troubled. He doesn't think we'll get approval without offering something. We discuss the merits of our proposal once more and in the end, we propose passing on the guarantee subject to conducting a full audit before funding. A full audit means we will physically check the machines and their underlying rental contracts, plus bookkeeping of each machine H.I. wants to finance in the respective packages. This, we feel, provides a good compromise. We finalise the application that afternoon. With a slap on my back, Kevin tells me to submit the application to our credit committee. "I'll send Willem an email; perhaps he can help us get the deal approved," he says as he returns to his office.

Late that afternoon, I receive a package from Charlton Hudson. The package contains the fresh audited reports for the last financial year. I run to the copier, making a copy of the whole document, then run it through the scanner and send it on to the credit committee. Before going home, I sit down and read the auditor's report. Much to my surprise, the report is even better than the interim statements Michalis had provided. That should bolster my application, which makes me feel elated as I put on my coat and head home.

On the commute home, I ponder on all of this; it's with a strange mixture of elation and apprehensiveness that I get home. We live in a semi-detached house that's been converted into two flats. It's okay, for me at least, but Emma keeps going on about how she wants to live in her own house. With the commission from the H.I. deal, I might just be able to afford something nicer, I think as I unlock the front door, but as I climb the steps to our first-floor flat, and before I take off my coat, I know something is wrong. Usually, Emma would come to the door, helping me out of my coat and kissing me. That evening, she's sitting in the kitchen, the biggest and warmest room in our flat, with a grim look. I know that look. She's spoiling for a fight.

"What's up?" I ask.

"That's what's up." She kicks the washing machine. The washing machine is as old as the kitchen units, which means very old. Twenty years is my guess. I bought it cheap, second-hand, and it's not been an ally. It tends to stop halfway through a washing cycle and won't budge. It's been the cause of many an argument.

"Oh."

"Oh," she mimics me. "The sodding thing has packed in again and the washing is still inside. I've been sitting here for hours waiting for you to come home. But no, Mr Wilson prefers to stay in the office playing corporate finance. Look at the clock, Neil."

I look at the big kitchen clock. 7 p.m. She always does this when she wants a battle. In the past, I would apologise and make a show of making up, cajoling a smile back on her face. Making up had been fun in the past, often ending up entwined on the sofa or in bed, but not anymore.

"I'll take a look in a moment," I say, too tired to make it sound convincing.

"You're never here, Neil." Emma looks down at the worn tabletop. There's a slight catch in her voice.

"I do have a demanding job, Emma." Even to my ears, it sounds lame.

She looks up, eyes burning. "Oh, and I don't?" she shrieks.

I prefer to say nothing. I walk over to the fridge and grab a beer.

"I want someone by my side who wants to spend time with me," she says with a sad tone. Her disappointment weighs heavy.

I say nothing. Too tired to care anymore. She rises, emitting a sob, and runs out of the kitchen, slamming the door shut on her way out.

"Fuck this," I say to the washing machine.

I try to find out what's wrong with the washing machine. But another two beers later, I still haven't figured it out. I've pressed all the buttons and tried to find a way of releasing the catch on the door but to no avail. I hear Emma moving about in the hall, so I get up, open the door and go out into the hall.

"Can't figure out what's wrong…" I say, but stop mid-sentence. Emma has changed. She's wearing a mini skirt with tights and a tight top, cut out low. She's dressed for going out. "Where are you going?"

"See, you don't even listen to me anymore, Neil," she exclaims. "Meeting Sally and Rachel for a drink. I *told* you."

I don't remember. "Dressed like that?"

"Yes, dressed like this. Everything else is in that sodding washing machine."

She marches out of the front door, leaving it for me to close.

I close the door behind her and walk into our lounge to the bay window. I see her in the street lamp's light, marching down the street. "The pub's the other way, love," I say to her, disappearing back. I know where she's going.

I return to the kitchen, grab my fourth beer from the fridge and sink down at the kitchen table. I look around – the kitchen is the only homely place in our flat. There are many photos pinned to the walls and sticking to the fridge with magnets. Photos from holidays and dinner parties – most of them held here in our kitchen. It's big enough to easily fit ten or twelve. Good times now long gone. Feeling despondent, I empty half the bottle in one go. Shit, I think, all this hassle. Just what I need. Although I've been promoted to key account manager, my salary hasn't increased much; my income is dependent on commissions. If H.I. goes through, I can expect a significant commission. But not until then. And until then, it's life on a small budget. I kick the washing machine the same way Emma did.

"I don't have enough money to buy a new bloody washing machine," I say out loud.

I'll have to get someone in to try and fix it. The doorbell rings. I get up and walk to the door. I open it and am about to walk down the steps, but stop as I realise the shape I can see through the frosted glass is not Emma. I rush into the front room, to the bay window where I stood just minutes before, and look down into the sodium light from the street lamp. A black-dressed figure is about to get into a black Jaguar. I shoot back round to the door of our flat, peering down. Flicking on the light in the stairwell, I see something poking through the flap. I slowly go down the steps, wondering who this could be. I open the front door. On the doorstep stands an enormous basket. I pick it up and the envelope poking in the flap, carry it upstairs and put it on the kitchen table. It's a Fortnum and Mason hamper wrapped in cellophane. The envelope is addressed to me. A card is inside with a voucher worth £500. I turn the card over and a message says "With best wishes from Holden Industrial".

I sit for an hour staring at the hamper.

5

"Good morning, gentlemen." The voice comes through the conference speaker before the video link is able to establish itself. But then he's there: Willem de Vries. CEO of Hamlays and our last hope.

"Good morning, Willem," Kevin and I said in unison.

Willem is sitting at his oversized desk. The camera is mounted on his computer monitor, angling slightly down but still showing the famous view across London through the windows behind him. But I don't really care for the view; I am desperate at this moment.

Kevin clears his throat. "Willem, the credit committee has turned down our application for Holden Industrial. We're astounded and a bit disappointed, to say the least. Neil did an excellent job and we felt confident that we'd get a positive signal to move forward with this account. The financial statements are sound, a superb annual report, excellent track record over years and good valuable equipment."

"What reason does the committee give?" Willem asks.

"It's the structure they don't like," Kevin replies. "We proposed a sale-and-lease-back with a right to sublet. It's important to H.I. to structure the deal in this way in order to maintain face-to-the-customer. And the benefit for us is that we finance the machines and not bits and pieces. A sale-and-lease-back makes perfect sense and H.I. is an exceptionally good credit risk."

"Well, you know the policies, Kevin," Willem says, but I can tell he's weighing up the pros and cons. "Policies are a guideline," he adds after a moment. "But it doesn't mean there shouldn't be exceptions." And I feel some hope rising in me. I'd been devastated by the committee's decision and hadn't been able to contain my anger as I sat talking it through with Kevin.

"Exactly," Kevin agrees. "It's the only point. Even Hamilton said he's okay with the structure."

"Did he?" Willem leans back and starts twiddling his pen. "Well, a big disappointment. I can understand your frustration, Neil."

"Too bloody right," I mumble, inaudible to Willem. Kevin shushes me with a raised finger.

"The point is, Willem, the request we submitted is sound. As I said, given Holden Industrial's track record, financial status is more than good and the structure is acceptable."

"I agree, Kevin. Totally. I see no reason to turn the credit request down," Willem says.

I look at Kevin. "What the hell is going on, then?" I whisper.

Kevin ignores me. "Willem, if we are all in agreement that this is a sound proposal, what are we going to do about it?"

There's an audible sigh through the loudspeaker. "Let me have a chat with head of credit. I have no power to overrule Andrew's authority, as you know. I'll need to convince him. After all, as far as I can see, it's only the policy that's the issue here, isn't it? Or is there something else I need to know?"

I wonder just how much Willem knows. I gather he's read the credit application. I hadn't left anything out and

I assume he knows about the controversy surrounding Alexis Theophilou and his silly attempt at establishing that family tree. Is that the reason, maybe? But that was years ago now and surely wouldn't stand in the way of doing business with an otherwise healthy and reputable company.

"No," Kevin replies. "Nothing that we are aware of. We were thorough, and Neil put a lot of time and effort into compiling the application."

"Yes, a good job, Neil. Very impressed by your work."

Receiving a compliment like this from the CEO is a boost to my morale, but more than anything, I want the application to succeed. Not just for my ego but because I need the commission.

"Okay, gents, I'll see what I can do," Willem says. "Anything else?"

Kevin looks at me. "Anything else?"

"No, not at the moment. What do I say to Michalis?"

"Just tell him we're still in the process. He won't be happy. It's been what, two weeks now?" Willem asks.

"Four," I correct. It has been four long weeks since putting in the application. Five since our meeting with H.I.

"Four?" Willem exclaims. "I'll ring Alexis. Leave it with me."

We terminate the call, the screen reverting to black as the video link disconnects.

"Nothing unusual in this, Neil," Kevin says, looking at me. "Patience."

"Okay, seems a bit weird, though. A very good client and we stumble on a technicality."

"Policies are what banks rely on, Neil. They are implemented for good reasons. There are risks in such a structure, but in principle, I agree with you."

35

It takes four more gruelling weeks. Every time I ring Michalis, I feel so embarrassed. What can I say? He's non-committal and just thanks me for keeping him updated. Then, one September morning, I receive an email from Willem. I click to open it.

Good news, Neil. I have managed to secure an approval. Credit will approve 25 million. Sale-and-lease-back and sublet, as requested. Well done. Willem.

I thump the desk with joy and relief. Great. I forward the email to Kevin, who replies immediately.

Told you, patience pays off. Wait until you have written confirmation from Credit. And then go get them. Kevin.

Waiting for confirmation takes two more nerve-wracking days. But finally, with the written confirmation printed out and lying before me on my desk, I ring Michalis.

"Good morning, Michalis," I say as the call connects and his gruff sandpaper voice comes through the line. "Good news, at last," I say. "I have approval from our credit people." Adding with nonchalance, "For the twenty-five million at present." I continue. "And structure as discussed. A small 'however', though," I say with reluctance, before adding, "subject to a full audit and floor check." I sit waiting for his response.

"At what price?" comes his answer.

"Pricing will depend on the actual size of the packages you want to finance and the handling necessary. I suggest I come by and we can discuss."

"A price indication will do for the time being," he replies.

"Right, okay. Shall I put together a proposal and a quote for you based on some parameters, and then we can go through it once you've had time to peruse it?"

"Sure. You do that."

"Fantastic, I'll be in touch soon," I say, but he's hung up.

He keeps me waiting for another six weeks. Six weeks in which I send one proposal and quote after another. But it's never right. Our pricing is too high. That's his response to each proposal I send. I sit with Kevin every time I get a reply, and we redraft the proposal and our pricing. I'm beginning to lose faith in ever receiving a positive response.

I'm out on a client call to one of my other new accounts when my mobile rings. A call from a phone number I haven't encountered so far.

"Neil Wilson, Hamlays Asset Finance," I say, expecting a client to be ringing.

"Willem here."

"Willem," I say, surprised.

"Just wanted to hear what the latest is with Holden Industrial?"

"Ah, to be frank, no progress, unfortunately. Still trying to get pricing agreed. Michalis is playing hard to get."

"That *klootzak*!" he exclaims.

"Pardon me?"

"Sorry, that was Dutch. *Klootzak*, as in arsehole." He laughs.

"Quite," I agree, laughing too. "A right *klootzak*, if you don't mind me saying."

"Leave it with me," he replies.

"Certainly, Willem."

On my return to the office, an email from Michalis is waiting for me. I open it immediately, wondering what he has to tell me.

Your last pricing is acceptable. Please draw up the contracts.

My word, Willem is a fast mover and certainly has clout. I'm impressed seeing that our pricing wasn't the best. I know we would have reduced it further still, but I'm not going to complain.

Despite Willem's intervention and Michalis's greenlight, progress is still painfully slow. I had the contracts drawn up, I sent them out to Michalis, and since then I've been waiting. And I'm waiting some more. It's not that they've queried them or disputed clauses, which I would have expected. I just haven't received a reply. Nothing. My calls go unanswered; I assume they're just too busy. But still, it unnerves me. I begin thinking it might be the floor check that they can't be bothered with and so, in desperation, I ring the managing director, Willoughby. Being the MD, he will have to sign the contracts anyway, so I feel it's legitimate to ring him. I've never had dealings with him so far, but I'm desperate for an answer. The switchboard puts me through.

"Willoughby." A voice as gruff and unfriendly as Michalis's.

"Neil Wilson here. Hamlays Asset Finance. Good morning, Mr Willoughby." No response. Nothing. I carry on. "I'm ringing regarding the contracts I sent Michalis – I mean Mr Likidis." No response. "Just wondering if you have received them and whether you might have any questions concerning the documentation?" Still no response. "If you do, I will be happy to discuss them with you."

I wait.

"What contracts?" the voice says after a full minute.

"The contracts concerning the financing of the drilling machines," I reply.

"You'll have to speak to Michalis."

"Okay, right," I say. The managing director has no idea about a major funding project? "And regarding the floor check, I want to ask if you have set a date yet?"

"The what?" The voice is getting annoyed.

"The floor check. It's a condition of the financing approval," I soldier on, feeling equally annoyed.

"Flipping heck," Willoughby grumbles.

"Sorry?"

"Speak to Michalis." He hangs up.

6

Frustrated from the day's events and just about keeping a lid on smouldering anger, I unlock the front door. Mrs Pearson, the elderly lady who lives in the ground-floor flat, is in the hallway, shopping bag by her feet, trying to get her key into the lock.

"Hello, Mrs Pearson," I say out loud. She's hard of hearing and jumps easily.

"Oh, Neil," she says, smiling at me. I take her key and unlock the door for her.

She's a sweet lady and has a passion for pink. We sometimes sit down together over a cup of tea and chat. She keeps a keen eye on everyone and everything, especially us. Often, I make fun of her and call her Miss Marple, but she never makes the connection. She thinks I'm just teasing her and giggles every time I do so.

"Has Emma gone on a holiday?" she asks.

"On a holiday?" I ask. "No. Why?"

"Oh, it's just that she left a couple of hours ago with two suitcases. And the gentleman that was with her had bags, too."

I climb the stairs to our flat, phone in hand. I do a quick tour of the flat. Emma has packed clothes and toiletries and taken them with her. I ring her number.

"Neil," she says as the call connects.

"Emma, what's going on?"

"Neil, I'm sorry," she says. I can tell she's crying.

"Sorry?" I ask, but I'm not surprised. I knew it was coming but wasn't expecting it to be like this.

"I can't go on like this anymore," she sobs into the phone.

"And so, you just pack some cases and bags and disappear?" I can feel the hot anger bubbling up again.

"It's best for us this way."

"You're dumping me like this?" I can hardly contain the sarcasm.

"No, Neil," she replies, her voice hard now, no more sobbing. "You dumped me ages ago, but you just couldn't be bothered to say it out loud."

I sit down at the kitchen table.

"Neil?"

"Yes, Emma, I'm here." My anger has evaporated. Totally deflated, I sit and wonder how I should be feeling and what I should say.

"Neil, it's better for us."

"But you don't just pack bags and go. You tell me face to face. Not over the phone."

"I have, Neil, on plenty of occasions. But you never listen. So now I'm gone. It's best for us."

"I can't believe it, Emma. Never thought you'd be like this. Dumping me over the phone."

"I'm sorry, Neil, but I couldn't face it. This way, we talk and I'm certain that you're listening."

Truth is, I know she has another bloke. Tristan. Her boss at work. The gentleman who carried the bags.

"Emma, just for the record, I never had someone lined up like you." It's a mean blow, but I can't stop myself.

Silence on the other end of the line. My guess is he's sitting next to her and listening to our conversation.

"I'm sorry, Neil," she says after a while, and I can feel from the way she says it that she really is sorry. "Unlike you, I want a partner in my life, Neil. You know, giving and taking, for better or worse and on equal terms."

I scored a hit but it doesn't make me feel better. And, to be honest, she has every right to be happy. I failed in making her happy, and she's the one who has built up her courage to end our relationship. Not me. I was just waiting. Waiting for something to happen. And now it has. Can I really blame her?

"What's to happen with the flat?" I ask. Tristan has a bedsit, and they'll be looking to keep this place for the time being at least. Finding a flat elsewhere will be challenging and I certainly don't want to stay here.

"Well, unless you want to keep it, I— Well, we…" She doesn't finish the sentence and lets her words trail off.

"You have it," I say.

"Okay, but where will you go? And for the holidays?" she asks.

"Not sure. I'll find something. And as for Christmas, either stay here or Ben's, perhaps," I say. Ben, my brother down in Worthing. Fortunately, I have some time off over the Christmas period coming up. I weigh up staying here or going to Ben's. Better at Ben's than here on my own.

"Neil," she says.

"Yes, Emma."

"Neil, you need to think about yourself. And your life. And what you want from life," she says. I don't know if she's expecting me to answer. I sit, waiting for what she has to say.

"All this career stuff. It'll get you nowhere unless it's all you want from life."

"All I want?" I ask, not understanding what she's leading up to.

"Yes, if it's all you want, then fine, but don't forget there's more to life than just career and money."

"Is there?" I say, meaning it to be sarcastic, but failing.

7

I trail along at the end of the group, marching across the vast tarmacked yard to the workshop at the end of the line of six units. There's three to this audit team and four more on the team that will be going through the paperwork. Floor checkers they're called. Leading is H.I.'s foreman, a tall, thick-set guy in blue overalls. The floor checkers' team leader is half of him. Small, lean with an athletic figure. The other two on the team are like him, equally lean and somehow uniform. It's not just that they look alike; it's their dress, too. They are wearing jeans, white sweaters and black boots. As the group marches across the yard, I see some H.I. workmen in their blue overalls peeking out of the doors at the side of the hangar-like units. I notice the big hangar doors, which had all been open when we met with Michalis, are closed. It seems odd to me, but I push the thought aside.

We get to the end unit, and the foreman opens the door at the side of the building next to the hangar doors. As we walk into the brightly lit space I can see various types of machines lined up in two rows. I quickly scan the machines and count sixteen. Six big machines on the left and ten smaller ones on the right. I mentally do some quick arithmetic; in total, there are sixty machines to be checked.

I watch the foreman talking to the team leader and his two floor checkers. He's taking his time, and the team leader is nodding and looking at his watch. I can see that he wants to get started. After a long while the foreman concludes his speech and, at a nod from the team leader, the floor checkers start scrambling around the machines, making notes and taking photos of the serial numbers and of the machines themselves. I meander up the row of parked machines, mainly not to get in the way of the floor checkers going about their business but also to have a nose around. The tall unit is made of prefabricated concrete pillars and walls with a concrete floor and metalled roof. Purpose-built to a standard design, I'd guess. The front end, with its sliding hangar-like doors and two separate entrances left and right, is mirrored at the rear end with the same setup. I wonder what lies behind, but the doors are shut and there are no windows. Probably another tarmacked area, in one side and out the other. Along the sides of the unit stand racks with components, spares and floor checkers of oil and grease. Next to these are some transport boxes, packaging and other bits and pieces. It looks organised in a haphazard way. The floor checkers make quick progress and the foreman leads them back to the side door at the front of the unit. He opens the door, gesturing for them to move through and I hasten to follow. The foreman is on his way through the door. He hasn't really noticed me so far, and whilst I hurry along to catch up with the disappearing back of the foreman, I hear a noise behind me. Glancing back, I see the big sliding doors of the unit start to move. Someone from the outside is starting to slide them open.

I catch up with the group; the foreman gives me a startled look as he realises there's one more person on the team. I give him what I hope is a reassuring smile. "All okay, I'm with the party," I say to him. He frowns but doesn't say a word.

We move on to the next unit, again entering through the side door. As we walk in, I'm struck by the fact that the lighting is a lot dimmer here. Otherwise, it's the same setup. The machines are parked up in two rows. This time, there are six of the bigger machines on the left and eight on the right. The floor checkers are about to swarm out, but the foreman asks them over and does some more explaining. I can see the floor checkers getting impatient; the foreman carries on unperturbed. He glances over once or twice in my direction, especially as I start wandering off, pretending to be inspecting the machines. I turn my back to the group, pretending to be absorbed with looking at the mechanics of one of the large machines, but again, I glance around, having a good look around in all the corners. The structure is identical to the first unit we'd been in. Sliding doors at front and back, flanked by two standard-size doors left and right of the hangar doors. High ceiling, lighting suspended from the metal girders supporting the metal roof. Apart from the dimmed lighting it's the same setup.

I turn around, surprised to see the foreman still talking at rather than to the floor checkers. They're showing their impatience, and the team leader looks at his watch. I hear a beeping sound from outside, not loud but audible enough. The foreman's head twitches and he stops his talk and lets the floor checkers get on with their task. I realise he's heard the beep, too, and can't help but think it must have been a signal. He glances at me, clocking my position. A floor checker calls out to him, and he walks over to the man crouched at the side of a drilling machine pointing. I do a quick about-turn and walk the line of parked machines. There's nothing out of the ordinary except that the machines closest to the sliding doors at the rear of the unit are all standing on long, flat-wheeled trolleys, whereas the ones further up are not. I remember seeing these when we first visited and workmen in forklift trucks were towing or pushing the machines. In the other unit had they stood on their wheels or tracks or on trolleys like these?

The floor checking is taking a lot longer in this unit. I can see the floor checkers are having difficulties getting readable photos of the plates showing the serial numbers. A lot of flash photos are being taken. After a good while, the floor checkers are done and the foreman gathers them together. This time, he keeps a lookout for me, and we exit this unit and move on to the next.

The third unit is a lot more cramped. The machines are not in neat rows but squashed in any old way. There's far more stuff standing around, too: boxes, packaging, drums and all other sorts of bits and pieces. Whilst the other two units had been open right up to the roof, this unit has an additional first floor. It makes the unit smaller and dense. The lighting is even poorer and glancing up, I can see that some of the neon tubes aren't working or perhaps aren't switched on.

The floor checkers are looking grim as they survey the machines crammed into the unit. Almost as if stepping out from behind the curtains, Michalis appears. He's all smiles and apologetic regarding the poor lighting. He has papers with him and gives a set to each floor checker. I move closer, hoping to hear what he's saying. He spends a long time going through them, explaining that of the total number of machines in the list, fifteen machines are packaged and in the yard. Five machines are in assembly in Unit 1, and five are at the paint shop getting their bespoke livery. He has the papers to show which machines these are. The discussion goes on for a long time; there seems to be some confusion and I can sense the floor checkers' impatience growing. They want to get the job done and judging by the expression on their faces, I can see that from their point of view time is being wasted.

Michalis and his foreman debate one point in particular but being out of earshot, I can't hear what it is. The floor checkers are looking from one to the other like spectators at a tennis match. In the meantime, I stand in the middle of the unit and do a slow 360-degree turn. All the machines here stand on transport trolleys. All the machines are of the same types we've seen in the other two units. I would have thought there'd be more different types, but I just guess that's how things are. But it's striking that, in contrast to the neat rows in the first two units, it looks like the machines have just been stuffed into this unit any old way. I do a mental shrug. I have no idea if what I'm seeing is out of the ordinary, but it is frustrating the floor checkers – that much is apparent. Finally, after much debate, the floor checkers start and hastily take their photos and make notes.

As I stand watching them, Michalis appears at my side. I smell the strong tobacco stench that clings to him before I see him, but I can't help feeling he tried to creep up on me. He's a head shorter than me. I notice he has gel in his salt-and-pepper hair, which strikes me as odd given his otherwise scruffy appearance and drab clothes. Grey jeans and a black sweater. But it's his eyes that grab me; given his dark skin and hair, they are startlingly blue.

"Interesting experience for you?" he asks.

"My first time on a floor check," I say. "Impressive setup you have here," I add.

"You have the contracts with you?" he asks. I nod in confirmation. I brought another set just in case. "Okay, then we can take a look at those later on. And Alexis wants to have a look at them, so we'll go over to his office."

We watch the floor checkers, and the little group sets off to the next unit. As we exit into the yard, Michalis taps me on the arm, pointing to the office block. We break away from the group and start walking over.

"Tedious business these audits," he says.

"Quite," I agree.

"We have so many machines all about the place, it's difficult to track which machine is where at any given time. Your auditors want to see every piece of paper, and woe betide you have something not in the right order. These audits take up so much time and cost too much," he grumbles.

I understand his point, for it's not just the machines we've been inspecting here on the premises but also the ones out on rental. They are all over the country, and identical teams have been in the field checking these. The organisational aspects and expense are considerable. I've forgotten about the second half of the team, which I can now see sitting in the conference room on the first floor as we walk closer. I see them in the brightly lit conference room, checking files and scribbling on pads as we walk past below. I assume we're heading to the office building and am surprised as Michalis keeps going straight, and I realise we're heading for the path that leads to the rear of the mansion. There's an expanse of lawn and a path leading through some bushes and trees. It's like stepping into another world. Once on the path, it veers to the left behind some high-growing bush and continues to meander left and right as it snakes its way up to the mansion.

"Good gosh. I didn't expect this," I exclaim as I follow Michalis along the path, the white gravel stones crunching underneath. He turns to grin at me.

"Yes, it's quite amazing. Wait until you see the house," he says.

Amazing? Well, I'd seen the house, at least the front of it, from the road and I'm beginning to wonder if there's a significant difference in terms of taste and aesthetics between Michalis and me when the path comes to an end and we stand at the foot of the garden. Beyond the garden, on top of a slight slope, lies the house. Admittedly, I'm speechless.

To me, the most striking aspect is that it's in the wrong country. Or, put more fairly, in the wrong countryside. It belongs somewhere in Spain or Italy, maybe, or yes, as the thought makes a click in my mind, perhaps somewhere in Greece or Cyprus. I can see a vast glass frontage, floor-to-ceiling glass walls, three terraced floors, concrete upright slabs made of a concrete that shimmers silver in the fading afternoon light. Interspersed with stone-clad pillars, the concrete roof sits heavily like a massive tabletop. The roof overlaps the patio, designed to provide shade from a hot Mediterranean sun but in England, in December, its purpose seems to be to provide cover from the English drizzle. Apart from the size of the house, it's the centre that grabs the attention. It stands out like a keep. Formed like the letter "H" but topped off with what appears to my eye like a massive concrete lid, it towers higher than the three floors.

My eyes drift back down to the lawns. They are immaculate, which is a major feat given that we are now in late December. Not a leaf in sight despite the plane trees and bushes artfully spaced out. We walk up some steps, turn right and follow another gravelled pathway that's set to the side of the lawn and leads up to the house.

At the top of the slope, the lawn gives way to teak decking surrounding a large rectangular swimming pool, set at a right angle to the building. Beyond the teak decking, white marble flooring forms a terrace that wraps itself all the way around the house and mirrors the overlap of the concrete roof. Outdoor sofas and easy chairs, stacked and covered up for the winter, stand in one corner under the overlapping roof but easily provide comfortable seating for fifteen or more people in the summer. Dotted around the immense terraced area stand more weatherproof chairs, outdoor dining tables and recliners all covered up but easily providing seating for forty.

A number of sliding glass doors are set in the glass walls, one pair partly open. My eyes are drawn to the towering keep which rises up before me. Between the massive concrete pillars, the expanse is one piece of smoked glass rising up three floors. I've never seen anything like it before. I can't help but feel that it's impressive but not welcoming. We walk up to the glass sliding doors and before we enter, I reach out and touch the concrete. It's smooth and there's a sheen to it, like a gloss.

"That's Roman concrete," Michalis says. "It's laid rather than poured. An ancient craftsmanship."

I have no clue about Roman concrete, but even I can tell it's special. We enter into an open-spaced area. The same white marble on the floor. Dimmed indirect lighting and a few spots, their beams directed at oil paintings hanging on the walls. To the right, sunken into the ground, a square sofa space. And behind that a stone wall of the same grey and roughly hewn stone outside. Fixed to the wall is a massive screen, easily the size any cinema would boast.

To the left, a dining area with a wide white high-gloss cabinet set against the wall, an oversized abstract crimson red painting above, and a white fitted carpet on the floor. On this stands a rectangular oak table big enough to seat all of King Arthur's knights. I hadn't noticed but I'd stopped to take it all in. Michalis stands next to me, watching me. With a smile, he gestures towards a central open passage built of the same roughly hewn grey stone interspersed with more ceiling-to-floor glass walls. At the end, an open gun-metal steel staircase with white marble steps leads upwards. I'm speechless as I cast a look back whilst we climb the stairs. How much is all this worth? I wonder. I try to get a glimpse of the rooms on the first floor but that's not possible. The first floor appears to be taken up by the private rooms. All doors shut, allowing no glimpse of what lies behind. We carry on, climbing up to the second floor.

This floor is exclusively reserved for Alexis. That becomes immediately clear. I can sense it and smell it. A mixture of varnish, leather and old smoke lies in the air. A square landing and ahead a wood-panelled – or it might even be solid wood – wall set within what must be the upper part of the H-shaped keep. To the left and right, doors lead off to other rooms, but again the doors are shut. I love to see what might lie behind them. Michalis knocks on the tall door set into the wooden wall. He doesn't wait and pushes the door open and walks, with me following behind him.

This is totally out of keeping with the rest of the house. The first thing I notice is a large Persian rug covering the floor. Up against the glass wall was an enormous mahogany desk with green leather topping. Behind it, with his back to the glass wall, I see the head and torso of a man hunching over an illuminated magnifying glass, studying something he holds up into the light with tweezers. It looks like a stamp to me.

"Alexis," Michalis speaks as he crosses to the desk, "this is young Mister Wilson."

I'm standing just inside the door, mesmerised. I feel like I've stepped into a different, old-fashioned world. Whereas below, everything is high gloss and minimalist papers stacked on top. The room isn't so much an office but a den. Michalis half-turns in my direction and stretches out his arm and hand as if presenting me to royalty. To me, this is a more than a strange gesture. The big man looks up slowly from his scrutiny, white-bearded face turning towards me and fixes me with intense blue eyes. Something he has in common with Michalis. He gives me a quick once-over and rises from a creaking, old-fashioned leather swivel desk chair. It seems like he's unfolding himself, for as he comes around his desk towards me, he seems to grow larger with every slow step and by the time he stands before me, he seems a giant.

"So pleased to meet you, young Mister Wilson," he says in a deep rumble of a voice, over-emphasising the "young" and holding out his hand for me to shake. And there it is, that instant, when you meet somebody you instantly take to, with a voice that makes you want to laugh and the humorous twinkle in the eye, and you know this is going to be great.

I shake the proffered hand, a big grin on my face. Alexis laughs and slaps my shoulder.

"Come in, my friend. Take a seat." He gestures to the black sofa against the side wall. "Coffee, tea?"

"Coffee would be great, thanks," I say, knowing I won't need to worry about spilling anything here as the coffee will come in a mug.

Michalis slips out to fetch the coffee, and Holden lowers himself onto the sofa. It is not an easy task for him; the sofa is too low even for me. We sit, half-twisted towards each other.

"Bugger this bloody sofa," he says with a smile, and I laugh. "It's been here, God knows how long. Just can't get rid of it," he explains, patting the armrest.

Two hours go by in a flash and we seem to touch on everything. He asks plenty of questions about me, my life and where I come from. It's so easy to talk to him. I come close to telling him about the split-up with Emma but something stops me. He asks me about my job, whether I'm enjoying my new position and whether the money I'm now earning makes it worthwhile. I hesitate to answer that particular question, but the conversation drifts along easily. I thank him for the hamper, saying it had been too much, but he waves it aside. I realise at this point that to him it really is nothing. A thousand pounds is small change in his world. He's charming, witty and his booming laugh puts me at ease. The more we speak, the more the awkward Englishness he affected to begin with is replaced by what I assume to be his natural Greek temperament. By the end of our chat, I'm awarded the honour of calling him Alexis or Alex, as I please. He makes me feel that we're best friends.

"Neil," he says, "by the way, we have our company Christmas party today and I'm sure you have other plans, but you'd make me very happy if you join us. We can have some beers and ouzo together, my friend." He beams at me, and I know extracting myself from this sudden invitation will be difficult.

"Well, Alexis, I'm not sure. It's your company party. You surely don't want outsiders joining in. Especially not boring bankers like myself." But in a way, I'm keen to stay. I have nowhere else to go this Friday evening and I'm interested in seeing what a company party at H.I. is like. They are famous events by all accounts.

"Nonsense, my friend. We have a party together with all our friends, not just employees. We are family, you know."

"Well, I suppose I could stay a while. Maybe for a drink or two."

"Good boy!" he exclaims in that booming, laughing voice. "Don't worry if you get carried away; we have accommodation in our little guest annex."

And with that and another slap on my shoulder, he shows me out onto the landing where Michalis stands waiting.

"Oh, the draft contracts," I say, suddenly remembering.

"Leave them with Michalis," he says and gives him a wink. "Neil will be joining us today," he says to Michalis, who just nods. For a moment, I think of saying that I sent the contracts to him weeks ago but I pass on it, not wanting to spoil the atmosphere.

Michalis leads me downstairs and back out through the sliding glass doors on to the terrace. It's dark now and the house is lit up. There's nobody else visible in the house and for a moment, I feel this is all fake, like a film set. But the house is real enough, and as we step out, a cool wind blows across and I'm grateful for some fresh air to clear my head. We stand and I admire the house, the terrace and the pool's indirect lighting.

"Does anybody ever swim in there?" I ask Michalis.

"You're welcome to do so if you like, but maybe better not tonight," he replies.

I wonder what it would be like to own a place like this. A brief fantasy gallops through my head: an image of me swimming in the pool, stretching out on the sunbeds, owning all of this. I do a mental shrug and push it aside. Never ever will I own a place like this.

Michalis walks me along the terrace back the way we came but veers off to the right before we reach the end of the decking. We follow a short path to the guest annex, tucked away behind some high-growing reed. I certainly hadn't noticed it when we came up.

"We have a guest annex here and I've reserved a room for you. You can freshen up if you like and then come down to the office at six p.m." Michalis gives me a tight smile and again that particular little gesture of the outstretched arm and hand, pointing me towards the door to the guest annex. I'm amazed by this unexpected turn of events and the hospitality shown to me. And whilst I hesitate to accept this invitation, I am very interested in having a look inside, so I step forward and head over to the glass door ahead of me, of course, set in a floor-to-ceiling glass frontage. I turn back to say thanks, but Michalis has gone. I have by now decided to make the most of this invitation, so I happily step through the door and walk along the white-marbled corridor.

The annex has been built using the same materials as the main house but it's scaled down. The short corridor leads to an open lounge area with more glass and stone walls and it sports a glass roof. Similar to the main house, a large flat screen hangs on one of the stone walls. Below this is a white high-gloss low cabinet including, as I discover, a well-stocked fridge. I turn and see a little illuminated panel fixed to a stone pillar. On it, glowing letters say "Welcome Mr Neil Wilson. Your room is *Famagusta* on the lower level. Enjoy your stay".

Only now do I notice the spiral staircase in the corner leading down, and I head down the staircase to the lower level. My presence activates indirect lighting. Ahead, a wide door, which, as I try the handle, opens to reveal an indoor swimming pool, a bar and what looks like a sauna and steam room. To the left, another wide door reveals a games room with a full-size snooker table, a table football, a bar along the back wall and easy chairs spread around. There's a large flat screen in the corner, shelving with books and what I like best, a glitter disco ball hanging from the ceiling.

I close the door, turn right and walk down the corridor. Doors left and right, these must be the guest rooms. At the end, a door and glowing faintly, a small screen set next to it: "Famagusta" it reads.

The door's not locked and I walk in. Light sensors trigger the spots, and I stand there, taking in the biggest double bed I've ever seen. Bathroom off to the left, with an oversized bathtub that easily accommodates two, a walk-in shower, two sinks and large mirror. I walk back into the room, taking in the fitted high-gloss furniture with white frontages like in the main house. Glass sliding doors lead on to a small patio. The quality of the furniture and décor is amazing – at least compared to what I am used to. In comparison, my flat is a shack. I stand looking with awe at the room. The most intriguing aspect, however, is the large mirror fixed to the ceiling over the bed.

8

I must have fallen asleep because it's gone 6 p.m. when I wake. With a start, I get up, put on the clothes I'd been wearing, and get myself ready. I'd treated myself to a long, hot shower and put on the sumptuous bathrobe hanging in the bathroom before relaxing on the soft bed. Now, I'm grateful for the toothbrush and paste that has been provided. I feel quite refreshed and ready. I look around for a key to lock the room whilst I'm out, but there isn't one. This isn't a hotel, I remind myself, but Alexis's private home. No need for keys.

I walk up the spiral staircase and out onto the decking. A fine but persistent drizzle strong enough to soak through to the skin mists the air. A smell of log fire comes drifting across from the direction of the workshops. I take a look around. The house is completely lit up, all three levels. But there's no one to be seen – not a soul. Surely, if the Christmas party is due to take place here, there'd be people. There must be staff, I think, an event of this size requiring cooks and service staff. I recall Michalis saying to come down to the office, so the party must be down where the workshops are. I turn, pulling up the hood on my parka and walk down the pathway to the bottom of the garden, lights in the shrubs illuminating the trees and showing me the way. As I reach the bottom of the pathway, I see the car park is full. The pool car I came in, which stood forlornly in the car park earlier on, has cars next to it and there are cars parked on the tarmacked yard.

More cars are arriving and people are getting out and setting off across the yard to the workshop units. Further along I now see fire pits standing to the right of the big units and the stream of people are walking towards these. I see people walking past the fire pits and turning left as they move past the first of the units, going behind it.

The office block is now in darkness, and I assume Michalis has gone over to the party location, so I follow the trail of people, wondering with growing excitement where we're heading. As I walk around the big unit at the end of the line, I see with some surprise more units behind the back. They are a lot older, smaller and lower than the big concrete ones standing in front of them. They are not visible from the office building, which is why I never expected them to be here. Illuminated by powerful multicoloured beams spread out along the tarmacked area between the two rows of workshops, I notice, judging by their worn and weathered red bricks, that they must have been built decades ago. I count eight, differing in height and width, as I walk along. The further along I walk and peering out under my hood, I see that the location for the party has to be the last building in the row, right at the end. More fire pits stand spaced out on the tarmac in front of the old workshop buildings and a marquee has been set up in front of the entrance, providing some cover from the drizzle. People are milling around, drinks and cigarettes in hand. Additional illumination comes from spotlights mounted on lighting towers, their beams cutting through the drizzle and soaking the area in front of the entrance in bright light, adding an eerie quality.

As I walk nearer, I hear music and feel the bass coming from high-powered speakers inside. I stop on the edge of the marquee, taking in the scene. Guests standing outside drinking, chatting and smoking. It's a mix of young people. The men are probably workers from the complex here in suits and sporting gelled hair. The girls are in tight, thin dresses, shivering in the cold. A universal sight at company parties, I think to myself. Even at Hamlays the scene wouldn't be any different. Loud voices accompany the loud music coming from inside the building as guests try to converse over the loudness. A puff of fog suddenly rises like a cloud from inside, rushing out of the entrance and lifting up into the air. Someone is operating a fog generator. More billows of the stuff come out into the wide-open entrance. Now, I can explain the diffused lighting as the fog rises slowly into the sky, enveloping the light towers.

A gap in the throng opens, and I see a low vehicle standing behind the marquee. Intrigued, I walk over a few steps to see what it is. It's an old but perfectly maintained tracked vehicle. A Universal Carrier, I realise, what my dad always called a "Bren Gun Carrier" and, according to legend, the nucleus of Holden Industrial's existence. It's been put in a scene, illuminated from below by more spots, glistening in the liquid light from the drizzle.

Following the throng of people, I push my way through the crowd, standing under the marquee and walk into the building. I can only assume it's an old workshop from the days when Holden Industrial was a metal-working business. The building is made of red bricks and is a lot lower than the concrete workshops opposite. It has some depth, though, as I stand near the entrance, I can't see to the rear end. Okay, it's in darkness but even so, there are plenty of people milling about. To the left and right, two bars, seemingly made from old pallets, have been set up, and suspended from the roof is a gridded

61

truss with multicoloured beams and lasers. I cast a look around and there must be two hundred people or more inside. I walk around, getting a feel for the venue and come across a covered passage that connects this building to the next. I walk through and this is where the catering has been set up. Along the back wall stands a long counter sporting a battery of buffet hot stoves. There's another bar, cocktail waiters mixing up elaborate drinks, and tables and chairs spaced out with potted plants between them. In the far corner stands a large Christmas tree, lights blinking and the only recognisable sign that this is indeed a Christmas party. Groups of people sit around, animatedly talking and laughing. I walk back through to the other workshop, ready for a beer.

I head for the nearest bar to get a bottled Beck's. I'm thirsty and down it one. Without saying a word, the attentive barman gets me a new one. I lean against the bar, taking my time with this one, and survey the scene. Some of the younger guests are already on the dance floor. The flashy lads strutting their stuff and the girls watching and giggling whilst coyly moving to the music. Around the dance floor, the slow starters stand watching, commenting on the action, drinks in hand. Over at the other bar, on the left side of the building, stands a group of older men methodically working their way through their beers. And in the corners stand more little groups chatting, their faces hardly discernible in the harsh flashing lights and deep shadows. I don't recognise anyone and wonder if I might be the only outsider here.

Two young men in jeans, ironed shirts and gel in their hair appear at my side and get their drinks. I smile at them, partly because I'm amused by their similarity in appearance, except one is much taller than the other and partly in greeting. They nod to me. The taller one looks vaguely familiar, and I think I recognise him from the audit today.

"Good evening," I say, and get a "hello" back.

I lean in a bit closer, addressing the one I think I recognise. "You work here, don't you?"

"Yes," he says guardedly, trying to work out who I am.

"I still haven't quite worked out the setup," I hear myself saying, unsure where that has sprung from.

He looks at me, not understanding.

"I mean, the setup of these workshops." I have to shout over the music. "The big ones in front and then the smaller ones here. What's the history of these units? They're a lot older."

"Oh, right," he shouts in reply. "These are the original workshops from the old days. This is the old part. These used to be the workshops from when old Terence Holden had the metal business."

"Oh right," I say, my earlier guess proving correct. "Just seems a bit weird that they're set back so far from the access road, the main entrance and office building."

As the young man leans closer, I can smell his overpowering cologne. "No, it was the other way round in the past. The old access road is the other side of this building." He points vaguely in the direction behind the building. "It's a sunken road now. You can't see it from where the offices are. In fact, you can't see it at all unless you know it's there. Over the other side, that's the new access road, see, from the eighties. Couldn't get the big lorries up the old road."

"Sunken road," I echo. "Never realised."

"Yeah, this was the first building on the site in the old days. When you come up the old access road and turn into the yard, this was the first building. Now, from the other side, it's the last. Old Holden had his office up there on the first floor, overlooking the entrance to the yard so that he could keep an eye on who was coming and going."

First floor? I look up and then I see it, to the left of the bar on the other side. A metal staircase leading up to a higher floor. The guy follows my gaze, pointing and nodding in confirmation. "Yes, there's a couple of offices and other rooms up there," he shouts into my ear. "That's where Holden had his office."

He looks at me a bit more closely. "Are you with the company? Haven't seen you before."

"No, I'm from Hamlays, the bank. We do some of the financing for the equipment," I say and hold out my hand. "Neil Wilson," I say, and he shakes my hand. "Tom," he says but nothing more.

"We did an audit here today," I say, but he doesn't understand me. "A floor check. On the machines here," I say louder.

This time Tom and his colleague hear me well enough. They exchange a long look and I'm about to say, "What?" when the smaller guy nudges his mate, points to the entrance where a couple of men are standing. With a "see you then" they take off. Something about their exchange of looks strikes me as odd, and I'm still wondering about that exchange of looks when a powerful spotlight comes on and dances across the floor. This is accompanied by music from Vangelis, "Chariots of Fire". The spotlight meanders back and forth, picking out people standing around before swivelling up to the upper floor, picking out Alexis standing on the landing of the steel staircase. Next to him stand Michalis and a couple of other men, one I recognise as the foreman, who had led us through the units earlier during the day. The beam of the spotlight rests on Alexis, who stands arms outstretched like a minister. He's dressed in a long white robe with red fur – the opposite to Santa Claus. With his white beard and long white hair he looks religious. The music ends and after some applause, during which Alexis stands still, his pose with arms outstretched fixed. The applause and the voices trail off as everyone stands looking up, mesmerised just like myself, waiting to hear the man's words.

"Friends!" Alexis's voice booms out, and he brings his arms down to his sides and smiles at everyone gathered. "As we bring another successful year to an end, welcome to our year-end festivities. You have all been amazing, and your dedication and loyalty to Holden Industrial is what makes us so successful." A cheer goes up from the crowd. Alexis raises his hand and silence descends. "May we have many more successful years like this one. And may the party begin," he concludes with a big grin, slipping a red and white Santa hat on his head. The crowd cheers and laughs and claps. Then, seemingly as an afterthought, he adds, "And the buffet is now open." More cheers and applause from the crowd. He brings his hands together as if praying, bows slightly and then waves to all. "Have a brilliant evening!" he shouts as the DJ flips on a new track, the disco lights come back to life and the fog generator emits a big cloud. Now the real party has started.

I watch as Alexis makes his way down the metal stairs, followed by his entourage. At the bottom of the stairs, the waiting fans greet him like a star. He shakes hands, slaps backs, big smiles all around, and slowly makes his way across the floor, greeting everyone. He works his way across to the passageway, stopping to greet and talk to everyone before disappearing through the passage to the other workshop. I turn back to the now-heaving dance floor and watch the action. Ten minutes later, I feel a big, heavy hand on my shoulder. I turn and there he stands, beaming at me.

"Young Neil, there you are," Alexis says. "Having fun?"

I smile and am about to reply when a man appears at Alexis's side and starts shouting at him. Alexis is visibly startled and horrified. The man is standing very close; I can feel Alexis's revulsion. I'd say he's middle-aged, as in forty to forty-five, but that's difficult to be certain of, for he has blotched skin and greasy hair. He looks dishevelled and unkempt. Alexis has taken a few steps back by now, the man still right up close to him, and I'm moving with them, wondering who this man is and what he's up to, but ready to grab him if he becomes violent. I can't understand all of what's being said as Alexis is now turning and walking faster, trying to get space between himself and this man. He's following, finger jabbing into the air and shouting. The music's too loud to hear what he's saying and now Michalis has appeared, stepping in to intervene. I hear him say, "Matlock, what the devil…" But the rest of the words are lost as shrill whoops rise from the crowd as a young bloke attempts to break dance on the dance floor. The bundle of men, which it has become now, with Alexis in the middle and the man – Matlock? – now grabbing his arm, Michalis trying to drag him off and the big foreman trying to shield Alexis, spills out of the entrance and out into the darkness and drizzle. I follow and out here it's still loud, but I can hear the voices clearly even as I move a few steps to the side, keeping a discrete distance.

Alexis now stands like a tower in front of the man, who is still jabbing a finger into the air. "…it's not enough. I'm taking all the risk…" he's saying.

Suddenly aware of where he's standing and the spectators close by, Alexis grabs the man's sleeve and pulls him further away from the entrance. He pushes him around the back of the tracked Universal Carrier. Michalis follows, keeping close behind the two men. The big foreman moves to the left and takes a few steps forward, keeping a close eye on his boss, ready to rush in if necessary. I stand to the right of the entrance and realise they are unaware of me being here. I carefully move some more to the right, further into the shadows.

"You have some nerve, Mr Matlock," Alexis is saying, barely suppressing his anger.

"No, I don't Mr Holden," he says in a squeaky voice. "As I said, it's getting tight. The partners are getting suspicious. I can't cover this up forever."

I gulp, now feeling embarrassed at hearing this. This is something personal and I shouldn't be listening in. But I'm stuck. I'll have to stand here in the shadows until they finish their conversation.

"Not now, Matlock," Alexis hisses. "You come here Sunday, and then we'll discuss."

"Okay, Mr Holden," he squeaks again. "What time?"

"Three p.m.?" Alexis says but it's not directed at Matlock. He's looking at Michalis, who is standing behind Matlock.

He shakes his head. "Not this Sunday."

"Next Sunday, then, Mr Matlock, three p.m.," Alexis says, leaning forward, his eyes boring into the other man's. "Got that?"

"Okay," the man called Matlock replies.

"Right. Now, Mr Matlock, I want you to leave."

They are standing just a few feet away from me; between us is the vehicle. The illumination from below the Universal Carrier throws light onto both men's features. I can't believe it. The man's face turns sad. His shoulders slump and he looks defeated. Surely, he wasn't expecting to be invited into the party, I think as I stand watching them. Not after creating such a scene.

"You should show more gratitude," Matlock says, and now his voice doesn't squeak.

Alexis straightens, his look softens. He pats the man on his upper arm. "A week Sunday, Mr Matlock. We'll speak about everything then."

Alexis walks past Matlock and heads not back to the party but away along the tarmacked area, followed by Michalis and the foreman. Matlock turns, watching the figures depart. He sighs and casts a glance at the entrance, where the reflections of the flashing lights dance in the night air and the beat of the music bounces off the walls. He turns and walks off…into the darkness. I follow him with my eyes and move a few hurried steps to see where he's going and am just able to make out his figure descending a slight slope before disappearing into absolute darkness. I'm baffled for an instant before I remember the sunken road.

9

The dance floor is heaving. I glance briefly at my watch, it's coming up to 10 p.m. Not late yet but the older folk have gone home, only the hardcore is left. But the party is really going and I have to hand it to the H.I. crew – they're good party people. I've had a few beers but I'm not drunk. The thought crosses my mind that now might be the right time to call it a day. I take another look around but there's no sign of Alexis or Michalis. They haven't reappeared since the episode with Matlock. I decide to finish my beer and then I'll head home. Fortunately, I'm allowed to keep the pool car overnight, which saves me making trips back and forth. The plan is to drop the pool car off at Hamlays' offices on Sunday and then take the train to Worthing. I'll be on leave as from Monday and have arranged to spend Christmas down at Ben's. It's not what I want. I'd have preferred to go skiing or something like that, but there wasn't time to organise something and nobody's available either. With my split-up from Emma, I've lost fifty per cent of my friends. I'm sort of ticking off the checklist in my mind when out of the corner of my eye, I see movement behind the dance floor. A black theatre curtain begins to rise. New clouds of fog billow from the generator, obscuring the view. The music stops. Everyone stands in total surprise, watching and waiting. As the fog rises slowly, a stage is revealed on which eight figures stand, black capes covering them. A track begins and each figure is picked out by a beam from the suspended grid above the dance floor. Slowly at first, the figures begin to move and as the music picks up speed, the figures throw off the capes. Eight very attractive young female dancers step away from the discarded capes and up to the edge of the stage. Wolf-whistles pierce the air, the crowd is clapping and laughing. I clap, too. Nice touch, I think, cool!

They are wearing sky-blue stewardess uniforms with zips down the front of their outfits. They perform some dance moves and then, in a theatrical and somewhat seedy gesture, pull the zips all the way down and remove their tunics. The crowd surges forward, especially the lads. I watch in amusement. In deft movements, the dancers undo the zips of their sky-blue dresses, discarding them, too, with exaggerated gestures. Underneath, they are wearing shiny silver hot pants and tops. Catcalls and whistles pierce the air, my ears ringing painfully. The mob is going crazy; they're loving it. The girls stand on the stage, animating the crowd. The party is rolling. I remind myself that I'm a free man now and throwing my mental time schedule and checklist into the bin, I decide to join the melee and get into the groove.

After about an hour of strutting my stuff, I return to the bar and get myself a fresh beer. I look around and am really surprised. Everybody is having a great time and to me it seems the number of people present has increased. Ah well, in for a penny in for a pound, I think and sinking the beer, return to the mad cauldron of the dance floor. The dancers left the stage after a while and have been in with the crowd on the dance floor, animating the throng and whipping up the heaving mob with each new track. At some point, I had a blonde and a brunette beside me, dancing provocatively and lavishing their attention on me.

I return to the spot where I'd been and within seconds, they're back. It's hot, sweaty stuff by now, but the girls still look fresh, and I wonder how they do it.

It's probably just a trick of the imagination but somehow they seem to be focused on me. It can't be my dancing, I'm no great mover, much to Emma's disappointment. I've had a few beers and have discarded any ideas of driving home tonight. Also, I'm feeling quite merry by now and simply don't want to leave. I'm enjoying myself too much, especially with the girls so close. I decide another beer is needed and make a move for the bar. This time, the girls wave to me and the blonde even blows me a kiss. If it weren't for the fact that I need a short breather and something to drink I'd stay.

As I stand at the bar waiting for my turn to order, there's a tap on my shoulder and I turn to see that they are standing right behind me, smiling. In need of a drink, too, apparently, so I ask the blonde one what she'd like to drink. The music's too loud, I can't hear what she says, so she leans into me and speaks into my ear. "We want champagne," she says, her lips brushing my ear and sending tingles down my spine. Her accent is foreign, that much I can make out, and I get their drinks for them. I'm just glad it's all for free here as I watch them knock back the champagne in one gulp. They laugh at my shocked expression and press in on me, pinning me to the bar, the brunette beckoning the barman.

"Champagne for us," she says to the barman. And then to me, "You must drink champagne with us."

I don't like champagne much, but who am I to say no when two beautiful girls insist in such a persuasive way. We stand at the bar, dancing and swaying, the girls moving ever closer. The champagne keeps coming, the barman winks at me and seems to be serving only us. I'm in heaven.

The more champagne I drink, the more things start to blur. There's something else but I can't grasp it. The girls are very close, dancing where we stand, their bodies moving against mine. I'm getting oblivious to my surroundings, all I feel is the alcohol in my head and the bodies of two gorgeous girls rubbing up against me. Their hands are all over me, and I'm getting increasingly excited by the feel of their bodies against me, and I'm sure I've had a hand or two on my growing bulge as we dance away in a tight little bundle.

10

Slowly, like a submarine rising from the depths of the ocean, I awake. At first, I can't work out where I am. Nor can I read my wristwatch. My head is throbbing and I feel nauseous. I feel around for a light but find nothing. Where the fuck am I? I crawl out of bed, realising with a moan that I'm naked and stumble in the direction of a small source a light: curtains. I push them aside and blinded at first, I fumble to open the sliding doors. Cold December air hits me and I gulp down deep lungfuls of it. I turn and look around the room. I can't believe the state the place is in. A wave of nausea rushes through me and I stumble to the bathroom and throw up. Oh God, I feel so rough. I drag myself into the shower and stand under the hot water for ages. I towel myself dry, take the toothbrush glass and gulp down water from the tap.

It takes me a little longer to stop feeling dizzy; I sit on the loo waiting for it to pass. I return to the bedroom and take stock. My clothes are lying everywhere and the room looks a right mess. It's almost as if I've been in a fight. The bed is severely messed up and when I pull the duvet aside, there are dark stains on the sheet and on the cover. It doesn't take an expert to realise the dark stains are blood. I rush back to the bathroom, checking my face in the mirror. Did I have a nosebleed in the night? No, no signs of that, the blood isn't mine. I walk back into the room. What the fuck happened here? I can't remember a thing.

I gather up my stuff. My shirt is torn, several buttons missing, as if it's been ripped open. Jeez, I mumble to myself, what's going on? Trying to tidy up as much as I can, I stop and examine the duvet. The stains will take some explaining, so I strip the bed, fold everything up and put the cleaner side of the duvet on top. I just want to get away.

I let myself out of the room and climb the steps one cautious step at a time. I hope and pray I won't bump into anybody. Upstairs, all is clear and I sneak out of the guest annex and onto the decking. I know I should pay my respects and say thank you, but I'm jittery. Something's just not right. Now I notice the light is beginning to fade. What time is it? It must be late afternoon. My watch has stopped. I take a look at the house. It's in darkness. I just want to get away now, so I follow the pathway down through the garden to the car park. Mine's the only car there. Searching for the key, I feel panic rising and jump into the car as soon as I can unlock the doors. "Start the bloody engine," I say out loud. Not bothering with the seat belt, I throw the car into reverse, then into "D" and floor it. Sod the noise the cold engine is making as I put my foot down, I take the car out of the car park as quick as I can and onto the main road, accelerating hard in the direction of London.

I speed up the A24, still feeling dizzy and weirdly detached. I make it home to the flat but have no clear recollection of how I got there. I bump into Mrs Pearson in the hallway. With a concerned look she asks if I'm okay. I give her a mad grin, stumble up the stairs, straight into the bedroom and dive onto the bed.

I awake the following morning in my bed, which is reassuring. I'm still wearing my dirty and torn clothes, which isn't so reassuring. It's an instant reminder of what's happened and worse, I still have no recollection of it. I can't fathom it out. I've been drunk before, many a time, but never like this. Plus, the nausea and giddiness. I've never experienced anything like that before. I get up, make coffee. Mug in hand, I sit down trying desperately to get my brain and my memory into gear. Failing to do so, I head for the shower. Catching a glimpse of my back in the mirror, I gasp as I see long scratch marks down the whole length of my back. Panicking, I give the rest of my body a thorough check. There are scratches everywhere, especially on my back and thighs and forcing myself to look, I whimper as I discover bite marks all around my groin. Of fuck, I gasp, whimpering some more as I carefully check out my dick and balls for damage. Luckily, there's nothing serious, just more scratch marks, a few bite marks, too, but much less nasty.

I pack my bags in silent rage, but I need to do something physical. Walking back and forth, from one room to another, I sort through my stuff and pack things into my big holdall. The realisation bubbles to the surface that this is the end of my life here and that I won't be coming back to this flat apart from to pick up the rest of my stuff. It's Emma's now. Emma and Tristan. Despite everything, a sudden sadness overwhelms me and I have to sit down. For a few minutes whilst I sit at the kitchen table I deliberate if I have the strength to face the trip to Worthing. If only I could remember what had happened. A total blackout. Given the state I'm in, I'd have no objections to staying here at the flat for another day or two, just to rest, but I've promised Ben. And also, I admit to myself, I don't want to be on my own.

With a sigh, I push my emotions away and focus on the task of packing and travelling. I'm putting my passport and wallet into my backpack as, with a startling flash, a piece of memory returns: Matlock! I remember now. Blotched face and greasy hair. Mad look on his face as he appeared out of the blue, shouting at Alexis. I have to sit down, so vivid is the scene in my head. I probe my memory, and more surfaces. Standing outside the unit, squeezed into the shadows, Alexis and Matlock talking. "*You come here Sunday, and then we'll discuss,*" Alexis had said. That's today, I realise.

I wish I could go and sit on the wall like a fly listening. It sounded so intriguing. But it's none of my business and now I remember feeling embarrassed at overhearing this private conversation. Another morsel of memory pops into my head: not this Sunday, next. I remember that detail now. Either way, not my concern, so I push it aside. I urge my memory to spew up more. And it obligingly does. In a series of flashbacks, I see in my mind what seems like sequences from a video, the dancers on the stage, then down in the dancing mob and then bang, it's there: the blonde and the brunette, moving in on me, dancing close at the bar, hands everywhere, champagne and then…lights out!

Lights out, absolutely. Total darkness from then on. My memory is unable to dig up anything more.

11

R u on the train?

Yep.

Good, be here in time for dinner. Smiley face.

Can u pick me up pls? I write. I know Ben won't want to, but I can't face taking the bus from the station and then the walk from the bus stop.

U can walk u lazy sod!

Pleeeease.

I can see he's typing his response, but then a pause. After a moment: *U ok?*

No. Not feeling good, I type.

Still hungover? Two smiley faces.

No, feel ill. I've been debating with myself if I should share what I now believe to have happened. I've spent the best part of the train ride researching it. But I hesitate. It feels odd to put into writing that I'm convinced I was drugged. Especially as I know Ben won't believe a word and will persist in taking the piss out of me for days.

Great. Comes here ill. F**k off back to London. Smiley face.

I know he's joking, but I can't be bothered, so don't reply. After a while, he comes back online and types, *Sure bro. Will come pick u up. Wots up?*

Dunno. I think there's been an incident.

I regret "incident" as soon as I've sent it. It means I'll have to explain. I should have written something like "worst hangover ever", but it's too late now. Plus, I'm so confused that I feel the need to discuss my suspicions with someone.

The train rattles over the Ouse Valley Viaduct, which for me has always been the point at which I discard my professional London life and return to being the Worthing lad. I love the viaduct and the countryside, and from this point I always look forward to coming home. Coming home to my family, my friends and the town in which I grew up. Home, where I can be me and where I know myself to be safe. To feel safe – that's what I need right now. The amnesia that I have concerning several hours of that night, coupled with the state the room was in – and me, too, for that matter – has left an uneasy feeling of total vulnerability. For a few hours of that night, I was totally in the hands of someone who wanted me to be in such a state. The questions that are at the forefront of my mind now are: who and why?

Ben's waiting for me outside the station. I'm more than glad to see him and doubly so, as it's raining by now.

"Hey, Neil," he says as I get in.

Ben is six years older than me but at first glance, we look like twins. We're the same height and have the same physique. He'd look younger than his thirty-five years if it wasn't for the receding hair that has been troubling him for some time. In an effort to cover this up, he combs his hair forward. He's the brother I have the closest relationship with. Doug and Will, much older than me, have always been aloof or at least that's my impression. Both moved away, pursuing their careers overseas. Doug, the oldest brother, is a lawyer in New York and hardly ever comes back to England. Apart from Mum, we don't miss him. Will, a partner in one of the big accounting firms, moved to Australia a couple of years ago. He, too, has detached himself from the family. Both are by appearance and character my dad's sons, whereas Ben and I take after my mother. Apart from video calls at Christmas, we never talk.

"Ben, thanks. Really grateful."

We try to hug in the confined space. He looks at me, giving me a close inspection.

"No, no bruises and no cuts," he concludes.

"Not in the face, no," I say.

"What?" he asks, and I can see he's getting concerned now.

"I have bruises and cuts and bite marks all over me," I say, not being able to hold it back.

"What happened? Who did that?"

"I wish I knew."

Claire brings in two mugs of strong tea and some digestives. I say thanks, Ben nods his thanks in her direction. Claire is Ben's wife. They've been together forever, since sixth form days. I can't see what Ben finds attractive about her. She's dour and boring. Amazingly, she works in marketing and public relations. I've never understood how someone so obviously lacking any communication skills is able to excel in a job where these are paramount. But, somehow, she does, so it must be my view of her that's wrong. Tall, brown hair but no style to it. She's turned plump over the years – I know it's nasty of me to say so. It's just that I've never liked her much, especially as Claire always got on well with Emma and used to keep going at Emma to dump me. Claire has always despised me. She thinks I'm superficial and arrogant. And she always resented me for treating Emma the way I did. Now that we've split up, Claire feels vindicated and thinks I deserve no better. But even she could tell I'm not well and for once, she showed some concern for me when I walked into their house.

"You should go to the hospital," Ben says. "I'm sure they can still find traces even now. It's not even forty-eight hours, is it?" We're sitting in his study-cum-office. Ben is self-employed and works from home. He creates and designs websites and things like that. He's a digital nerd – something I never was or will be.

"I guess so, but what's the point?"

"The point?" Ben exclaims. "The point is, you've been drugged – probably. That's a criminal offence."

Ben is full of righteous anger at what has happened to me, and I'm grateful for his concern. I've told him most of what's happened, leaving out some of the details, like the two girls and the blood on the sheets. He's right, of course. And we've been discussing this back and forth for some time now. Go to the hospital and to the police. And yes, I should. But I feel inhibited to do so. For a start, I feel embarrassed enough as it is and if I go to the police, they'll ask for details. I can't really describe the girls. Blonde and brunette with beautiful figures and their hands all over me. That's what I remember. But did they administer the drugs? And, the other thing is, I still can't understand the *why*. I'd have gone with them willingly – a dream come true. Plus, if I go to the police, I will need to say where I was and that will mean Alexis becoming involved. He was the host. I don't want that even if Ben has forced a thought into my head. A thought that's going round and round. Was Alexis involved? It's something I don't want to believe – or to even consider. Why would he do that? Silly, really, to think he might have been involved in any way.

Fortunately, Claire calls out that dinner's ready, which puts a temporary end to Ben's nagging insistence to go to the hospital. I'll give Claire one thing, though, she's a great cook and her Sunday roasts are amongst the best. I tuck in, happily accepting the offer of seconds. I didn't realise how hungry I was until I started smelling the sweet aroma of roast chicken. Feeling famished, I eat heartily, not being able to remember whether I'd eaten since Friday or not.

12

"Go to the hospital whilst we're out, Neil," he says as I reach out for the next plate to dry up. "At least that way you'll know for sure. Even if you don't go to the police."

We're standing in the kitchen, which in Ben's house is situated at the back and looks out onto the garden. I like Ben's house – always have. It's a two-up two-down but on a larger scale as is common. At least it strikes me so, as it's far more spacious than most other two-ups I've seen. Viewed from the front, the proportions are deceptive. It looks narrow at first glance but once you enter, the rooms are longer than they are wide. Ben and Claire, they had an extension built when they bought it. The extension is where he has his study-cum-office on the ground floor. Above is the en suite bathroom to their bedroom. What was left of the old patio was converted into a conservatory. Beyond that they have put down some teak decking and there's still enough garden left for it to look harmonious. They had the pebbledash painted white and latticed windows fitted. It's a cosy house now, and I always enjoy staying here.

"If you want you can take the scooter," he says, wiping down the sink. Despite having a dishwasher, the breakfast dishes are always washed by hand. It's a Wilson thing, passed on to us from our mother. "As you usually do," he adds with a smile.

Ben has a 400cc scooter. A big, powerful machine, but nippy and good to get about town or even for a tour, say to Brighton. I always get to use it when I'm down.

The build-up to Christmas is always a big thing in our family. It doesn't matter that we'll only be four. Apart from Doug and Will, we're one more down as Emma is no longer part of our family Christmas. Ben and Claire plan to go shopping this morning. They don't want me to come as I always get in the way and they have a carefully organised shopping list that follows the layout of the supermarket's aisles. Ben has convinced Mum to spend Christmas here rather than us going to her house, so they're doing the shopping. Whilst they're out, I set up my work laptop on the little desk in the front bedroom and log on to my account. As it fires up, I take in the room and the subtle changes that have occurred over time. I remember this room being decorated in bright colours, in anticipation of conversion into a nursery and, in time, a child's room. The child never came and over the years, the colours and furniture have been replaced. It's a guest and storage room now. Despite being on holiday, I scan the emails but there's nothing of interest in my inbox. I'm expecting the audit report from the floor check to come in, but that probably won't be until the afternoon.

Sitting at my computer, my mind wanders back to the events of Friday night. Should I go to the hospital to have a test? I can't decide, fearing the consequences of what will happen if I do get confirmation and make it known. I'm good at that – procrastination. To delay having to make a decision, I decide to go for a walk along the seafront and pop in to see Mum. It's less than a mile from here to my mum's house and a walk will do me good.

"Hello, sunshine," she says, opening the door. As I walk into the hallway, we manage to hug in the confined space.

"Hello, Mum," I manage to say as we disengage. "Getting smaller," I say, smiling as I appraise her. She just about reaches my chest.

"Cheeky sod," she says, laughing. But my mum has shrunk. At sixty-five, she's still a very fit woman. Silver-haired, slim and smartly dressed in Marks and Spark's latest fashions, she's still a force to be reckoned with. She's active in several organisations and clubs. Her energy is amazing despite the toils of bringing up four kids and having to live with my dad. Since his demise, she's blossomed.

We sit in her overcrowded lounge and chat. Whilst we sit, I can't help but feel that Mum is becoming a hoarder. The lounge, as the rest of the rooms in her house, is full with bags and boxes, things she says she's put aside to clear out. Except that they have been parked in the corners for years. Mum lives in a semi-detached house close to town. Built in the thirties, with brown pebbledash, now a shade too brown from rain and decay, the house looks worn. Mum brought all the old furniture with her when she moved, despite the rooms being too small. The result being a small woman living in a worn and crowded house. It's a stark contrast to her otherwise active character. It doesn't take long for the conversation to drift towards the inevitable.

"Neil, what happened to you and Emma? She's such a sweet girl."

"Yes, she is, but we weren't compatible."

"But you were such a sweet couple," she replies. As if being a sweet couple is the most important aspect in a relationship, I think but don't say it.

"You are twenty-nine," she says.

"So I am," I say, trying to keep it humorous.

"It's about time you settled down."

"Is it?"

"You young people, I don't get it. All you seem to want is material things and an easy life. No commitments," she replies.

We've had this conversation many a time.

"You're too much like your dad," she says in an offhand way.

This is news to me. "In what way?"

"He wanted too much out of life. A family just got in his way," she says with a touch of old sorrow in her voice.

This certainly is news to me. "What do you mean?"

"Oh, he had dreams. Dreams of success and money. But we had Doug when I was still so young, and he had to give up on his big ideas. He never forgave me, and he took it out on you kids."

That certainly explains his behaviour to a certain degree, I think, but again, I keep the thought to myself. All the more reason not to make the same mistake. But I'm intrigued; we've never had this conversation before. "What kind of dreams did he have?"

"Your father was a complex man, Neil. What's the saying? He had ideas above his station. He was envious of successful people and despised his peers that had done better in life than he had. After he was bypassed for promotion, he went so far as to fiddle accounts. I don't know the details, but it had something to do with awarding contracts to companies and taking a commission for it. It cost him his job. But he never accepted it, claiming he was framed, but I always felt it was true. He went freelance after that, but he was never successful."

My word, to say I'm shocked is an understatement. A deep family secret shared in such a blasé way – I'm lost for words. All I know is that my father was a conceited patriarch, always right in everything and with a strong right arm to dispense *his* justice on us kids. A bigot and, so it seems, a fraud. And on top of that, my mother claims I'm like him? That's too much to bear. I decide to drop the subject, focusing instead on the usual banalities of our conversational topics.

After another hour, I'm glad to get away. I walk back along the back roads, mulling over the conversation in my head. I'm amazed and shocked at my mother's revelations; I never knew any of this. Above, seagulls circle, their screeches loud and grating. Normally I like seagulls, to me they are part of what makes the seaside so special, but today I feel like they are laughing at me.

13

Late in the afternoon, the audit report is sent through. I'm back in the front bedroom of Ben's house, staring at the laptop, but my head is full with my mother's revelations. I'm wondering if Ben is aware of any of this as my mind registers the new email highlighted in my inbox.

The email from the floor checkers is long, mainly disclaimers, so I pass over it, clicking on the PDF attachment. There's a management summary followed by pages and pages of reporting. They're obviously being paid by the page. The authors describe in length the approach to the floor check, the exact steps of what they did and where. I search for the result – their verdict on the floor check – and after some scrolling, I find the passage.

Just then, my phone rings. Kevin.

"Hi, Neil, you read the report?"

"In the process," I say, trying to read the passage. Kevin waits patiently whilst I scroll and read.

They write that ultimately, as far as can be said, followed by more disclaimers, the floor check showed no serious findings apart from a few machines not being where they were supposed to be and rental contracts not being up to scratch. Fundamentally, as far as floor checks go, the report concludes all is well.

"Here, got it," I say. "All well. Wow, cool." That's a relief. A positive audit is a pre-condition to the payout of the first five million.

"Congrats, Neil."

"Thanks, Kevin." So, now the deal can go through once the documents have been signed, and I get to book my first major deal…and earn some commission.

"Are the contracts in yet?" Kevin asks, spoiling my dream.

"No." I'm immediately on the defence. I know what's coming.

"Get it sorted, Neil, holidays or not. We have three weeks left to book in this year."

For a moment I hesitate, but if I'm going to mention what happened, now would be the time. But I don't. Instead, I say, "Yes, right, on to it," despising the greedy capitalist system that enslaves us and which has now put even more pressure on me. And then I think of the commission I will be earning from this deal and it doesn't seem quite so despicable.

Kevin says his goodbyes and galvanised into action, I pick up the phone, scroll down to Michalis in my contacts and am about to dial his number when something makes me stop. I try to bring back that feeling of elation I had, but I feel wary and I realise, given the incidents of that Friday night, a bit suspicious.

Instead, I return to the PDF file of the audit on my screen and start going through the report properly. The first section deals with the machines that had been checked in the field. This means on location on the various building sites or literally out in a field, depending on the job that was being performed. The floor checkers report that they carried out this exercise in Horsham. They'd picked a number of machines at random and all had been where they were supposed to be. There's a detailed report on each machine. Each page deals with one machine: its position, the third party renting the machine, the job currently being performed and extensive checks of documents, including payments received. Some documents are not quite complete, but on the whole, all machines are accounted for.

The second section concerns the machines that were at H.I.'s site in Horsham – the floor check I attended. These machines have all been ticked off: checked visually and photos taken. Machines not at the site at the time of the audit have been listed and their whereabouts explained by H.I.'s management. Some have not been assembled yet; some were at a paint shop getting a bespoke livery sprayed. All the machines we inspected are documented and at least three photos per machine have been taken. One photo of the plaque showing the serial number and two of the machine from different angles. I glance through the photos, but there's nothing untoward about them. I look to see if the floor checkers have commented on the worsening conditions as we moved through the units – the lighting getting worse and the growing disorder until finally everything was jammed in haphazardly. There's only a brief mention of the organisation becoming less stringent during the course of the audit and that due to this, the time needed to complete the audit increased as the audit progressed. Which, incidentally, means a significant increase in their bill too.

I dither some more, reluctant to speak to Michalis. Get a grip, you twit, I chide myself. I take a deep breath, and then I hear the ringing tone in my ear. The call goes to his voicemail. I put on a cheerful air and record my good news. "...and before we can process any packages for payout, we need the contracts and documentation signed and returned to us as soon as possible," I conclude before adding a cheery thank you. I hang up. For good measure

I send an email too, basically reiterating the message I've just left.

Done.

I sit clicking back and forth on the laptop until the conversation I had with the workman at the Christmas party, Tom, pops into my head. I remember what he said about the sunken road. On impulse I switch to Maps and zoom in on H.I.'s site in Horsham. I'm intrigued by the sunken road and sure enough, after some zooming in and out and switching to satellite mode, I find the contours of it. I track the sunken road, finding the access point, which is of a smaller road close to the A24. I zoom in and out; it seems quite easy to find. And suddenly an idea forms in my head. A stupid crazy idea, but it provides me with a way to deal with my unease about the events of that Friday night. Furthermore, although I'd put it aside as it's none of my business, I also recall the conversation between Alexis and Matlock outside the old unit on that night, too. I replay the memory of that in my head. What had he said? Then I remember his words: "*As I said, it's getting tight. The partners are getting suspicious. I can't cover this up forever.*"

"I can't cover this up forever." The sentence bounces around in my head. What was he referring to?

I check the weather forecast. The next days will be dry, sunny and not too cold. Perfect for an outing.

14

I'd memorised the map as best as possible and as soon as I get south of Horsham, I look for the landmarks I've picked out on Maps. The sunken road is accessed off a minor road that turns off from the A24. According to Maps there's an old pub on the corner. Despite using the navigation mode on my mobile, I still have to stop several times before I find it.

Fortunately, it's not a private road but is apparently used mainly by agricultural vehicles, so it's hard to spot. There are high trees on both sides, now devoid of leaves, and some hedges. I stop the scooter, peering along the road. It's very secluded and I can't see very far into the darkness of the bushes and trees which stand tall on both sides and on the verges. I drive along the sunken road for a while, a lot further than I'd have anticipated, before spotting the old entrance to H.I.'s site. I motor past, glancing into the yard as I pass, and am glad to see there's nobody about. It's a Sunday, after all, and I would be surprised if there was much activity. I turn the scooter around and drive back and up to the edge of the site access. I keep to the edge, hopefully out of view. There's a slight slope leading up to the site, which provides some additional cover. I switch off the engine and standing beside the scooter, wait a couple of minutes. I'm glad I'm wearing Ben's black motorcycle gear and his black helmet. Black against black, I should be hard to spot.

All's quiet. I walk as close to the site entrance as possible, keeping to the side of the road and the bushes. I peer through the foliage and can see the front of the old workshop where the party had been. I walk a bit up the slope, keeping under cover as much as possible. I can now see down the line of the old workshops and the rear ends of the units which stand in front of them. The tarmacked space between the two lines of units is about ten metres wide. Wide enough to accommodate two cars or vans side by side and enough space to turn a car or van around in the confined space. A forklift, however, no problem. I'd seen those shunting the machines around on their transport trolleys.

I scrutinise the unit closest to me, the location of the event. Red-bricked, built stone by stone, unlike the concrete units opposite. I look up to the first level where I can now see the windows along the side of the old building. There's one quite close to the corner of the workshop – this must be where old Holden had his office. I remember the workman, Tom, saying Holden could see who came onto the site by looking through his window. I doubt he'd be able to see anything nowadays; the windows are very grimy. They don't appear to have been cleaned in years. I check my watch; I still have plenty of time. The appointment Alexis has with Matlock is at 3 p.m. – at least, that's what I overheard. I try to see if there are any signs of movement behind the glass but from this angle, it's not likely to spot any movement unless someone stands right by the window. In any case, even at this time of day, my impression is without lights, it will be too dark inside. Nothing to be seen, which is good, but doesn't account for much. I have no idea if the appointment is still on; it might have changed. And the meeting might take place elsewhere, but I remember Alexis saying, "*You come here*," and something in my gut tells me that he means exactly here. Even if they don't appear, it'll be no loss. It's better to do something even if it gets me nowhere.

I take a deep breath and dash up the sloped access to the side of the old workshop building. Peeping around the corner, I check to see whether there are any CCTV cameras mounted on the workshops on either side of the line of units but can't spot any. I still have the helmet on and the visor is tinted, which limits the view, so not being one hundred per cent sure, I return to my earlier vantage point and remove the helmet. I'm glad for the balaclava I am wearing underneath; my face will be unrecognisable at a first glance. Not that I want to bump into anyone – how would I explain my presence here?

I stand waiting for a while deliberating if I should drive back to the pub on the corner of the road and warm myself up. I still have more than an hour to go. I move over to the scooter, where I am out of sight, and dig into the pockets for a chocolate bar. It's getting cold and some energy will do me good.

Faintly at first but then clearly discernible I hear the engine of a car. Wondering if it's coming up the sunken lane, I move closer into the bushes. But then I realise it's coming from the lane between the units, the sound of the engine bouncing off the walls of the buildings on either side. I move back to the bottom of the slope, where I can now see a black Jaguar pulling up in front of the old workshop.

The driver's door opens and a man in black jeans and a black leather bomber jacket gets out. He's wearing a black baseball cap; I can't make out his features. Then the rear passenger door opens and out climbs Alexis. He's wearing a long black overcoat and black trousers. Only his silver hair provides a contrast to the blackness of his and his driver's outfits.

Alexis unlocks the workshop doors, pulls the right-hand door open – it opens outwards; I remember that detail now too – and disappears inside. Dim lighting flickers into life from within the workshop. The driver gets back inside the car and I watch as the car makes a three-point turn and drives slowly away. I switch my gaze back to the workshop where now a light has come on in Holden's office.

Right, I think the appointment is on.

I wait watching. I check my watch, coming up to 3 p.m.

Every minute or so, I stand on tiptoe, looking along the length of tarmacked space between the units waiting to see if the man in the leather jacket will return. Then he does, and a few metres behind there's another figure. As they walk closer, I recognise the second man. Matlock.

In contrast to the other two black-clad men, he's wearing a beige rain mac and what looks like red trousers. From my vantage point here at the bottom of the slope, I can see the mac's creased and dirty and the trousers baggy and worn. He looks like a tramp.

Bomber Jacket pulls open the right-hand door and gestures to Matlock inside.

Matlock walks past the man in his bomber jacket keeping as much distance from him as possible. His posture and the quick steps he makes give the impression he's wary of the man. Bomber Jacket moves a bit closer to the entrance and I can see he's straining to hear. I can't make out any words from this distance but he nods and walks away, leaving the right-hand door open.

I wait until he's well out of sight and with a thumping heart, cross to the other side of the slope and, keeping to the bushes, slowly walk up the slope to the edge of the workshop. The door stands open, wide enough to provide cover, and with a rush of adrenaline, I move up to the open door.

I pause by the open door, straining to listen. I lean forward, taking a quick peek into the inside of the unit. All clear. Taking a deep breath and trying to calm my nerves, I quickly walk inside, keeping to the right.

Where the makeshift bar stood are now pallets stacked high. I move into the shadows behind them and take stock. The floor space, which had been used as the dance floor, is full with crates and boxes. A forklift stands a midst the various boxes and crates. I look up to the upper floor. The door to the office stands slightly open, faint light spilling out onto the metal landing. Waiting for my eyes to adjust to the dim light in the workshop, I notice the truss with the lights and lasers is still hanging from the metal grids supporting the roof. I guess it's permanently mounted there. Beyond the pallets, I can see the stage. Perhaps a permanent fixture, too. There are grimy skylights set into the roof, allowing some daylight. But it's getting darker now so there isn't much light coming in. I take another deep breath and strain my ears once more to hear any movement or voices. Nothing.

I creep around the pallets, putting them between me and the door. Who knows, Bomber Jacket might appear any moment. Given the dark and damp smell of old bricks, it's difficult to visualise the sights and sounds of the party location. I had hoped that coming back here might trigger some more memories of what happened, but my mind and memory remains blank. I push that aside;

what I want is to get up onto the first floor and close to that partly open door.

Using the cover the pallets provide, I edge my way as close as possible to the metal steps that lead up to the first floor. A gap of a few feet with no cover remains between me and the steps. A last look at the open door of the unit and with my heart hammering in my chest, I rush across and put some weight onto the first metal step. The metal step is solid. Very slowly, I make my way up step by step. The grated metal steps are well-worn with use but thankfully emit no sound as I climb to the top of the staircase and stand on the long steel landing running the length of the building. I halt, listening and looking. I turn towards the partly open door. On tiptoe, I move to the door, light from the room spilling out onto the landing. If anyone comes out through this door now, I've had it. I'm totally exposed. I go down onto my knees and move my upper body forward. I want to look into the room, but I don't dare. But this close, I can now hear.

"No, Mr Holden."

A soft voice, hard to hear even from where I'm positioned. It must be Matlock speaking.

A sigh. That must be Alexis.

"The price you are paying me is not enough," the first voice again, but now firmer. Matlock.

"So, what do you think is the right price?" the second voice says, and I can clearly identify Alexis's deep rumble.

"I know what you are planning," Matlock says. "I think two hundred and fifty is a fair share."

"What? That is outrageous!" Alexis exclaims.

"It's not outrageous." Matlock's voice is now louder, agitated. "I've been looking after your books for eight years now and you wouldn't be where you are without me…"

No reply. There's a pause. "And given what you plan to pull off, two fifty is nothing." Matlock is speaking again. "That's my price, Mr Holden. Two hundred and fifty thousand. And make it euros."

"Okay, Mr Matlock," Alexis says, seemingly resigned, but there's a grim note to his voice.

I hear a screeching sound from below. Someone is opening the doors to the unit, the hinges complaining as the doors are opened wide. As fast as I can, I move along the landing to the far end, which is in absolute darkness. I peer below. Bomber Jacket has returned, whistling some tune. He walks to the forklift. He starts the vehicle, the motor soundless, it must be an electric version. He raises the forks, picks up a pallet and reverses the vehicle out of the entrance.

I creep back up the landing to Holden's office. Just as I'm about to resume my position, the door is shut in my face. I almost have a heart attack – that was close. Nothing more to be gained now, so I make my way down the metal stairs and to the entrance. Both doors stand wide open. I inch forward, peer around the doors in both directions: the coast is clear. Hugging the wall of the unit for as long as possible, I rush to the slope and down into the sunken road wondering who on earth is this guy Matlock!

15

Walking briskly through Homefield Park and past the hospital, I reach the seafront and march along the promenade to Splash Point. I should have brought my running shoes and then I could have got it out of my system. Instead, I march at top speed along the promenade. Only as I reach the pier do I slow down. Turning on to the pier's eastern promenade, I stroll along the thick planked walkway, stopping at the plaque commemorating the poor souls of a crashed Lancaster bomber during the war. I always pass this spot and pause for a while to read the plaque and the names. The guys on that plane had all been younger than me. They had their lives still ahead of them, their dreams and hopes extinguished in a few agony-filled moments. They'd fought and died to make a better world and here I stand, having to tell them that it was all in vain – it hasn't become a better one.

My head swirling with the chaos of my thoughts, I walk on to the end of the pier, where the anglers stand, and watch them for a few minutes. The wind is strong, black clouds racing in from the west, bringing with them the promise of rain. The tide is in and I watch the waves as they march by below me like rows of soldiers to throw themselves onto the beach. The air is laden with salt spray, the seagulls circling above, their screeches loud and shrill as they effortlessly ride out the gusts. Breathing in the cold salt air, I try to bring order into my mind.

I now know who Matlock is.

I spent Sunday evening researching. It took a while but I found him. From what I overheard of the conversation, I thought he might be an employee. H.I.'s bookkeeper, perhaps. But he isn't. He's H.I.'s accountant. He's a senior manager – so his title – at Charlton Hudson, H.I.'s firm of accountants. I started with a name search. "Matlock" brought up the results one would expect, which was irritating as it wasn't the TV series I was interested in, and it took a while to refine the search before I found what I was looking for. As soon as I saw the name of the accountancy firm, it clicked. I went through their "About us" and then on to "Our team", and there he was: Peter Matlock, Senior Manager. I'd never have recognised him, though. The photo of the man on the company's website must be a few years old. The man I have now seen twice is a mere shadow of his photographed self.

Having been able to identify him and his job, the conversation between Alexis and Matlock has now taken on a different dimension, the bits I overheard pointing in a totally different direction. His words, "*I've been looking after your books for eight years now and you wouldn't be where you are without me…*" have been tumbling around in my head. Sunday night, lying sleeplessly in bed, it dawned on me. Matlock has been manipulating Holden Industrial's accounts. Quite simple really. We were all surprised by H.I.'s financial figures.

Towards dawn, I'd just about come to terms with my mind's deductions when another snippet of the conversation between Alexis and Matlock barged its way to the forefront of my mind: "*And given what you plan to pull off, two fifty is nothing*".

Those had been his exact words, and they had me sitting upright in bed.

I'm no Sherlock Holmes, but even I can work out that the manipulation of accounts serves one purpose: to fool everyone as to the performance of the company. I had concluded by this point that this was what Matlock had been talking about and that his reward for performing such special services was *two fifty* – I'm sure he was referring to thousands too. *Two hundred and fifty thousand. And make it euros*, he'd said. A tidy sum for a guy who looked like a tramp.

But what had me sitting upright in bed had been the other bit in that sentence: "*And given what you plan to pull off*".

Now why would he say that unless something unusual was being prepared? And the way he'd said it had given it a negative connotation that my brain had picked up. My mind was reeling, trying to make sense of it, when it literally hit me in the face.

Knocking over the bottle of water on the bedside table as I struggled to sit upright and switch on the bedside lamp triggered it. Desperately scrambling to get hold of the bottle before it crashed to the ground, I caught my notepad with the audit report on top and it toppled over and fell onto the bed. I gathered them up, one page with a photo of one of the machines ending up on top. I stared at it as my mind made the connection.

I head back along the pier and on impulse, take a detour through the amusement arcade situated halfway along the pier. Nothing's changed is my first impression. It's the same cramped, noisy atmosphere as I remember from my youth. The same antiquated machines burbling out their tinny jingles at full volume through tired speakers. I stop at some of the machines, trying to work out what they do. It beats me how any of the games on offer can entice anyone to part with their money. One machine catches my eye, though; it's one of those old claw crane machines where you try to position the claw through a joystick and then let it fall, hoping the claw will close successfully on the prize and bring it to you. It's the only machine I ever played.

Something about the claw crane machine triggers my thinking. Most arcade machines require little skill level. You just pop your money into the slot, press a button or pull a lever. With the claw crane, the arcade lets you think that you can influence the outcome with the right amount of skill. You might be able to position the claw just right, but it slips off the prize when the claw falls. Or your position might be a millimetre off and the claw bounces of the side of the prize. But still, you have hope because it's your skill that you are pitching against the mechanics of the machine. Until you come to realise that behind the visible mechanics of the claw crane, there are more little levers and cogs in place that will manipulate the outcome in favour of the arcade. Behind the flashing lights and garish jingles there's a mastermind programming the little levers and cogs. And to me, this is the same with what is going on at Holden Industrial. Of course, I could – and should, for that matter – take my suspicions to my boss or go straight to the police. But I had already decided that morning, as I lay in bed, to tackle the mastermind. I walk back out of the arcade, grateful to leave the jarring sights and sounds behind me and head over to a corner where it's quiet and pull out my phone and ring Michalis.

He picks up on the first ring.

"Hello, Neil, I've been waiting for your call."

"Have you?" I ask, and Michalis picks on the undertone straight away. He doesn't answer my question. "I need to speak to Alexis," I say.

"Do you?"

"Indeed. Some irregularities."

"Irregularities? Concerning what?"

"Of the type that needs discussing with Alexis." I end the call.

Two minutes later, my phone rings.

"*Neil*, my young friend," the familiar voice booms through the earpiece and into my ear. My name drawn out once more like an accordion.

"Alexis, we need to talk."

"Do we?" he replies. This is like table tennis.

"Oh yes, we do," I say.

There's a moment's silence. The mastermind is trying to read my mind, I think.

"Okay, where? When? It's nearly Christmas. Isabelle and I are flying to Cyprus this evening from Gatwick."

"Well, that's good enough for me," I say. "Gatwick," I add.

"Can't it wait until I'm back?"

"Of course. But the deal might be called off by then," I say.

Another long pause. I can hear him thinking. "Okay," he says. "There's a Sofitel close to the North Terminal. Let's meet there. I can send a car. Six p.m.?"

"No car, I'll find my own transport. Six p.m. Meet you there."

16

A car would be sensible. It's cold and it's started raining. The big black clouds have hit land, bringing with them that awful persistent drizzle from the sea. But I want to be inconspicuous and unencumbered by the restrictions a car brings with it. Ben's scooter is ideal. I don't need a car parking space and it's nippy, just in case. Just in case? My brain trips over that, a knot tying itself in my stomach.

The roads are slick with the film of rain that's settled on them. I drive carefully and by the time I get to Gatwick, I'm soaked through despite my rain gear. I park the scooter close to the underground car park. I've brought a change of clothes, stored in the top case of Ben's scooter. I slip into the hotel through the entrance from the underground parking area. Seeking out a gent's toilet, I dart inside a cubicle. Changing out of my wet clothes, I dry myself with a towel I had grabbed on the way out and change into jeans, shirt and jumper. I check my watch. Ten to six. My mind wanders back to the morning's discussion with Ben.

"Ben, can you take a look at this please," I asked as I came into the kitchen. He was sitting on a stool at the kitchen bar, eating his toast and reading the news on his tablet.

"Sure," he said, looking up, catching the expression on my face. "What's the matter?"

I handed him the audit report. "Take a look at the photos will you?" I asked, pointing to the pages of the machines we'd inspected at H.I.'s Horsham facility.

Looking at them, he said, "What am I looking for, Neil?"

"Would you be able to tell if the photos have been manipulated?"

He scrutinised them. "No, not from these. They are printouts and not particularly high definition either. If you have the photos as such, I could get a better look."

"Okay," I say. "I just wanted your opinion."

"Do you think they have been manipulated?" he asks. And it's a good question. It's a piece in this unexpected puzzle I can't make to fit. But if something big were planned, involving the financing of these machines, then to me, that would be the obvious approach. At least, that's what my sleep-deprived mind has been stumbling over again and again.

"I don't know," I admit.

He turns back to his toast and takes a bite. "But then again," he says, "you wouldn't need to manipulate photos, would you?"

"Meaning?"

He looks up at me. "Well, just exchange the serial numbers," he says, stating the brutal obvious.

I take a deep breath, stow my wet gear in the big bag and store it in the top case. I walk up the stairs to the reception area and look around. A lounge area, low sofas, coffee tables, and dimmed lighting adjoin the reception. I see Alexis sitting on a sofa in a corner at the very back of the lounge, reading a newspaper. He sits relaxed, legs stretched out, at peace with himself and the world. He's dressed casually: dark cotton trousers, a shirt and a comfortable jumper. A man waiting to be picked up, destined for a flight home for Christmas. I walk over, my heart pounding. He looks up from his newspaper as he sees me approach. No big smile this time. As I come closer, a tough-looking, lean man detaches himself from the shadows. All I notice at first is the black bomber jacket. As he intercepts me, I see a face like a boxer. He stops in front of me.

"I need to check you," he says. He's the guy who drove the Jaguar and manoeuvred the forklift out of the workshop, no doubt. Short hair, cut army style. He's shorter than me but where I have loose skin and flab, he has muscles. Not the type to pick a fight with. I nod. He frisks me, quick but thorough. A few people sit further away, closer to the lobby and the main entrance. But apart from us three, there's no one here. Done, he nods to Alexis and steps aside.

"Sit, Neil, and tell me what this about," Alexis says. His tone's a mixture of curiosity and annoyance. To make sure I get the hint, he makes a show of looking at his big, gold wristwatch. I sit down opposite and fix him with a long look. He returns my look but bides his time. We both sit there looking at each other, not flinching. I take a deep breath and steady my nerves.

"The floor check has come up with some irregularities," I say. "Management is concerned and has asked me to clarify."

"Really?" he asks, one eyebrow lifted. "So, this is official?"

"Unofficially official, yes," I reply, nodding my head for emphasis. He gives me a long look, suppressing a smile like one tries to suppress a yawn.

"So, what kind of irregularities?" he asks. I hesitate. "I do need to know, otherwise I can't comment on them."

"The auditors have suspicions that some photos show false serial numbers," I say.

He takes this in and gives a low whistle. "Ah well, I'm sure it can be cleared up." The smile is back. "I'll get Michalis to sort it out."

"I believe they are right," I say unperturbed. This time he gives me a searching look. "I have checked the photos and I think they are right. The serial numbers match the list, but I think they have been manipulated. I attended the floor check and the further we moved along the line of workshops, the checks became more arduous. The lighting got worse; the machines were in no order like in the first couple of units. The checks slowed down. It took us longer and longer to perform the checks the further we moved down the line. I think it was deliberate. I think machines were moved from one unit to another. Once we had checked the machines parked in one unit and moved on to the next, I think the machines were manhandled out of the unit we had just checked and moved further down the line. That would explain why the order got messed up the further we got to the end. The light was dimmer and I think your people stuck plaques with serial numbers embossed over the ones that were there before. I have counted at least twenty machines where I believe this was done so."

He just sits there looking at me, measuring me.

"I'm sure this can be sorted out," he says, but his voice isn't quite so confident now.

"Alexis, I have enough data to be sure that the floor check was manipulated. The photos support this. The question is, for me, why? Why should a floor check be manipulated unless there is a motive behind it? After all, we are about to fund twenty-five million quids' worth of these machines through a sale-and-lease-back."

"So, what do you plan to do?"

"Obviously, the course to take would be to report this to my boss and the credit committee and stop the deal going forward."

He nods as if agreeing, rubs his beard and then his forehead.

"Talking of photos," he murmurs and glances briefly in the direction of my left shoulder.

The bloke with the boxer's face appears from behind. He leans over and puts down a brown envelope on the coffee table in front of me.

"I hate doing this, Neil, I really do," Alexis says from his sofa across the table.

I look at him, wondering what this is about. He gestures towards the envelope. I pick it up, open the flap and look inside. Inside are cards or prints. I reach in and pull them out, realising they are photos. High-resolution, enlarged photos taken from a video apparently. I sink back into the chair and start going through them. The photos, or the video from which they have been taken, are of me. In the guestroom in Alexis's house. With the two girls from the party. The questions that have been haunting me for the last few weeks have now been answered, my suspicions confirmed. The shots show me and the girls performing various sexual activities and in multiple positions. The last two photos make me jump. In the first, the threesome has been extended to a foursome. A man I don't recognise has joined in and is performing oral sex on me. The second photo shows me being pushed into a position of performing the same on him. Looking at the photo, one can sense my reluctance, my horror even. The girls are pushing me and the man is forcing my head down. My right arm is pulled back, hand balled into a fist. I feel the anger rise like a volcano and I almost leap out of my chair.

"What the fuck?" I yell. A few heads turn at the sudden noise, but I'm oblivious to them. I now remember the barman, who had almost exclusively served us and I remember the face now, too. It's the guy in the photo. I'm aware of Boxer Face standing very close to my left shoulder. My anger is still there, but I start laughing as much to Alexis's surprise as my own.

"What the fuck is this, Alexis? What's the point of all this? I don't get it."

"Neil, I like you. I really do," he says with what sounds like regret. "I don't approve of this, but consider it a sort of insurance. By the way, you broke his nose."

It explains the blood, but that's of no significance now. "Insurance? For what?"

"Insurance isn't perhaps the best term. Call it motivational assistance, if you like."

That makes me laugh. "Okay, I'm getting the picture," I say. "You set me up at the party, you drug me, get me into this situation," I add, gesturing at the photos now lying on top of the brown envelope on the table. "Then you take photos – or a video apparently – and now you put the thumbscrews on me. You call this insurance? But at the time this little merry game was being carried out, there was nothing that needed insuring – or, as you say, motivationally assisting. I didn't realise about the serial numbers until after the results from the audit came in. In fact, I didn't realise until this morning. So – thinking aloud here, Alexis – you set this up in case something *might* arise.

Which means with forethought and foreplanning. You *knew* there was something amiss right from the start, because you planned it. And now, it's come to life because I did notice something. What are you playing at, Alexis?"

He just sits there looking at me, his face a mask.

"What we are doing, Neil, is securing finance for the company," he says after a moment. "At the end of the day, it won't matter if one or two machines are missing. The money will be used to expand H.I.'s basis and secure its growth. We will be securing jobs."

"What? Don't give me that, Alexis," I say, my anger returning. "A few machines missing? Securing jobs? Are you doing this for the benefit of the company and its employees? Saint Alexis? You are doing this for other reasons. And what you are doing is criminal."

"Criminal?" he says, derision now in his voice. "Grow up. Business is never honest, Neil. I learnt that many years ago. Nothing is ever honest or fair. Business isn't and life isn't. But, apart from that, I can assure you we are taking on finance for the company. Admittedly, things haven't been running well. The figures are good but the underlying trend is not so favourable." I can see he's making this up as he's going along. For the moment, he seems to have forgotten that the annual report showed a superb performance, but he keeps going. "We need to invest to keep the company on a growth path. We are planning investments that will keep the company on its course. There is nothing criminal in that."

I'm close to saying that I know the financial data has been manipulated but I restrain myself. "Are you kidding me? The fact that the floor check was manipulated is a serious issue, Alexis."

He sighs. "Neil, as I said, I like you. You are the kind of young man that I would employ myself." I suppress a snort at that. "But in this matter, you are a pawn." He holds up a hand as I begin to react. "Let me explain, Neil. There are other powers active in this game. People are supporting this as they know it will be a good investment."

"Meaning what?" I ask, totally at a loss as to where this is heading.

"Meaning that there are stakeholders – interested parties – who have a firm interest in helping H.I. move along. People in your company, Neil."

"Alexis, who and what are you talking about?"

"Let me make it a bit clearer for you. You don't really believe it was just your good write-up that secured this deal?" I look at him, my bewilderment apparently obvious to him. "Your boss has a firm interest and commitment to make sure we get this finance in place."

"Kevin?" I ask, not believing my ears.

"No, not Kevin. Think higher up the ladder."

My brain's in overdrive until I realise that Willem had been a strong supporter and instrumental in making the deal go through. I hesitate before I'm able to say the name. "Willem?"

Alexis nods. "He has supported our activities – not just H.I.'s – for many years."

The implications of this are mind-boggling if they are true. I'm trying to think fast, trying to absorb the information and to plot my course anew.

"Okay, well, in that case, I'll ask Willem, then."

Alexis gives a little laugh.

The words bounce around in my head. "Alexis, you are telling me that…that…" I struggle to get the words out. I breathe in and steady myself. "Are you telling me, Willem de Vries, the CEO of Hamlays, is taking money from you?"

Alexis fixes me with his blue eyes and smiles.

Desperately I try to get a fix on this, but my mind is unable to. I'm lost for words, the implications are mind-boggling. I'm aware my mouth is wide open and I'm making strange noises, failing in my attempt to form the words that are rushing around my head.

He gives me a long, sly look and reaches for his wallet. I bristle as I wonder what comes next, but all he does is take out a business card, turns it over and scribbles a number on the back. He passes it to me.

"You think about all this, my friend, and then call me when you're ready. And that number is my private and very personal number."

He gets up, ready to go. I stand, too, thoughts somersaulting in my head.

The goon is standing with his back to us, surveying the lobby. Alexis stands for a while, looking at me. For a moment, I think he's about to hold out his hand or some such gesture but he doesn't.

"Hold on a sec," I say.

"Yes?"

"What's in it for me?"

"You what?" he says. It's his turn to look bewildered.

"You have painted a gloomy picture of my position and my prospects, Alexis. Whatever I do, I'm fucked for life – that's your message to me. You are blackmailing me with those." I point to the brown envelope in his hand. "And with whatever your *stakeholders* might do to stop me."

"I wouldn't call it blackmail, Neil—" he says, but I don't let him finish.

"Cut the crap, Alexis. You and obviously others don't want me to rock the boat, isn't that so? See the deal through, right? And I'm asking you what's in it for me?"

I can see he's weighing me up. He can't tell for sure if I'm bluffing. Nor can I, for that matter, but I want an answer to that question. Just how far is *he* willing to go?

"I meant it, Neil. I like you, and a young man like you would be an asset in my organisation. I just want you to know that. But you need to be clear about your intentions, Neil. Is this just a casual temptation? No way back for you if it is."

He leaves, the goon following him, taking the photos with him.

17

I ring Willem's office number, but his PA picks up.

"Neil Wilson here," I say. "I have a message from Willem saying he wants me to ring him."

"He's on leave," she replies, her tone of voice conveying the end of the line for me.

"So am I," I say, "but he asked me to ring him, which I'm now doing."

A long sigh. Then she says, "Have you got a pen?"

Equipped with his mobile number, I enter the digits. My mind is still awash with conflicting thoughts from yesterday's meeting with Alexis. Another sleepless night lies behind me. *In this matter, you are a pawn*, he'd said. It kept me awake all night. The photos, the veiled threat. No way out for me, so the picture he drew. And now the summons to call Willem – surprise, surprise.

As the phone busies itself dialling, the thought strikes me how odd it would be to see myself and Willem from one of those satellite perspectives one sees in films, where they zoom in from space to the protagonists. The camera would zoom in on me in my brother's cramped front bedroom, with the single bed in the corner, next to it the little desk where I'm now sitting. Zooming in on Willem, the camera would show him driving up the gravel driveway in his Jaguar to his mansion, where his beautiful wife stands with her favourite horse, returning from a brisk gallop across the meadows.

Willem picks up the phone. "Willem here."

"Ah, Willem, it's Neil Wilson. You wanted me to call you?"

"Ah, yes, Neil." He sounds out of breath. "Sorry, I'm in the garden with my wife, tidying up the pots and the mess."

"Oh, right. Sorry. Bad time to call?"

"No, no, glad for the break, good excuse to go in and warm up. My wife is a terrible boss." He, the CEO of one of the major banks in the UK, laughs at his little joke.

"So, Neil, how's it going? You settled into the new position?"

"Er, yes, thank you. Fine," I lie.

"Deal closed yet? All documents in place? I think the first tranche of five million payout is due this week or next?"

"Er, no, not quite," I mumble.

"Ah," he says. "Neil, I have a personal interest in this. Want to see it through to a successful conclusion. Good show so far, Neil. Twenty-five million new business right from the start, really good performance from your side, but I want that deal booked." Then a pause designed to let the words sink in. They do, and I'm wondering wtf is he telling me.

"Alexis is difficult to handle, I know that," he continues. "But get it done. This will commend you for other key accounts, Neil. You're my rising star now." He laughs, and I wonder what's so funny.

"Yes, Alexis is quite a character. Very special person. He has his own ways and special views on business and such," I say, trying to draw him out. Willem takes his time to respond and when he does, his tone is less jovial and charming. "Yes, but he is loyal and can be quite generous too."

What the hell is he implying? "He certainly has his methods," I say. "He beat me." And that's no lie. I feel bruised and battered after yesterday's meeting.

"Well, as you English say," Willem replies, "if you can't beat them, join them. Ah, my wife…" He says something in Dutch, then comes back. "Have to go, Neil. Good to chat. Speak soon."

And he's gone.

I look at my phone, unable to make sense of what I've just heard. I must assume Alexis has briefed him. "*If you can't beat them, join them*" – is that an encouragement to switch sides?

That night, I lie in bed and can't sleep, again. My mind is running a marathon. Hold it, not running, sprinting. I'm so restless, tossing and turning non-stop. What on earth should I do? Go to Kevin is the obvious. Go to the police, is the next obvious. Report it anonymously to the fraud squad or whatever they are called – another sensible option. The least sensible, however, is the one that keeps me tossing and turning. *What's in it for me?*

I've played all options through in my mind. I've imagined a meeting with Kevin: "*Kevin, there's something I need to tell you…*"

I've imagined going to the police: "*I'd like to report a date rape, a blackmail and a fraud in the making…*"

And I've imagined sending an email to the fraud squad.

And my dilemma is that out of all the options available to me, none of them appeal. All of them are akin to climbing insurmountable mountains. For a start, no one will believe me. I only have flimsy evidence. Anything I put forward can easily be opposed. And then, the photos. I've spent hours thinking about those and asking myself what harm can they do? Plenty is the conclusion I've come to. And I don't just mean the embarrassment.

And so, I've imagined doing nothing, letting them succeed and get away with it.

Thing is, I can't do that either.

I've spent the night pondering the meaning of "*If you can't beat them, join them*". I know the original meaning of that saying means to adapt and use your opponent's methods. Out of all the possible options, it's the only one that makes sense to me. If everyone else is on the take, why shouldn't I? Of course, I say to myself, not for my own personal gain but as evidence.

At 4 a.m. my phone beeps. A text message. A number I don't recognise. The message is short. It reads: *And?*

I sit up in bed, staring at it. I realise it's from a Cypriot telephone number.

I think for a moment, impulse driving me to enter my answer: *I want 100 grand.*

A few seconds later, the answering beep of a new message. *Ring Michalis.*

18

Becoming a criminal isn't easy. I realise that as soon as I think about how to go about it. How do you negotiate your illegal reward? It's not like you set up a contract and sue the counterpart when it's not fulfilled. I mean, there are no YouTube tutorials for this kind of stuff. It's intuitive and it's based on trust. Trusting criminals is contradictory. By definition, doing something criminal is illicit, deplorable and dishonest. Do you expect a criminal to keep his word? Certainly not. I've been pondering this for some time now and am wondering how to discuss this matter with Michalis.

I feel odd – that much I will admit. I've never ever done anything like this, not even contemplated it. I feel guilty as anything: it is not only immoral, it is illegal. I push that aside, saying to myself I'm doing this to collect evidence. And force myself to concentrate on my tactics. The only course of action open to me is to play my cards close to my chest and – as a trump up my sleeve – keep the threat open to publish my discoveries if word is not kept. Of course, that won't save my neck. I know that, but it would bring the whole house down, so that's surely worth something.

I take a deep breath and ring Michalis. He picks up immediately.

"Michalis," I begin, trying to put a casualness into my voice that I don't feel. He puts the phone down on me. I sit looking at the dead phone, bewildered. Two seconds later it rings, number withheld. I pick up.

"Hello," I said into the microphone.

"Get a burner," comes the reply. "Never use your official phone."

"Okay," I say, embarrassed and feeling like a bloody amateur.

"It's straightforward," Michalis says in his sandpaper voice. "You get the deal through and everything sorted. Once it's done and only then, do we settle. And we settle in cash. We don't deliver; you pick it up. Details then, when all is done. And get a burner, do you hear?"

19

With a couple of days left before moving up to Kingston upon Thames, I'm sitting comfortably in the lounge reading a car magazine. Everything's running well. I've managed to get the first H.I. package processed through the system and booked. Five million paid out. The second package is ready to be processed next week. Another five million. Ten million quid in total, and fifteen to go. A nice commission in the pipeline and a big *bonus* to be expected at the end of the project. That bonus is twice my annual salary from Hamlays – and tax free, cash in hand. And not to mention illegal. But within a few days, I've succeeded in getting used to ignoring that aspect. One hundred grand in my pocket – wow! I've found a flat, a nice place slightly above my income bracket, but I'm confident I'll be earning big time soon. Plus, with a hundred grand in my pocket I can do some cross-subsidising.

Got to keep cool, though. I know I went a bit over the top at Christmas and New Year, splashing out on nice presents for all and champagne for New Year. I caught Ben looking at me, but I ignored him. I just wanted everyone to have a good time.

"Hey, bro," he says, walking into the lounge.

I look up. "Hi, Ben," I say. "All good?"

"Neil," he says, with the intonation that comes with an awkward message one feels compelled but embarrassed to convey.

"Yeah?" I turn back to my magazine. I'm not really interested in what he has on his mind.

"Can't help but notice your generosity at Christmas and New Year, Neil."

"Sure, you're welcome. You've put me up for three weeks, so more than deserved."

"Sure… Sure…" His resolve falters. Whatever he wanted to say, he's put aside. Okay with me. "It's just, well, too generous. You spent loads. Claire… Well, she's embarrassed and wants you to take her present back. Far too expensive – excessively so."

"No way, Ben," I say. "I don't want anything back. You've supported me for so long and you let me stay here every time and never let me contribute. So, please, let's leave it at that, okay?"

Ben nods, keeps his mouth closed and we have lunch together.

The second package booked, the third lined up, and I'm on a high. New flat, new super-sized TV, new PlayStation. Even thinking of buying a car. Not that I need one – certainly not for work and I get to use the pool cars for my appointments – but I've always fancied a TVR.

I'm cruising along the motorway on my way back from a new and quite promising account, dreaming of sitting in a powerful TVR, when my phone rings.

"Kevin, hi," I say as the call connects.

"Hi, Neil," he replies, coming through loud and clear on the car's speakers.

"Good meeting," I say, thinking he's ringing to ask how the meeting went.

"Great, you can tell me all about it when you're back. Listen, Credit have been in touch; they want to do a quick review of H.I.'s financial status before the third package is processed. You need to get fresh interim figures from them. Okay? Do it now – better to get it out of the way."

"Sure," I say.

I'm not panicky, but of course, it's more than annoying. I think briefly of ringing Willem and asking for his personal intervention in our mutual interest but no, it's just a routine thing. I ring Michalis instead. Our interaction in the last weeks has been regular and absolutely neutral. Purely business related. No mention of anything other than business. I feel good, so I ring him, expecting him to say no worries, I'll get some up-to-date financials to you right away.

"Hey, Michalis," I say as he picks up and grunts his hello. I'm used to that by now, so I push on. "Credit want to do a quick review before we pay out number three package, so if you could send me the latest interim figures, that would be great."

"You what?" he barks. "Why?"

A bit taken aback, I say, "It's nothing serious, Michalis. It's routine."

"Your part of the deal, Neil, is to make sure everything goes through without a glitch," he snarls, and I'm sitting upright.

"Well, Michalis, it's normal procedure. And it's surely not a big deal to get the latest interim statements sent over?" Especially as you're getting special service from Matlock, I think but don't say. There's loud breathing coming through the speakers; I can tell he's really pissed off.

"How much time have we got?" he asks, agitated. "I have nothing ready and that wanker Matlock is pissing around."

I don't think he intended saying the name outright and I can sense his stricken silence on the other end. A long silence.

"I'll get it sorted," Michalis grumbles and hangs up.

I continue driving but thinking now about the conversation rather than TVRs. No way I'd be able to turn down Credit's request for fresh financial statements. It's not unreasonable of them to want them. But still, I'm wondering why Michalis was so pissed off. Probably because Matlock will have to put them together. For a moment, it makes my stomach churn and the guilt hits me. I'm pulled out of my gloom by my phone ringing again. I push the green call button.

"Neil Wilson speaking."

"Hi, Neil, this is Helen Carr, Credit Team." Her voice comes through my loudspeakers. "I'm ringing about Holden Industrial. I think there are some discrepancies. You are the key account manager, so you should be able to help me."

"How can I help you, Helen?"

"Well, as you know, there is a payout due and we'd like some up-to-date financial data."

I sigh with relief. "Yes, I've been in touch with our client. All in hand," I say.

"Oh good," she says, and I'm glad that's all. But then she adds, "Also, I've checked the documents and encountered some discrepancies in the floor checking audit report."

Jeeeeez... I have to force myself to stay calm. "What kind of discrepancies?" I ask as cool as I can.

"Well, it's not my job, but I think we're missing some machines in the report. I counted them all through and I think the audit report missed ten machines. Not much in

122

terms of total numbers but in terms of aggregate value, it mounts up to over a million. And we're meant to be paying out five million. So, I might be mistaken, of course, but I think we should have clarification given the values."

My heart is pounding but it now sounds less ominous. "I'll look into it when I'm back in the office," I say, trying to sound cheerful.

"Good, I've sent you an email with the details."

"Oh great," I say. "Thanks. That'll help."

I end the call. To say I'm surprised by this is an understatement. If anyone read the audit report in detail, it was me; and whilst I didn't count and add everything up, I did check them off against the audit list. How could I not see ten machines unaccounted for?

When I get to the office and after checking the pool car back in, I run to my desk, hook up my laptop and scan my emails. I click on Helen's email, read her summary and open the attached Excel file. She's been thorough. I pull up the files containing the asset lists – which are the machines we're funding – and the audit report. And then I go through the whole lot with a fine-tooth comb.

She's right – ten machines are missing from the audit report. I sit at my desk thinking. There's no way I can explain this, so I grab my phone, retire to a meeting room with my laptop and ring Michalis. As it's official business, I should use my real phone and not the burner. But we might have to be creative, so I use the burner.

"What now?" he says.

"Michalis, we have a slight issue."

"Great. Another issue. What is it?"

"Someone on the Credit Team has been poking her nose into stuff that shouldn't be her concern and has discovered that we have ten machines missing. They are on the asset list in the package we're about to fund, but they were not included in the audit. They weren't on the list for the audit. But they should have been. According to the asset list, they should have been in Horsham at the time when we were there."

"How often will I have to remind you what your part of the deal is, Neil? Your job is to make sure nobody goes around poking their noses into things that aren't their concern."

"Can't just make them disappear off the list you submitted, Michalis."

He sighs. "Which ones?"

I give him the serial numbers and hear him clicking away on his computer. After a few minutes, he comes back on the line, sounding much more at ease. "They were destined for a rental firm in Stockport and Manchester," he says with relief. "Shipped them the day before the audit."

"Excellent. Can you get the documents to me, shipping bill and all that?"

"Of course," he says before the sound of him lighting up a cigarette comes crackling through the phone.

20

Mesmerised, I watch the processes being played through in our systems. For a few weeks, I'm in a trance-like state, just sorting out issues, watching and cajoling, and babysitting everyone involved in the financing of H.I.'s machines, and that includes Michalis. The remaining three packages just seem to float in and glide through Hamlays' apparatus as if on greased runners. Like a spectator at a sports event, I watch as the last deal is booked, the payout of five million is flagged in the system and the money is transferred to H.I.'s bank account. A grand total of twenty-five million pounds in the space of less than three months.

That evening I sit in my lounge, an open bottle of champagne in front of me on the glass table with the chrome legs. Not that I like it much but it's solid, it looks classy and it cost a few bob too. My flat has experienced a transformation in the last weeks. I have acquired a leather sofa, a matching reclining armchair with a massage function and a new hi-fi system that blows the cobwebs away. In fact, I'm beginning to feel I need a bigger place to accommodate all the gadgets I've bought. I've spent a lot but the money's coming soon, so I'm chilled about it. I'm really fantasising about a TVR, but I'm going to have to wait a bit. In any case, I'm celebrating tonight. Celebrating the successful conclusion of the H.I. finance deal. Twenty-five million is cool. I raise my glass, sip the champagne. I don't like it much. Given its price tag, I expected more but it just tastes sour. One thing left to sort out. I take another sip and ring Michalis on the burner phone.

"Neil," he says in his usual gruff way as the call connects.

"Michalis," I reply as kindly as I can muster. I'm beginning to hate him and his condescending manners. "All sorted," I say, "last deal processed, payout affected this afternoon. Funds should be in your account tomorrow."

"Great," he says.

"So, I was wondering," I say, not sure how to put what I want to know into words. "What would be the next steps?"

"Next steps?" he asks.

I'm sick of his games by now. "Do I need to speak to Alexis to get a sensible answer?" I ask, imitating his gruffness.

There's a pause on the other end of the line. "Sunday, two p.m. Your slot. We'll get in touch beforehand."

"My…" I manage to swallow the words before they come out. My slot? Did he mean to say that? I can't imagine so. I just hope it doesn't register with him that it's registered with me. *Your slot…* That must mean there are several appointments planned for Sunday. Now that's interesting. But I needn't have worried; he's terminated the call.

I sip my champagne, wondering if Willem gets the same treatment and a summons to pick up his share. I can't imagine so. For a start, he's the CEO and secondly, I can't imagine him taking cash. I spend some time thinking about how they actually go about it. I have no idea how much Willem is taking, but it won't be a miserly hundred grand. And it certainly won't be two fifty grand, like Matlock, either. It must be a lot more. And for that they must use a far more elaborate scheme to transfer large sums of money. Bank transfers to offshore accounts. But for small fry like me, and I suppose Matlock, it's the tradesman's entrance. I start thinking if anybody else – and who – might have an appointment for Sunday, apart from presumably Matlock and me. I have already decided to stake out H.I.'s site to see who might come by to pick up their special commission. And, equally important, to get some evidence. I grab a piece of paper from the desk by the window and my new Montblanc pen and start jotting down things I need to take: binoculars, camera…

On to the second bottle of champagne now and I get quite excited at the idea of holding a big package of banknotes in my hands. In fact, it makes me wonder how big a bundle it will actually be. I have no idea. But I'll need to carry it. One hundred grand, it won't be that heavy, I suppose. I have an inspiration and stand up – a bit too quickly and my head starts spinning – and go over to the kitchen, which I've just had done, and search for the digital weighing machine. I walk into the hall – shit, a bit unsteady now – and get my wallet. Returning to the kitchen, I take out all my notes and start weighing them.

The champagne has gone to my head and I have difficulties completing the task. But after a while, I manage to extract one useful piece of information: pound notes are not heavy. Roughly one gram per note.

Total weight will depend on whether they choose ten-pound notes or twenty-pound notes or fifty-pound notes. I assume higher denominations as they won't want to lug heavy bags around, unless they want to enjoy a joke at my expense. I give up in the end as I feel ridiculous. Bloody amateur.

Returning to the lounge and my third bottle of champagne, I start planning. How do I get there and by which mode of transport? By car seems the obvious choice. But I don't have one. I could hire one, of course. But where do I park it? And if I want to stake out H.I.'s site, which might mean spending a few hours before and after my appointment hiding and observing, where do I put it so that it's not noticed? I'm convinced the handover will take place in the old workshop, where Alexis and Matlock met, so the sunken road will be the best way to approach H.I.'s site. But a car parked there will be conspicuous and a hindrance if I need to get away quickly.

The best way to go about it, I conclude, is to use Ben's scooter. Or any scooter. I don't want to ask Ben again and if I do end up asking him, it means going down to Worthing to pick it up. An additional trip that'll take time.

My head is spinning not just from the booze but also from too much bloody thinking. I lie down on the sofa just to stretch out, and my last conscious thought is where do I get a scooter from?

21

I find what I'm looking for parked on the pavement outside a motorcycle dealer in Richmond. A second-hand 300cc scooter with a large top case. I walk up to the sales guy, proclaiming my interest in buying it but I want to rent it for the weekend.

"We don't do rentals," he says.

"Sure, but I want to test it before I buy it. If I can try it out over the weekend, I'll know for sure if it's right for me," I say.

He looks like he's trying to find the right words to turn me down.

"I'll make it worth your while," I say, reaching for my wallet and casually flicking through a big wad of bank notes. That seems to be the incentive needed to make him more accommodating, especially as I add, "And I need a black helmet with tinted visor, a warm motorcycle jacket and gloves." He's grinning by the time we end up at the till, with me paying a premium to keep him happy.

Next, I pop into a big electronics store in Brentford and purchase a bridge camera with a massive zoom and binoculars with high magnification. After that, I kit myself out with a camouflage poncho and waterproof boots, waterproof trousers and a thermal balaclava. It's March, after all, and the forecast is wet and cold. For good measure, I buy a Thermos flask. Returning to my flat, I lay everything out on my bed together with the small backpack, my sling shoulder bag, which has my passport, wallet and keys, and try the gear on. I look at myself in the mirror grinning. I feel like special forces.

I set off, mindful of speed limits and ever-present road cameras. I ride defensively, I don't want anything to happen on this trip. I know where I'm going, which makes the drive easy. I get to the turning in good time. The pub on the corner is closed, not a single light showing, and behind it the sunken lane lies in complete darkness. I stop at the pub and walk around. My plan is to get a taxi from here for the short drive round to Holden Industrial's offices.

At a slow pace, I drive up the sunken lane to the familiar H.I. site entrance.

I pull up past the slope up to the site, keeping close to the bushes and kill the engine. I find a spot where the scooter is well concealed, put it on its stand and watch and listen. Nothing. Not even a bird. Absolute silence. Pulling on the camouflage poncho, I hang the binoculars around my neck. Next, the black balaclava and the hood over that. Ready, I walk back the few steps to the foot of the slope.

In a crouch, I walk up the slope, keeping close to the bushes and trees that line the side on the right, the side where the big concrete units stand. Every few steps I stop, listening and watching for any movement, my heart beating loudly in my ears. It's as quiet as a cemetery. I walk up to the edge of the site access and check once more for movement.

Standing in the bushes on the edge, the old, red-bricked workshop is just opposite. The doors are closed, a big padlock and chain fixed through the handles of the wooden doors. The first in the line of big concrete workshops is directly ahead of me. In a crouch, I move to the corner of the building and squeeze in between the outer wall and the bushes lining the side. Keeping low, I can wriggle through, and on my hands and knees, I fight my way through the narrow gap between concrete wall and bush to the end of the unit's outer wall. Here I lie down and peek around the corner. Before me is the wide tarmacked yard. And beyond that at the other end stands the office building.

The tarmacked area in front of the workshops is clear. I lie in the dirt and put the binoculars to my eyes, adjusting the sights. I focus on the office building and find the conference room on the first floor. All is dark and deserted. Grey rain-swollen clouds race across, occasional gaps allowing daylight through, lighting up my surroundings. I quickly scan the building before the next clouds come rushing across, spotting video cameras on the roof. Three at least, one trained in this direction, one towards the area leading to the older units, tucked behind the big concrete units and one trained on the car park.

As the next gap in the clouds opens up, I focus on the office building and the conference room. If the handover is to take place there, the view from my position will be good. They'll have to switch a light on, I think, and then I should be able to pick out details, like faces. I try out the camera, zooming in on the conference room and take a couple of photos. Bringing them up on the device's monitor, I'm satisfied that the zoom is good and the sharpness too.

I crawl back the way I came and return to the edge of the concrete unit and the area in front of the old brick workshops. I lie down and survey the old workshop buildings one by one. The one opposite, the venue of the party with Alexis's office on the first floor, doesn't appear to have any cameras. But from where I'm lying, I can't be sure there aren't any mounted on the roof. I scan the neighbouring workshop building and the ones further along, searching for signs of life and cameras. They, too, lie in darkness, locked up, big chains and padlocks visible on the doors. I scan the top of the buildings with the binoculars but can't see any cameras. I crawl forward a bit so that I can now see down the line of the concrete units with their hangar-like doors and bingo! At the far end of the line, mounted on the wall of the workshop furthest along, I see a camera facing this way. So, they do have a clear view down the length of the yard between the concrete and the brick workshops. I would have been surprised if they didn't. They are able to see any movement here. Accordingly, they can see any person or vehicle that comes up through the entrance from the sunken lane. I just hope they didn't see me on my first sortie here, but I doubt it. Also, I can't imagine anybody sitting at the monitors on a Sunday. Of course, they probably will be making a recording. Something to bear in mind for later on.

I decide to stay put and wait. I'll move back to the other end of the unit and scan the office building in a while but for the moment, I'll just stay here and have some coffee. I creep under the cover of the bushes, sit with my back to the concrete wall and fill the cup from the Thermos flask. Despite the thermal underwear, it's cold and I can feel the chill climbing into my body.

A car! I can hear its engine. I lie flat on my belly and edge forward to the corner of the wall. The same black Jaguar is driving slowly along the space between the workshops and draws up in front of the workshop right opposite. I'm sure whoever's in the car can't see me. I'm flat to the ground, the hood of the poncho pulled right down. It's still quite dark, a grey March morning.

The driver's door opens and the goon with the boxer jacket gets out. He opens the rear door. Out climbs Alexis, his big frame awkwardly rising from the car. The other rear passenger door opens and out gets Michalis. Once more, they are dressed in black. Black boots, black trousers and black overcoats. I can't help thinking of members of a secret society on a clandestine operation. Alexis makes his way to the double doors and inserts a key into the padlock. He removes the chain and opens the right-hand wooden door. Bomber Jacket and Michalis walk to the rear of the Jaguar and open the boot. They lift out four canvas bags, heavy bags too, judging by the effort. Alexis has both doors open wide now, and I can see him standing just inside as fluorescent lights flicker on. He turns as the two men walk past him. I can see them turning to the left, where I know the metal stairs lead to the upper floor and Alexis's office.

My assumption has been confirmed. The handover will take place here. Hidden away from sight and as discrete a location as one can ask for. I remain sprawled out on the ground, watching and waiting. Half an hour goes by, and then Bomber Jacket comes out, gets in the car, does a three-point turn and drives it away. Ten minutes later, he's back, a backpack on his shoulder. He walks into the workshop, closing the left door but leaving the right one ajar. I crawl out of the bushes and dash across the ten metres separating the units hoping and praying that no one is sitting at the monitors of the surveillance cameras.

I hug the wall and slowly move up to the door that is standing ajar. Here I pause, straining to hear anything from the inside. Nothing. I check my watch, still plenty of time.

With a start, I notice that the right door is moving. It stands further ajar than before. I hold my breath, glued to the wall. A gust of wind or a draught has forced it open further just that little bit. I relax, taking a deep breath and trying to steady my nerves. I look down the units towards the camera mounted on the wall of the workshop at the end of the line. The door is obscuring me from the camera's view. A rush of adrenaline shoots through my body even before I've committed myself. In a swift move, I'm through the door.

A quick glance left and right and I'm heading to the right, slipping behind stacked boxes. I look up to where Alexis's office is. The door stands open, light spilling out onto the metal landing. Slowly, I tiptoe over to the metal staircase and in a crouch, slip underneath it. I take the balaclava off and now I can hear them talking. Alexis's booming voice, the words haven't quite manifested themselves yet, but I hear the other two laughing. I try to steady my breathing, subdue my pounding heart and the buzzing in my ears. I manage to control my breathing and the words became distinguishable.

"So, all set up, Vincent?" I hear Alexis loud and clearly. Bomber Jacket has a name.

"Yes," a muffled but audible reply. "Cameras and microphones set up, monitor is ready."

"Okay. When's Matlock coming?"

"Twelve noon," Michalis's sandpaper voice.

"Right, and Wilson at two p.m.," Alexis's voice.

"I still think we should have just left," Michalis replies.

"Michalis, my friend, how many times do I have to tell you? We're buying time. Nobody needs to know we're clearing out. Before they realise what's happened, we'll be long gone."

No response to that.

"You've completed the transfer?" Alexis's voice again.

"Yes," Michalis replies. "Wired through to our bank in Vilnius and from there to Cyprus via Serbia."

"Who's taking over here?" says Alexis.

"Willoughby. There are sufficient cash reserves until the end of April. Wages covered. Then the well runs dry." A pause. He continues. "Officially, we are on an extended business trip, prospecting new investments in Croatia. No one should realise anything until then."

Alexis's loud laugh reverberates through the whole building.

I can't believe what I'm hearing.

They're doing a runner! Clearing out with Hamlays' twenty-five million.

I'm crouched under the metal staircase, frozen to the spot. Totally and utterly paralysed. I scramble to get my brain moving. I need to get out of here but I can't get myself to move. They are leaving. Abandoning the sinking ship. Leaving everything behind. The company will run dry within six weeks. Oh my God. They've planned everything, transferred the money and now wrapping up the loose ends. The consequences will be devastating. The company will fold. And, they are filming and recording everything here. For fun?

But why wait? Why pay us fools our money? Buying time, Alexis said. Yes, of course. Undoubtedly, Matlock, the unstable loose cannon, he might just spill the beans if he turns up and no one's here. And me? Well, I guess they have no idea what I might do. And now I understand, my demand for one hundred grand – the amount was never questioned, no negotiations. I did wonder about that. Bloody fool. If you're in the process of reaping in twenty-five million, then one hundred grand is small change.

And still, I'm shocked by the revelation. The whole thing will collapse like a house of cards. But why? And why now? Why not wait until a better opportunity arises? I guess because for them this is the ideal opportunity. Bloody hell.

This puts a new perspective on everything. I try to think through what will happen to me. With H.I. collapsing, there will be investigations. Auditors will pour over everything. The cooked books, the discrepancies in the floor checking report. Everything will come to light, including my involvement of course. And Willem's involvement. Is this the reason they're pulling the plug now?

I force myself to focus on my predicament. It will not only cost me my job, but there will be proceedings against me too. Aiding and abetting, or whatever you call it. And Alexis and his cronies, they will be long gone. And here I am, waiting patiently for my appointment to collect my share and doing a bit of clandestine observation on the side. Just as well that I did. Oh fuck, I should do a runner, now.

But I don't. I'm glued to the spot. Even if I do run now, I'm in too deep. I'll have to go to the authorities and spill the beans, say I went along with it to collect evidence. That was the plan after all, I remind myself. And then I'd still be in up to my neck. I can only hope for some easier sentence. A lesser conviction. Or whatever legal options there might be in such cases. Or carry on, pull this off, see how the wind blows and disappear myself. But with one hundred grand, I won't get far. Oh fuck.

My attention is pulled back to the here and now. Vincent is coming down the stairs. I've missed out on what has been happening, being totally immersed in my thoughts.

Alexis's booming voice follows him as he comes down the metal stairs. "And make sure he has no mic on him, I've never trusted that bastard."

I glance at my watch. It's a quarter to twelve. Matlock's appointed time. I shrink back into the shadows as far as I can. Vincent walks up to the doors, pushes them wide open and disappears. If you're going to clear out, do it now, I think, but I hear the conversation taken up again upstairs.

"And we tell him that all is well, Michalis. We tell him we continue to need his services. Anything to keep him relaxed and comfortable, okay?"

"Okay, okay," Michalis says. "But the guy is a nervous wreck. He's a walking liability, Alexis."

"Yes, but as from this evening, we don't need to worry anymore. And what he does when he finds out is no longer our concern."

A coughing fit. Michalis or Alexis, I can't make it out. Long rasping coughs. Not sounding good.

"Relax, Michalis. Here, your tea. Not long, my friend, and we'll be home." I hear that it's Alexis speaking with genuine empathy in his voice.

I'm standing in the shadows behind boxes, waiting. Part of me wants to run, but another part wants to wait and see what happens. The noise of a car's engine fills the air as it screeches to a halt outside. The engine's cut off and agitated voices can be heard from outside. There seems to be a commotion. Then shouts, which brings Alexis, and following a step or two behind Michalis, to the top of the staircase. They are about to run down the stairs when a figure comes rushing in. Matlock. Following close behind an out-of-breath Vincent. Matlock stops and looks up at Alexis and Michalis.

Matlock's face is flushed red. Vincent is panting as he tries to speak. "He saw me… And accelerated like crazy… Had to jump out of the way. Bastard," he manages to get out, trying to catch his breath.

"Mr Matlock," Alexis oozes, descending the stairs slowly, trying for reassurance. Matlock stands still, staring at him.

"I want my money!" he shouts.

"Of course, that's why we're here," Alexis says, trying to calm him. He's fixed his most charming smile into place. He stops about halfway down. "Come on up. It's all prepared."

"Bring it down," Matlock hisses.

Alexis smiles at him. "Now come, Mr Matlock, it's all laid out for you. You'll want to count it, won't you? Plus, you have some documents for Michalis, I believe."

Matlock, a puzzled look on his face, becomes aware of the briefcase in his hand. He shakes his head in wonderment and moves slowly across to the staircase. Alexis opens his arms in a welcome gesture, turns and begins climbing back up the metal stairs. "Michalis," he says, "let's make Mr Matlock a nice cup of tea, shall we?"

He walks past Michalis, who's standing at the top of the landing looking, and back into the office. Matlock hesitates a moment on the last step, eyeing Michalis, who takes a step back and half-turns and holds out his arm and hand with that exaggerated gesture I've seen him do, showing Matlock towards Alexis's office. Matlock holds his briefcase to his chest as he walks past him and into the office. Michalis, with an evil grin, follows him and closes the door. Vincent sprints up the metal stairs, his soles making no sound, hurries along the landing to the next office, opens the door and disappears inside.

I wait a couple of minutes, but I can't hear anything through the closed door. I creep out from behind the stack of boxes and make my way over to the entrance. The doors stand wide open and checking to see that all is clear, I edge my way out, past Matlock's old, battered Citroen, which is parked just outside the doors, and dash for the slope.

22

My mind is whirling with the information I have just picked up. My instincts tell me to get away immediately and ring the police. Perhaps it's the fog in my brain but my mind is still weighing up options: run without the money, run and keep the money, sit it out, or pretend I had no clue. That won't work, I know that. I'm not really sure why, but I decide to stay and see it through to the end. Part of me still wants that money.

I glance at my watch. Time is running out. I take off the poncho and waterproof trousers. My plan was to drive the scooter down to the pub and take a taxi. Now I remember there being a footpath, at least it was marked as such when I did my research. I walk up the sunken road but after a short distance, the road peters out, turning into a deeply rutted track providing access to the fields further along. It must be the other side, then. I retrace my steps, walk quickly past the site access and carry on searching. About sixty yards further, I find the path. I set off down the footpath, which leads past some copses with horses on the left and on the right trees and bushes to the rear of the old workshops. The path is dry and I make it to the A24 with not much mud on my boots. What little there is I scrape off as I walk the narrow tarmacked path running alongside the A24 at this point. I arrive at the turning that leads to the H.I. site with time to spare and keeping out of sight, I wait.

At ten to the hour, I walk up the short access road, past Alexis's matchbox house on my right and follow the bend to the site entrance. I feel very nervous by now and my senses are on high alert. I walk past the car park, up to the office building and stand waiting outside the entrance. The building is in darkness, doors locked. There's no one to be seen, which at least gives me some comfort that there's no one sitting at the camera monitors.

A voice from behind me makes me jump, and I turn to find the guy with the boxer face standing within a yard from me, hands in his pockets. Vincent.

"What, no motor, Mr Wilson?" he asks, eyeing me from top to bottom.

"No," I say, "not here, at least."

"Right, follow me, then," he says and starts off across the tarmacked yard. I follow him, a step behind, and we walk across the yard – the same route I'd taken on the night of the fateful party. As we turn the corner and commence walking up the lane separating the new and old workshops, I note with relief that Matlock's car has disappeared. Vincent walks up to the open doors of the unit and stands to one side, letting me through. As I attempt to walk past him, he holds out an arm, blocking my way.

"Just a quick check, Mr Wilson."

"Sure, as long as you don't mind me giving you a quick check too?"

He grins at me, a grin that conveys he does indeed mind, so we stand facing each other, forced smiles fixed, eyes like daggers.

"Let him through, Vincent," a voice booms from within. Vincent, his grin still fixed, takes a demonstrative step to the side and I walk past him into the workshop.

Alexis is standing just inside, a big friendly smile on his face.

"Good to see you, young Mr Wilson," he says in his most charming manner as if greeting an old friend. I know it all to be lies, so I don't bother replying. It's all a game, as I now well knew. I stand before him, no expression on my face, just waiting and keen to get things over. His smile fades and he gestures wordlessly to the metal stairs that lead up to his office.

I walk ahead, climbing the steps fast, my senses wired, not knowing what to expect as I'm now about to walk into this office for the first time. At the top of the stairs, I stop on the metal landing, waiting for Alexis to catch up, and cast a glance around. From above, I can see that my earlier hiding places were well chosen; from here the space below is in almost complete darkness. A long mental sigh of relief and as Alexis walks past me towards his office, I see Vincent standing below, looking up at me with a murderous expression.

I follow Alexis into the office, trying to take in as much as I can. It's a complete mess. Boxes stand everywhere on the floor, papers heaped on top. Having seen the mess in Alexis's den in his house, I'm not sure if this is normal or if someone is in the midst of a massive clean-up. If they are, I certainly know why. A quick glance around and over to the windows. I'm relieved to see they are so dirty it's impossible to see anything through them. It's an old office in an old building. A sticky and dirty PVC flooring, well-worn with dark patches and chunks missing. Old wooden filing cabinets line the wall, boxes upon boxes stacked above. There's a smell of oil and musty damp in the room. The only clear surface is that of the dark wooden desk which stands towards the rear wall of the office. A wooden swivel chair behind it. My eyes are drawn to a stacked heap of banknotes lying on top under the extended illuminated desk lamp. It casts a yellow shine on the plastic notes. Despite my nervousness and heightened state of alarm, seeing that heap is bewildering. There lies my money.

"You'll want to count it," a voice says from behind me, piercing through the bubble of my reverie. I turn and only now do I see Michalis, whom I'd completely forgotten about, sitting in an old, worn chair in the opposite corner, looking small and pale.

Alexis has manoeuvred his heavy frame around the desk and sinks into the old, tatty swivel chair. It creaks under his weight. Picking up a bundle of fresh twenty-pound notes, with an elastic band holding them together, he holds it out to me. I thumb through the notes, trying to assess how much one bundle amounts to and trying to count the number of bundles on the table. I've never seen one hundred grand in cash before. My nervousness returns; I'm suddenly conscious of both men sitting there watching me.

"I guess it's all in order," I say, looking at Alexis for confirmation.

He gives a little shrug. "Count it."

I feel at a loss, too nervous to do so. Now that I'm here, I just want it to be over and be gone. And only now do I realise I haven't brought a bag.

"Er, would you happen to have a bag?" I ask, raising a merry laugh from both men.

"Sure, Neil, sure," Alexis says, rummaging in his desk drawers. He takes his time, no doubt enjoying my discomfort and embarrassment. Whilst he plays his little game, I try to compose myself, remembering the words I want to say and rehearsed on the walk over.

"So, what do you plan to do with the money from Hamlays?" I ask. My voice and my words sound false and tense, but I'm talking to and for the camera's benefit.

Alexis looks up, shooting me a probing look. "What do you mean?"

"Well, you're investing it in the company, aren't you? That's what you said."

"Sure, all in hand. New machines and investment in the property," he says with as much sincerity as I've got acting ability. It sounds false, and he knows it, too.

"So, the funds from Hamlays are being channelled into investments here?"

Alexis pauses and fixes me with a long and assessing look. He's no doubt wondering what the hell I'm doing. He doesn't bother to answer. I decide not to push it any further and leave it at that. Bored with his little game, he hands me a plastic Tesco bag.

I scoop up the bundles of cash and stuff them into the bag. When I'm done, I look at Alexis and he nods. I give the room a brief once-over, trying to spot any cameras but can't see any. They're well hidden. I turn. Michalis is busy lighting a cigarette and doesn't take his eyes of his match as I march past him towards the door.

"Goodbye, Neil," Alexis says to my back.

I run down the metal steps, out through the door and straight down the slope to the scooter, almost expecting to see Vincent suddenly appear behind me, but no one's following me. Why should they? The transaction's done. They'll be clearing out soon enough themselves. I push the scooter off its stand, the Tesco bag still in my hand, and run, pushing the scooter.

After a good few yards, I start the engine, jump on, and speed off. Only now do I notice the rain. It must have started whilst I was inside. I'm getting soaked. I skid to a halt, get the rain gear and the helmet from the top box, and stuff the bag with the money in its place. I struggle to get into the waterproof trousers and abandon the attempt as I'm losing too much time. The poncho will have to do until I'm clear of this sorry place. I jump back onto the scooter and open the throttle.

About two-thirds along the lane, I see a car. I slow down, the rain driving into my eyes as I put the visor up. Here the road is wider with grass banks on either side. Rain ditches line the sides before the banks rise steeply, covered with bushes and trees. The car is half on the grass bank, half on the road. The front of the car, on the driver's side, is slightly askew, where the front wheel has dropped into the ditch. As I come closer, I see it's white. An old, battered Citroen – it's Matlock's car.

I stop the scooter just behind it, dismount and look around before walking alongside to peer inside. There's a figure slumped to the side, head resting against the driver's side window. I open the passenger side door, looking inside. It's Matlock. So far in my life I've been spared the sight of dead people, but even I can tell he's dead. Nonetheless, I reach in, touch his shoulder and gasp as he falls forward. I retreat, my heart thumping. I check once more to see if anybody might be approaching, steady my nerves and kneeling on the seat, feel for a pulse. Nothing. One knee on the seat, I stretch myself forward and, overcoming my reluctance, push his body back. It's heavy and my angle not favourable, so I push harder and this time his chest and head flop back into the seat; I recoil as his head turns and his wide-open eyes lock onto me. I steady myself and feel once more for a pulse but nothing.

He *is* dead.

Still with one knee on the passenger seat, I survey the inside of the car. A total mess. Plastic bottles, the remains of sandwich and sweet wrappers, papers and all other kinds of rubbish lie on the floor and on the rear seat. I swallow hard and search his pockets. Apart from his passport, I find a wallet with photos of Matlock and what I assume must be his wife and probably his daughter. Tucked inside his passport is an airline ticket for an evening flight from Heathrow to Sydney. He obviously planned on doing a runner, too.

On the back seat behind Matlock, I spot a canvas bag. Both knees on the passenger seat, I lean between the front seats and grab it. Near panic, I pull the bag forward and through the gap. It knocks his head, which drops forward. I drag it out and put in on the wet bonnet. Another quick look in all directions, all is still clear. The rain is belting down now and I rush to open the zipper. Inside, there are bundles of cash. Euros and underneath pounds. I briefly wonder why euros but push that aside. I also wonder how on earth he'd planned to get this on board a flight to Australia. But I chide myself – that's of no issue now. Keep focused. I can't tell how much it is but the number of bundles is significantly higher than my heap, and then I remember his demands for two hundred and fifty grand. But I'd think there's more in here. I pull the zipper shut, give the crumpled, sad figure one more look and, taking the bag, return to my scooter. I stuff the bag into the top case, push my Tesco bag on top, struggle into my waterproof trousers and speed off.

Only as I get close to the A24 do I realise that I've just left my fingerprints all over the car. Shit! Once onto the A24, and heading back towards Horsham town and beyond that London, I begin to think my position through. Realising that I'm now truly fucked, I take the next turning off the A24 and stop the scooter. I quickly go through my options. I have a hundred grand plus a big heap of bundles that are Matlock's. Two fifty minimum. I could and should go straight to the police. That would be the morally right and only sensible thing to do. Yes, I think, do that. But I hesitate, my resolve being washed away with the rain. It's clear that whatever I do, there's no way out for me. Unless…

I get back on the scooter, only to skid to a stop at the next turning. I stop the scooter, get off and walk back and forth, trying to get some rational thinking done. A thought has barged its way to the front of my mind. But, no, I can't possibly do that. Unless… Unless… Apart from turning myself in, the only other option I have is to hide somewhere, well away and out of the immediate reach of those who will come searching for me. A corpse will undoubtedly add even more drama to the whole damn mess, even if death came through natural causes, as I firmly believe. But Matlock's car and body, so close to H.I.'s premises, will certainly add to the long list of questions anybody will have on their list, especially with Alexis, Michalis and the rest of their gang absent and my fingerprints all over the bloody car.

"I need a diversion, a false trail," I say to myself, surprised at my own voice under the helmet. Yes, and then head off somewhere where you can think and plan… And then it strikes me: Uncle George's yacht in Shoreham. I know where he keeps the spare key. Maybe I can hide there for a day or two and plan my next steps. But I need to have them looking for me somewhere else. I get back on the scooter, a plan now in my head.

I turn the scooter around, drive back onto the A24 towards Horsham and the signs for Gatwick.

I drive as fast as I can, given the conditions. I make it to Gatwick in one peace and park the scooter beside several others just outside the terminal building. I stow the helmet and rain gear in the top case, take the canvas carry-all, stuff my Tesco bag inside, slip on the backpack and my shoulder bag. At first glance, I should pass as a passenger on his way to his flight. Trying to look like the casual traveller, I enter the terminal building. I walk around as nonchalantly as possible, hoping to be picked up by as many cameras as possible. Let them think I boarded a flight.

Despite the adrenaline surging through me and every instinct telling me to flee, I even manage to buy a coffee and sit in a café, the heavy canvas bag between my feet, looking up at the departures board. Despite everything, my involvement and my illegal gains lying by my feet, I'm still contemplating whether or not I should turn myself in. I feel angry about how they manipulated me and roped me into this. Admittedly, it was me who demanded a hundred grand. I was just turning the tables, though, wasn't I? Getting evidence. They, Alexis and Michalis, and even Willem, had no qualms whatsoever about using me for their plans. Of course, the simple thing to do would be to walk into any police station and confess the whole story. Why don't I? Perhaps, in a way, part of me is no better than those I'm condemning. I have a big bag full of money at my feet and a plan, however simplistic and naïve. Deep inside, I know I'm not being honest. I'm savouring the excitement. Perhaps it's the adrenaline and my high-flying nerves, but in this rush of excitement, my deeds are opposite to my thoughts.

A few more minutes and I feel I've spent enough time now. I get up and go to the gents. I remove my jacket, stuff it into the holdall. Putting on my baseball cap, I pull it down over my eyes and leave the terminal building at the nearest exit. I go to the train station and buy a ticket to Brighton.

Arriving at Brighton, it's dark now, and I get off the train, putting the jacket and poncho back on and walk to Shoreham. It's not that far, but it's still raining and a cold wind strikes my numb face. As I approach the marina, I check for activity and cameras. All is in darkness and the marina is deserted on this cold and wet Sunday evening. I wait, standing in a dark corner close by the locked gate. After a while, I get lucky, a man appears, manhandling gear for his boat. He walks right past me, not seeing me, and opens the gate with his keycard. Just before the heavy gate swings shut, I slip through the gate. I make my way to Uncle George's yacht, which is lying in its usual position. I quickly climb on board, retrieve the key, which is tucked inside a fender cover at the rear, and with as little noise as possible, slide the hatch open and slip inside. I slide the hatch closed, sinking down onto the cold boards. Only now that I'm safe inside do I feel the adrenalin that's kept me going since the morning recede. With a groan I can't subdue, I collapse; and fuelled by exhaustion and self-pity, I cry my eyes out.

23

I must have fallen asleep because when I awake, it is pitch dark, outside and inside. I check the clock on the phone and it's past 2 a.m. It's freezing cold inside and I shiver from the cold and exhaustion. Numb with fatigue, I get to my feet and peer out through the side windows. No one about, which is what one would expect at this time of the night. I grope around in the dark and finally find one of Uncle George's many head torches. He has a selection, some with red LEDs. It's one of those I want, the red light much less visible from the outside. I don't want anyone seeing a light coming from inside the yacht. I switch it on, grateful for the two red LEDs that provide enough light for me to see what I'm doing. I move forward to the front cabin, where George keeps the sleeping bags and pillows. I drag the canvas bag into the forward cabin, place it on the mattress and wrap a sleeping bag around me, and then grab a second one for my legs. Opening the zip, I up-end the bag. Putting my Tesco bag to the side, I sort through the contents now sprawled on the mattress between my legs. Apart from Matlock's bundles of money, I'm grateful to find chocolate bars, crisps and some bottles of water. I open one of these and greedily drink the icy water. I start counting the money, my lot first. One hundred grand, as agreed. Matlock's heap of bundles next. I lose track a couple of times and have to start afresh, but in the end, I count two hundred and fifty thousand euros and fifty thousand pounds. Enough to start a new life.

I push everything back inside and sit and think. My plan, if you can call it that, was to spend just the night here and then think of somewhere else I can go. Wales or Scotland – somewhere remote. I realise as I think it through that anywhere in the UK will be risky. With the money I now have, I can live for a long time. Another idea starts forming. I'm sitting on an ocean-going yacht. Knowing Uncle George, it will be tanked up, engine well maintained and ready to sail. What if I sail to the Continent? I have sailed the Channel a couple of times with George and whilst I've never done this on my own, I feel confident enough that I can do it. It seems doable. And accordingly, a real possibility. Sail across the Channel to Calais or maybe Ostend and hide out in France or Belgium. For a while at least. I have my passport and as long as nothing untoward happens, there shouldn't be any issues. I guess any harbourmaster on the other side of the Channel will be curious as to why a solitary Englishman should suddenly appear, especially in mid-March before the season starts, but we have a reputation for being mad, so that should help.

Galvanised into action, I struggle free of my sleeping bag and check for charts. George is meticulous about these things, so I soon find what I'm looking for. I study the tide tables and as I remember, I can clear the lock here in Shoreham at full tide. I check and that should be at roughly 8 a.m., going by the tide tables. Madness, I know, but a chance for me to get away.

But then there's the harbourmaster. He will be suspicious of me taking the yacht, but George and I are roughly the same build and if I don his gear and life vest plus his cap, I might just be able to pass as him. From a distance anyway. I know he's had some modifications done to the engine, so if anybody challenges me, I can maybe just buy some time by saying I'm trying out the engine. I'll have to try and sound like him and pull my cap down low.

I feel invigorated by this new plan and pushing away my fears, I start preparing, trying to make as little noise as possible. In the growing daylight, I climb up the steps of the companionway and check the rigging. George has rigged up, which is great; he always is keen to get out as early in the season as possible. I check the tank, which is full. Batteries charged too. The only thing I don't have is freshwater, but I shouldn't need it; with luck, it will be a trip of several hours across the Channel. I check the weather forecast on my smartphone and it seems I'll be having some strong winds on the way, but at least they'll be coming from the west. My newly formed plan might just work.

The only thing that makes me pause is my family. What will they say? I push that thought to the back of my mind, promising myself I will contact them once I'm on the other side. And then the memory of poor Matlock in his car surfaces. God knows if anybody has found him yet. I debate ringing the police but decide against going down that route. I then remember from my research that the SFO (Serious Fraud Office) had an array of hotline numbers on their website. Perhaps I'll ring them and note down the number. Once I'm out in the Channel, I can ring them. It's not just Matlock's demise, but also the premeditated disappearance of Alexis and his cronies with twenty-five million in their pockets. Despite everything – and in particular my own role in this situation – I do feel that pulling the plug on this whole nasty scheme is the right thing to do. But will turning myself in be the right thing to do too? No, I won't. I'll run and see where life takes me.

I get myself ready and counting down the remaining hours and minutes, I then climb up on deck. I do my checks on the boat all the while checking for movement. I remove the covers from the sails, get them readied but keep them secured. So far so good. I look around – there's nobody about. It's Monday morning, not much activity to be expected. I open the fuel supply, start the engine and switch on the sat nav plotter. I'm ready.

I slip the mooring lines and engage the propeller. I cautiously manoeuvre out of the box and into the Channel leading up to the lock. I look back – still nobody to be seen. I head up to the lock and my new future. Adrenaline pumping through me, scared stupid but determined to give it a go. A fugitive on the run. My new status. So be it.

Part Two

24

I know I should say I'm sorry, but I don't. Sorry is too inadequate a term. I could say I'm revolted by my actions, by my deplorable behaviour, disgusted with myself – yes, that would be more adequate, but there's no point in that. Besides, it wouldn't quite fit the truth. So, I just say I've taken your boat and sailed it to Ostend. I add quickly that I haven't damaged it, but I've used most of the fuel. I've moored it in the Royal North Sea Yacht Club to be precise and I've paid the fees for a week.

I've put what I hope is enough as compensation in Uncle George's secret little kitty tucked away in the forward cabin, but I know he won't ever touch that money. By the time Uncle George gets here, the news will have spread, and my involvement in the H.I. fraud will be known to all. Undoubtedly the police will have been to see my mum and Ben by then. I've yet to send him an email, but that's next on the list and will be even harder to write.

I know, too, that there's no point in explaining how it all happened and that despite being a willing party – even if I was tricked – I never foresaw the dimension of the ploy. This must surely be one of the biggest fraud schemes in recent times and my involvement was instrumental in making it happen. That's why I know that Uncle George will never touch the money I've left for him, and Mum and Ben will never cease to wonder what got into me. I end the email stating that I know he will never be able to forgive me and that I would have to live with that.

I leave the email open and start on the one to Ben. I want to send them off together and then get the hell out of here.

As far as writing an email to Ben is concerned, converting my thoughts into words is so much more difficult. It's because I'm writing to Mum, too. Mum doesn't have email, so I'm addressing Mum through Ben. But what can I say? I'm sorry for betraying my family. For committing a crime that I know will blacken their lives for years to come. Sorrow for the disappointment they will feel every time my name is mentioned. For running away?

I sit, unable to write anything.

After a while, I realise several pairs of eyes in the internet café are on me, and I've been sitting here staring at the computer screen for ages. I'd better get a move on as there's one thing I don't want and that's eyes on me, storing my image in their memories. I let out a sigh and decide to make it short:

> *Dear Ben,*
> *Nothing I can say apart from sorry.*
> *I'm gone. Better for all.*
> *Give my love to Mum. She'll hate me for a while –*
> *you'll hate me a lot longer – but nothing I can do about*
> *that now.*
> *Must go,*
> *Love Neil.*

With that, I finish and send off both emails. I grab my canvas holdall from between my feet and head off to the railway station. Monday evening, the station is fairly empty, but still I feel conspicuous. I check the available trains and spot an Intercity heading for Brussels. I buy a ticket, grateful to use some of the euros from the stash and board the train. The train is half-empty as it's late, and the daily commuters are heading back this way from Brussels. I find a window seat, sink into it and place my bag between my feet, securing the strap to my leg. This bag contains my new life: two hundred and fifty thousand euros and one hundred and fifty thousand pounds sterling. It's everything I have; I must guard it as best I can. I almost instantly feel the weight of my body bearing down and my eyes flickering as I fall into a dream-filled sleep, reliving last night's crossing of the Channel.

I take the yacht, *Florence*, out through the canal and into the open grey sea. Grey clouds above, even the seagulls looking down on me are grey. Despite the greyness surrounding me I feel buoyant and alive. A westerly wind is blowing, still moderate, but forecast to pick up during the day. I set a general heading on the sat nav plotter for Beachy Head but maintain my southerly course to get more space between me and the shoreline. I remember Uncle George saying that one needs to overcome one's fear and the desire to hug the coast and get enough clearance. High tide and I'm expecting the tidal streams to push me along. The trip should be straightforward, but I've never done this on my own; and, to be honest, I'm shitting myself.

I'm running the boat on the engine; no experiments as far as I'm concerned. Straight out a few nautical miles, then swing round onto the heading that will take me past

Beachy Head. That's phase one. After that, I've put in a way point and a heading to Dungeness, where I will have to steer out into the Channel and cross the shipping lanes. That's phase two. I've logged in Ostend as I've been there once before with Uncle George, but I guess anywhere on the French or Belgian coast will do. A total of about 130 nautical miles and I'm terrified. I'm praying for moderate winds and no nasty surprises.

The further out I steer the boat, the stronger the wind becomes and the waves are beginning to slap into the side as I'm keeping *Florence* on a southerly course. The waves are coming at a right angle, and, running along on the motor, the effect is slightly unnerving. Once I swing round onto my course to Beachy Head, the waves will be coming from behind, which should give me more speed. The engine is running smoothly; it's only a twenty bhp diesel engine, but Uncle George has had it refurbished and it's chugging away nicely. *Florence* and I are cruising at six knots, which feels good to me, but given the total distance of roughly 130 nautical miles, it'll take me about twenty-two hours at this speed.

Once on course to Beachy Head, I might unfurl some of the jib sail to give the boat some added propulsion and stabilise her. I must conserve the fuel. The engine will use about two litres per hour at current rpm, which currently amounts to six knots. The engine will get through approximately forty-two to forty-five litres at this speed. Uncle George has a seventy-five-litre tank plus reserve canisters, so fuel should be plenty, but I don't want to be caught out. I have calculated back and forth and know I'm being over-cautious, but my nerves are shredded to bits. I can't believe that my life was so totally different just a day ago.

I never dreamt I would be on the run with a big canvas bag full of money, which is now lying in the forward cabin. Most of it is Matlock's money, and his sad demise made this plan come alive. Without his money on top of mine, I'd never have embarked on this adventure. Money stolen from Hamlays or Holden Industrial, depending on whichever way you look at it. I've stolen his stolen money, adding another criminal act to the list I have been accumulating. But that doesn't matter now. I dig in my pockets for my work phone. Let Hamlays pay for this call, I'm doing it for them and for Matlock, who is probably still lying dead in his car. I ring the Fraud Office hotline I noted down. After some waiting, I am connected to a real-life person. The young woman launches into her rehearsed greeting.

"Good morning, Serious Fraud Office Hotline. How…?"

I interrupt the usual introductory spiel. "Good morning, please listen and listen well," I say. "If you can record this, please do so and then you can forward this to whoever is responsible."

"Sir," she says, but I interrupt.

"I'm sorry I don't have time, so please listen. I'm calling to report a fraud of significant magnitude that has taken place over the last days. It concerns Hamlays Bank in London that has been defrauded by its corporate customer, Horsham-based Holden Industrial. The perpetrators are Alexis Theophilou and his right-hand man, Michalis Likidis. I also have reason to believe that Hamlays CEO, Mr Willem de Vries, is involved. Please contact Mr Kevin Sunderland, the Head of the Key Account Management Team at Hamlays Bank. The fraud concerns the financing of horizontal drilling machines to the amount of twenty-five million pounds."

"Sir," she tries again but I don't let her.

"The perpetrators have transferred the money out of the country using several offshore accounts."

"Sir, I need to know who you…" she tries yet again.

"Please just let me finish and then I'll let you ask your questions," I say. "There's another thing. A Mr Peter Matlock, Senior Manager at accountants Charlton Hudson, who was responsible for manipulating Holden Industrial's financial data over the last few years, died yesterday afternoon. He was lying in his car in the sunken road behind H.I.'s complex in Horsham. That's where I found him. Unfortunately, I had to leave him there."

And then I disconnect the call and switch off the phone.

After about an hour and a half, I feel I can't take much more of this uncomfortable course. At six knots, I must be about nine nautical miles off the coast by now, and I'm hoping this will give me enough clearance to get past Beachy Head. I'm hoping that the wind and tidal stream will help push me along.

I decide to change course and bring *Florence* onto the new heading. I mark the point on the sat nav plotter, bring the boat around onto an easterly course and set a fixing for Beachy Head. Instantly, the boat starts rising and falling like on a seesaw: the waves are now coming from behind and running under the boat. I disengage the autopilot and prepare myself to unfurl the jib. Inch by inch, I let out enough sailcloth to give me more speed and stability. With about a third of the sail unfurled, I can sense the boat picking up speed and rather than being lifted by the waves passing under the hull, the yacht is now overtaking them, and *Florence* is surfing down the waves. It's tiring business riding out the waves, but once I feel comfortable that *Florence* is steady enough on her course, I engage the autopilot again and adjust the settings to match the compass bearing for Beachy Head. The yacht is now running at nine knots, which is great.

Despite the boat's movements being unsettling, I begin to relax. All good so far. My nautical skills have never been good, but I'm coping. I put the engine into neutral to see if it slows me down, but I'm still running at eight knots. I hesitate to switch the engine off, so decide to leave it running in neutral for a while. I check the battery gauge and the batteries are fully charged. There shouldn't be any reason for the engine not to start, but still, I'm reluctant to do so. Uncle George would have a fit if he could see me. "Switch it off," he'd say. Better on than off, I think. There's no way I want to have any trouble starting it if I need to in a hurry.

Only now do I realise how cold it is and that I'm beginning to shiver. My shredded nerves, fatigue and the cold are wearing me out. I need warmer clothes. I go below for a thicker sweater, warmer gloves and a blanket. A hot cup of tea would be great, but with the boat's movement increasing in the choppy sea, I don't want to fumble around with putting water into the kettle, lighting the gas stove and making tea. Under deck, the movement makes me feel seasick, so I climb back up the companionway and settle in the cockpit, padded out in several layers of clothing. I feel better and despite the cold, I'm certainly more comfortable. I just hope I can handle the cold and exhaustion. I've still got a long way to go.

Uncle George has installed an inflatable life raft in a container to the rear guardrail, so I huddle up in the shelter it provides from the wind. I wrap myself in a blanket, checking autopilot and general course occasionally. I never even notice that I fall asleep.

A persistent beeping jerks me awake. The sat nav plotter is warning me that it can't hold the course and with a pounding heart, I realise I'm too close to the coast. I check the plotter, panic rising as I see that I'm heading directly onto the cliffs. I can see Beachy Head lighthouse ahead of me and galvanised into action, I disengage the autopilot, engage the propeller, thankful that the engine is still running, furl away the jib and floor the power lever to head out into open waters.

"Jesus, bloody hell!" I scream into the cold morning air.

Fortunately – and once safely heading away from the cliffs – I realise that I still had enough time and space, but nonetheless, it's precisely the kind of situation I was desperate to avoid. My heart thumping, I watch as the cliffs slowly recede and *Florence* methodically works her way back out into open water.

After an hour of motoring, looking out at a grey sea with occasional whitecaps rising off the top of the waves as the wind catches the water, I swing the boat around to a new easterly heading that will take me up to Dungeness. This will be my starting point for the crossing over to the Continent. I unfurl the jib again, the wind still coming from aft, just enough to give me more speed. *Florence* settles on the new course, the speed showing nine knots again. Just don't fall asleep again, I chide myself.

After what seems an eternity, I've lost count of the hours I've been sitting here; and with darkness now descending, I reach the way point I've set on the plotter. For me, this is the point of no return. Crossing the

Channel on a cold March night isn't a sailor's dream. For me, it's a nightmare. I have prepared as well as I can. Position lights on, chocolate bars and icy bottled water by my side, wrapped up like an Eskimo, I steel myself for the next phase.

Supported by the jib, I have made good time despite the many hours that have slipped by since leaving Shoreham. The engine is ticking over; fuel consumption is okay. I have switched on the diesel-powered heating in the cabin and am sitting in the hatch with my feet on the companionway steps as the cold is unbearable. I'm just glad it's dry. Wet and cold would be my end. In theory, I must cross the shipping lanes at a right angle. The fastest way through is my priority. I have plotted a course through the shipping lanes on the sat nav plotter. I have the paper charts in their protective covers by my side. The westerly wind is favourable and it's calmed a bit. The wind gauge is showing a steady four Beaufort with occasional gusts of five. As I will be on a beam reach, my plan is to overcome my fear and sail this boat across rather than just motor. For speed and stability, I will need the sails.

Having prepared the sails, I turn into the wind, and grateful that all sails can be operated from the safety of the cockpit, I raise the main sail as far as the first reef and turn the boat back onto its course. I then unfurl the jib two-thirds and put the engine into neutral. *Florence* picks up speed; despite the reefs, I'm making eight knots. I check the plotter; the course is good. I pluck up my courage, turn the boat back into the wind, raise the main sail up to the second reef and slowly adjust back onto my course. With more wind in the sails, *Florence* leans over but the speedometer shows nine knots, then ten.

Happy with my speed, I engage the autopilot once more and concentrate on crossing the shipping lanes. In the darkness of the night, I scan the horizon for lights of moving ships and compare their positions with their corresponding little black triangles on the plotter. I'm luckier than I deserve to be as there aren't many ships about, and those that appear are well spaced out, so I can sail straight through without having to take any evasive action. With a big sigh of relief, I make it across into French coastal waters.

I start thinking that any French marina will be just as good as Ostend, but I'm unfamiliar with the French coastal towns and the layout of the marinas. Uncle George has a complete library of nautical almanacs and guides to all marinas on the French and Belgian coasts, but I decide to stick with Ostend, as I have some recollection of the layout despite now running solely on adrenaline. Besides, I don't want to have to navigate my way into a French marina in darkness. I've lost all sense of time; I'm just functioning. I set the course for Ostend and with daylight slowly growing on the distant horizon, I finally reach Ostend in the early morning.

I can make out the Royal North Sea Yacht Club in the growing daylight and approach the marina at what seems like a crawling snail's pace. I hasten to prepare the mooring lines, careful not to slip on the wet deck. Very slowly, I approach an empty berth, not caring if it's reserved or not, which I doubt given the time of year, and ease *Florence* into the box, securing the mooring lines even before the bow is anywhere near the jetty. Finished, I stand, survey the boat, adjust some fenders and look around. Fortunately, there is no one about. After twenty-two hours, I switch off the engine, climb down below, ease myself out of my life vest, sailing jacket and boots, fall onto the mattress in the forward cabin and am instantly asleep.

A hand shaking my shoulder jerks me awake from the replay of the Channel crossing in my mind. I'm sweating, beads running down my face. A man in his forties in a leather jacket is leaning over me, speaking in French or Dutch – I can't make it out. I feel panic rising in me as I stare wide-eyed at the man.

"What?" I say.

"This is Bruxelles, Monsieur. The train stops here."

I must have been fast asleep throughout the train ride. It seems that only now has my subconscious found the time to process that cross-Channel trip. In itself, I guess it was nothing spectacular and I was very lucky with the weather, but to me it was a daunting and draining experience, both physically and mentally.

I shake myself awake. The train has come to a halt and, looking out of the window, I see the platform and a sign reading "Bruxelles – Gare Centrale". Just as well the train ends here, God knows where I might have ended up. As the man moves away, I gather my belongings, hoist my holdall onto my shoulder and exit onto the platform. It's way past 10 p.m., so I set off in search of a hotel.

25

I walk the streets for hours and it doesn't take long before I come to the conclusion that Brussels isn't for me. I mean, not totally, as I've been here a couple of times and liked the city. But it's the combination of time of year, which being March is cold and wet, and the overall sordid atmosphere and the seedy-looking people multiplied by my tiredness. And the simple but amazing fact that I can't get a room. All I want is a bed and a shower. I thought I'd treat myself to somewhere nice and classy. After all, for once, I have the means to pay for it. But all the classy hotels I have entered so far either don't have a free room or, if they do, they want my passport and payment by credit card only. My offer to pay cash has been met with frowns and confused expressions. I can only guess that there's concern that an unwashed and unshaven individual like me might not be able to cover his bill despite the offer of cash. But no, so I'm told it's the law. I pound the pavement, entering one hotel after another. Each time, I lower my standards a notch, finally focusing on finding a place that doesn't look too much like a brothel or appear even more tired than I am. I eventually find a hotel that is prepared to take my cash, doesn't care about my passport and doesn't ask any further questions.

As soon as I enter the room, I know why. The room's worn out, dilapidated even. I groan inwardly when I see the mirror attached to the ceiling above the bed.

Surprisingly, the mattress is good and the shower's hot. It's all I need for my first night.

I'm prepared to give Brussels a second chance and at first, I enjoy walking around the old city centre, taking in the tourist sights. After a while, I start getting tired and with rain setting in, I'm happy to find a free table in the corner of a café off the *Grote Markt*. I sit and think about my next steps. First, I need to get a backpack rather than lug this canvas bag around. It's uncomfortable, and I fear it can easily be pulled off my shoulder. I'd be buggered if that happens. I certainly don't feel at ease carrying all this cash around with me, and I keep thinking where I can stash it. I wonder whether there are luggage lockers at the train station, so I decide go to the train station and check it out after coffee, something to eat and the rain stopping.

After a couple of hours looking at the pouring rain beating up the paving of the *Grote Markt* through the large café window, I come to a decision. Fuck bloody Brussels, why not go south to sunnier climates. Happy with this idea, I gather my belongings, pay my bill and head through the rain to the station not to check out the lockers but with a new plan.

For no other reason than the fact that Isabelle, the girl I'd had a fling with at university, and who then claimed to be pregnant, came from Montpellier, do I decide to make my way there. Not that I have any plans or ideas of meeting her, it just strikes me as a nice destination. It's a long, slow trip. I sit looking out of the carriage window as the train rattles and bumps along, heading further south on its tracks. Most of the time, I sit watching the scenery pass by, occasionally noticing the changes in landscape the further we get south. Usually, I'd be distracting myself with my smartphone, playing games or texting, but they are stashed away in my new backpack, switched off and out of bounds. On one of the frequent stops, an elderly man boards the train and ends up sitting opposite me.

He attempts to read his newspaper but seemingly bored with it, he turns to me and starts chatting. He's friendly and tries to engage me in conversation, but I don't understand much of what he's saying. I nod politely, smiling. I'm happy to have company, but reluctant to answer his questions, especially in my poor French. He's been scrutinising me, but in a friendly way, and I'm startled when he suddenly asks me in English, "Monsieur, you are English, non?"

"Ah, well, yes," I say.

"Ah, I thought so," he says, smiling.

"Do I look English, then?" I ask him.

"Monsieur, forgive my rudeness, but yes, I suppose you do."

I laugh, and he joins me laughing, too.

"You are on holiday?"

"Sort of," I say, mindful of what I should disclose. "On my way to Montpellier to visit an old friend," I add.

"Ah, Montpellier, a wonderful city. Your friend has chosen well if he lives there."

I smile at him, hoping it's the end of his questions.

He returns to his paper, turns the pages quickly as he scans the articles, making disapproving noises when he lingers on an article that doesn't agree with him. Turning to the next page, he neatly folds the pages over, and I nearly jump out of my seat when I see the article that is now on the page facing me.

"I'm sorry," I say and he looks up expectantly. "May I just see that article?"

"Of course, which one?"

I point, and he passes me the paper.

It's the business section but it's the photo of Hamlays Bank's corporate sign outside the head office in London that has grabbed me. I try to read the article but fail to get the meaning of the words.

"Excuse me," I say, "what does it say?"

I hand him back the paper, and he looks at the article. "Let me see," he says and then starts translating. Bit by bit, we work our way through the article, the old man translating and me supplying the odd word or two. In the end, it reads like this:

British Bank Hamlays Rocked by Major Fraud.

According to a spokesman for London-based Hamlays Bank plc, the bank's asset finance division has been hit by a major fraud case. It is reported that the fraud involving the funding of a GBP 25 million package of horizontal drilling equipment was carried out by staff and management of one of the bank's major customers, Holden Industrial. Unconfirmed reports state that some members of staff of Hamlays Bank's asset finance division, Hamlays Asset Finance Ltd., were involved. Sources close to the investigation have disclosed that Hamlays Bank CEO, Willem de Vries, left the country on Sunday night and is suspected of involvement. It has been confirmed that the UK authorities were first made aware of the fraud by an anonymous whistle-blower on Monday. Officers of UK's fraud investigation agencies are asking the whistle-blower to come forward...

The rest of the article goes on to describe the fraud and speculates on the perpetrators. Many questions centre on the possible identity of the culprits and how they were able

168

to carry this off. Questions but no answers. But I know all about that.

As far as the *whistle-blower* is concerned and the paper repeats the investigators plea for the person they identify as a young man to come forward, I need not look far. The old man raises an eyebrow when he reads out that bit and gives me a long look. It takes a conscious effort to keep my face clear of any expression. "I used to work there," I say to him. "Some years ago," I add hastily.

"Ah," he says, his friendly smile back in place.

Looking out through the window as the train pulls into the next station, he quickly grabs his coat and hat. "My station," he says. "Bon voyage and a good time in Montpellier." He hands me his paper as he heads out into the aisle.

I sit with the paper in my lap and wave to him as he passes by the window. Well, well, the whistle-blower... I can't help but feel it's so obvious that's me, and as the train pulls away, I feel like I want to sink into the cushions of my seat and be invisible. Briefly, I sit thinking they might not have identified me yet but, of course, they have. It's Tuesday and by now, all will be on the table. I've been gone since Sunday. They will have been in touch with Mum and Ben, and I'm sure they have the emails from the internet café in Ostend. They know I'm on the Continent. It means being even more careful and not use my passport or credit cards or my phones.

As much as the first part of my journey was boring and monotonous, the second part, after reading the paper article, is spent in a heightened state of nervousness. I jump every time the train stops and I see someone in uniform walking up the platform, even if it's just an SNCF official. I urge the train to get to Montpellier. Eight hours after leaving Brussels, it does.

Despite my giddy nerves, I can't help but feel it was worth it as I step down onto the platform. It's fifteen degrees centigrade and sunny. Friendly, smiling people – so much nicer than Brussels.

I make my way from the station to the city centre. I do the tourist thing for a couple of hours, walking the city with my massive backpack. I pop into a couple of hotels, asking for room prices and presenting my offer to pay cash. The staff behind the counter react the same way as their colleagues in Brussels. Credit cards only.

After the second or third hotel, my spirits come crashing down again.

Down by the river Lez I come across an Irish pub. Early evening, not much business yet, but on an impulse I walk in thirsty for solace in a beer. The staff is the usual mix of young English, Irish and Australian lads and girls. Easy-going, friendly, and most of them backpacking their way through Europe. Stopping along the backpackers' trail for a while, happy to earn some cash, before moving on. I sit at the bar, down the first pint, get another and start chatting to the barman who, within a few minutes, informs me he's a backpacker from Sydney. He points at my oversized rucksack and assumes I'm the same. I can't fault him, as I've now got plenty of stubble and my clothes look in need of a wash. After a couple more beers and a burger, I ask him if he knows where I could stay for a few days, hinting that despite my appetite, my budget is small and I'd be happy to crash out for a few days somewhere cheap and cheerful.

"No worries, mate," he says in what seems to be the standard Aussie reply.

He walks off to talk to a girl who's loading up a tray with beers. He nods in my direction, her glance following his gesture and settling on me. She gives me a long, appraising look, but the smile that then spreads across her face is genuine. On her way back from bringing her tray of beers to a table packed with leering and thirsty local lads, she stops by my side. Close up, she's even prettier than she was just now standing at the bar. A petite blonde with sparkling blue eyes, freckles and a smile that has me going weak at the knees. As it turns out, she's from Australia, too.

She has a small flat she shares with a girlfriend who's presently travelling. If I pay cash and behave, she can let me have her girlfriend's room for a while. Bingo, I think, with a big grin.

To say thanks, I give her and the barman some drinks and a big tip. This elevates my status to "mate" and sure enough, within minutes, I'm on first-name terms with Carl, the barman, and Milly, my new landlady. As I have to wait for her shift to end and I don't want to spend the whole night drinking beers, I jokingly say I could do some washing-up, which makes her laugh. But Carl is looking at me with a serious expression.

"Seriously," I say.

Milly just shrugs, it's no concern to her, but Carl, who turns out to be the assistant manager, is happy to have me work in the kitchen. And so, at the end of my first evening in Montpellier, I have a home and a job.

26

It must be 3 a.m. when the place finally closes and Carl boots out the last punters. Some of the staff get together for a quick drink as Carl pays the staff their day's wage. It seems a normal thing in the pub business down here. Carl pours drinks and sets a beer in front of me on the bar. He takes some money from the till and hands it to me for my work. I decline and tell him to give it to Milly, my first day's rent. They both laugh, but I notice Milly doesn't hesitate long before pocketing the money.

It was 4 a.m. when we got to Milly's flat. I'm too tired to notice much of the streets we walked, but we have a lively chat on the way, and after climbing what feels like a small Mount Everest to me, up five floors to her flat under the roof, she unlocks the door and shows me in.

There isn't much in the way of furniture, and what's there is old and mismatched. But I don't care; I'm too knackered and I'm just grateful to have a roof over my head and hopefully a soft bed. The room Milly leads me into is big and the bed, which stands directly beneath a skylight, is queen-sized and irresistibly inviting. I head in that direction, bang my head on one of the prominent rafters and collapse on the bed. I hear Milly laughing by the door. She gives me some instructions, but I'm struggling to get out of the backpack and my jacket and off with my shoes before I hit the pillow and am gone.

I awake, still dressed in my jeans and shirt. I need a second to realise where I am and with a bolt of panic, I sit

172

up searching for my backpack. The panic subsides as quickly as it rises; my backpack is lying next to the bed under the skylight. I lie back, the sun's up and through the skylight, I can see it's a fine morning. It's bright outside. I rub my eyes to get them to focus and check the time. 11 a.m. Seven hours of sleep, then, that's all. I groan and lie back, slowly coming back to life.

I take stock of my new home. The room is pleasant enough, albeit worn and old. The skylight provides the only source of daylight, but it's big and the room is bathed in light. It'll be unbearable in summer under the roof and with a skylight so large. Several posters are stuck to the sloping walls, some of groups I've never heard of and some old movie posters. There are plenty of photos, too, Blu-tacked to the sloped walls and to the knee wall, which runs the length of the room where the roof slopes down to the eaves. Photos of smiling young people on beaches, climbing mountains or on ski slopes. On the wall next to the bed is an assortment of photos showing a brunette, arm in arm, with an athletic-looking surfer type. I assume this must be the girlfriend whose room I'm now living in, and I say thanks to her and her decision to be absent on my arrival. Just then, there's a knock on the door.

"Yes," I manage to croak, only now noticing how dry my mouth is.

The door opens a crack and Milly peeks in. She laughs as she sees my sleep-fuddled, crunched-up face, hair sticking up in all directions.

"Now, if that's your usual morning face, Neil, you have some work to do to get that straightened." She laughs. "First night's rent includes breakfast, so rise, shine, and shower. You stink." She bangs the door shut.

I get up, stretch and, avoiding the rafters, grab my wash bag from the backpack. I feel the reassuring lumps of cash stashed away in the various compartments and pockets. I feel uneasy leaving my backpack prone on the floor, but I don't think Milly's the kind to go searching through it as soon as I'm under the shower. I open the door, happy to see Milly busy at the hob, tucked into the corner of what is a living room, kitchen and dining room all in one. She turns as I walk in, her smile genuine and warm.

"It takes a lot of trust letting a stranger into your home in such an easy, relaxed way," I say as I lean against one of the rafters that divide the room into its functional areas and sip coffee from the mug Milly has thrust into my hand.

She laughs. "I had a good impression of you, Neil," she replies. "I can tell straight away who's a dick and who's okay." She sees the expression on my face and adds, "And I can defend myself in many a painful way."

She insists on me having a shower first – no breakfast until I'm clean and presentable. The bathroom is cramped, the sloping roof taking away most of the headroom. Nonetheless, I manage to stand upright in one corner and let the hot water run down my body.

Milly has set the table: there's orange juice, croissants, baguette, butter and a pan full of scrambled eggs and ham. And most importantly, a large cafetière with steaming black coffee.

We sit and chat and after a while – it doesn't take long at all – I realise what a lovely, cute and pretty person she is. She's warm, with sparkling blue eyes and freckles. A sun-kissed beach beauty from down under. She insists on telling me her story first. Initially from the outskirts of Melbourne, she took off with her hometown bestie to discover the world. First travelling through Australia and New Zealand, they soon got the appetite for more.

"It was like being on a drug," she says. "It was wonderful to see all these fascinating places. We just couldn't get enough." The travel bug had taken hold and after touring Indonesia, Malaysia and Vietnam, they'd made their way to Europe. "We did London, Berlin, Paris and now here, Montpellier," she says, taking a bit off her croissant and dunking it in the coffee, true French style. She's sitting opposite me with one foot up on her chair, hair hanging down one side. "But this is only a stop. We're saving up for the next big destinations: Spain, Italy, Greece, and we want to go see Croatia and all those places you only ever hear of when you're down under."

I sit listening to Milly, her lovely Australian accent making me laugh. She reminds me of a young Kylie Minogue and she's full of laughter. I've never seen anyone laugh so much. She's only twenty-two, which also knocks me for six.

"I'm amazed, Milly, I really am. So much energy and initiative – I've not met anyone like you," I say, and I mean it too.

"Yeah, but if you come from a dead outpost of a village like I do, there's not much choice."

If she'd grown up in Melbourne or Sydney, she and Allison, her friend, probably would not have developed this urge to get away and see the world, she explains.

"And travelling really is a drug," she goes on. "Once you get hooked, it's difficult to stop." She rattles off even more countries and towns she and Allison want to see: Scandinavia, the Baltic region, Saint Petersburg, Moscow. They have their plans, and nobody's going to stop them.

"At this point in life, boyfriends have non-permanent status," she says, and I feel a sharp prick of disappointment. "Once that changes, it's time to go home." She stops there, fixes me with those lovely blue eyes, slowly raises her mug to her lips, and en route asks the question I've been dreading. "So, what brings you here?"

"Oh, I'm taking a year out," I say, having prepared my story whilst she was telling me hers.

"Really? Bit old for that, aren't you?" she says, winking at me.

I smile at her. "This old man might be twenty-nine but never too old for adventures." I wink back at her, which makes her laugh. "Seriously, a year out after a big project at work, which went disastrously wrong," I lie truthfully. "Plus, a nasty split-up from my girlfriend." This is equally not quite the truth but true enough.

"I felt burnt out after these two experiences and wanted time to get my life back together," I say, warming to my story and yes, it kind of makes sense and, to a certain point, is the truth too. Milly seems to believe me as I take her through my hastily concocted story. She sits opposite me, one knee up on the chair, hand supporting her chin, blue eyes fixed on me. Her look is mesmerising, so I expand on my story just to keep the moment going for as long as I can.

Milly cuts short my dreamy, soft-focus reverie by taking a long swig of mineral water from a bottle and burping loudly. She laughs at my expression of utter surprise, reminding me that she's a gal from down under, mate. After washing up, she takes me out on a tour of the city.

Over the next weeks, we settle into a routine which, to me, is pure bliss. We work together at the Irish pub, Milly serving and me in the kitchen. We work until the early hours and get paid cash in hand. I give her rent money and when off duty, we hang out, go shopping and cook together, which is so intimate, I feel we're becoming a couple. On our few days off, she introduces me to her friends – mostly backpackers – and we go out partying. If someone knows someone with a car, we jump in and drive down to the beaches on the Med. Carnon Plage is a spot Milly likes and where she occasionally helps out at a beach club for kids. She loves kids and for her, it's a certainty that one day she'll have a family. And a husband too, of course, she'd add, smiling at me.

It's not until a couple of weeks have gone by that I first think about getting in touch with home. With a start and a shot of guilt, I realise that I haven't sent one message. But I feel like I've been on a holiday, so absorbed have I become in this wonderful life here together with Milly.

I have watched her sending message after message to her elder brother and sister. Both live in Melbourne, and they chat regularly via apps like FaceTime. At some weekends they set up a video group call together with her parents, which last for hours despite the differing time zones.

"Don't you get on with your family, assuming you have one and you're not the product of some botched-up laboratory experiment," she teases me after one of her family video chats. "I never see you talking or chatting to anybody back home. In fact, come to think of it, I've never seen you with a phone. Don't you have one?" she asks, triggering a terrible pang of guilt in me.

I'm evasive in my answer, but I start to feel the heavy burden of having left without a word and not being in touch since. I admit, I've blocked it all out so far but listening to Molly and her family chatting away happily, brings it home.

I know I can't use any of my phones except the burner, maybe as calls from phones can be traced, so I go in search of an internet café. I work myself up to a near level of hysteria as I contemplate what might be going on regarding the H.I. fraud. I must assume the police or whoever investigates financial crime is looking for me. I know emails can be traced, too, and getting in touch will be dangerous for me. My imagination runs wild and I have nightmares about being caught by the police in the midst of exchanging emails with Ben. That one newspaper article is the only piece of news I've seen and to be honest, I haven't gone looking. I've spent the last weeks totally absorbed in a comfortable fantasy and distracted from the realities that brought me here. Now, they have come back to haunt me.

Crazy with anxiety, I skip a day at the pub, grab some money from my backpack and borrow a car of one of Milly's friends. I pay him well and he asks no questions despite the number of kilometres I travel in one day. For fear of being traced to Montpellier, I travel all the way to Girona in Spain. I find an internet café and hope that if anyone picks up the email I plan to send they'll think I'm in Spain. I'm not thinking straight because it's only when I get back that I realise I'll have to return to see if there's a reply – or find another way of accessing my emails without giving away where I am. I know what Michalis would say: bloody amateur.

Sitting in the café I access my account. The number of emails that have been sent is staggering. I scan them quickly. There are emails from Hamlays and even Kevin has sent a few to my private email address. I hesitate to open any of those and check for emails from Ben.

The first one I read is in reply to my email from Ostend. It reads:

Neil,
What the hell have you done? Get in touch immediately.
Ben.

The second is from a couple of days after that:

Neil,
Police have been here and two investigators from the NCA. They are looking for you. They know you were in Ostend.
Get in touch quickly before you make things worse for yourself.
Ben.

And then there's a third:

Neil,
Get in touch! Mum and I are going mad! Where the hell are you? Let us at least know you're safe!
Ben.

I put aside the text I'd prepared. I sit and think. What can I say? With trembling hands, I write:

Dear Ben,
Sorry to have caused you so much worry. I'm fine. Please tell Mum I'm okay.
I can't tell you where I am and I'm not going to try to explain what I did. I can only say I was tricked.
Love you guys, but I can't come back.
Neil.

It's all I'm capable of writing. I feel sick and dispirited. I return to the car and drive back to Montpellier and the sweet bubble of delusion I have created for myself there.

A week later, Milly's twenty-third birthday comes up. Carl and the gang at the pub kick out the punters on the dot at midnight and with cries of surprise and "happy birthday" get a private party going. It's an exclusive insiders-only do for Milly. Not expecting this, she's totally agog that everyone has made such an effort on her behalf. Her modesty and genuine happiness make my heart leap with joy for her. She's the centre of attention, but that doesn't stop her coming to look for me in the kitchen. "Come out and celebrate my birthday with me, you dickhead!" she yells, so I drop the tea towel and join her party.

The place is heaving. Carl has got a DJ in who's spinning the records. Tables and chairs are pushed aside, and the floor becomes a dance floor, flashing lights and all. The locals are all trying to get in, but Carl has locked the doors. It's a fantastic party, and I can see Milly's really enjoying herself. I have no idea what time it is when we finally get home. It isn't quite day yet, but the sky is getting lighter on the fringes of the eastern horizon. Milly's happily drunk, leaning on me and wanting to be carried up to the flat. It's my birthday, she insists. Who am I not to help a fair maiden and much to her amusement and giggles, I carry her all the way up. She's a lightweight and it's no burden to carry Milly up five floors. We struggle to get through the door into the flat and I gently set her down in the living room. She clings to me and, looking up into my eyes, she grins and says, "I want you to fuck me, Neil."

"Do you?" I gulp, more than surprised at this unexpected but very pleasant turn of events.

"Yes, you dickhead. All the way, mate."

And with that, she leads me into her bedroom and onto the bed.

The next two weeks are indescribable. Our little routine of working together, shopping and cooking, excursions and evenings out has now been augmented by sleeping together. Her appetite for sex is even greater than mine and not only do we fall into bed together after getting back from work at the pub, but we also grab any free minute for a quickie. Sex with Milly is relaxed and unencumbered. She has fun and that's all she wants. She has her own funny names for things. She says, "The reception bay is ready," or "The cream is waiting," meaning she's covered herself with whipped cream and I have the joyful task of licking it off.

I can't help but compare it to sex with Emma. I recall how, over time, that became hard work. It was like having to get over an obstacle course, as if sex was only permissible against the backdrop of the greater goal: getting married, getting a house in suburbia and having kids. I always thought of it like going through a pre-flight check. The points had to be ticked off in the affirmative before she'd let go and really get down to it.

But what I don't realise is that Milly is getting ready to let me go. I'm happy as a bee, living in my bubble, feeling deliriously happy, but Milly has a different plan. Allison had rang a few days earlier and I'd even been privy to the call. I heard her say she was coming back soon. But I failed to link up the dots.

She tells me on a Sunday morning as we lie in bed. It knocks me for six, my bubble bursting and I hit the

181

ground hard. I have to concede that Milly has a tough side to her that I wouldn't have thought possible. From her perspective it's simple. We've had fun together over the last couple of months and serious relationships are forbidden at this stage.

"So, Neil," she says, "I'm sorry, but this is where our fun ends. You'd better move on," she adds, "because Allison and I will be shortly."

In a way, I knew it would turn out this way, but still I'm saddened by it. More than that, I'm shattered. I really like Milly. In fact, I realise, but don't say it, I've fallen in love with her. But that was the deal, and there's no negotiation. I can't make her love me and I'd never want to stand in her way.

Even in terminating our arrangement, Milly proves to be generous and caring. She's arranged for me to work and stay in Cannes, where friends of hers run a campsite. She has asked, and her friends can fix me up with a job for the summer season, which is now beginning. The campsite, which is part of the backpackers' trail through France, has plenty of jobs going and there will be other backpackers working there, too. We separate with plenty of kisses and hugs, and grudgingly I set off to Cannes and the campsite on the fringes of town.

27

I sit watching but not seeing the landscape pass by from the carriage window. I feel totally deflated. The weeks with Milly had been wonderful. *Had been*, I have to admit to myself, past tense now. I'd been living a frugal life. We hadn't needed much but had lived life to the full. In the weeks I was there, I hadn't touched any of my stash of money apart from some euros to pay for the use of a car. But, as I now sum it all up, it had been worth it. Despairing, I sit on this train feeling so lonely now, totally out of touch with family and friends back home. I haven't allowed myself to think much about them, and apart from that one trip to Girona a couple of weeks ago, I haven't been in touch. And now I ask myself, what are you going to do?

I'm greeted by a woman – Joanne – in her mid-thirties and, going by the backpackers' rules, definitely outside of the typical backpacker age bracket. She's Australian, too, but has settled here, committing that backpacker's sin of meeting a Frenchman and deciding to abandon the backpacker's dream. She married him, has kids and manages the campsite in Cannes that belongs to her husband's family. There are more, she informs me, dotted around Nice and Cannes.

I strain to come across as a jovial, highly motivated backpacker exploring France on his year out, and I can't help but feel that she sees straight through my fake story.

But she seems quite happy to accept my tale and gives me a job.

Joanne shows me around the campsite, which turns out to be massive. It has two swimming pools, two restaurants and several bars, a supermarket and a couple of kiosks, as she calls them, selling ice cream, drinks and other bits and pieces. There's a big kid's playground and a central meeting area where people can get together for events, barbecues and games. It's more like a holiday camp than just a campsite. Joanne says I can work in the kitchens, in the bar or both, and that it's expected of me to help out in any capacity as required when they hold their events. I agree to everything, but secretly I vow to myself that I'll clear the hell out of here as soon as possible.

At the end of our tour, she shows me the staff living quarters, which are at the back of the campsite next to the main road and strictly off limits to guests. She emphasises that particular piece of information, and I nod obediently. Staff live in old caravans, small prefabricated huts on a wheeled chassis or containers, specifically designed as living accommodation. Small but clean, she says, and I can either share or have a *demi*, as she calls them, apologising for her use of French words whenever she forgets the English term. A demi is a container that boasts two small living quarters with separate access. I opt for one of these as I want some privacy.

The rent will be deducted from the money I earn, but food is included unless I want to cook for myself, Joanne explains as I struggle with my backpack to get it through the door. The demi is okay – if you're not much bigger than a mouse. It's basically one room with a little pantry-style gas hob, a small fridge, a small table with a couple of foldaway chairs and a minute bedroom, separated by a curtain. There's just enough space to stand and a couple of cupboards mounted above the bed for my stuff. But I want this accommodation as I want my privacy and at least some security for the stash of money. No toilet and no shower, Joanne explains, as she stands at the door watching me drop my backpack into a corner. I'll have to use the communal washrooms that are a stone's throw from my demi. Joanne says I can start in the morning, so I have the evening for myself.

Joanne closes the door, and I sink down onto the springy bed, gloom settling over me. Here I am with thousands of pounds and euros in my backpack, living like a pauper, housing in a one-man cell. This is not what I wanted. I thought I'd be able to live life, enjoy myself even if on the run. But I've come to realise, that despite a backpack stuffed with money, I'm homeless. Cash won't let you lead a life unless you have all the other little things that you need. Simple things, like an identity. Of course, I have one, my own real identity. But I can't use it. And that's the only good thing about this backpacker's trail. Here, my identity doesn't matter. At least, so far, no one has asked me to identify myself. I'm living on the fringe of society, work paid in cash and no questions asked. And now I realise, too, what the difference is between people like Alexis and me. Alexis not only has the means and the resources, but he has a plan. Alexis would never lead a life like this. Without an identity, I can't live. I have all this money, but I can't enjoy it. What a bloody amateur I am.

The campsite provides mountain bikes for hire, so I take one to cycle down the hill into Cannes. I'm not interested in the sights of the town, although I do notice the boulevards, the classy crowd and the long promenade. I find what I'm looking for in one of the less salubrious

185

side roads near the station. I stand outside for a moment, taking a deep breath. As I walk into the internet café, I know what I'm doing is stupid and reckless, but at this moment in time I don't care. I log in to my email account and quickly scan the emails. Two weeks have passed since I drove down to Girona. I sent my email, and Ben answered in less than twenty-four hours. I was happy in my bubble at that time, but now I'm close to giving up. It's his last email, sent four days ago, that grabs my attention:

Neil,

The police have been here again. A guy called John Williams and a lady from the Fraud Office or whatever they're called, Alice Jefferson. They have traced your last email to Girona in Spain. They say it's only a matter of time until the police get you. You can't hide from them forever, they say. They want to talk to you. They have a proposal. They say it's your ticket back to a normal life. Get in touch. Do it, Neil. I'm sure you're not happy wherever you are now.

Ben.

They traced the email back to Girona… For a moment I'm furious with Ben for passing the email on until I realise that he didn't necessarily do so. They have probably got inside my email account. They'll have the powers and the means to do so. And then I realise that I need to get the hell out of here, as I'm sure somewhere an alarm will be ringing. I log out and leave the internet café. I cross the road, find a corner where I can observe the other side of the road from the shadows and wait.

Sure enough, within less than ten minutes, a dark blue Peugeot pulls up outside the internet café and a guy wearing jeans and a light sand-coloured blouson jacket gets out and walks inside. He could be anybody, but it's the holster on his belt that confirms his role.

I jump onto my bike and cycle back to the campsite. To say I'm nervous is an understatement. What an idiot I am. I've led them right here to Cannes. I can only hope they think I might be on my way somewhere else, but I'll have to be careful. If only I had an identity I could use.

Next morning, I'm up early, sleep having evaded me once more. I shower and prepare for work. I'm glad the demi has a solid metal door and a key, and I feel reasonably comfortable leaving my backpack where it is under the bed. Joanna takes me round to the kitchen. The staff is mixed, with some local French and the usual assortment of backpackers. A jovial crowd apart from the *chef de cuisine*, basically the boss in the kitchen, who turns out to be a right bastard. It's clear from the start that he hates everyone who isn't French, and especially the backpackers. I smile to myself; the guy is so comical, but he's wielding a big knife as he berates all and everyone.

I'm put into the washing-up gang, and I don't understand a word of his strangely guttural French as he screams at me. The less I understand, the louder he gets, until his face is bright red. He insults me even more, but I have no idea what he wants until a black guy steps forward and takes charge of me, de-escalating the situation. He leads me away, hands me a rubber apron and positions me at a big sink. His name is Gilbert, he says, speaking French to me. I say my thanks and start working. Gilbert stays close by, guiding me through the morning's work and we start talking. He surprises me by switching to perfect English mid-sentence, grinning at my nonplussed expression. From here, we get on like a house on fire.

I manage to get through the first week of working, eating and sleeping. I don't set a foot outside the campsite for fear of being arrested. My routine and my apparent diligence pacify the choleric *chef de cuisine*, but I'm functioning on autopilot. I do the work assigned to me, never complaining. But underneath, I'm preoccupied with how to escape my predicament. It's the only thing keeping me going. What can I do and where can I go? And how can I get a new identity that'll enable me to get a foothold? Or do I give in? The only social contact I have is Gilbert. He's a local guy, who lives the other side of the motorway in a part of town tourists never see. He has a small room in a shared house in a dead-end part of town. We talk, and share jokes and stories. He doesn't ask questions about me, and I don't ask questions about him. I get the feeling he's on the run from something – just like me.

By this point, thoughts of home and family never leave me; I've never experienced such gloom before. I realise it must have become noticeable as Joanne comes up to me after two weeks and tells me I can have the Sunday off.

"Go and see Cannes," she says. "Clear your head and have some fun."

It sounds like an order, but I agree to the day off and putting on shades and a baseball cap, I head into town. Cannes is beautiful, money is on display everywhere and I watch the rich people and the tourists enjoying life. But it just makes things worse. It's the proverbial salt in the wound. Sitting outside a café down by the old harbour, sipping my overpriced coffee whilst watching the crowds of happy people all about me, I have to concede this is it: the point of no return.

I go in search of an internet café and log in to my account. I ignore all the emails and scroll to Ben's last email. I click on it and press the reply button.

Ben,

Tell them to give me a number to call.

I'm packing it in. I'm coming home.

Neil.

28

I borrow a bicycle and cycle down to a spot called *Plage Robinson*. There aren't that many tourists here, and that's why I like it. Gilbert has set me up with a French prepaid mobile with enough credit for what I guess might be a long call. I enter the digits of the number Ben sent me in his last email. *Just ring them*, he urged. I'd dithered a few days, but now I'm ready.

There's some clicking as the call is routed through. Then a voice. "Jefferson here."

"I hear you have a proposal for me," I say.

"Neil, good to hear your voice," the woman replies.

"The proposal, what is it?" I say again.

"Neil," the woman called Jefferson says, heaps of sincerity and empathy in that one word. "I'm so glad you called. Let me introduce myself, my name is Alice Jefferson. I'm with the NCA and I'm an investigator looking into the Hamlays fraud."

Hamlays, not Holden Industrial, I note.

"Neil, first of all, please let me know you're well," she says, pausing and waiting for my response.

"I'm well," I say after a while.

"That's good. Neil, we have a solution for you," she carries on. "We can help you extricate yourself from your current predicament." It seems to me that she's rushing to get it all out, perhaps afraid I'll hang up. It sounds rehearsed, and I also notice she keeps saying my name.

"Neil, we can get you re-established. You can have your life back." She's said my name five times in as many sentences. And as far as "you can have your life back" goes, I have my doubts. I sit looking out at the Mediterranean and the setting sun glistening off a thousand little mirrors on the blue sea. I sigh, but I agree; I want an end to my current predicament, as she's put it.

"What do you want me to do?" I ask.

I sit outside on the steps of my demi, my half hut as I like to call it, sipping a beer. I have spoken to Alice several times now and they are coming over to Cannes. They'll be here this afternoon and I will go to meet them tomorrow morning. That's the plan. They have assured me that they've called a halt to the police searching for me on the condition I show up. If I don't, then the search for me continues. They know I'm in Cannes. They traced the call, but I also told them. No point in not telling them. I'm done with hiding.

For the first time in over four months, I have charged my phones and switched them on: work and private phone but not the burner, which I keep switched off. They are lying beside me, beeping like mad with all the messages they're downloading. I'm surprised both are still working, but as far as my private phone is concerned, the monthly fees are being charged to my bank account back in the UK, and I'm surprised I have credit left in the bank.

The fact that they're coming to Cannes astonishes me, but Alice confirmed that they are. They want to talk to me here, she'd explained, and didn't expect me to return to the UK for the talks at this point. That's kind of nice, but I wonder about the why. The plan is straightforward enough – I'm to go to their hotel at 10 a.m. She would send me the hotel's address via SMS to my French phone, she'd said.

Alice explained that she's an NCA investigator. But there's a joint agencies' unit investigating this fraud and other similar cases. She mentioned the SFO, the NCA and the City of London Police. The other bloke that's coming is police, she'd told me. John Williams his name. To me it just sounded confusing, but I don't care. They have a proposal and that's all I'm interested in.

She'd also told me some details over the phone: they'd had tabs on Holden Industrial and Alexis Theophilou for ages but not because of a potential fraud based on the financing of machines like in the Hamlays case but because of other activities. There was some inside info linking staff at Hamlays to these activities but it was not strong enough to act on. Willem de Vries was a prime suspect she said, especially after he'd disappeared that same Sunday. And my predecessor, apparently. He'd vanished months ago; no one knew anything about his fate. She didn't ask me specifically about my role, but she said she'd listened to the recording of the call I'd made and felt that deep inside I didn't really want to be a part of it. And she is sure I don't want to be where I now am. That's what she thinks, she'd emphasised. I'd gone along with that, agreeing with her – I don't want to be where I now am. I want to be somewhere else, enjoying my life. But I kept that to myself. But I had said, and it had been truthful, that I am desperately unhappy. I miss my family and I miss a normal life. I explained that I'd never had great plans for my life, but I certainly hadn't envisaged a fugitive's life. I didn't say I hadn't expected a fugitive's life to be so frustrating.

"Do you have a guilty conscience?" she'd asked during our longest telephone call.

The answer I gave didn't correspond to what I really thought in the moment she asked me. No, I didn't feel guilty and I still don't. It had been exhilarating. It had been so tempting. Tempting... I thought back to my conversation with Alexis in the hotel at Gatwick, as Alexis had asked, is this a *casual temptation* for me? Which meant what? A casual thing as in a one-off? No, I think I'd have carried on taking backhanders if they had been offered. But they did a runner and that changed everything. But it's not what I told her.

"Yes, I do have a guilty conscience," I said to her. "It was wrong to take the money."

But it's an astounding thing when you realise what you're capable of doing. And lying is one of these skills I never knew I had.

Technically, she went on to explain that they can't arrest me. The French police would do that, on request of the British authorities for my role in the fraud. But for the time being, that's not what she – what they – want. They want to talk to me, and they want me to listen to what they have to say. For the moment, I'm prepared to trust them.

My phone has finished beeping and I look to see what's come in. There are plenty of messages, especially in the first weeks of my disappearance. Messages from friends asking where I am. After the fraud made the headlines, the number of messages exploded. Friends asking about my involvement, photographed news articles sent asking if the person referred to was me. Even Kevin sent a couple of messages asking where I was and what I had done. We texted occasionally via our private phones, mostly sharing jokes, and he tried to contact me via my work phone before switching to my private one.

Ben sent some text messages on top of the emails and kept it up much longer than anyone else. Angry at first, his messages softened over the weeks I was away. He'd been very worried, that much was clear. He wrote saying that they had filed a missing persons alert but now assumed I might be hiding somewhere or, worse, that something had happened to me. He had pleaded for me to get in touch. Reading his messages, now weeks old, I feel the despair he had felt. That makes me feel really rotten inside.

I'm studying the messages, lost in my thoughts, when I hear my name being called. I look up to see Gilbert standing a couple of feet away from me. I laugh, I didn't see him, and he's obviously called out my name a couple of times already.

"I know, black guy standing against a black background," he says in reply to my laughter. He has a plastic bag in one hand. It looks bulky and heavy.

"What's in there?" I ask.

"Beer and ice and a bottle of Ricard, dude. I wondered where you were. You left our shift without a word. You haven't looked happy, so I thought I'd come look see what's eating at you."

He came up the steps and sat down next to me. "Wanna talk?"

"Sure, but not about my problems. Nothing worse than other people's problems."

"Rubbish, got plenty of those myself. Always good to talk. You have to air your problems. Especially if it's woman probs, mate." His time to laugh.

"I wish it was just that. And she's history now. Left that problem in Montpellier," I say, unable to disguise a note of sadness.

"Here's one for you," he says, taking an ice-cold beer from the bag.

We sit in comfortable silence for a bit. Despite my vow not to mention anything, I feel it bubbling up inside me.

"Ever done something really stupid?"

"Sure, that's why I'm here. Here as in this shithole campsite. And not where I belong."

I turn to look at him. He's staring into nothingness.

"Where you belong? Where's that?"

"Not even sure anymore. Anywhere I suppose but here."

"You kill somebody?" I ask, not meaning it seriously.

"In the army, yes," he says. "But that's not it. Got a medal for that. But the army, that's a fucked-up world. Makes you go mad," he says, finger pointing to his head. "I was a tough, mean soldier. My background was ideal for it. I grew up in a world where discussions are resolved with fists. Started at school and it's never stopped." Not sure how to respond to that, I don't say anything and we sit sipping our beers.

"No, I got involved with the wrong people in Paris, got caught, went to jail. Fucked up my life for good. Unemployable now, apart from working here 'under the table' as the French say."

"How come your English is so good?" I ask.

"Simple, really," he says, a smile spreading on his face. "Coz I am. Born and grew up in Luton. Joined the army to get away from the hell that was home. Left that lot and joined the French Foreign Legion. Got French citizenship

195

for my service. Went to Paris. Then jail. Came here. Couldn't go back to Blighty."

"Christ, really?" I exclaim. I'd never have expected any of this.

"Yeah, if I did, they'd put me away."

We sit in silence once more for a few moments. I want to say it's a comfortable silence, but it's not. I'm wondering just who I've got for company and what on earth he's implying. I'm a bit nervous to say the least.

"I had a good job in Paris," he continues, oblivious to the thoughts racing in my head. "Got into computers. Was good at it too, you know. Setting up internet sites and web shops. Good money, but business was volatile so I was very happy when I got a job working in the IT department of a bank in Paris until I got sweet-talked by a bunch of criminals. Wish I'd never met them." He takes a long sip of his beer. I let him arrange his thoughts and decide if he wants to tell me more.

"They were into all sorts of cyber-crime," he continues after a few moments. "They started off with petty stuff, nicking credit cards and identity thefts, but over time, they developed a scheme where they'd falsify invoices. You know, they'd send invoices with manipulated bank details and the customers would pay them rather than the original company who sent the invoice. That was far more lucrative. They got someone on the inside of a big utilities and engineering company, and this someone would send them genuine invoices. And then they'd manipulate them before sending them on to the customers for payment. It was easy, but they needed a constant supply of invoices that they could manipulate. The well ran dry and they were scouting around for opportunities to intercept other invoices. Plus, they had a problem with the banks."

I look at him not really understanding. He sees the question marks in my expression.

"You know," he continues, "you can't just walk into a bank and open phony accounts. They had to have a proper account. You know, to put on the invoices they were manipulating. And to open a genuine account you need ID and an address and all that. They'd done all that, but they weren't comfortable with it because it meant that one real identity was lodged in a bank's IT system. And if their venture went belly up, that ID would lead the police on to the next and so forth." Gilbert takes a long swig of beer, and I can sense a reel of recollections passing through his mind.

"Yeah, that's how stupid me got involved. Big mouth here said I could set up phony accounts in our IT system. I had their attention. They asked how and I explained that working in the IT department, I knew my way around. They charmed me and promised me loads, and I fell for it. Setting up the accounts in the IT system was risky, of course, but I could do it. I had all the necessary admin rights for the IT system and I was able to disguise the phony accounts to a certain extent. But to be honest, I was amazed at how easy it was to fool the customers. Hardly anyone challenged the altered bank details on the invoices. They even went so far as to put a flag on the invoices, saying please use the new bank account. Amazing."

He pauses and takes another swig of beer. "But the setup was too cumbersome. And in the end, too risky. They kept it going for too long. Of course, after a while, the suppliers whose invoices had been altered would come forward demanding payment. The customers would say 'we paid' and would show the transaction receipt. That started the ball rolling. In the end, the police came calling and the internal auditors started doing their investigative work and it didn't take long until they found my digital DNA and then bang. My jolly friends took off with the thousands or maybe even millions they raked in and left me in the lurch. I did a runner but got caught. Went to prison and on being released, came here. Been here ever since. The money I got, I spent of course. Bought stupid, flashy stuff. Didn't think it through. Now I'm stuck here."

I sit, mouth wide open. I can't get my words out; my thoughts are too jumbled up. "Bloody hell, how did…? I mean, how long did you, or better said, they run the scheme?"

"Don't really know. Six months, I guess. I sat watching the account we'd set up. The money just kept pouring in. I even helped doing the invoices. They had it all wrong, so I did some of the first invoices. You know, high quality scan and then superimpose our bank details, making them look real. Once that was sorted, I took a back seat. Thousands of invoices, thousands of customers tricked. Must have been millions in the end."

I let out a low whistle. Millions.

"Should have done a big one-off and then absconded," I say.

"Oh yes, but they were greedy. Kept it going for too long."

For a moment, I want to tell him my story. The beer has made me lightheaded, and I want to offload and cleanse my conscience. And, in a way, we're partners in the same crime. Brothers in fraud, so to speak.

"Got another beer in that bag?" I ask after a while.

"Sure," he says, handing me another beer. "But, you know, I had that idea, too. A big one-off. I found a way to do that. Use the bank's software rather than manipulate invoices. Had it all worked out, but then the police came knocking. End of the line for me, that was."

We sit sipping our beers. The silence weighs heavy. And with the silence, there's the burden of our mutual experiences.

"You know," I say after a long pause, "I did something equally stupid. I took a bribe. A bribe to keep my eyes closed to a crime in progress."

"Really?" The look on his face shows only limited surprise. "I somehow thought there was more to that story of yours about taking a year out."

And so, I tell him. Albeit an edited version. I leave out most of the details and certainly don't say a word about the stash of cash in my backpack under my bed just behind our backs. I don't trust him enough not to want to take it. After all, and by his own account, he's stuck here and he might have few qualms to take what he wants. His life's a mess and a stack of cash is readily available; that might just be incentive enough.

29

A figure appears dressed in a bathrobe. Quite early for a morning swim; it's not even 6 a.m. She takes it off, displaying a bikini rather than a swimsuit. A bit daring, I think, but I'm not going to complain. A nice figure, I have to say. She climbs into the pool and sets off, pulling quick, energetic lanes. Thirty minutes she keeps it going, which is impressive. She gets out, dries herself off and disappears.

I'm dead knackered, not having slept at all and the beers have left a bitter taste in my mouth. Once the alcohol wore off, I realised how much I'd told Gilbert. Far too much. Idiot. But I needed to offload. I haven't spoken to anybody about my experiences. I suddenly felt wary, ideas of dangers lurking all around me, so I got up at three in the morning, packed my backpack and as quiet as a mouse, made my way to where the bikes are parked and cycled here.

The hotel is a horrible seventies affair. Concrete matchboxes stacked on top of each other. The rooms facing the front have a grandstand view of the motorway. The ones at the back at least have a view across Cannes. I suppose they cost a premium. The only good thing is the long pool, with some strips of lawn to the left and right with sunbeds and chairs. And the accompanying pool bar with a patio and chairs and tables, which is where I'm now sitting.

Twenty minutes later, the woman reappears. Now dressed in dark trousers, sensible shoes and a white blouse. She carries a tray with a plate of croissants and a big cup of coffee. She sits down at a table under the sunshade of the pool bar and sips her drink. Definitely not a tourist and not a businesswoman either. She has an aura about her that cries out English and civil servant. It has to be the woman I'd spoken to: Alice Jefferson. I watch her dunk her croissant in the coffee, then she lifts it up to peer at it before nibbling a corner. If I need any confirmation, then that's it. I get up, hoist the backpack onto one shoulder, walk over and scare the living daylights out of her as I pull out one of the metal chairs next to hers, the legs scraping over the concrete.

She looks at me, an expression of shocked surprise frozen on her face. But there's recognition too. "God, you gave me a start there, Neil," she says, and I can tell that despite my friendliest smile, she wants to punch me in the face.

"Sorry, ma'am," I say, not meaning it.

"You're early, too."

"Yes, had to move. Sorry, it's been a rough night and I'm dead tired. And hungry," I say, eyeing her croissants and coffee.

"Hold on a moment," she says, rising from her chair. A few minutes later, she returns with another tray laden with croissants and a cup of coffee. She sets it down in front of me, and smiles. "At your Majesty's invitation," she says, sitting back down. I nod thanks, grab a croissant and dunk it full speed into the coffee, the French way. Alice smiles. She's kind enough to wait until I've eaten the first and have reached for the second croissant before speaking. "Okay, what brings you here so early, then? You said a rough night?"

I ignore her, not because I'm rude but because I'm hungry and too busy dunking and biting into the croissant. I get fractious when I'm hungry, but I see her appraising me as she sips her coffee. I do some clandestine appraising, too: she's fortyish, blonde shoulder-length hair, cut in a business style, which means easy to deal with. She has blue or green eyes, but I'm not sure as the light is diffuse and I don't want to make it obvious that I'm checking her out.

"Sorry about that," I say after washing down the third croissant with a sip of coffee. "Famished." I sit back, with a big cup in my hands. "I decided to clear out in the middle of the night and, with nowhere else to go, came here," I tell her but not wanting to delve into any details. "I hope I'm not inconveniencing you. I'm sure you have everything prepared, so I didn't think it too impolite to come a bit earlier."

She leans back in her chair. "No, it's fine, Neil. We're here for you, so it doesn't matter what time you arrive. I'm glad you've decided to come."

Definitely blue eyes. I can tell now that I'm sitting upright and she's fixing me with her look. Longish face too, and intelligence written all over her. She's early forties, I now reckon: the little lines around her eyes and the permanent frown on her forehead give her away. She reminds me of a young Jodie Foster.

I had no intention of replying at first but realising first impressions are important and this woman might be the solution to my current predicament, I decide to be nice. "I'm glad you reached out to me and I'm glad you made the effort to come here," I say. "Right, well, what do we do, Alice? How does this work?"

She smiles, keeping her eyes fixed on mine, before replying, "I suggest we get some more of these—" pointing at the croissants "—and another coffee, and then I'll get John to join us in my room where we can talk about everything in peace and quiet."

"Okay with me," I say.

She gets up, I get up and we stand looking at each other. Now that we're standing and smiling at each other, I realise she's quite small. A bit taller than Milly maybe, but five feet two max. I'm over six foot, in metric terms one metre eighty-five. She's slim and fit by what I could judge watching her swim. Her appearance and her demeanour aren't so that she eludes instant likeability, but I have to say that I like her already.

I can hear the phone ring through the wall in the neighbouring room. "Good morning, John," Alice speaks into the phone. "He's here."

"Be right over," a man's deep voice replies. The walls are so thin there's no need for a phone.

Three seconds later, there's a knock at the door. Alice rises to let the man in. As he comes in, I check him out. My size, roughly my build, too, but the muscle is turning flabby and the paunch a sign of fading vigour. Hair going grey at the sides and thinning a bit. Fiftyish, I surmise.

"Neil, this is John Williams. John, Neil," Alice introduces us.

We stand awkwardly, as there's a chair missing, so Alice sits on the bed, notepad in her lap, and John pulls the small table forward, places himself in a chair that he's brought in from the tiny balcony, and I squeeze behind the table to sit in the plastic chair that matches the plastic table.

"A bit cramped in here," I offer with a smile, but John ignores me.

He turns to look at Alice.

"We're NCA investigators, Neil," she says, facing me. "Mr John Williams—" she points unnecessarily at the man now sitting opposite me "—is the section head and I'm on his team. We are investigating the fraud involving Holden Industrial and Hamlays Bank. Both of course are familiar to you."

I nod in confirmation.

"You are suspected of direct involvement in this case, which has led to the collapse of Holden Industrial and put Hamlays Bank in a serious position. As you undoubtedly know, the damage the fraud caused was twenty-five million pounds, plus a lot more in collateral damage and knock-on effects, given the collapse of the H.I. Group. The damage to the bank and the banking sector runs a lot higher than the sum of the fraud with a loss in trust and reputation."

I gulp at this, nerves suddenly on edge. I hope they're not going to put all the blame on me.

"Now, at this stage, we're here to talk to you and we have – as I explained on the phone – a proposal by which we can hopefully give you your life back. All this is subject to you cooperating with us," Alice explains. Then adding after a short pause, "Fully."

Williams leans back in his chair, crossing his arms. I look at him, his body language, and his facial expression hostile. I can only assume it's preplanned and aimed at intimidating me. I can't help but feel it's a bit over the top.

We sit in silence for a while until I realise they're waiting for me to say something.

"What do you want to know and what's the proposal?" I ask.

"Let's get started with how it all started, Neil," Alice says, leaning forward towards me. I nod in assent and, taking a deep breath, begin to tell my tale.

"Well, I assume you know the details of my employment history at Hamlays?" Both nod. "So, you know I was appointed as a key account manager in March last year and that Holden Industrial was one of the accounts assigned to me."

"Yes, we know all that," Alice says. "Please focus on the fraud and your involvement," she says.

"Okay," I try to arrange my thoughts. "It started with H.I.'s Christmas event. That was the day we did the floor check." I can see they don't know the meaning of that term. "That's the audit we did of the machines that were destined for financing. We had approved a sale-and-lease-back transaction. That's where the client sells us assets – in this case, horizontal drilling machines – that they were holding on their balance sheet." I look up at them, but it seems they know what a sale-and-lease-back is.

"Right, so I went to the audit and joined the group that was checking the machines on the premises. I can't remember how many we checked, but it was a fairly large number and we spent most of the morning going from one workshop unit to the next, checking them off and taking photos. I didn't notice anything untoward at the time apart from the fact that the conditions got worse as we went from one unit to the next.

"The machines in the first unit were parked in two lines, all neat and tidy. The lighting was good and the floor

205

checkers were done in a few minutes. We moved on to the next unit and there was some considerable delay as the foreman was talking ages. I remember the floor checkers getting impatient. Oh, and I remember when we moved from the first unit to the second, there was a low whistle or something. I remember being surprised by this but didn't think anything more about it at the time."

"A low whistle?" John interrupts me.

"Yes, a low whistle from outside the closed hangar doors. You know the workshop units have hangar doors both ends. And I heard this low whistle outside the rear doors of that first workshop just before we left to go through to the second unit."

"Go on," he says.

"In the second unit, things were still orderly but less so than in the first one. And I remember the lighting was more subdued. And the foreman spent even more time talking. I was watching the floor checkers, who were getting more and more impatient.

"In the third unit, things started deteriorating. Bad lighting, machines standing around in any old way, you know. The floor checkers spent a lot more time checking the machines getting the photos done. And here – with the benefit of hindsight, I guess – I started thinking they're playing for time. These delays are on purpose."

"Because?" John asks.

"My theory is they were manhandling machines out of the first two units and stuffing them into the other workshops. That takes time. And sticking plaques with fake serial numbers over the real ones."

"Did you mention anything to the team leader at the time?" John asks.

"No, it was my first ever floor check and at that point, it never occurred to me that they might be doing this. I had no suspicions at the time."

"Okay. And then?"

"At some point Michalis, that's Alexis's right-hand man, came up to me and said that Alexis wanted to meet me.

"So, you left the floor check at that point?"

I look at Alice and in reply, say to her, "Yes, we left the floor check at that point. But I recall it went on for some considerable time. There were still other machines parked outside of the units to be checked, and then they were also auditing the books, you know, the files belonging to each machine. H.I. primarily rent out the machines, so there are rental contracts and payment streams and other stuff to check, too."

"What's the purpose of the audit – or floor check?" John asks.

"To make sure that all the machines Hamlays was financing were accounted for and that all the documents were in order. It's the only way to ensure that the machines are physically present. They are the bank's collateral."

"And then you met the big man himself?" Alice asks.

"Yes, in his study in the main house."

"And what happened there?" she asks, looking up from her notepad.

"Not much, really. We had a long chat. It was the first time I'd met him."

"Did he propose anything to you?" John asks.

"Propose?" I ask, unsure of his meaning.

"As in a bribe," Alice explains.

"No. He never proposed anything," I say, and realise I've just committed an error.

"He never proposed anything to you…" John says, looking at Alice, who's making a note of my words on her pad. "We'll come back to that in a moment," he says, turning his eyes back onto me.

"Apart from me joining their corporate Christmas event," I say.

"Right. Go on."

"The H.I. events were notorious according to rumour within the key account management team. And I was intrigued to have been invited, and they also let me have a room in the guest annexe. I had nowhere else to go, so I decided to stay."

"And was it notorious?" John asks.

"Yes, very much so, considering they drugged me and arranged a rape—"

"You what?" John exclaims. Even Alice looks up from her pad, surprise on her face.

"Yes. It's still very hazy in my memory – I still can't put all the pieces into place – but I ended up getting quite drunk and then there were these dancers, and they zoomed in on me. I just thought it was fun, but I ended up waking up in the guest room and it was all a mess, like as if there'd been a fight. Blood everywhere…" I let my words trail off, the recollection rising like bile in my throat.

"Are you saying they drugged and forced you to engage in sexual activities – against your will?" John asks, but he has a stupid grin on his face.

"Yes, that's exactly what I'm saying." I can feel the anger rising up inside me at the memory. "They did so to blackmail me."

"To blackmail you?" John echoes my words, except his sound doubtful.

"Yes."

"Why did they blackmail you?" he asks, eyes fixed on me.

"Because I found out that the floor check had been manipulated."

"Okay, let's just go a step back," John says. "If they drugged you and set you up like you describe – but this was before you found out the floor check had been manipulated, right?"

I nod in agreement.

"Okay," he says, acknowledging my nod, "then why didn't you go to the police?"

"Ah, well…" I know that whatever I say now will come across as stupid.

"Ah well…?" he echoes me again.

"At the time, I just wasn't sure."

He says, "There are tests."

"I know, but I just wasn't sure. And I thought that if I go to the hospital and the police, I'd only be rocking the boat. I was convinced nobody would believe me and I'd be potentially endangering the deal. Just imagine the implications. I had no idea that Alexis orchestrated this until he showed me the photos."

"And when did he do that?"

"I was confused. I just couldn't understand why anybody would do this. I mean the two girls were delicious and I'd have gone willingly with them. I just couldn't work out why anybody would have an interest in doing this. I got suspicious, and then I realised the floor check had been manipulated. So, I rang Alexis. And we met at Gatwick, and then it all came out."

"You met at Gatwick?"

"Yes, before he flew home to Cyprus for the Christmas holidays."

"And what happened at this meeting?"

I can see Alice scribbling away on her notepad. Her tongue is darting back and forth as she writes. I think back to that meeting. And how it all started there. What should I say? After all, it was me who initiated it. *What's in it for me?* had been my words.

"I confronted him with the manipulated floor check. I had no proof, just a hunch. And then he drops the photos in my lap. And says, 'I'm just a pawn.' And that Willem will make sure I'll never work again in the banking sector if I don't keep shtum about it."

"So, you knew that Willem was involved?" John asks, and I can see out of the corner of my eye that Alice has her pen poised, waiting for me to answer.

"Alexis didn't say so directly, but he implied that Willem had a personal interest. He made it clear to me that his personal interest was very personal and there was no way out for me."

"The easiest way out would have been to come to us," John says, watching me closely.

"Yes, I did think of that. But then I thought if Willem's involved, then there might be others, too. And I thought there might be a way of finding out and gathering evidence."

"So, you did what?" he asks, driving me all the more into a corner.

"So, I decided to take another route. I said to him, 'What's in it for me?'"

30

John returns with a few bottles of water. He smells of cigarette smoke. In the meantime, Alice and I have been sitting here. A chance for me to catch my breath and think my story through. I noticed Alice watching me closely. She's been forming an opinion. And I realise a none too favourable one. I fear that they don't believe what I've told them about the drugging and the rape incident. That I was blackmailed seems beyond their powers of imagination. Also, the story I've upheld in my mind, and which I put on the table, that I went along with the fraud to gather evidence sounds hollow. The fact that it was me who initiated the bribe, if that's what you want to call it, hangs like an invisible fog in the room. I wasn't lured by the villains – it was me who suggested it.

She hasn't commented on it. She asked some additional questions about the night of the Christmas event, but that has been all. Now John has taken his place again and is fixing me with his dark eyes. He has eyes like dark pits, devoid of any warmth.

He pops a chewing gum into his mouth and starts chomping it. The sound he's making is irritating. He's watching me, assessing me, provoking me. I return his stare, keeping my face expressionless.

After a while, he sighs. "Okay, so how much did you get?"

I struggle to keep my face expressionless. This is the question I've been waiting for. I've stuffed fifty thousand euros in a vest I bought at Brussels station and which I have on underneath my shirt. The rest is in the backpack.

"I got a hundred grand. Pounds, that is."

He whistles. "A hundred grand. Alice, did you hear?" he says, looking across at Alice, who nods.

"And how much did Matlock have?"

"He had two hundred grand in euros and fifty grand in pounds."

"Nice," he says, still chomping away. "And where is the money now?"

I nod in the direction of my backpack. "It's in there."

"And how much of it is left?" he asks.

"All of it," I say. "Apart from a couple of hundred – I needed to pay for the use of a car to get to Girona and back."

"Ah, yes, the email from Girona." He smiles at me, and I smile back at him.

I thought they'd jump up and search the backpack, but neither of them move. Instead, they remain seated, watching me.

"Right, Neil," he says, "why are you lying to us?"

I'm caught off-guard, but perhaps that was the idea. "Lying?"

"Yes, lying. That story about being drugged and blackmailed doesn't make much sense."

"Do you think Alexis isn't capable of pulling off something like that?" I ask and judging by his expression, and Alice's for that matter, I see that they do think he's capable of that. "I can only assume it was something they did to ensure my co-operation in case of… In case of what, I don't know. Perhaps it was Willem's idea. Perhaps he perceived me of being a bigger threat to him than to Alexis. I don't know. All I do know is that they pulled off that little number before I had noticed the manipulation of the serial numbers. So, it was done with forethought and foreplanning."

"Okay," he says. Tired of chomping on his gum, he removes it, as much to Alice's relief as mine. "And this story about collecting evidence – what's all that about?"

I sigh. "When Alexis made it clear to me that I had no options and that whichever way I turn, be it to report the incident to my boss or take it to the police, I knew I'd have the burden of proving my story. They'd be able to cover up the issue with the serial numbers, I was pretty sure of that. So, they wanted me to sit still and keep quiet. That's why the blackmail. I didn't agree with that. I thought there might well be others involved. I wanted to find out who that might be and build a case against them. I identified Matlock. He'd been manipulating their accounts and financial statements for years. I went to the H.I. site and was witness to a conversation between Alexis and Matlock."

Alice looks up from her notes. "Do you have any evidence of that meeting and conversation?"

"No, unfortunately, I don't."

Her disappointment is tangible.

"And what did you plan to do with the money?" he asks, before adding, "apart from buying tons of stuff, like a new PlayStation, telly and so forth."

"I don't know," I say, tiring of this discussion.

He slams his hand down on the table, jerking us upright.

"Neil, you do realise that you played a major role in this fraud? And that fraud is a criminal offence? You committed a crime! Aiding and abetting and God knows what. You also let Matlock die in that car, for Christ's sake!"

"He was already dead!" I can't help but shout. "I felt for his pulse. There wasn't one."

"How can you be sure?" John asks. "Are you a doctor now too?" His eyes are boring into mine.

"I… I…" But I don't get any further. I can't find any words to say. I was convinced he was dead.

"Your fingerprints were everywhere in that car, Neil."

I slump forward, head in my hands.

"How could you be so stupid, Neil?" he exclaims. It's formulated as a question but it's a statement. "You were there for the money. That was your motive. Given what you're telling us, it looks like you'd do it all again, Neil," he says.

"Good lord, no," I reply. "I admit the temptation was there and I succumbed to it. I felt I was in a situation with no options left open. And the way they manipulated things, it put the blinkers on me."

"The simplest and decent thing would have been to come to us," Williams says again.

"Yes, I suppose so," I say, defeat in my voice and in my thoughts.

"But you didn't. You saw an opportunity to rake in one hundred grand. And when you came across Matlock in his car, you saw an opportunity to grab another big pile of money and so you left him there and took off."

"No, it's not like that. When I drove up to the H.I. site on that Sunday – the day of the handover – I was prepared and equipped to collect evidence. I had the camera and all that. I made sure I was there really early so I could see who'd be coming apart from me. But in the end it was only Matlock, and I knew all about him already. But the thing is, it wasn't until that morning when I was hiding in the old workshop, that I overheard them say they were clearing out. And I panicked."

"You overheard them?" Alice says.

"Yes, before Matlock came, they were upstairs in old Holden's office and I crept in and overheard the whole thing. They were going to clear out. They were leaving the country and leaving H.I. to crash against the wall."

"But yet, they still paid you?" John asks.

"Yes, I was just as bewildered. I heard Michalis say that he thought they should have just left. But Alexis replied that they were proceeding as planned in order to buy time. Incredible," I say, thinking back to that cold Sunday morning and how my little bubble had burst. "That gave everything a new spin, and I panicked."

John looks pensive for a moment.

"Matlock had his slot at noon. I was due at two p.m. Matlock arrived, and I had to get out and get ready for my slot. I had some clothes stowed away in the top case of the scooter."

I watch Alice scribble notes and putting question marks behind every note she jots down.

"I walked from the sunken road, where I'd hidden the scooter, round to the office building, and there Alexis's bodyguard-cum-driver – a guy called Vincent – met me and escorted me to the old unit. And then I got my—" I hesitate briefly "—payment."

"And then?" Williams asks.

"I knew they were recording the handover and I wanted to do the same, record the conversation as evidence, but in my panic I forgot to activate the recording app on my smartphone. They gave me my money and I made sure I got the hell out of there. I dashed down to the sunken lane, jumped on the scooter and drove off. Halfway down the lane I came across Matlock's car."

"And that's when you helped yourself to Matlock's payment," Williams says.

"Yes, I did," I say – no point denying anything now. "He was dead, I swear. He had an airline ticket in his pocket for Sydney. He was planning to clear out, too. I thought it's a chance to lead a new life. I had the one hundred grand but I knew if they disappeared, then one hundred grand won't get me far. But with Matlock's money I'd have enough to fund a new life."

Williams shakes his head. "You must realise it could never have worked, Neil," he says with a tone of bewilderment in his voice. "All it amounts to is an act of desperation. No plan – just wild, headless activism. The scooter, walking around Gatwick…" He sighs. "And then you ring the hotline from out in the Channel and those emails from Ostend. By the way, I appreciate you rang the hotline. It shows you're not rotten to the core. Not yet, at least. But you were driven by greed and opportunity. Your actions all along have been amateurish, Neil. We'd have got you sooner rather than later – and we weren't even trying up to this point. We had the number plate of the car you were driving… Oh yes, there is photo evidence from CCTV and the number plate recognition system from the motorway," he says as he sees the expression of surprise on my face. "We – with support from our Spanish and French colleagues – traced the car to a Matthieu Dubois in Montpellier. And then Cannes. We had that all worked out," he says with calm confidence.

"Then why didn't you come and arrest me?" I ask.

"We wanted you to come to us, Neil," he says. "You just needed to work that out for yourself."

I sit with my head in my hands. I can't bear to look up. I feel so humiliated.

"I won't comment any further on your motives and your moral compass. Here's a chance to make amends and redeem yourself." He sighs a long sigh of disappointment. "All in all, and if we sum it all up, there's enough here to put you away for years. And unlike the threats made by Alexis, that really *will* leave you with no options for the future, Neil."

31

There's a knock at the door. Alice rises and walks the few steps to the door. Outside stands a man in his thirties with neatly trimmed black hair and a little moustache. He's smartly dressed in a blue summer weight suit and behind him, I can see the partially obscured figure of a uniformed policeman with a briefcase chained to his wrist. The suited man holds out a French police warrant card. He introduces himself as Inspector Dubarry. She lets both in, and the room is now full to bursting. Williams stands and shakes hands with the inspector and then turns to me.

"Neil, the money goes with the police for obvious reasons. I have arranged for you to remain free if you agree to wear a GPS ankle tag."

I nod, rise from my plastic chair and squeeze around the table. The inspector gives a signal to the uniformed policeman, who opens the briefcase, taking out the device. The policeman indicates for me to raise my right leg and fixes the ankle tag on my right foot. Done, I stand upright, the heavy device resting on my ankle, and squeeze back past the inspector and Williams and return to my place behind the table.

I watch as Williams, Alice and the policeman place my backpack on the bed and take everything out. Dubarry supervises. They place my personal stuff on one side and the bundles of cash on the other. Then begins the painstaking process of counting and recounting the money. They pack the bundles into the briefcase. Williams confirms the total amount and signs a chit. The policeman closes and locks the briefcase, fixing the chain to his wrist. Williams guides the inspector towards the door and into the corridor, exchanging a few words in hushed tones. He returns and takes his place at the table looking at me. In that exact moment I remember the vest I'm wearing with fifty thousand euros stuffed inside. I can feel my face go red.

"Do you think we could get some more water, maybe?" I ask. "It's hot in here and I'm feeling a bit dizzy."

Williams checks his watch. "Sure," he says, gets up and leaves the room.

"What happens now?" I ask Alice, who is sitting on the edge of the bed.

"We'll get to that shortly," she replies. We sit and wait, exchanging not a word. Eventually, Williams returns with a tray loaded with water bottles and baguettes with cheese and ham.

He offers me a baguette, and I suddenly feel hungry. We eat some food in silence. Williams rolls up his shirtsleeves, moves the plates from the table and fixes his gaze on me. Gone is the hostility; he addresses me in a more considerate manner.

"Neil," he begins, and I wait to see what comes next. "You realise by now your involvement, actions and subsequent flight puts you – legally – in a tight spot. I won't go over this again, but there is little doubt that you'll be sentenced to jail for many years in a court of law. How many years you'll get, I can't say. Some mitigating factors, pleading guilty and a good lawyer, will undoubtedly soften the conviction. Nonetheless, you'll be fucked for life."

I can't argue with that.

He pauses for dramatic effect. Then continues, "We have authority to make you an offer." He looks across at Alice, who nods assent. "The agency, together with the CPS, has approved an exceptional move. Despite – and I emphasise *despite* – there being enough calls from within the agency for you to be brought in front of a court. You understand that fraud is a major crime, and the government's policy is to take a tough stance."

He pauses once more, letting the words sink in. I just look at him and Alice in turn, wondering where this is heading.

"We can give you your life back – within limits – if you are willing to agree to cooperate fully."

I now begin to feel apprehensive but still say nothing.

"The CPS is willing to lessen the charge, maybe even drop all charges, if you consent to our proposal. The proposal is that we want to get you into Alexis's organisation as an undercover operative of the agency," he says, looking at me. I don't quite get it at first, but then, after the words sink in, I look from one to the other. I can't help myself, perhaps it's my nerves, but I burst out laughing.

I'm laughing like one does when a mate tells a good joke. It's hilarious, ludicrous even. "*We want to get you into Alexis's organisation as an undercover operative*" buzzes and bounces inside my head. Up until now he has been smacking me in the face for my crimes and now, he wants me to become an undercover agent. How funny. I have tears rolling down my face.

Alice is the first to pull her eyes away from me. She turns to look at her boss. Her look is fixed on him; she's waiting to see his reaction. I switch my gaze from her to

Williams, too. He sits there, his face quite devoid of any expression, staring at me and waiting for me to finish.

"Right, Neil," Williams says, holding up a device that looks like a bulky smartphone. "This is the receiver of the GPS ankle tag. I have reserved a room for you next to mine, two down from Alice's room here. I can see where you are at any point with this." He taps the device. "You will be free to move around the hotel but not leave without us. If you do, the device will trigger an alarm and you will be arrested. Is that clear?" I nod. "Okay," he continues, "our proposal to you is based on our plan to get you into Alexis's organisation. If you decide against it, I will ring Dubarry and you will be arrested, interned and sent back to England to face charges. If you try to leave the hotel, the same will happen."

"And how do you plan to do that? Get me into his organisation?" I interrupt him. "And what if it doesn't work?" I say, hearing the panic in my voice. "And what if it does, but they find out I'm a plant and decide to get rid of me? It's my fucking life you're playing with." It doesn't register with me, but I'm shouting.

We sit there staring at each other, the anger burning inside me. "*You're expendable*," Alexis had said to me all those months ago, and I feel like someone has decided once more that I am expendable. Dead quiet. Although my eyes are burning into Williams's, I hear Alice release the breath she can no longer hold.

Williams makes a physical effort to relax. He still takes his time before answering. "Neil, listen to me first, okay? I'll explain." His voice is now soothing and calming. "From what you have said, Alexis took a shine to you. Of course, he might have just said all that to lull you into going along with what they had planned for you. But on

221

the other hand, he might have meant it. We know that his sidekick, Michalis, is the brains behind his organisation. And we also know that Michalis is seriously ill. We have intelligence that he is, in fact, terminally ill. This might be an opportunity for us. We have tried for a considerable time to access his organisation but have had no luck. Even the guy they left behind in England to hold the fort, Willoughby, and who is now out on a limb, won't say a word. We want to get someone into the organisation and feel we have an opportunity – with you."

I hear the words, but I can't believe my ears.

"You have, as you said yourself, Alexis's and Michalis's numbers. We want you to get in touch with Alexis or Michalis and offer your services. If you speak to Michalis, word will get to Alexis. He will talk to you – of that I'm convinced. We will work out the plan and a detailed story in the next few days. I believe he won't even be surprised if you contact him. Of course, he won't *appear* to jump with joy when you ring him but, in fact, I reckon he's waiting for you to contact him. That's my hunch. He needs people for his organisation. And it's not as if he can post a recruitment ad on the web. He has experienced how you act in a tight spot and, irrespective of what I think about such things, I believe you have what he's looking for. We will go through it all with you bit by bit. We want to see how he reacts. If he tells you to sod off, okay. We will keep our promise to you. But if he shows interest, we can exploit that opportunity. And, if we can get you on the inside – in whatever capacity – then we can expand on that. We are not expecting you to go live with him but, of course, that would be a bonus." Williams tries to make it sound like a joke, but I'm not laughing. "You are a young man with no obligations. You are on the run and you're not averse to a bit of adventure. We will design everything around the reaction he shows."

My thoughts are galloping. "But what do I tell them?"

"We will work every angle in the next days, Neil. If we succeed, great. If it fails, we stand by our word to you."

I notice Alice looking from me to Williams. Her facial expression tells me everything I need to know. They don't have a clue how this mad plan is meant to succeed. To me it all sounds hollow…*amateurish*. Now that the words have been spoken, I can tell that even to their ears it sounds futile.

"Which is exactly?" I ask.

"As we said—" Williams looks at Alice, perhaps to show me that this is a team plan, and I see her nodding in confirmation "—we can end your life on the run and give you back a life in the UK."

I have to believe them even if the offer amounts to nothing. It's just words. Their plan is rubbish, but I keep that to myself. A vague promise based on even vaguer assumptions. Why should Alexis be interested in talking to me? I serve no purpose to him anymore.

Her eyes turn back to me. I scrutinise her face, wishing I could read her mind. She turns slightly red in the face, and I realise it must have been her idea. With a discernible effort, she pulls herself together and tries to give me a confidence-boosting look. I think about it all for a moment. But once more, there's no way out for me. What can I do but play their game?

Much to their surprise, I nod and say, "Okay, why not."

32

I sit in my room, on the bed. My few belongings are heaped at the foot of the bed, the now empty backpack in the corner. I just can't believe it. From the frying pan into the fire. How do they think this crazy plan could work? Scrap plan – there *is* no plan. It's a wild attempt and sure to fail. But I agreed. Mainly to bring the day to an end. My head is spinning and what other options do I have? I'm in their hands now.

Williams escorted me to the room, taking my passport, mobile phones and wallet. For a moment, I feared he'd do a body search but he didn't. I took off the vest as soon as he left and for the moment, I've placed it under the mattress. I've searched the tiny room for a good hiding place as there's no safe but so far, I haven't found anywhere to store it.

The ankle tag is a solid piece. Steel with reinforced plastic. No way to get that off without tools. No money, no passport and nowhere I can go with this thing around my ankle. I don't doubt his warning to me either. The ankle tag and the sudden appearance of the police really brought it home. I'm a criminal. And a failed one too. All this effort for nothing. But I have to concede, I haven't been a happy fugitive either. I didn't touch the money in all these weeks and I didn't have a clue how to live constantly on the run. I hit rock bottom after the ankle tag had been fixed. What a failure. And what a mess.

I decide to take a shower. The shower is hot and the water washes away some of my gloom. The hotel phone starts ringing and I pick it up. Alice.

"Hey, Neil, you okay?"

"Sure," I say. She hesitates for a moment before carrying on.

"Want something to eat? The hotel restaurant is pretty shit, but they do some okay pizzas down at the pool bar."

"Pizza sounds good as long as I don't have to sit with you two," I say.

"No, I can understand that." She even manages to sound sincere.

"Am I allowed a beer or two or three with the pizza or does that exceed my status?" I can't hide the sarcasm. "Can't pay for them myself, unfortunately," I add with even more sarcasm.

"Sure, Neil," she replies. "I'll bring it up to you."

"Oh, great. Room service extraordinaire."

"We're not your enemies, Neil," she replies. "We can't undo what's been done. It was your decision to get involved with them and it's the result of your doing that you are where you are. Don't forget that, Neil. We're here offering you a hand to pull you out of the water."

"Sure, I'm sorry, Alice. Feeling just that little bit fucked," I say apologetically. She is right.

"What topping?" she asks.

I laugh. "Yes, sorry – don't know. Anything without fishy stuff."

About half an hour later, there's a knock on the door. I open it to find Alice outside with a pizza carton in one hand and a carrier bag in the other. She walks in, puts the stuff on the little plastic table in the corner. "Salami, ham, mushrooms," she says. "No fishy stuff."

She takes out two beers and hands me one. I look around for a bottle opener, but they're screw tops and Alice has the cap off in a second. She walks out onto the small balcony, and I go out after her. We stand there with the beers in our hands, looking out across the lights of Cannes below.

"Nice," she says.

"Have you been down to the waterfront? The classy bit?"

"No. Only managed a brief outing to a little restaurant around the corner."

"Shame," I reply. "Definitely worth a visit. But then, you're not on your hols are you."

"No, definitely not. Strictly business," she says with a sigh.

I'm pensive for a bit. Not sure whether I really want to ask. But then, my inquisitiveness gets the better of me.

"Tell me, Alice, honestly, how do you think this can work?"

She turns to look at me and then glances around to see whether anybody might be in earshot. "Let's discuss this inside."

We go back in, and I push the balcony door shut. Alice has taken the only chair, so I sit on the bed.

"In my experience and especially in John's, who's been a copper for thirty plus years, a setup like Alexis's is a tightly knit community. It's family based most of the time. Alexis has an extensive network of legal and illegal activities. He has built a spider web of fronts and operations. But essentially, he's an opportunist. And like every opportunist, he seeks new opportunities all the time. He's not happy just to settle down and live off the fruits of his labour. Of course, he will have no immediate need for an outsider like you, to join his inner circle. But he will listen to what you have to offer."

I raise an eyebrow at that. An offer?

"Yes, an offer," she says, noticing my quizzical look. "We're here to work this out with you, Neil. You are the first person we've met who's had close contact with Alexis and who isn't part of his entourage. You have had meetings with him, you have talked to him and, although you're not quite aware of it, you have gained insight into how he works, how he interacts, his emotions. We want to get that out of you and then we can think of how we can get a better grip on the whole thing. I know we're asking a lot and if it all fails, we will stand by our word and get you rehabilitated as much as we can."

"This was your idea, wasn't it?"

She looks at me for a long time before answering my question. "Yes, it was my idea." She sighs. "When I heard the recording of your call to the hotline, I felt that you wanted to make amends. That you didn't really want to be part of the scheme and you'd been lured into a trap. At the same time, I also felt you're not averse to a little bit of excitement and adventure. This is a chance, Neil, to take on an active role, but this time on the side of a good cause. That's why I put the idea to John and our director, Giles Carmichael. It took some persuading, but we're here now and it's down to you to decide what you want to do."

33

I'm up early and rested after a good night's sleep, I sit on the balcony, enjoying the early morning coolness. It's going to be another hot day – that much I can foresee. I watch as Alice appears down by the pool. I smile as she undoes the bathrobe revealing the same skimpy bikini. Who brings a bikini on a trip like this, I think. But she's worth watching, as she climbs into the pool and sets off. Creepy perv, I chide myself, but can't draw my eyes away. She's fast, pulling off one lane after another. As she climbs out of the pool and stands drying herself, she happens to glance up. I give her a cheery wave.

I go downstairs to get some breakfast. I sit alone, with no sign of my new companions. I grab another coffee from the machine in the hotel restaurant and go looking for them. I ask at reception, and they point towards a corridor that runs along the side of the hotel that faces the road. Surprised they have any, I wander along the corridor and come across a conference room with an open door. Voices from the inside. I walk up to the open door to find Williams and Alice standing inside, their backs to me. Williams is pushing a whiteboard on wheels into position next to a conference table that sits four. On the other side stands a flipchart. He's put an assortment of marker pens and multicoloured Post-its on the table. On a sideboard stand bottles of water and two big Thermos flasks of coffee.

"Quite a setup, John," Alice says, bemused. He turns to look at her.

"Yes, I want a business-like atmosphere, and a cramped hotel room isn't the right kind of environment. I just hope Neil is willing to get positively involved."

"I think he will," she says.

"Heard my name," I say as I walk into the room, smiling at both of them.

Williams and Alice exchange glances. I look from one to the other. "What?"

Williams laughs, the first sign that he is capable of a positive emotion, and invites Alice and me to sit. He produces a basket with croissants from the sideboard, puts a Thermos flask of coffee on the table and takes his place between whiteboard and flipchart. He gives me a long, assessing look, and I realise he's trying to gauge my mindset through his policeman's eyes. I raise my hands in mock defence.

"It's okay, John," I say, smiling at the older man. "I've had time to think. And I think your plan is not bad, even if you don't have one. I'm ready to help. In fact, I want to help."

He sits looking at me, an expression of surprise on his face. "Just to be clear," he says, "as much as I'm happy to see you've changed your view on this, I don't want you getting over zealous. Let's start with more analysis of your meetings and then move on, based on your input, with how we can formulate a plan."

I nod in approval, waiting to see what he has in mind.

We commence and for most of the day, the focus is on my few meetings and interactions with Alexis and Michalis. Every little piece of information and impression I'm able to provide is written down and dissected. He jots

229

down every detail on the whiteboard and the flipcharts, sticking these to the walls and taking photos. It's a tiring business with only a brief stop for lunch, but it's fascinating stuff seeing the trained policeman in action. I can tell Alice is exhausted by the time John looks at his watch and suggests ending for the day. He then takes them down, rolls them up and places them on the conference table, stressing that no data is to be left here in the room. He sits down, and we sit in silence, looking at each other.

"Very impressive performance today," he says. "A good haul from the ocean of your memory, Neil."

I nod. "What next?" I ask.

"A beer and, I suppose, another bloody pizza," he says, patting his paunch.

"No, let's go to that restaurant," Alice suggests.

We meet in the lobby. John adjusts the GPS tolerance of the ankle tag on his device. "I'll be setting that back to the hotel perimeter when we get back," he says as we walk through the hotel door. I shrug, not expecting anything else.

It's a warm evening after a hot summer's day. A pleasant breeze is coming in from the sea. We walk downhill and I trot along, following whichever way they turn. In the end, we stop outside the restaurant, a Corsican place. Apparently, they came here on their first evening. The waiter finds a table on the patio for us with a view of Cannes and the sea below.

John orders an aperitif, Ricard on ice, and raises his glass. "Thanks to Her Majesty, who's sponsoring this tonight." I cringe inwardly but sip my Ricard. The meal is good but typical of French dinners – not enough to fill the stomach. John orders a new bottle of wine whenever a bottle is emptied. He keeps my glass filled, and I realise he's trying to get me inebriated, no doubt to get me talkative.

"So, Neil," he says after the plates are cleared, "tell me about your family."

The interrogation begins, I think to myself.

"What would you like to know?"

"Tell me about your father," he says, leaning back, smelling the cognac that has just been brought by the waiter.

Good lord, my father. I groan inwardly. I have no idea what he wants to know, so my replies are guarded. He switches suddenly to my meeting with Alexis at Gatwick.

"How did Alexis react when you said to him what's in it for me?"

"Oh, he was surprised. I don't think he expected me to say something like that. He asked me whether this was just a casual temptation on my side."

"A casual temptation?" John looks puzzled. "What's that?"

"I don't know. I suppose a one-off. You know, as in a one-off affair."

"A casual one-off affair," he echoes. "And was it?"

I make a show of thinking about it, but I know for me, it would have been a drug. Once tempted, I guess I'd have gone back for more. "Absolutely," I lie. "Look where it's brought me," and I laugh, opening my arms wide to embrace the view of Cannes, the restaurant and the warm evening.

34

I go down to the meeting room only to find the door locked. I'm not surprised and I have to grin thinking back to the evening out. John had succeeded in getting himself and Alice more drunk than me. What a laugh. The special investigators sent by the agency end up in a passionate affair. Ha ha, I was laughing even now. And they'd been passionate – and loud with it. Should have closed the balcony door, but I don't think they'd been able to do so even if they'd thought of it. I'm sure the whole hotel had been listening. Well, none of my concern; despite the noise, I'd fallen asleep.

I get myself a coffee and sit out by the pool and think. I now know their assessment of me. And I know I can't trust them. After we got back to the hotel, and Alice had retired to her room, leaving the door a fraction open as I noticed John stopped outside my hotel room door.

"Neil, I'd like to thank you for your positive contribution today," he said in slurred words. Then he startled me when adding, "Perhaps you want to call your family tomorrow?"

I'd nodded a yes, and he gave me a friendly, buddy-like thump on my shoulder. Then he turned and went to his room. I stood just behind my door and within minutes, I heard his footfall in the corridor heading back past my door. Less than a minute passed before I heard footsteps again walking past and heading for the staircase. I opened my door and saw the backs of John and Alice disappearing down the stairs.

I followed them quietly as they made their way out to the pool bar, a bottle of red wine in John's hand and two glasses in Alice's. They found a table in a dark corner. I crept up the rear side of the bar, keeping to the shadows and got as close to them as I could.

"A good day's work," I heard him say. "What did you make of him?" he asked, trying to keep his voice low but failing.

"An opportunist, I think," she replied, her speech showing signs of too much wine.

"Yes, absolutely. But they got on well together, so there might be a bond there we can work on."

"Can't really trust him," she says with effort.

"No, he's an opportunist. Runs in the family, apparently. His father was no different."

"Do you think he'll do it?"

"Sure, he has no other options," he replies.

"God, I fancy a fag."

I sit sipping my coffee and thinking about John's suggestion the previous evening and I wonder if he remembers. Now that he's put the idea to me, I'm desperate to do so. Up to now, I haven't dared to think about it. John still has my phones and, of course, I can just use any phone, but I want his okay first. For the time being, I have decided to play by his rules. I still have no idea where this thing is heading, but I know that now I'm even further away from home than I was before. Whatever their plan, I won't be seeing my family for a long time.

John is the first to arrive. He's showered and groomed, has put on a fresh shirt and trousers, but the small eyes with the dark rings give him away. He sits down next to me with his coffee.

"Sleep all right?" he asks.

"Yes, like a log," I lie. He seems relieved by this.

"Seen Alice?" he asks.

"No, not yet. Seems we all had a bit too much to drink last night," I say, grinning inwardly.

He nods and drinks his coffee. After a while, Alice appears armed with a big mug of coffee, looking pale and hungover. They keep their greetings brief, which almost makes me laugh. Now that we are assembled, John gets up and we follow him in single file to the conference room.

"Okay," John begins once we're settled. "Let's do a brief review." He sticks the flipcharts back onto the wall with Sellotape. "We've established quite a bit of data – thanks, Neil, for your input. Combining our knowledge – yours of Alexis and his close entourage, and ours of his international organisation – I think we can say that our profile so far allows us to make some assumptions." He pauses, moving from one flipchart to the next, collecting his thoughts.

"Alexis has a widespread organisation. He never appears as a director or general manager. He has stooges for that, like Willoughby, who acted as general manager for Holden Industrial." He points a finger at me, and I acknowledge his statement. It had been Willoughby who had been listed as company director and who had signed the documents. "That means he never holds a corporate position and can never be held directly accountable. All his assets are owned by offshore companies, like his house in Horsham, owned by a real estate investment company and let out to H.I. In turn, that company is owned by another offshore holding company, which again is owned by another offshore company in Panama, and so on.

"We know he has a wide international network of operational companies, some real and legitimate, others existing only on paper. He also has companies that don't do anything. They don't trade; they don't manufacture any goods but still generate revenues and invoices. These are purely vehicles for tax frauds, like VAT fraud schemes or to facilitate other entities immersed in the multiple chains of deception. He mixes legitimate companies' business activities with fake ones, thereby covering tracks, evading tax and providing support for his schemes.

"He has, as we have been able to establish, money laundering activities, VAT scams and all other kinds of operations running. Apart from the H.I. fraud, which made the headlines, he keeps his operations low-scale and virtually invisible. H.I. has been the exception. Why?

"We have discussed the H.I. fraud in detail and I think – we all agree here – that he deliberately drove H.I. into the wall to bring the scheme to an end. Supported by your observations and the conversations you overheard, Neil, I'd say he did so because there were too many outsiders involved, for instance, Willem de Vries, Matlock, and the partners in the firm of accountants – although they deny any knowledge – and because it was too elaborate. And the company was going down the drain. They'd been cooking the books for years. And then you, Neil, come along, notice the switch of the serial numbers and confront Alexis. He has his insurance ready and blackmails you. This proves to you that something is up and unexpectedly—" he turns to me at that point with a wicked grin "—you invite yourself to the party rather than report the planned fraud and claim your bit."

I smile an embarrassed smile. He continues. "Alexis goes along, although from a financial perspective, your contribution to the scheme was minimal. Why? I think at that point – as you were saying – he was buying time. He still needed some bits and pieces to complete the scheme. As you have said, Neil, Matlock seemed almost totally out of control and was a potential threat. By the way, Neil, Matlock passed away from a heart attack, but they – I mean Alexis and Michalis – decided to clear out before the house of cards came crashing down. Willem de Vries, CEO of Hamlays, was directly involved, and we have evidence that he was also involved in other schemes, some involving H.I. in other banking activities." He pauses, turns to me. "It appears your predecessor might have been involved." He turns back to the flipchart. "De Vries cleared out, too, no doubt having been forewarned by Alexis." He sits down, looking at Alice and me in turn. "H.I. was the unplanned exception and it does not fit the pattern we have of Alexis's other activities."

He pauses, letting us digest his summary and conclusions.

"One more aspect," he says. "The linchpin in the whole structure appears to be Michalis, his chief henchman. We don't know much about him apart from the fact that they have family ties. Michalis is the operations man: he controls the organisation and the flow of money. He also seems to be the man who sets up the schemes, invents new ones and manages everything on Alexis's behalf. He seems astute, is totally loyal to Alexis and, as we have also confirmed, is terminally ill. Who in the clan – I think we can call it a clan – might likely succeed him? We don't know."

John returns to the table and sits down. He pours himself a coffee and glances from one flipchart to another. "Any additions?"

Alice clears her throat. "We have been unable to penetrate the organisation," she says. "Not a single employee at management level, who must have insight into some of the dealings, like Willoughby, has spilled a bean. On an international level, the same thing. An insider at one of Alexis's Croatian entities came forward and provided some information into a VAT scam, but he has withdrawn his statements and disappeared. If foul play is involved there," she says, looking at John, "we can't tell. Alexis seems to pay well and is rewarded with total loyalty. We have data supporting this. Willoughby, for instance, was extremely well paid for his position as managing director of what amounts to a mid-sized engineering company, and our investigations have shown that he has accumulated assets and wealth far beyond his salary level."

"From a personal perspective," John says, taking over, "we gather from your input, Neil, that Alexis keeps a tight ship. The inner circle is long-serving, mostly family and loyal friends. He did, and that's my conclusion – and I think Alice will agree—" he looks in her direction "—show interest in you. You say that in the conversations you had with him, he – on several occasions – indicated that he might have use for somebody like you." I nod in affirmation. He did say that a couple of times, but did he mean it? I have no idea. "We think he might well have taken a liking to you." He pauses, waiting to see if I might disagree or comment. "It's too much to expect, but he may be looking for new members to join his organisation, especially if he needs to replace Michalis. From what you have said, we think he will be willing to talk to you and maybe meet with you."

I look from one to the other. "But surely that's not it?"

"What do you mean?" John asks.

"Surely just talking to him or maybe meeting with him won't get us far. What's that going to get *us*?" I emphasise the "us" to show this is now our joint mission, but I've started thinking along different lines. "We want more than just talking? He won't give much away in a phone call or over a cup of coffee, is he?"

"No, but we hope that we can get you to re-establish a connection. Of course, it will take time and we're not sure at this point how we can capitalise on it down the line, but we're hoping we can – how can I say it – get you connected in a way that'll give us insight into his activities… Well, maybe not activities, but processes…" John's voice trails off.

It sounds lame, and he knows it. It's not a plan. It's nothing.

"John." I make a controlled effort to keep the exasperation out of my voice. "I'm sorry, but this is rubbish." The look he gives me is one of suppressed indignation and agreement, all rolled into one. "I know what we can do," I say.

They both look at me, faces showing their expectation.

"One thing that made my time on the run so frustrating is the fact that I had no identity I could use. My own identity was off limits to me. I had to stay under the radar. I had money but no opportunity to use it without running the risk of having to identify myself. And I soon noticed you can't do much with just cash. You need a bank

238

account, for which you need an ID and so forth. If there's one thing Alexis knows, it's how to establish identities. It's a simple thing that we'll do: I will ring him and ask if he can get me an identity. It'll be a business proposition. I won't ask it as a favour; I'll propose to pay him for his services."

35

I watch as my phone runs through the start-up procedures and logs into the French network. I ignore all the beeps as it downloads messages, connect it to the hotel's Wi-Fi and open the chat app. I scroll through the contacts, and there he is. He's online.

I press the call symbol, the call is routed through and I hear the ringing tone. He takes his time before answering. His voice comes through loud and clear in my ear and in my head.

"Hello," he says.

"It's me," I say.

"Oh, not the police, then," comes his answer.

"No, not the police. They're downstairs."

"I hope you're in a cell and they've handcuffed you," he says.

"Well, I've got an ankle tag. It's sort of handcuffs if you like."

"Good," he replies, and then there's a lengthy pause.

"Ah, Ben, good to hear your voice," I say, giving in. "What can I say? Where do I start?"

"How the fuck should I know? It's your story – you decide." The anger in his voice is tangible. I sigh. He's right. Where should I start? I decide to just talk, but he gets in before me.

"So, fuckwit," he says, his voice has softened now. "Start at the beginning. Tell me your story."

And so, I do.

The first hour flashes by. He listens, not saying much.

"So, you were drugged," he says when I'm done.

"Yes, I was. They were blackmailing me."

"And that's why you didn't want to go to the police," he adds.

I think he's misheard me, but I don't say so. An unexpected way out of having to repeat my sinful story yet again, so I grab the chance. "Yes."

"And now you're working for the agency as an undercover agent? Sounds exciting."

"Only if you're into James Bond films," I answer.

36

Watching Alice go about her morning swim, I wonder briefly about the nature of their relationship. John and her. I can't imagine relationships in a government agency like the NCA are approved of. But I suppose the work they do, the long hours, must bring people together. But hey, I think it's no concern of mine. Suddenly, the chair next to me is scraped over the floor, startling me. John sits down with a plate full of croissants and a big mug of coffee. He started dipping the first croissant into the coffee.

"A habit everyone seems to pick up when in France," I say.

"Normally I can't stand them – croissants that is – but here they taste okay, and all the other stuff is awful," he says between bites.

"So, what do we do today?" I ask.

"Ring Alexis," he says.

"Good. We ought to go through it. The call, I mean. Prepare it."

"Sure," he replies, dipping another croissant.

"Hungry?" I say, amused.

"Always," comes the reply. He doesn't stop, fully focused on scoffing one croissant after the other.

Alice climbs out of the pool, wraps herself in a big towel and comes over. She sits down and quickly grabs the last croissant on his plate. He lets her.

She then sits, one leg up, and studies my face. "How was your call with family?"

"Great," I say. "After a while," I add. "Hard going at first – as to be expected."

She nods. John sits sipping the remnants of his coffee, watching me. "Let's get started," he says after a moment.

In the conference room, we quickly go through the various possible angles of my call and the possible replies. John does his usual, noting down likely questions and answers on several flipcharts that he Sellotapes to the wall. I let him, but I think it's pointless. Done, he gets up, walks over to his shoulder bag propped in a corner and takes out a small device. He sets it on the table, and I realise it's a small conference speaker.

"You need to activate your Bluetooth," he says, sitting back down. John positions the chairs so that Alice and he are sitting at right angles to me. Nothing like a bit of pressure with them two sitting so close and yards of flipchart Sellotaped to the wall opposite.

"Okay," I say, taking a deep breath.

The burner phone only has two numbers stored on it: Michalis and Alexis. I dial Alexis's number. The ringing tone comes through loud on the conference speaker, and John quickly turns the volume down. We let it ring and ring and then, nothing. The phone ends the call. The disappointment is tangible. We all look at each other. John is scratching the stubble on his chin. Alice just looks blank. I check my watch. Coming up to 10 a.m. here, but God knows where he is. It could be any time. The phone rang, so it's on. But perhaps he doesn't use it anymore. All these thoughts are running through my head. I keep my face blank but inwardly, I can't help thinking what did they expect?

And then my phone rings.

I press the green call button and after a second or two, a voice comes through on the loudspeaker.

"Who's this?" the voice says.

"It's Neil," I reply.

"Neil, who?"

"Neil Wilson."

"And who is Neil Wilson?"

I look at John, unsure what to say, but he just makes an impatient movement with his hand for me to carry on.

"Neil Wilson. And I'm calling to speak to Alexis."

"Why?"

"That's for me and Alexis to discuss." I recognised Alexis's voice right from the start despite the charade. "Oh, come on, Alexis, you know who I am."

That booming laugh; I have to smile.

"Neil, my friend," he says. "To what do I owe this pleasant surprise?"

"Alexis," I say, making my voice sound more relaxed, "how are you?"

"I'm always fine, my friend. Enjoying life. Are you?"

"Well, it's a challenge," I say now, letting some resignation slide into my voice. It's a game, and I'm warming to it.

"So, where have you been these last few months?"

"Travelling."

"No doubt."

There's a pause, and I know I have to keep it going. "Alexis, I need to call on your services."

A thumbs-up from John.

"My services?"

"Yes, your professional services. It's a service I'm happy to pay for."

"Such as?"

"Services that'll make my life easier." Another pause. I carry on. "Life without an identity is difficult."

A booming laugh comes through on the speaker. "So, your casual temptation isn't quite so casual as you thought, eh?"

"No, admittedly, it's not. But there's no way back for me. And I'll pay the going rate."

Silence. And then I realise the phone has gone dead. I look at it and then at John. "Was that a sod off?"

But John holds up his hand, indicating to wait. The phone rings again. Number withheld.

I swipe the green button, connecting the call.

"What did Michalis tell you about phones, Neil? You're ringing from a UK registered phone." The familiar deep voice coming through loud and clear again.

"I know, Alexis. I did listen. It's my old burner phone and it's been off for months and you see, that's all part of the issue of why I'm ringing you."

John nods his approval.

"So, where are you, Neil?"

I look across at John, who gives me an affirmation to go on. "I'm in Cannes."

"Okay," he says, seemingly not surprised at all. "There's a little place I like at the Plage L'Ecrin. Just off the Boulevard de la Croisette near the Square de Verdun. Meet you there the day after tomorrow. One p.m. We'll have lunch together."

Wow, I think. I look at John and Alice. They're both beaming with pleasure and nodding their approval.

"Yes, sounds excellent, Alexis. Glad we can meet up so quickly."

"Sure," he says before disconnecting.

37

John marches out of the conference room and orders a cab at reception. He's all policeman now as we set off to check out the venue. The cab takes us downtown, and I stare out at the tourists walking along the promenade in the afternoon heat. It seems a different and bizarre world. The cafés and bars along the Boulevard de Croisette are jampacked, the holiday season at its peak.

The cab drops us off at the Square de Verdun and we walk the few metres to the Plage L'Ecrin. The beach is full, tourists and locals lying in the hot sun or in the shade of the multicoloured parasols strung out along the bleached sand. Kids are playing in the sea. Screams of fun and laughter bubbling through the baking hot air. I can see Alice taking in the holiday atmosphere, but John is focused on the restaurant, the layout of the place, especially the vast decked patio. We walk around, surveying the place. Across from the restaurant is the marina, Port Pierre Canto. The big boats lying tied up in their berths with their sterns to the promenade. I can't help but notice the number of ensigns sporting the Union Jack flying from the biggest yachts. There's parking space for cars by the marina, and the models parked there are all top of the range. Big Mercs, Range Rovers, Jags, Maseratis and one or two Ferraris. This is the life, I think to myself.

Seeing none of this, John is checking out observation angles. We walk into the restaurant, John ignoring the waiter who comes up to us. He mumbles something about looking for someone, and we trail behind him as he walks to and fro, out onto the patio and back inside, the waiter following us, desperately calling for support. Some of the outside tables have fabric screens between them, providing some privacy to the diners. He frowns as he takes this in. We stick out like sore thumbs. Heads begin to turn and the waiter rushes off, summoning the head waiter or security to deal with this intrusion. I decide to return inside, close to the entrance. I have my shades on and a baseball cap, hoping Alexis isn't sitting amongst the diners. John has stirred up quite a commotion, but he's oblivious to it.

John comes marching back through the restaurant, Alice close behind, ignoring the head waiter, who's now trying to block his path, and walks out onto the concourse in front of the restaurant. I wait a few seconds, and then follow as inconspicuously as possible. Under the palm trees, there's a public sports arena with gym equipment. Suntanned and oiled young men are going through their routines, being watched by tourists milling about, ice creams or soft drinks in their hands. John does a full circle, taking it all in before walking back across the Square de Verdun to the Boulevard de Croisette. Here, he turns, casts one final look around, and then walks across to the marina. We follow him like sheep. He finds a bench in the shade and sits down. The heat is unbearable, and we're all sweating. John wipes the sweat off his brow, and I can see that his shirt is soaked. Even Alice looks hot and flustered.

"That was fun," I say, earning myself a furious look from John.

"From a surveillance perspective, this place is a nightmare," is his conclusion. "You'd need a complete team to cover this place, and then you'd still not be able to see into every corner. Shit."

I know it's not conducive to the overall situation but I say, "I can't see how it's going to make much of a difference one way or another." John shrugs and chooses not to reply to my comment. "Anyway, on a different note, if I'm going to meet him here for lunch, then I need to get some clothing. All I have is worn out or not appropriate. I don't think I'd make a suitable impression if I turn up in shorts and an old T-shirt."

Alice looks at John, anticipating his reaction. Before he can speak, she says, "I think he's right. Nothing too fancy but smart enough. Appearances could be important here." John agonises over this, no doubt thinking of the expenses, before agreeing. He'll have some explaining to do, but he has some success to report too, so he just shrugs.

We catch a cab back into town. The taxi drops us at the Galeries Lafayette in the rue du Maréchal Foch. We leave John in a small, air-conditioned café, and Alice and I set off to buy some smart but not too expensive new clothes. Alice, grateful for the break and the air-conditioning in the department store, provides the fashion support and the cash. As we present John with the bill, he frowns but doesn't comment. Finally, we take a cab back to the hotel.

We're hot, sweaty and dusty. For the first time since coming to the hotel, I take to the pool, ignoring the ankle tag, which arouses plenty of suspicious looks and hushed conversations. I have to laugh as one mother grabs her child and carries it to safety.

I do some lanes, joined after a few minutes by Alice. She swims some lanes, too, but we give up after a while and just lie in the water cooling off.

"So, how do you feel about meeting Alexis again?" she asks.

"Not sure." I really don't know how I feel about it. On the one hand I have him to blame for everything that has happened in the last five months. But not entirely. I'm painfully aware of my own role in the whole thing.

"Where's John?" I ask. "He hasn't said a word since leaving the Square de Verdun."

"On the phone to London, I assume," she replies. "Reporting and getting new instructions, no doubt," she ventures.

"Fancy a lemonade?" I suggest, and we swim over to the ladder closest to the pool bar. I order two Oranginas and we sit down at one of the tables in the shade.

"Always loved these as a kid," she says, sipping the fizzy orange drink.

I sit watching her. "Tell me, Alice," I say. "I take it this little clandestine operation really is approved by your superiors."

She gives me an inquisitive look. "Why else would we be here?"

"Well, the more I think about it, the more it seems to be outside the remit of a government agency."

"In this case, it isn't," she says, and her voice is a bit brittle.

"But it puzzles me," I say. "The NCA, or whoever it is you work for, endorses such a mission. Okay. We've contacted him. He´s agreed to meet me. And then?" She hesitates to answer, so I carry on. "I mean, it can't be the plan just to have the chat. He's not going to say much. He isn't going to give away any secrets now, is he? He'll be on his guard. And even if he is willing to help me get a new identity, which we know will be a fake one, then of course

249

that makes him guilty of some sort of crime, but that isn't enough, is it? And even if we get on well, it doesn't mean he'll share inside knowledge with me or invite me to join his organisation."

"We've discussed all this already, Neil," she says.

"Yes, but it's all too vague."

She looks around to see if we can be overheard. "We want you on the inside."

"Yes, I know." I'm not willing to let this go. "But how? It can only really work if he takes me into his organisation."

She looks into my eyes. "Yes, we want to get you into his team."

"But that means I have to go with him. We've touched on this, but you guys aren't answering the questions."

She just sits there, a slow smile forming on her lips. "You got any other plans, Neil?"

"I can think of a few," I say.

She gives me a long, assessing look. "You want to go, Neil," she says after a moment.

I think for a moment, wondering just what their expectations are. "That definitely has to be outside of the remit of your organisation."

"That part is true," she concedes.

"So, I'm out on a limb."

"Yep, secret agent," she says, making it sound like a game.

"What about the risks? If they find out who I'm working for?" I let it hang there, but she has no answer. "And there's no reward for me," I add.

"Your old life back," she replies. "If it works out right."

I leave it there. It's pointless to discuss it any further. She doesn't want to understand my worries. And I was about to say it's not enough, this vague promise of *your old life back*. But I keep my mouth shut. I've had a different thought.

38

"Come on, Neil," John says, "you need to keep focused. It's a turning point, that meeting tomorrow. After that, we'll know for sure what the options are."

I shrug. I'm not prepared to commit unless I have that reassurance. John sighs. He gets up, brings out his phone and dials a number. After the call connects, he says a few words and then hands the phone to me.

"Neil, good morning to you," the voice on the other end says. It's a cultivated upper-class voice. A voice of authority. "Carmichael here. I'm the director general. The work you are doing is splendid. We're glad you decided to cooperate with us. Now, Williams tells me you are seeking some assurance from the agency concerning the treatment you will be likely to expect on your return to the UK given the background of your involvement in the H.I. fraud," the voice says. He doesn't wait for me to answer. "Well, I can assure you that your co-operation will be honoured accordingly. Your efforts are vital in clearing up the background of this fraud case, which has inflicted significant damage to the British system and is costing taxpayers dearly. Not to mention your critical support in building the case against Mr Theophilou and his network. Also, your role in this mission going forward will certainly positively impact the outcome of any proceedings against you." There's a pause. Perhaps he's expecting me to say my humble thanks or to be jubilant and show my instant gratitude. I say nothing. "Of that, I can personally assure you," he adds after a moment.

I thank him and assure him that I'm truly appreciative of his personal commitment, but I don't believe a word. They are offering me nothing.

"Right then, carry on the good work," he says in a superb caricature of an upper-class officer, and I pass the phone back to John. John turns away and exchanges some more mumbled words with Carmichael. All I hear is, "Yes, sir," and "No, sir," and then he finishes the call.

John returns to the table and looks expectantly me at me. "Satisfied?" he asks.

"Sure, of course," I reply, but I think he's disappointed by my tepid reaction. I'm convinced now that whatever happens out there, I'm on my own.

He passes over an envelope and gestures for me to look inside. There's a bundle of euros inside. I look at him, not understanding. "Four thousand euros," he says. "To cover upcoming expenses."

39

The taxi ride through town down to the Square de Verdun takes about thirty minutes, and I'm grateful for the taxi's air-conditioning. It's baking hot outside.

I sit in the back of the car, thinking ahead to the meeting with Alexis. I have no idea what to expect. I watch the city pass by but don't take anything in. The taxi stops, and I get out. I look around; nothing looks any different than two days before. But why should it? It's just another baking hot summer day in Cannes.

I check my watch; it's close to the agreed time. I walk across to the restaurant. A waiter comes across with a questioning look. *"Bonjour,"* I say. *"J'ai un rendezvous avec Monsieur…"* (I have an appointment with Mr…) But I don't get to finish the sentence. I hear the familiar booming laughter coming from outside. *"Je l'entends,"* I say, indicating that I've heard him, and he grins, nodding.

I make my way through the restaurant and out onto the decked patio, where every table is taken by groups and couples sitting under big sunshades. All I have to do is follow the laughter. I draw up in front of a group sitting under a large sunshade, screens providing privacy between the bordering tables but with an undisturbed view of the beach and the sea. I'm about to make myself noticed when a big, dark figure appears by my side – Vincent. I'd obviously walked straight past him. Now, as I stand before his boss, he's jumped up to provide protection if necessary. I turn to look at him; he looks fleshier than I remember. But the added flesh is flab rather than muscle. Life has been good.

I turn back to face the table, and there he is, Alexis. He's sitting in the corner chair directly next to the beach. He looks up at me, not recognising me, so it seems, so I take off my sunglasses. Recognition dawns on his face, and he beams at me, erupting into a joyous cry.

"Neil, my friend!" he bellows. I can feel rather than see the faces of his party looking up at me. He tries to get up, failing to get a hold on his seat. His frame has increased greatly since our last encounter. Life has been even better for him.

I put up a hand to gesture that he remain seated, with an even bigger smile on my face. He gratefully drops back into his chair. Only now do I take in his entourage. Next to him is a small, suntanned woman in her fifties I'd guess, but it's difficult to say given the enormous sunglasses and the artificial smoothness of her skin that's visible to me. She has blonde hair styled in a long bob. Dressed smartly, draped in rings, bracelets, and a necklace that even I can tell must be worth a fair bit, she exudes classiness. Opposite sit two men in their early forties, sporting designer sunglasses. Both have short black hair, are deeply tanned and dressed in smart casual wear. The one on the right, sitting directly opposite Alexis, is wearing a blue polo shirt and I can just about make out an embroidered symbol and some letters below. "Axe" or something like that. The other guy is wearing a light blue cotton shirt. All sun-glassed faces are turned towards me, the conversation having stopped.

"Vincent, get our guest a chair," Alexis barks, and Vincent turns and disappears from my field of vision. Whilst I stand waiting, I take in Alexis. He's sporting a

255

cream-coloured linen shirt that is straining to cover his large stomach. I can see the heat is getting to him – he has sweat beads on his forehead and dark patches under his arms. His white hair is tied back into a ponytail and his long beard is bushy but carefully trimmed. He looks like an off-duty Father Christmas on his summer holidays. Large sunglasses are propped on his forehead.

Vincent reappears and shoves a chair into the back of my knees. As I sit down, I notice the table is full of plates and various dishes of food. Seafood, various meat dishes and several bottles of wine in coolers. A half-empty bottle of red stands next to Alexis's plate. There's hardly any space left for me, but I notice that a place has been laid out. So, they had been expecting me – maybe.

Alexis busies himself, barking orders at his table guests to pour me some champagne and for me to help myself. I'm totally surprised; I didn't expect to be gatecrashing a lunch party. I thought it would be just Alexis, me, and his constant shadow, Vincent.

Alexis introduces the blonde woman, "Isabelle, my wife." I can't see much of her face; her sunglasses are so oversized they cover most of it. What I do see seems frozen into place and she strains to smile at me. He gestures to the men opposite. "Marcel and Gioti."

I say a hello, then shake hands with each of them.

"First we eat, Neil, then we talk," he commands and makes a gesture for me to tuck in whilst spreading an oversized napkin back over his massive stomach.

The conversation restarts where it finished before I appeared. I sip some champagne and look at my lunch companions. I hadn't expected any of this. I take some morsels of food from the closest dishes. It's an incredible array of food – more than four or five people can eat.

Crammed onto the table are elaborate fish and meat dishes, salads and the ubiquitous baguettes. I can sense Vincent sitting close behind me; in fact, I'm convinced I can feel his hot breath down my neck. I turn my head, trying to see where he is, and out of the corner of my eye, I see him behind my right shoulder at a separate table. But fortunately, it's not his hot breath I feel on my neck – it's the sun.

Around me, the conversation is going on as if I wasn't there. It's a mix of French and Greek, and now and again a bit of English thrown in. Alexis is telling the guy sitting opposite, Gioti – if I heard correctly, a long story. I don't understand a word, for they are speaking Greek. Isabelle and Marcel are speaking French, but their conversation ends as Alexis's tale becomes louder. His story is elaborate and ends in a big guffaw. Gioti laughs and even Isabelle and Marcel, the other guy sitting next to me, join in.

I allow myself a discreet glance to my left and right in search of John and Alice, but I can't see them. As I look back towards the table, I notice Alexis's eyes on me. He's still laughing but his eyes aren't. I smile boldly at him, showing my willingness to join in. He's a big storyteller; nothing's changed. But he's sharp as an eagle, and I hope he hasn't noticed my searching glances.

The first hour goes by and I sit there feeling superfluous. Alexis never stops telling anecdotes, some in English for my benefit and I join in, laughing whenever everybody else does. I wonder how long this will go on and if coming here has been a mistake. Perhaps he's just toying with me and wants to enjoy my discomfort.

After the second hour, I start to feel annoyed.

Fortunately, the third hour is slowly filling up, and we're past coffee and dessert by now; Marcel makes a show of looking at his watch. *"Mon Dieu!"* he cries out. "Isabelle, if we want to look at the new collection, we'd better make a move." Isabelle looks at her watch and chides Alexis for not reminding her. They make to leave. Gioti, taking his cue from the other two, says he'd better get back, too, as it's a longish drive to Saint Tropez. They say their goodbyes and suddenly it's just me and Alexis and, of course, the ever-present Vincent.

Alexis leans back in his chair, extracting a cheroot from his breast pocket. He gives me his best smile. "Neil," he says, "come sit opposite me." As I rise, Vincent is at my side.

"Need to give you a quick check, and I need your mobile phone and anything else in your pockets," he says. I look first at him and then at Alexis, but he's busying himself with lighting his cheroot. I let him perform a quick frisk and hand over my smartphone and my wallet, which he takes over to the table where he's been sitting and places them on the seat next to him.

As I stand, I notice that the outside dining area and restaurant are empty. The restaurant is closed. It's just the three of us now. Staff are busy tidying up outside and inside. They don't glance once in our direction. Alexis gestures towards the chair opposite.

"Sit down, Neil," he says, sounding a lot more business-like.

I sit down. Alexis pours himself the last from a bottle of red, puffing away at his cheroot.

"Well, then, my friend, tell me your story."

"What I want to ask you," I say, feeling that he wants me to get down to the request I have on my mind, "is whether you have the means to get me a new identity, as in a passport." I'm about to launch into why I need one,

258

but he holds up his hand, stopping me. He looks at me with half-closed eyes, whether from the smoke or alcohol-induced tiredness, I can't tell.

"No, not just yet. Tell me your story from when you left the workshop with your plastic bag under your arm."

"Oh, okay," I reply but, in my head, I'm thinking shit, I should have expected this. What do I tell him? After a few seconds to sort out my thoughts, I start. "Well, I drove home at first. Come Monday morning, I received a phone call from my boss. I'd taken the day off, you see, and he rang me at home. He said I had to come into work. There was a lot of commotion. He said there was something wrong. Police and investigators had arrived, swarming all over the place, and they wanted to speak to me. A major fraud involving H.I., he said. A whistle-blower had informed the SFO, as I found out later in the newspapers. I tried to act normal but of course, I knew. Willem de Vries had vanished, he told me and asked what the hell was going on. I said I didn't know. I panicked then, as you can imagine. I didn't know you'd absconded." I laugh at that point. "See, you didn't forewarn me," I say, making light of it. His half-closed eyes are fixed on me, but he shows no reaction. I now suddenly realise there's so much I want to ask him, but I don't. Not now, I say to myself.

"No way was I going to go into work," I say resuming my story. "I thought about what to do. I decided to clear out. I took a train down to Brighton and then walked to Shoreham, where my uncle has a yacht. I thought I'd stay there for a day, lie low and think about what to do and where to go. And then I had an idea. I decided to take my uncle's boat and sail it across the Channel. I got to Ostend and from there, I made my way to Brussels. But I needed to keep below the radar, as you can imagine, so I moved on, and travelled by train to Montpellier. There, I came across the backpacker fraternity – young people from around the world travelling around Europe on a shoestring budget. I got a job in a pub, and found some cheap accommodation where you pay cash, no questions asked. I moved on from there and ended up here in Cannes, working in the kitchens of a campsite up near the motorway. It's a barren, hand-to-mouth type of existence but no questions asked. Ironically, I have money but without an identity, I can't use it. I've been working for cash to have a roof over my head and keeping under the radar. It's not the kind of existence I want, Alexis."

He sits there opposite me, listening, not interrupting once and showing no reaction. Once I'm done, he sits upright, looking directly at me.

"So, you took your uncle's boat and sailed it single-handed to Ostend. Not bad," he says with a smile on his lips. "Bet that went down well with him."

"Oh yes, hates my guts, but I think he enjoyed the trip back across the Channel," I say.

"And since then, you've been playing the backpacker?"

"Yes, not very glamorous, I admit."

"No, I guess not," he concedes. "Neil, my friend, what can I say? A fine mess we got you into, eh? But that's the way it goes. At least you have the money," he says, with one eyebrow raised. I realise it's a question.

"Well, most of it. I've had some expenses along the way."

He gives me one of his inscrutable looks. And then he just shrugs. It's not his concern.

"My friend, I owe you that one favour. No doubt. Despite everything, I am a man of honour," he says, his voice heavy. "To answer your question, yes, I can arrange for that. But it's not so that I can just post it to you. It takes time and it can't be done here." I breathe in deeply, my heartbeat increasing. "There's one comfortable way we can do this, my friend," he says, smiling at me. "Come with me to Cyprus."

I cast a nervous glance in Vincent's direction. Alexis sees me glance over and laughs.

"No fear, my friend. You will be my guest." He puffs the last of his cheroot, crushing it out in the ashtray. "Unless you have better things to do, of course."

"No, it's not that I have a full agenda. But how do I join you? I can't get on a plane unless I use my real passport. I have no idea if I'd get through security."

He laughs. "We have better methods, Neil. Simple, you come back here in—" he looks at his massive wristwatch "—let me think. Saturday next week. Same place, same time. And then we set off. You will be my guest, so don't worry. Just bring whatever you want to take with you. You won't need much. Just yourself." He gives me a big grin.

He takes out another cheroot, lighting it, and then turns to look out over the beach and the sea.

"Just keep your head under the radar one more week, Neil. Can you do that?" he says, glancing at me, before turning once more to take in the late afternoon sun glistening on the lazy waves of the Mediterranean. Vincent appears at the head of the table holding out my belongings to me. I get the hint. I stand up, about to say thanks, but he just waves, and I turn and walk through the restaurant to the entrance.

40

I walk into the lobby, looking for John and Alice. I walk over to the conference room, but the door is locked. Where are they? I stride across to the pool bar, where I find them sitting at a table in the shade. They have beers on the table and are busy studying their mobile phones. John has his laptop open on the table in front of him and his messenger bag by his feet. They look like they've been sitting there for a while. They don't bother saying anything to me as I walk up to them and sit down. After a while, John looks up.

"Get a beer," he says.

I do as I'm told, wondering what the hell is going on. As I sit down, beer in hand, I study them both. They look knackered. Alice has sunburn on her arms and her face is red, too. John looks equally red and sore. I don't say a word. Finally, John leans back in his chair, lets out a sigh and looks at me. Alice does the same. Both are staring at me now.

"What?" I say, their looks making me nervous.

"So," John says, "how was your lunch? Didn't eat much."

I look at him. "Did I do something wrong?"

"No, it's just we spent fruitless hours watching you. Got a few photos, but that was all."

"Not my fault," I say.

"Just knackered, Neil," John says with another long sigh. "It was hot and, as you see, milling around in the hot August sun for hours leaves its mark."

"Well, what can I say? It's not that I had much say in the matter. Alexis left me sitting there waiting for hours."

"Yes, we saw that. What came out of it in the end?"

"Alexis says he can get me a new passport. But he can't just post it to me. He wants me to go with him to Cyprus."

"Good. A result," John says after a minute's contemplation. "It shows he has resources, and it shows he's willing to support you. It's what we expected. You going?" John is fixing me steadily.

"Wasn't that the plan?" I ask after a moment's thought. What the hell has got into these two?

"Of course. Just make sure you keep in touch with us. Oh, that reminds me, let me have your mobile phone."

I hand it over, unsure what he's intending to do. He looks at my phone, takes a connecting cable and hooks it up to his laptop. John taps on the keyboard and watches the screen as some program is carried out. He disconnects my phone and passes it back to me.

"I have installed a tracker and an app enabling you to communicate with us by text and voice. It also has an alarm function if there's an emergency. It connects you automatically to the agency's communication system and it will send your position to our crisis unit as long as you are logged on to a mobile network or Wi-Fi. If you're not, it will record your message and relay it to us once you're back in a cell or Wi-Fi network. We can alert the police or whatever service is appropriate. But the main function is that it enables you to talk to us securely. The calls or texts you send will be encoded. The app is disguised as a calculator. Quite useful actually if you need to do some calculations, and it's accessed by pressing the calculator icon in the top corner. You have to draw this pattern to enter the app."

He shows me. Indeed, it looks harmless, a clever disguise, and I hope to God I won't need the emergency bit.

"Okay," I say, "got it." I look at him. "What happens next?"

"We fly back to the UK tomorrow. We're done here for the time being. When are you meeting him?"

"Next week Saturday. Same place."

"Did he say how you will be travelling?"

"No, just said for me to be there. Same place. Same time."

If John has any concerns for my safety, he doesn't show it. He just nods.

"Okay. If you change your mind, ring me or Alice. You have our numbers, or you use the app. Obviously, don't call us on our mobile numbers once you're with Alexis. Not much else we can do at this stage, so we've been ordered back to London."

Now I understand the change in mood. Their little adventure as agents in the field has come to an end.

He gives me another envelope with euros.

"This is all we can give you. Make it last," he says. I do a quick count. Five thousand. He then hands me two receipts to sign. One for the first amount of cash and one for the second. "And remember," he says, his tone serious, his look a warning, "if you don't honour our agreement, we will find you."

"Of course, I'll honour the agreement," I say.

"You better," he says, before rising and putting away his computer. "Time to pack."

Right, I think, mission completed. Dismissed.

41

I lie on the recliner in the sun, an iced coffee on the small table beside me. One question plays on my mind – what do I do when it's done?

One week to kill. And then I start a new chapter in my life. I have no doubt that Alexis will honour his promise to me. I have no clue how long it takes for him to get me a new passport but when it's done and I have a new passport, I can move on. Where to? I have no idea at the moment. I have roughly sixty thousand euros cash. How long can I live on that? I'll need to find a job. Somewhere. Somewhere where John and Alice won't find me. But where could that be?

But I have no intention of joining Alexis's organisation. For a start, why should I? And I doubt that he will propose such a thing to me. Ridiculous. But I have also made a promise to John and Alice. And I will try to give them something, for a while anyway, to make them happy. And to buy myself time. Time to plan. But I certainly don't trust them. And I don't want to go back to the UK. Not yet and not on their terms.

I'm now stuck between the two.

Even if there is an opportunity and Alexis does have use for me, do I want to be part of Alexis's organisation? Even if it is on behalf of the agency? What do I owe them? They promised me my old life, but do I want it back? No.

With a new passport and a new identity, then why not take my life back into my own hands? When it's done, pay him for his service and move on. That sounds the best option to me, even if I can't answer the questions that come with it: where to and to do what?

Ah, well, I think, cross that bridge when I get to it. I settle deeper in my recliner, close my eyes and let the sun's rays warm me.

It slaps me in the face. The little bit that's been hanging on to the end of my thoughts for days and which I've been ignoring. I decide to allow it to surface.

When John, Alice and I had first thought about how to approach Alexis, the focus had been centred on proposing something to him. This had evolved into asking him if he could get me a new passport and identity, but the initial idea has remained inside my head.

A proposal.

I sit upright. I look left and right, ridiculously sure that my thoughts are visible. Indeed, that little persistent tag on the end of my thoughts, it might just qualify as a proposal. But I need to talk to Gilbert first.

Galvanised into action, I get up, rush to my room, which the agency has kindly paid for until the end of the week, and get dressed. I scout around the hotel grounds for the bike I liberated when I'd taken off from the campsite not even two weeks ago and had deposited in a corner of the hotel grounds. To my amazement, it's still there. I grab it and cycle up the hill to the campsite.

I stand near the main entrance but am anxious to stay out of sight of the office. I don't want to have to explain myself after my sudden departure, especially to Joanne. For a moment, I'm struck at how radically different my life has changed once more. Two weeks ago, I was living a fearful and uncomfortable life on the backpackers' trail with a sack full of money. Now, I've surrendered the sack full of money but have a legitimate purpose and a view to doing something else.

I stand watching and waiting. It's coming up to 4 p.m. and if Gilbert is still working here, and he's on the day shift, then he should be coming off now. I know he'll be using the top entrance, as it's closest to the bus stop where he catches the bus home.

I keep well back. I feel nervous. I mean, I did a runner because of Gilbert. He scared me right enough. Ex-soldier. Seen action and all that, and now here I am, waiting desperately for him to appear and to share an idea with him.

It's 4:30 p.m. by now, Gilbert hasn't shown and I curse under my breath. Okay, I'll come back tomorrow. I'm about to turn away when strong hands grab my neck.

"*Qu'est-ce que tu cherches ici*, motherfucker?" a voice hisses into my ear. *(What are you looking for here?)*

Apart from the fact that I can't breathe, it takes me a second to distinguish the pure English pronunciation of "motherfucker". I raise my hands in surrender, and the hands release their grip. I turn slowly to find Gilbert standing behind me, grinning.

"God, Neil, you'd never survive in the army, mate. I've been standing behind you for ten minutes minimum and you never noticed," he says, laughing his head off. "What the fuck are you doing here, you daft sod?"

I'm still in the process of recovering from my shock, unable to answer. He slaps me on the shoulder in encouragement. "Come on, spit it out, mate."

"Gilbert," I croak, "I've been waiting for you."

"What? Hiding here in the shadows and as far back as you can from the main gate and Joanne's eyes?"

"Yes, didn't want to bump into her. I left in a hurry and probably owe her money for the demi."

"That you do, but I don't think she'd come after you with daggers, mate. You're not the first backpacker to sod off without telling, and you won't be the last. Come on, you can accompany me to the bus stop and tell me what you've been up to in the last two weeks."

We set off up the hill.

"So, where have you been and what have you been up to? Disappears without a word, he does. Thought you'd gone to find that Aussie girl," Gilbert says as we walk side by side up the hill.

"Long story, Gilbert," I reply.

"You got fifteen minutes until my bus comes," he says, smiling at me.

"It'll take a lot longer than that, I'm afraid. You got anything planned? Can we go somewhere and I'll tell you."

His smile disappears. "You in trouble?"

"Sort of, yes."

"Okay, there's a café near my bus stop. Let's go there and you can tell me all, you sad loser," he says, a smile back in place.

We get a coffee each and find a quiet table outside in the late afternoon sun.

"Go on, then," he says.

"I left because I had an appointment," I begin. "That issue with the bribe, well, it's still current and the police have been after me. Well, not the police exactly, but the Serious Fraud Office." I pause for a moment. "Actually, they were National Crime Agency investigators."

"Okay, glad you know who's after you," he says, rolling his eyes.

"Yeah, it's confusing," I say, laughing. "The bribe I took, it enabled some bigger crooks to carry out a major fraud. A fraud that netted them twenty-five million pounds."

He's about to take a sip of his coffee but stops and lets out a low whistle. "Cool," he says.

"Not so cool, as they decided to do a runner, didn't bother telling me and left me behind."

I can see him thinking this through. "So that's why you end up here in hell's kitchen doing the dishes for your sins?"

"Yes."

"Okay, so what happened?"

"They, the NCA investigators, sent me a message via my brother. Said they wanted to talk to me."

"Nice," he replies. "So, you got all cosy with them somewhere romantic here in Cannes?"

"Sort of. But it wasn't romantic. They put the thumbscrews on me, drawing a lovely picture of my prospects if I don't collaborate with them. And they were close, too. Tracked most of my movements despite being careful and keeping beneath the radar."

"Well, you're still here, so you're collaborating with them?"

I nod.

"In what way?"

"Well, they're after the big crook. I had some dealings with him and I have his number. They suggested I ought to contact him and propose a deal. But they had no idea what this deal should be. They can't really propose something illegal. We spent some days juggling ideas but at the end of the day, it came down to me contacting him to ask that he get me a new identity and a new passport. Not as a favour, but as a business deal."

"Sounds good. I could do with a new identity, too." He grins.

"Yes, I can imagine. I can put a word in for you," I say, smiling back at him.

"Okay, so that's what you did. Rang him, and he said, 'Sure, no problem.'"

"Basically, yes. But I have to go with him."

He fixes me with his eyes. "Sounds a bit dodgy. And what's the deal with the NCA?"

"They want me to become an undercover agent. Ingratiate myself, spy on him, report back to London. Help them build their case against him."

"Fuck me," he says, a frown now set on his face. "A dangerous game they're asking you to play. What are they offering you in return?"

"Quite. They have no concern for my well-being. And their offer doesn't amount to much. Put in a good word for me with the CPS – that sort of stuff. Oh, and ten grand to cover my expenses."

He smiles at that. "Ten grand? Generous. But you've agreed to go along with their wonderful plan?"

"Yes. Not much else I can do. I'm stuck here. The French authorities have an eye on me and will put me in a sack and post me to England if I don't play by their rules."

Gilbert laughs. "Yes, I can imagine. The French don't like foreign criminals lying on their beaches, even if small fry. Mind you…" he says as an afterthought. "I can't really believe that the SFO or NCA, or whoever they were, would be empowered to set up a scheme like this. I mean, it's a bit of secret service kind of stuff. They're just using you and you're taking all the risks. They can wash their hands of you anytime." He's pensive for a moment. "And they're not really offering much, are they? Ten grand and a lighter sentence, you said."

"Precisely. That's what I keep thinking. I'm taking all the risks, aren't I?"

He sits looking at me. "So, what is it you want from me?"

I hesitate for a moment before answering. "Well, the big crook said he's willing to help me get a new identity. In fact, he says he owes me that one favour. Man of honour, and all that. The new identity is to be it: the favour. It means I will be going with him." I pause, wondering briefly if I should say where to. "To Cyprus."

"Cyprus?" Gilbert asks. "Plenty of fresh concrete going into new developments there."

I nod as the thought hits home. "As his guest, he points out. But I'm to spy on him, find out whatever I can and report it back to London. What if he finds out? These are professional criminals. I doubt they have qualms to get rid of me – permanently." Once more, my worries take a hold of me and I lose myself in them. "And even if I do get that shiny new passport, what next? If I decide to go off and start a new life, I'll need a job. But doing what? I have no qualifications I can show. If I apply for a job, it'll be with an empty CV."

He looks away. I can see he's following my train of thought and then I remember, he's been down this road before.

"If I'd known I was going down the drain, I'd have asked for a million."

He turns his head back to me and laughs. "A million. Ha ha. Rings a bell. I thought I'd make a million, too."

"See. But they ripped you off like they ripped me off. People like us don't win. We don't get the million because we're not smart enough."

He nods in confirmation.

"So, what's your answer, then?"

I've forgotten for the moment what he's referring to.

"What do you want from me?" he reminds me.

"Right, sorry. The thought crossed my mind, just as a backup, what if I do have a proposal for him? And maybe for me." I look him in the eyes. "A scheme that'll have him interested. Buy me at least some time."

He looks at me patiently, waiting for my answer to his question.

"Tell me how it works. That scheme with the invoices."

His features become stern. "I told you how it works," he says.

"You drew an outline. I want the details."

"Why?"

"Why? Because I have an idea what the proposal could be," I say, leaning back, smiling at him.

"What's in it for me?" he says, leaning back, too.

I laugh. "A million?"

"Not enough, mate."

"You decide, then," I reply.

He gives me a long look. "You fooling around, you daft sod." It's said as a statement, but there's a question in there too.

"Maybe not," I say. "Let me buy you dinner, and then we can bounce some ideas around – for fun."

"A ten grand dinner?" A big grin on his face.

"Fuck off. McDonalds, mate."

He laughs. "All right, then, but sod McDonalds. I know an African place. Costs the same but the food is much better."

Part Three

42

Once more, I climb out of the taxi at the Square de Verdun. Shouldering my holdall, I walk across the square to the restaurant. Walking in through the main entrance, I scan the tables packed with the usual lunch crowd. I'm expecting to find Alexis holding court again, but I can't spot him anywhere, so I stand waiting.

A waiter comes by and stops with a questioning look on his face.

"*Bonjour, je cherche Monsieur Theophilou,*" I say to him. *(Hello, I am looking for Mr. Theophilou.)*

"*Le patron?*" he asks. "*Le patron n'est pas là.*" *(The boss isn't here.)*

I think for a moment: *le patron* means boss or owner, and then it twigs. Alexis, *le patron* – he owns the bloody place. No wonder we sat here undisturbed way past closing time.

I feel a bit dumbfounded, seeing that he expressly told me to come here at 1 p.m. I look at my watch. It's 1:05 p.m. I stand there, holdall over my shoulder, at a loss and sticking out like a sore thumb, wondering if I have misunderstood or whether Alexis has decided to play another little game with me. It's then that I hear a voice behind me.

"Are you Neil?"

I turn and before me stands a young Asian woman. I'm taken aback. She is stunning. Beautiful. Incredibly so. Long black hair with some brown thrown in, an elf-like face, skin like silk. Brown eyes, but with a touch of chestnut and a sheen-like gloss. She's evenly tanned and physically... Well, what can I say? Trim would sum it up. To be honest, she has a lovely figure, which is undeniably and clearly visible in the close-fitting tank top and shorts she is wearing.

"Yes, I am," I manage to say after appraising her for too long.

She laughs at my embarrassment. "I'm Zuki," she says, her voice betraying an American accent.

"Nice to meet you, Suki," I say.

"*Zuki*," she says, "with a zee."

"Cee?" I ask. I'm confused.

"An American zee, Neil," she informs me.

"Ah, okay, Zuki – got it."

She smiles at me. "Follow me."

We walk out of the restaurant, and she turns left towards the marina. I know from our last visit here there are parking spaces along the marina access road, and I assume she's heading towards the cars parked there. I follow her and we cross the road rather than turning towards the parked cars. She keeps going, leading us onto the marina promenade. Along this stretch of the marina the biggest yachts are moored, and I'm just beginning to wonder where she's taking us when she stops at the gangway of a large, two-masted, blue-hulled yacht with white superstructure. The name *Axiom* is displayed on the

275

yacht's stern in raised gold letters. She gives me a brief encouraging smile and walks up the gangway onto the rear deck. I hesitate for a second before following her.

We now stand on the rear deck. Right in front of me is a massive teak table, cream-coloured canvas-covered seats on both sides. A matching canvas sunroof spans the whole deck. Beyond the smoked glass, sliding doors stand open. I hear music and voices coming from within. Zuki walks around the table and, through the open doors, disappears inside. I follow, tentatively stepping into the darkened interior.

The lounge we walk into is beyond anything I have encountered so far. A raised sitting area, two large leather armchairs on the left and right, with a massive glass-topped coffee table in the centre. We skirt around this and head down a few steps into the lower-lying section. This broad and deep lounge boasts heavy leather chairs and tables scattered around, plus leather-topped seating that's fixed to the sides and runs around the circumference of the lounge. A big bar stands in the corner on one side, where Alexis stands with several people apparently mixing drinks. Pop music is playing on hidden speakers and the atmosphere is of a party in progress. Zuki walks up to Alexis, who is standing at the bar with his back to me. She touches his arm, and he turns to face her and then, following her gesture, turns to me with a big smile on his face.

"Neeeeeiiiiil!" he cries, drawing out my name once more like on an accordion. He comes up towards me, arms outstretched and envelops me like a long-lost friend in a big bear hug. He draws away and looks me up and down. "You really have thinned out, Neil. And your hair, so long. You look more and more like that English footballer, what's his name, yes, McManaman."

I smile politely, thinking there's worse than being compared to McManaman, whom I admired as a kid. To me, Alexis looks more and more like a cross between Pavarotti and Vangelis, but I don't say it. His hair is longer than mine and white as snow. He looks like a wild Alaskan trapper with his hair and his bushy beard. A trapper plucked from Alaska and dumped onto Hawaii – judging by the garish Hawaiian shirt he's sporting.

He pats my arm and puts his hand on my shoulder. "Let me introduce you," he says, turning to face the crowd of people still occupied with mixing drinks. "Mizuki – Zuki – you have met. This is Sakura, her sister. This here is Fiona and that is her sister, Lee. Over there is Gioti, whom you have met, too. This here is Laki and over there is Marcel, who you have met also."

I look at them in turn. "Hello," I say. It's difficult to get an impression of the people standing so close together in the semi-darkness mixing drinks.

"Drop your bag and grab a drink, my friend. You're part of the family now," he exclaims, his booming voice reverberating around the lounge.

The young people don't take much notice of me, but I notice Sakura giving me the once-over. She is as stunningly beautiful as her sister but in a less refined way. She, too, is physically fit and looks the cheerleader type. Her face is rounder than Zuki's and her attitude certainly more brash. She pours me a large glass from the big bowl they are preparing, comes over and hands it to me. I can now see she's wearing shorts, too, and a T-shirt. Close up, her eyes are dark brown. Her look seems certainly more calculating than her sister's, and I can't help but think she's trouble.

"Come on, Neil, relax," Alexis says, eyeing me with an amused expression. Equipped with big glasses, we troop back out onto the rear deck. We sit down at the table, Alexis at the head. All eyes are now on me.

I lift the glass. "Thanks for having me," I say, not knowing what else to say. I take a sip. It's delicious. "What's this?" I ask.

"Gin and jam," Sakura says between long drags on her straw.

"Pink gin with tonic water and lots more," Alexis says. "The girls make it up as they go along," he adds. "Our daily lunchtime aperitif never tastes the same from one day to another." He laughs.

I look around, taking in the large rear deck, the seats and guard rails with their matching canvas screens, the canvas sunroof, all made of the same material. Pristine teak decking, the clean white of the superstructure. Judging by the look of everything I see, the furniture here and the fittings in the lounge, I can only guess what the rest of the yacht is like, but the yacht is in excellent condition, and I wonder just how many millions have been poured into this.

Ignoring the babble of conversation surrounding us, Alexis has his eyes on me. He's assessing me with that eagle-eyed look. I raise my glass to him, nodding a thanks. He smiles back at me.

"This is my pride and joy, Neil. This is where I can let my hair down," he says, shaking his loose hair for effect. "Even if my wife does not approve." He winks at me. "*Axiom* is a thirty-five-metre steel-hulled, schooner-rigged home away from home. I'll show you around later but as

278

an accomplished yachtsman, you will appreciate her beauty."

There's no denying that. "So, this is how we travel to Cyprus?"

"Ten days of pure enjoyment, my friend," he says, grinning at me. "It's about time you started enjoying yourself."

As discreetly as possible, I scrutinise the crowd I'm now apparently a part of. Gioti is wearing white cargo shorts and that same polo shirt. I can now read the letters embroidered onto the shirt: Axiom. Right, so he's a crew member. Apart from the shorts and polo shirt, he's wearing the same sunglasses, too. Laki is same type of man but taller. Muscular and the kind of deep suntan that comes from working in the sun for years. Black hair. Same outfit. Another crew member? Marcel, at the lunch meeting, he wore a light blue shirt and chinos. Now he's also in shorts, but the smart kind. Dark blue with a white polo shirt. And the girls, Fiona and what was it? Yes, Lee. Both are in their early twenties, I'd say, like Sakura and Zuki. College or uni friends, perhaps? In any case, they are pretty, but on the attractive side of pretty. A lot paler and, judging by their accents as they chat with Sakura, English. Shorts and T-shirts seem to be the uniform here.

We sit and drink and the afternoon passes in a gathering blur. The conversation is loud, fun-filled and inconsequential, Alexis and Sakura the drivers. They have a repartee going that has everybody in stitches. I'm the newbie here, the outsider, but soon enough laughing like the rest of them. At some point, lunch appears, seemingly from nowhere – salad, grilled meat and fish. I can only assume there must be staff somewhere, as none of the group sitting here has left at any point, except to get up and replenish drinks – and bring the plates and dishes through.

I'm beginning to feel the effect of the alcohol, so have started filling up my glass from the bottles of water that have also appeared. I'm determined to stay as sober as possible. Around me, the party is getting louder except for Zuki, who's doing the same as me, topping up her glass with water. We share a few looks and smiles.

Quite suddenly, there's movement, the big yacht swaying slightly as Vincent appears at the top of the gangway. Behind him, a small but elegantly dressed woman follows, whom I recognise as Isabelle, Alexis's wife. She gives me a smile and a wave as she walks by on the opposite side of the table. She stops next to Alexis, gives him a peck on the cheek and speaks quietly to him before moving on and through the open sliding glass door.

Vincent stands directly opposite me, and I just know he will be glaring at me, so I don't bother looking his way, but switch my attention back to Sakura, who's telling some story about university life in San Francisco. Soon after, Gioti rises, saying it's time to get the ship ready. Marcel rises, too, apologetically raising his mobile phone and saying he has some calls to make before we set off. Alexis lets out a long sigh, seemingly saddened by the sudden interruption of the party.

"Saki," he says, looking at Sakura. "Be so kind will you and show Neil his cabin. I think I might have to have a siesta."

Sakura gets up and beckons me to follow her. Zuki rises, too, and starts clearing the table. As I walk past her, she smiles at me. I wish Alexis had asked Zuki to show me my cabin.

Sakura leads me into the lounge, and I pick up my holdall. She takes me through the lounge and out into a hallway. Ahead lies another large lounge area with wraparound windows. I can see a solid dining table set against the forward windows. Companionways lead below and up on deck. To the left and right, there are cabins with their doors shut. Sakura takes the companionway down and I follow. A central corridor runs the length of the yacht. She turns left and walks some steps before stopping at a cabin door on the port side of the yacht – well, I guess ship is more accurate given the dimensions.

She opens the cabin door, steps in and I follow. The cabin is small, as to be expected, but it's superbly fitted out. Directly ahead, a bed is fitted into the space below a large porthole. Wood panelling on all sides with drawers fitted below the bed and a wardrobe to the side. Two brass reading lamps with cream-coloured shades are fitted above the matching cream headboard.

"There's a shower here," Sakura says, opening a door opposite the wardrobe. I hadn't noticed it at first glance as it looks like part of the wood panelling. Inside, a shower, toilet and washbasin have been crammed in. For a bloke my size, it's tight, but it will do perfectly well. I squeeze back out into the cabin, turning to face Sakura, who stands unnecessarily close to me. The cabin isn't that small, after all. Here we go, I think, but I smile at her.

"Zuki and I are next door," she says in a husky, alcoholic voice as she leans in even closer, looking up at me. "If you need anything, let me know." She grins like a cat finding a saucer of cream. "Sure, I will," I say, making a point of looking away from her. She takes the hint and makes for the cabin door.

"Oh," I say. Sakura turns and looks at me. "Just wondering, do I call you Saki or Sakura?"

Her demeanour changes in an instant. "No one ever calls me Saki except for Uncle Alexis," she hisses.

"Oh, okay." I smile back at her. She gives me a sour look and leaves the cabin shutting the door with a solid thump.

43

I unpack my holdall and stow my few belongings into the drawers and wardrobe. I lie on the bed, trying out the mattress. It's surprisingly soft, specially made to fit snugly into the space available and just about wide enough for two. I get up, lift up the mattress and examine the frame underneath. As I expected, there's a little nook in the woodwork at the foot of the mattress into which I stuff my cash.

After locking the cabin door, I take out my smartphone. Time to send a little report. I activate the app John installed by clicking on the calculator icon, pressing on the secret access button and drawing the pattern on the screen. The app has a simple design, and I go through the options offered to see what lies behind them – apart from the distress call, which I don't touch. It's comprehensive: a secure telephone mode, a texting facility and a GPS tracker. I can even take photos with the app. I decide to send a text message, assuming whoever receives the message will know who it was from.

Aboard Axiom *Yacht. Currently moored in Port Pierre harbour. Alexis confirms we are to sail to Cyprus.*

I tap the send button. The app confirms the sent status and saves my message with a symbol showing it to be an outgoing message. Within seconds a message comes back in.

Message received. Do you have an ETA for arrival in Cyprus and where?

Wow, I'm impressed. I reply, *No, estimate is 10 days travelling time. No idea of point of entry.*

I smile to myself; no one can say I'm not showing willingness to fulfil my side of the deal.

Vibrations in the hull startle me. I realise the engines have been started. We're off and feeling quite excited, I rush up on deck to watch our departure.

I feel the phone vibrate briefly in my back pocket as I walk through the lounge and climb the couple of steps to the rear deck. I'm expecting everybody to be here but they're not. Instead, two crew members in matching outfits of white cargo shorts and light blue T-shirts with *Axiom* embroidered on the back stand at the back guardrail hauling in the mooring lines. Down on the promenade, tourists have assembled watching the process and taking photos. The gangway is still extended, and I can sense movement coming from the gangway.

Vincent appears at the head of the gangway, dressed in black cargo shorts but same T-shirt as the two other members. He gives me a quick glance, but being busy, he forgets to put on his venomous look. Not sure where everybody else is, I suddenly feel very self-conscious.

Vincent walks over to a control box, lifting the lid, and pushes some buttons hidden in the recesses. Electric motors whine and mechanical levers and gears engage with a clanking noise as the handrails of the gangway fold inwards, and the gangway is drawn inwards into a hidden compartment below our feet. Vincent looks at me and points upwards.

"Up on the sun deck," he says.

I nod, walk through the lounge and out into the forward-facing lounge that I'd glimpsed earlier. I pause by the companionway leading up to the sundeck, whip out my smartphone, quickly click on the app and read the final message: *Good luck and take care.*

I'm sure now that Alice is on the other end. I smile and point the smartphone upwards, taking a photo. It's a silly thing to do, but I feel like sending her a parting shot. Up above, Alexis sits in the middle of a wide cushioned seating area, shaped like a half moon and which spans the back end of the large cockpit. The four girls – two each side – are kneeling on the cushions. They're facing out to the stern of the yacht, watching the departure and waving to the tourists standing on the promenade as *Axiom* slowly draws away from its berth. It's a funny sight, Alexis sitting like a fat Buddha, two bikini-clad bums either side of him. Although he hasn't seen me yet, a big grin sits on his face, like a cat that's had the cream.

I climb the few steps up onto the deck. Alexis looks up and his grin grows in size as he sees me and looks left and right, glancing at the girls to his side. I grin back and give him a thumbs-up.

This upper deck is a fly bridge and sitting area in one. Gioti is standing at the wheel to my right, manoeuvring the large vessel away from the promenade and towards the harbour mouth. Between the fly bridge and the seating area is a solid pedestal, which forms the base for eight winches of varying sizes. In the centre of this pedestal stands the solid main mast, as big as a tree, with its large boom. Behind the pedestal, the seating area with a fixed table with extension flaps, lowered to provide space, spans the width of the deck. Beyond that, laid out on the deck, an expanse of fitted mattresses and cushions for

285

sunbathing. A champagne cooler and an assortment of glasses and nibbles stand on the table. In the centre of the seating area, Alexis sits, arms folded across his chest, big grin still fixed on his face, with the girls either side of him laughing, chatting away, and still waving to the crowd on the promenade. This is the life, I think, and such a stark contrast to the existence I have been living over the last months.

I look to the front where Laki and another crewman are stowing away the thick mooring lines and readying the big boat for the open sea. Gioti accelerates, the yacht gliding through the waters towards the harbour entrance.

As I turn back towards Alexis, the girls have resumed their places and are sitting demurely left and right of Alexis, posing like photo models, shades covering their eyes, faces towards me. I can't stop myself from laughing and for the first time in ages, I feel happy.

"Sit down, Neil," Alexis says, "or would you prefer to take the wheel?" He reads my mind. "Gioti, let Neil have a go. He's an accomplished sailor."

Gioti turns to me, a smile on his face. Dark sunglasses cover his eyes. He moves aside, letting me take the big wheel.

"What course?" I ask.

"Two hundred degrees for a while, then we'll bring her on to a bearing of one hundred and eighty degrees until we have passed Île Sainte-Marguerite."

I bring *Axiom* on to a course of two hundred degrees and hold her steady. The island, roughly two kilometres from the coast of Cannes, grows as we draw closer. Zuki appears by my side. She has a man's straw hat on her head, tilted at an angle as it's far too large for her. She holds out a big glass for me.

"What's that?" I ask.

"Water, ice and some lemon," she says, her big brown eyes on me, smiling. She plucks the hat from her head and reaches up on tiptoe to plonk it on mine. "A gift from Alexis; he says you need to wear a hat." I turn to wave a thanks, and he raises his champagne glass to me. She touches my arm softly and turns to head back to the seating area. "When you're done here, come and talk to me, Neil," she says, with a look that increases my heart rate by a hundred. As she walks off, I can't help but admire her bikini-clad figure.

I have fun steering the boat for an hour. Gioti points out the landmarks as we pass Île Sainte-Marguerite, followed by Île Saint-Honorat. I hand over to Gioti and return to the seating area. The girls are lying on their towels on the mats behind the sitting area in the sun. Alexis has spread out on the seats and is snoring gently in the late afternoon sun. I sit down next to Zuki, who rolls onto her side, facing me.

"There you are," she says, pushing up her sunglasses. I can't help but check out her figure. She's slim, well-toned and evenly tanned. I'm grateful for my sunglasses and hope she doesn't notice my ogling. But I'm sure she does. Her smile and her unwavering eyes tell me so.

"Hello again, Zuki, with a zee."

She smiles at me, and my insides go all gooey.

"Tell me about yourself, Neil. Who are you?"

"What can I say? And where do I begin?"

Zuki is watching me, waiting. "Yes, well, I wanted some time off from my life and my job and an adventure on top, and so I came to France and did some touring around the country, working my way. And Alexis was so kind to offer me the opportunity to join you. I'd never say no to a nice sailing cruise in the Med and I've never been to Cyprus, so it seemed like a fantastic idea. Made all the nicer by cruising with such delightful ladies like you." That earns me a suppressed snort from Sakura.

The look Zuki gives me convinces me that she doesn't believe a word but fortunately, she doesn't push it.

"Ah, well, lucky you," she says instead. "And where are you from?"

"I'm from Worthing, on the south coast of England. Near Brighton. No one knows Worthing."

"Oh, we know Worthing," Zuki says.

"You do?" I say, startled.

Sakura sits up. "Yes, Dad worked near Worthing for a while. Alexis has a company near Worthing, in a town called Horseham."

"Horsham," Fiona said, sitting up, too.

"Oh yes, Horsham. Horseham. Sounds almost the same," Sakura replies.

Inside my head, alarm bells are ringing.

"Yeah," Sakura continues, "Fiona and Lee—" who are now both sitting up, looking at Sakura and me "—their dad was – is – the managing director of the company. What's it called?" she asks Fiona.

"Holden Industrial," Fiona says, the expression on her face full of worry.

I find it difficult to breathe. I'm speechless at this sudden revelation.

"Yeah, that's right," Sakura says. She pauses and there's a look on her face that makes me realise she's thinking what she should say. After a moment, she continues. "Well, anyway, some issues there, and Fiona and Lee, well, they're here with us on this holiday."

288

"Right," I say, trying to sound as relaxed as possible. But my heart is thumping away. I glance over to where Alexis is lying stretched out and his eyes are closed. The snoring has stopped, though, and I wonder if he's awake, listening to every word.

"Nothing like a nice cruise on a yacht such as this for a holiday," I say, trying to be as non-committal as possible. Change the topic, I think. "So, your dad, where's he, then?"

"Dad's in Cyprus," Zuki answers. "Not doing too well. In and out of hospital, undergoing tests."

"Oh dear," I say. "Hope nothing serious."

"Well," Zuki carries on, "cancer. He's had some issues lately." She sounds sad.

"Only got himself to blame," Sakura comments with a note of anger in her voice. "All those bloody cigarettes. Chain-smoker. What do you expect?"

Zuki shoots her an angry look. She turns to me. "Michalis, our dad, he's been with Alexis for decades. My earliest memories of Dad are always with a cigarette."

I nearly faint. My mouth is agape, and Zuki looks at me with a puzzled look on her face. I'm glad for my shades so she can't see my eyes. Aware of my mouth wide open, I make as if to sneeze. I shake my head, which serves to fool Zuki, but I, in truth, am overwhelmed by the information I have just been presented with. Not only are Fiona and Lee apparently Willoughby's daughters, but Zuki and Sakura are Michalis's daughters. I look once more at Alexis, who's still lying there, apparently asleep. My nerves are jangling; my blood pressure is dangerously high. Wtf! Alexis has a nerve. For a moment, I wonder if he has planned this, but he can't have. It's an unbelievable coincidence.

Alexis stirs, yawning and stretching as he rises to a sitting position. He looks at us, but then his eyes settle on me. He has a devilish gleam in his eyes, I'm sure. He laughs. "Having fun?" he says to us.

"Sure," Sakura answers, rising from her mat and stepping down to embrace Alexis. "Had a good snooze?" she asks, hugging him. "Time to get ready for dinner," she says to no one in particular.

Fiona and Lee rise, too, following Alexis and Sakura down the companionway to the lower deck. Zuki and I remain, watching their departure before looking at each other.

"There you have it, Neil," she says. I'm not sure what she's implying and I must have a bit of a blank expression on my face, for she adds, "Our current history in a nutshell."

"Yes, I'm a bit shocked to tell you truth."

"No need to be, Neil. It's not your life."

She totally misunderstands me, for which I'm grateful. I wish I could tell her how much it's at least partly my life, too, but I can't.

We sit talking some more and she tells me about her life: how her dad had met her mum, a Japanese-American, in Los Angeles as a young student. And how Sakura and she had grown up in Cyprus until her parents separated and her mum went back to America, eventually settling back in California. And how they'd gone to America with their mother, returning each summer to Cyprus or wherever her dad was working at the time. They'd grown up as American girls, fully immersed in the American way of life and seemingly shedding their Cypriot roots. But the roots were still there, she says, and it had been Alexis, their uncle as they called and thought of him, although they

290

weren't related by blood, who had ensured that they spent as much time with Michalis as possible. It had been Alexis, too, who had taken care of things when as teenagers they needed support and guidance. Zuki tells me that she finished university last year and has spent the time since travelling Europe. I briefly try to visualise her as a backpacker, but that's not her style, she says. Sakura finished university this summer and has come over for a long holiday before deciding what she wants to do.

Listening to Zuki is easy. She makes everything sound vibrant and she's witty. I get the feeling that she's had her ups and downs and that her parents' separation took its toll on both girls. But Zuki strikes me as having come through the emotional aspects a stronger person. She's immensely likeable and finally, when the little bell tolls below, announcing dinner is nearly ready, we reluctantly get up and make our way down to our cabins.

Dinner is served in the upper, forward-facing lounge with its solid fixed dining table and large panorama windows. The forward deck is bathed in light from the spots mounted on the forward mast, giving everything an almost old-fashioned atmosphere of a large turn-of-the-century steam liner. Despite all the décor and paraphernalia, starched tablecloth, heavy crystal wine glasses and silver cutlery, the atmosphere is relaxed. Fiona, Lee and Sakura have cooked, serving up pasta and salad. Wine stands in coolers on the table, but Alexis is again pouring champagne. Never have I seen so much champagne liberally consumed as here.

Dinner is a loud affair. Animated talk from all sides, in Greek, French and English. Alexis switches easily between all three languages, telling elaborate stories. Sakura reminds him repeatedly to speak English for my benefit.

He sits at the head of the table; a large cloth napkin tucked into his shirt. He has a massive appetite, which certainly explains his largely increased girth since I'd last seen him in Horsham. That to me seems like ages ago, but it's only been six months.

An array of empty bottles starts building up. I sit at the end of the table, with Fiona on my left and across from Lee and Zuki next to her. The two young English girls are subdued throughout dinner, and I can only imagine what they're thinking as their dad is right at this moment taking the brunt of the fraud investigation whilst his boss and the mastermind behind the fraud is sitting in the midst of the Med on his thirty-five-metre yacht holding court and having fun.

I switch my attention back to Alexis, who's never stopped talking since dinner began. He has a knack of drawing in all who sit at the table, but he largely leaves me out. I assume it's courtesy. After the main course, desert is brought up, tiramisu in large dishes. Alexis tucks into the tiramisu like a famished refugee.

There's no escaping the ouzo, though. The merrier Alexis becomes, the louder he is; and he suddenly cries out that he wants to hear his record. I wonder what he means and as he becomes more belligerent, Sakura gets up and walks over to the music system. I have to laugh when Erasure comes belting out of the hi-fi system: "Ship of Fools". He sings along loudly and laughs, shouting across the table at me, "*Ship of Fools*, Neil – do you get it?" I don't, but Fiona explains that he plays this track over and over every day on board *Axiom*. I have no idea what he's referring to – unless he deems all of us on board fools.

44

A knock on my cabin door has me jumping up in the hope that Zuki's found another reason to visit me. I open it to find Marcel standing there.

"Please come with me, Neil," he says with his heavy French accent. I follow him, and he takes me through the rear lounge onto the rear deck, where Alexis is sitting under the canvas sunroof, smoking a cigar and sipping cognac.

"Sit down, my friend," Alexis says.

I take the seat opposite him, and Marcel sits down next to Alexis.

"You enjoying yourself, Neil?" Alexis asks, watching me.

"Yes, absolutely," I say, smile in place but nerves tingling.

"Great," he says. "I see you're getting on well with Zuki."

My nerves accelerate to frantic tingling mode. "Yes, she's a wonderful person."

"Good, good," he replies, smiling back at me. But these smiles never reach his eyes, as I've come to notice about him. "Okay, let's talk some business. This new identity. What are you looking for?"

I look from him to Marcel. "It's okay," Alexis says, noticing. "Marcel will prepare things. We will be leaving you and the girls when we get to Cagliari. Some business, and then a flight back to Cyprus. You will be lucky enough to spend some more time in the company of the ladies. But—" he puts up a finger in mock warning "—I am leaving Vincent to keep a watchful eye on you, my friend," he says, winking at me.

I smile, trying to convey that butter won't melt in my mouth unless Zuki puts it there. Alexis raises his eyebrows. Oh yes, the unanswered question.

"Well, a passport under a different name," I say.

"A passport will get you in and out of a country, but that's about it. If you want to work and live somewhere, you need an identity, not just a passport. What are your plans?"

I look at him, trying to arrange my thoughts and how to play my cards. "I have no plans at the moment," I say. This is where I need to tread carefully.

"You want to go back home? To England."

"No," I say. "Not really. Too close to the fire."

He nods his understanding. "There's plenty you can do, my friend. Think about it. You have time now unless you spend that time exclusively with Zuki," he says, laughing.

I return to my cabin. My mind is in turmoil. I pick up the phone, thinking of sending a report to Alice, but I decide against it and put the phone back down.

45

Alexis, Isabelle and Marcel leave us in Cagliari and we set off the next day. Instantly, the mood on board changes. So far, all we've done is motor. Gioti sets the course, steering the boat out of the harbour and into the open sea.

"Right," he says after an hour. "Neil, the time has come. Let's get sailing."

I watch as the crew prepare everything for setting the sails. On a boat this size that's a major task. Gioti steers the yacht into the wind and the big electric winches whine as they start to take the strain of the heavy sheets. Slowly, the main sails are raised, filling with air as Gioti steers back onto the course. There's a noticeable shift as the big vessel begins to lean over and the crew trim the large sails. Next, the jibs are unfurled and the yacht's speed increases noticeably. Gioti stands on the fly bridge, directing the crew, occasionally issuing commands until *Axiom*'s sails stand perfectly. He calls me over and tells me to take the helm. It's exhilarating to steer such a large boat and despite its size, *Axiom* is sensitive to even the slightest adjustment of the wheel.

"Imagine owning a ship like this and not liking sailing!" Gioti yells into my ear.

"Unbelievable!" I yell back at him. This is it, I think, as the wind and the creaking of masts and boom mingle into one like music in my ears.

I quickly look back to where Zuki and the girls are sitting, wind in their hair and sunglasses on. Zuki smiles and waves. This is perfect, I think to myself, the previous night still fresh in my mind and the evening I spent with her. We stole away and walked around Cagliari until we found a Japanese restaurant. Zuki pulled me inside and spoke in Japanese to the owner, who came up to us with his large, laminated menus for tourists. He threw them aside and disappeared into the kitchen, returning with dishes he'd prepared solely for us. Zuki translated the various names and meanings to me, and explained so much about the customs whilst placing morsels from the dishes in my mouth with her *hashi*, which I learnt is Japanese for chopsticks. It was the most sensuous experience I've ever had. We walked back to the marina side by side, constantly brushing up against each other and fingers touching. We kissed goodnight and retired to our cabins. I lay in my bed, my heart beating fast, the sweet agony of longing keeping me awake.

As the afternoon wears on and the wind increases, I go up to the wheelhouse to see what the weather forecast has in store for us. Gioti is still relaxed, but the forecast is getting dramatic, and he states that we will have to bring in the sails soon and return to motoring.

"It's getting uncomfortable," he says, "and even under motor it will be rough."

We're bang in the middle of the Med and if there's a storm, we'll have to ride it out, I think to myself. Light is slowly beginning to fade, and my only concern is that if he's intending to bring in the sails, then better now than in darkness. It takes him another hour to make up his mind, and a series of strong gusts finally has him summoning the crew to bring in the sails. I watch as the crew don their life jackets.

I stand next to Gioti in the swaying wheelhouse, watching them go into action. Although I have faith in the strength of the ship's build to ride out a storm, I still feel uneasy as I stand watching the gusts and the whipped-up sea rock the ship. *Axiom* is rolling and swaying, and the crew are struggling to bring the sails down, their movements cumbersome on the rolling deck. I watch Vincent struggling with the big jib. Gioti turns to me with a pleading look. Being a guest, he could never ask, but I understand the meaning.

"Where's a life jacket?" I ask him.

"Over there in the cupboard." He points over my shoulder.

I grab one, put it on and rush out down to the foredeck, where Vincent is trying to furl the jib in. He has the thick jib sheet, which furls the jib on the drum on the winch, but he's not making any progress. I stagger up to the bowsprit, the ship rolling and lurching, where the drum for the jib is secured. Leaning forward, I can see that the sheet has caught up in the drum.

I stumble back to Vincent and yell into his ear that the sheet is caught. He goes forward to see for himself and I take his place on the winch. He tries to loosen the sheet in the drum by pulling and jerking but to no avail. Shifting position and trying to steady himself on the pitching deck, he yanks with all his strength on the rope but with no effect. A tremendous gust hits the boat and sends him flying to the side. He gets up painfully, and I see his foot catching in the slack control lines as another gust blows into the jib, filling it like a balloon. The lines tighten, whipping him off his feet. He's yanked to the side, seemingly hanging in the air for a moment, before toppling over the side guard rail.

I stand frozen in horror for what seems like ages before sprinting forward across the deck to where he's fallen overboard. As I get to the spot and lean over, I see him hanging upside down, his foot fortunately still tangled up in the sheets. He'd be in the sea if it hadn't been for that. I manage to grab hold of the lines and his foot. I need to secure him, and fast. I look around, desperate to find something that will help me secure him, and see a solid boat hook clipped to the guard rail a few feet away. I manage to reach it without letting Vincent go and leaning over the guard rail, manage to slip the hook into the belt of his life jacket. I pull with all my strength, yelling at him to grab the foot rail. He hears me and in a desperate sideways jerk manages to get a hold on the foot rail. I lean out further, praying that no more gusts will hit us side-on, boat hook in one arm, and manage to grab the strap of his life jacket. I desperately hold onto him, trying to pull him up by letting myself fall backwards, the roll of the boat nearly throwing me overboard. I feel the hull vibrating as the big engines kick in. The big boat swings into the wind, the rolling now replaced with pitching as *Axiom* rides out of the tossing sea head-on.

"Good man, Gioti," I say out loud into the roaring wind. As *Axiom* rises on a rolling wave, I manage to use the momentum to haul Vincent up onto the deck. As he comes over the top, arms reach past me from behind, grabbing him and we all crash backwards into a pile of arms, legs and bodies on the deck. Somebody's elbow rams into my face and in an explosion of pain, I feel blood rushing over my face and eyes. Blinded for the moment, I lie on the heaving deck, holding onto Vincent as he lies on top of me. The only sensation I register is the movement of the big boat as it rises and falls with each angry wave, and then a curious thought takes hold. I now know that through this selfless act, I have fully won Alexis over. He no longer owes me a favour; he now owes me everything, for I have saved Vincent's life.

Stunned and blinded by my blood, I lie choking on the deck, paralysed, until hands and arms lift me up and a cold, wet flannel or towel is pushed onto my face. The howling wind is deafening and the boat's movements so severe that I am unable to stand by myself. Strong arms support me as I'm led inside and placed on the floor. Zuki's voice comes through the mist in my brain as she directs whoever is standing around me to put a cushion under my head and to bring more wet towels to suppress the blood streaming from my nose. She fusses over me, concern in her voice, wiping my face and slowly, vision returns to my eyes as the blood is washed from my face.

"It's all right, Neil," she says, her voice soothing as she wipes away.

My sight restored, I see that she's kneeling beside me with Sakura on the other side of me, wringing out a towel in a bucket. Fiona bends down and hands Sakura something. Sakura tears off some plastic wrapping and hands what looks like cotton wool sticks to Zuki. She wipes my face and nose, pain flashing through me like an electric current, and slowly inserts the cotton wool sticks into my nose.

"Okay," she says, "that's just a temporary measure. We need to get you upright. Sakura, get behind him and support his back. Fiona, get a bowl from the galley." Both do as instructed. "Neil, I need you to lean over the bowl when Fiona brings it and then I will remove the tampons."

"Tampons?" I mumble.

"Yes," she says, laughing.

With the bowl in front of me and my head leaning over it, Zuki eases the tampons out of my nose. Blood gushes out and Sakura puts a wet, cold towel on my neck.

"Right," Zuki says, "now we wait a bit for the bleeding to stop. And then we need to fix your nose with tape. It's broken, Neil."

"Oh fuck," I mumble.

A figure appears and squats in front of me. I raise my eyes. Vincent.

"Malaka," he says. "You saved my life." He reaches for my arms and holds me. "I don't know what to say apart from thank you." He pats my shoulder. "Rest, buddy." He rises and stands for a few seconds, looking down at me. All I can see are his feet, but I hear him breathe in hard. "Take care of him, please." His tone of voice is heavy with emotion. "Now I kill that fool Gioti," he says, anger in his voice, and strides across to the companionway and up to the wheelhouse.

Zuki and Sakura help me to my cabin. Zuki commands me to lie down, which I gratefully do. She shoves cushions under my head to raise it up. She gets some tape from a first-aid kit that Sakura places on the bed beside my head. She carefully puts some gauze over my nose and, despite my attempts to push her hand away, tapes it into position, ignoring my protests. It hurts like hell. She sticks some more tape lengthwise across onto my cheeks to securely position my nose. I look up at her through one eye, the other now swelling shut, as she busies herself. She notices me looking at her and smiles.

"You ogling me again, Neil?"

"Nothing else here to ogle," I reply.

She smiles that wonderful smile, bends over and kisses me gently.

The storm continues through the night and I drift in and out of sleep despite the pain and the rocking sensation of the boat. Zuki sits beside me, alternately holding my hand and replacing the cold flannel on my forehead and the ice pack on my nose.

"We need to keep cooling it," she says, soothing me as I flinch once more, the pain shooting up into my head. Hours later, Gioti comes in and sits on the edge of the bed.

"How are you?" he asks, his voice tired.

"Dunno," I say. "Hurts like fuck, but glad all went well and we didn't lose Vincent."

"Yes, thanks to you, Neil. You saved his life and mine incidentally. Mind you, not sure if Vincent might still throw me overboard once the storm blows over. These medicane storms appear from nowhere," he says, trying to smile.

Not knowing what to say to that, I ask, "Did you get the jib sorted?"

"Yes, all secured, and we can sort out the drum when the storm's passed."

He leaves shortly after. Zuki gives me more painkillers and I drift off to sleep. Later in the night I awake to find Zuki curled up next to me, her head on my shoulder. She's fast asleep and I hold her in my arm, trying to breathe in her scent through my blocked and swollen nose. I suddenly feel a warmth spreading within me, a passionate and deep sensation. I hold her as tight as I dare, not wanting to wake her. I'm so grateful for her to be here, by my side. For the first time in my life, I know I am infinitely and desperately in love.

Zuki stirs, looks up and studies my face for signs of pain or discomfort. "Are you okay, Neil?" she asks, worry spreading across her face. When she sees my grin, she laughs.

"Feeling better, are we?" she says, smiling. I nod.

She kisses me. Carefully at first but then more passionately. I hold her tight, a moan of something else than pain escaping from deep inside me. She pulls away, studies my face again and slides her hand under the bedcover.

"Oh, my word, you still have blood inside you," she says, laughing as she discovers what is troubling me. "Naughty boy," she breathes into my ear as she pushes the bedcover aside, pulls my boxers out of the way and climbs on top of me.

46

"Roughly four hundred nautical miles," Gioti says. "Four days."

I sigh. Four days. It's more than I can be bothered with, but it also means four more days with Zuki. The days are blissful and I feel a lot better with every passing day.

We relax in the sun, spend lazy days sunbathing, sleeping, playing board and card games, drinking and eating as the minutes and hours tick away. Zuki spends every night with me, and we uninhibitedly make love all night. Nobody says a word, but nonetheless, it feels strange to me. I'm sure there's talk behind our backs, and I wonder whether I have crossed a line. But my status has been elevated; everyone – even Vincent – treats me like royalty. And my feelings for Zuki are genuine, and hers for me, too. I'm sure of that.

Arriving in Limassol, Vincent packs the gear into the car once *Axiom* is berthed and we say goodbye to Gioti and the crew. We all pile into a large seven-seater Land Cruiser and drive out of the marina gates. Vincent takes the car through town, and I sit looking out of the window as the city flashes by. To me it's a strange mix of modern and old. The flashy new developments close to the marina segue into grey concrete developments from the seventies. Occasionally, I catch a glimpse of some historic building, painstakingly preserved. He takes a major road out of town and within minutes, the scenery changes. The countryside becomes hilly, sun-bleached fields with bushes and scatterings of trees. I gaze out of the car, noting stones like oversized golf balls scattered in their thousands on the dusty ground. The car climbs further up into the mountains, the winding road cutting through forests of pine and cedars until we reach a turning. Vincent swings the car into a narrow, forested road and after about half a mile, he slows, pulling up to metal gates. He retrieves a remote control from the central armrest, presses a button and we wait as the gates open. He drives the big car onto a gravelled area, the tyres crunching on the gravel, before coming to a stop in front of worn stone steps leading up to large, time-old wooden doors. The house belonging to the doors is as old as history, made of rough grey- and sand-coloured stones from the surrounding hills.

As we get out of the car, the doors swing open and Alexis appears at the top of the steps with Isabelle behind him.

"Welcome back to Camiro!" his voice booms out, arms outstretched as he comes down the steps, followed by Isabelle. He embraces the girls, hugging them, and then stands before me. He smiles at me and studies my swollen, bruised face before wrapping me into a bear hug. "Neil, welcome. Welcome to my home. We are so thankful to you. Zuki—" he turns to her "—you took good care of this young man." He points at my nose. "Vincent," he calls out, who turns, pausing from unpacking the car, "you fool." He laughs, and Vincent just waves him away, returning to his duties. "Come inside," he commands, and we follow him up the steps into the house.

I stop as I enter, trying not to gape like a kid. Whereas the mansion in Horsham had been a cold, barren building made of silver concrete and glass walls, Camiro has been built entirely of roughly hewn stone of light grey, brown and yellow. The main house seems centuries old but has been fully modernised and converted. The rear end of the house is one wall of French windows standing open, letting in a cool and fresh breeze. Through these, I catch a glimpse of a courtyard swimming pool shaped like a cross. I walk across the central hall and through the open doors into the inner courtyard. Never have I seen anything quite like this. The courtyard pool is flanked by patios made of old flagstones on either side. Tiled roofs supported by wooden pillars and beams provide shadow for the patios. The pool is easily the size of a tennis court, though longer and narrower. Smaller buildings, which I assume must have formerly been outhouses, have been integrated, their old stonework merging into one large house with quaint nooks and latticed windows. A large patio lies beyond the rear of the courtyard pool, spanning the whole width of the property. Steps lead down to a manicured lawn with well-maintained shrubs and flowerbeds, providing a fantastic view of the hills rising up in the distance behind the house. There's a smell of pine in the air.

Everyone has drifted into the open-plan kitchen and as I join them, I hear the pop of corks flying from champagne bottles. "Let's have a drink on your safe return," he says, his booming voice reverberating through the open space. As Alexis pours the champagne into the glasses, Zuki comes to stand by my side. She takes my hand in what I assume is a little demonstration of our new status. This doesn't go unnoticed to Alexis, who beams a large smile at us as he hands us our glasses. He winks at us before turning to fill more glasses. I look down at Zuki, who smiles back at me.

Alexis calls me over and leads me into his study. He closes the door, walks to his large desk and slides open a drawer. "Sit down, Neil," he says in a business tone of voice and hands me a thick brown envelope. Not sure what this is all about, I take out the contents, almost dropping a crisp new passport.

"Your new identity," he says, sitting down behind his desk.

I pick it up, flicking through the pages, amazed that he has it all ready. I stop as I read the name: Jordan Epica.

"Jordan Epica?" I exclaim. "Who the fuck is Jordan Epica?" I ask, amused and bewildered at the same time.

Alexis laughs. "Jordan Epica is you. Your new identity. I told you, you don't just want a passport, Neil, you want a new identity. Jordan has a history. He has a life story to tell. He has roots in Cyprus. He was born here. He has a family. He has an education, a university degree. He has work experience. He also has a medical history; he has insurance. He has everything you need to be able to apply for a job, to work, to rent a house, to buy a house even. He has bank accounts, a driving licence, everything."

I look at him dumbfounded. Of course he's right. Having just a passport is nothing.

"Yes, okay, I understand," I say. "But… Well… Jordan Epica? Seriously, was there no other name going?"

"What's in a name, Neil? Jordan Epica sounds as good to my ears as Neil Wilson does. And besides, it's a real name too. That's the thing about an identity, Neil; it has a history, a present and, for you, a future. You can go anywhere now and build on that history." He pauses. "So, Neil, now that you have your new identity, you can think

306

about what you want to do. Have you thought about that?"

Once more, I sit in front of Alexis, my mind a blank. I still haven't thought about it. I've been enjoying myself too much. And I really don't have a clue. If it weren't for the secret mission that has been forced upon me, I'd be happy to just spend my time with Zuki.

47

Any progress?

A simple message, but it leaves me in turmoil. Zuki lies asleep but I'm restless and get up to fetch a glass of water. I know I should be doing *something*. Either honour the mission bestowed upon me or move on. Neither option is attractive to me. Alexis is happy for us to be here. In fact, he doesn't want us to leave. He enjoys us being here. Fiona and Lee have returned to England, but Zuki and Sakura have still got plenty of time and seem hesitant to make any real plans, mainly because of their dad's medical condition. Michalis: he's in a bad state, now indefinitely confined to hospital and in terminal decline. I haven't gone along to see him, finding excuses not to go. It's not that we became friends.

And I'm now in a relationship with his daughter. All I know is I want to stay here with Zuki, to support her and to be with her. But I also know I will have to make a decision soon. I'm convinced I could approach Alexis and ask him for a job. After saving Vincent from drowning in the Med, Alexis considers me part of the family. Once more, I have spent the days dithering, pushing the decision as far back as possible. Until now. The message reminds me that I need to act.

After breakfast, the girls leave to visit their dad, taking Isabelle with them. Vincent drives them. It's Alexis and me. He sits out by the pool, drinking coffee and reading the paper.

"Mind if I join you," I ask.

"Of course, Neil. Sit."

We sip our coffees for a moment. He's looking at me, an expression of worry spreading across his face.

"What's troubling you?" he asks.

"I was approached," I say, feeling guilty.

He looks nonplussed. "What? By whom?"

"By investigators looking into the H.I. fraud," I say, not wanting to hold anything back now.

He sits upright, scrutinising me. "And?"

"And they want me to spy on you."

"They sent you?"

"They put the thumbscrews on me and forced me to agree to their stupid scheme. I should try to get close to you. Ingratiate myself."

He slumps back into his chair, realisation hitting him. "They succeeded," he says, disappointment with a note of sadness in his voice.

"I haven't sent them anything, Alexis. It's their plan not mine. What I want is something totally different."

"Like what?" he asks, but his tone is one of distrust now.

Like a big bubble of air, it comes bursting to the surface: "I want to rob a bank."

Alexis bursts out laughing. "You what?" he says after he's stopped chuckling, wiping tears from his eyes.

"I'm serious," I say, laughing myself. "But not as in walking into a bank and robbing it at gunpoint."

"I'm glad to hear it. Your new identity will have been a waste," he says, smiling. "Good God, Neil. First, you confess to being a spy, and then you say you want to rob a bank. That's quite a rollercoaster ride in the space of a couple of seconds."

"A digital hit-and-run," I say, smiling back at him.

He has a quizzical look on his face. "Go on," he says.

"In my humble opinion, the thing with H.I. was that it was too destructive and too elaborate." I pause, watching him. The expression on his face is changing once more. This is now a very slippery slope.

"What do you mean?" he says after a moment.

"Well, I'm certainly no expert in these things, but you built up H.I. over years—"

"It was a genuine business," he interjects, and I can see the colour rising in his face. "You're doing well here, Neil," he growls.

I keep going, determined to get my message across. "Yes, but in the end, what happened?" I'm not expecting him to answer, so I carry on. "You built up a real company. You invested time, energy and money. But at some point, it became clear that the business was beginning to struggle. You could have sold it, you could have closed it down, whatever. But you didn't. You decided to develop a different plan." I stop, looking to gauge his reaction. His expression is devoid of any emotion but the colour is still in his neck. "That plan you put into action killed the company and your reputation, and it made the headlines. It was elaborate, it involved far too many people – it could have gone terribly wrong."

"I had my reasons, Neil. Believe me." His voice is hard.

"Really?" I can't hide the sarcastic undertone.

"Yes!" he bellows. "Apart from all you're saying, Neil, and you're right, I had a score to settle with that arrogant and patronising British establishment."

This halts me in my tracks. I look at him, not understanding.

"You have no idea," he says. "But I don't want to talk about it."

"But what about the collateral damage?" I ask him. "And people like Willoughby, who is now in the dock – for you? Alexis, they'll get you in the end."

His fiery look recedes. He leans back in his chair and lets out a long breath. "Willoughby is taken care of."

"And Fiona and Lee?"

He looks up at me. "They are, too." But it's said with not quite so much conviction.

I decide to leave it there. "There are different ways one can do what you did. What if one got into the inside of a bank's IT system and just twiddled a few settings?"

"What are you going on about, Neil?" There's a look of exasperation on his face.

"Okay, let's say one had the means to get into a bank's IT system; for example, a bank like Hamlays with an asset finance division and altered some settings?" His expression is now puzzled.

"A bank like Hamlays finances machines and vehicles and other stuff. A customer will typically finance his investment in assets by signing a finance contract. Hamlays pays the invoices on behalf of its customers as they want title to the equipment. It's their collateral, their security. Now Hamlays does this on a big scale. Hundreds of millions per annum. All these assets are processed through the IT systems. They are batched and paid out daily. Roughly speaking, Hamlays paid out thirty to fifty million per day. Every day. More so at the end of the financial year when customers rush to get their equipment and finance contracts sorted. The suppliers send their invoices to the bank. The bank enters the invoice details into the IT system. Name and address of the supplier,

311

bank details, asset type, etc. Just imagine one could get into the IT systems and modify the bank details. Just for one day." I sit back and watch him as it sinks in.

He's still frowning, but I can almost hear the gears engaging and the cogs turning in his head. Eventually, a smile appears on his face.

"But as you say, one would need to get into the IT system. How would you do that?"

"Oh, I know just the guy."

"You do?"

"Yes," I say with as much conviction as I can muster.

Alexis is deep in thought, stroking his beard. After a while, he looks up at me. "This is all hypothetical, isn't it? It's a sweet-sounding idea. Good luck with it. Now, how about another coffee?"

48

I lift the heavy shopping bags out of the car. As I turn, I see Alexis standing at the top of the old stairs in the doorway. He pecks Zuki on the cheek as she walks past him. He beckons for me to come with him, and I follow him into his study.

"Sit, Neil. I have something to discuss with you."

Oh shit, I think, feeling nervous. Perhaps I'd gone too far. Had I now outstayed my welcome?

"Neil, I have a proposition for you," he says. "I've spent time thinking about what you said."

He looks at me, his face hard. My heart crashes to the ground.

"Let's play their game," he says, a grin taking shape. He laughs at the look of relief on my face. "You will work for me. I will give you a position in the family company. You can spy on me and send them stuff. We'll have fun deciding what to send them."

I smile at him. Perfect, I think.

"But, Neil, you will have another role too. With Michalis being in the state he is, and we all know his strength and health are diminishing fast, you will also have a real job to do."

I nod. "Of course," I say.

"And you will have special projects."

I look up, surprised. "Special projects? Okay, that would be very exciting."

He laughs. "Excellent," he says, satisfied. "And talking of special projects, that particular project you mentioned, how would it work?"

How would it work? I have no bloody idea. I've never done anything like it or even contemplated such a scheme.

"How would it work?" I echo his question. "First of all, we would need to identify banks or asset financing companies that use a certain back-end system. And to be frank, we would need my friend to support *us*." I put emphasis on the "us". "This particular back-end system is commonly used throughout the industry, so I have no doubt that we can identify a number of banks who use it. And then we would have to narrow it down to one that fits the bill."

"Fits the bill in what way?"

"Oh, large enough, with the kind of business volume that is worth it. But not too big, as the bigger the bank the heavier the procedural controls."

"Okay, and then?"

"There's a particular blind spot in the system. We need to plant a wee little seed just there."

49

"And how does one get that little seed just there?" Alexis asks.

Gilbert leans forward, placing his elbows on the table. We're sitting in Alexis's office on the top floor of his office building in Limassol. Alexis has assured us the room is soundproof and that an electronic jammer suppresses all signals. He insisted on us handing in our smartphones at the front office, where Vincent put them in an insulated metal box.

Alexis sits at his desk, and both Gilbert and I are seated in front of him. Behind him, large floor-to-ceiling windows provide us with a grandstand view of the marina below. This office is in stark contrast to the messy den in Horsham. It's tidy and almost barren. I get the impression he doesn't use it much.

"Well, step one: get the seed into the system," Gilbert explains. "This can be done via email, for instance. However, you must have someone who will open the email – specifically the attachment, ideally a PDF document or something like that. The seed is then in the system. It is designed to lay dormant until activated. Step two: when triggered, it will worm its way through the system until it reaches the blind spot. Step three: there, it emulates a security patch und fills the gap. It remains dormant until, in step four, it's activated again and then it performs a script, overwriting the existing data with our data. When the batches are processed for payment, the system will read the files and transfer the data from the back-end system via the interface into the banking software. But the details will have been overwritten. The payment is automated as all the checks will have been performed in the back-end system. The payment system doesn't perform a check on the account numbers and stuff, so the payment is affected based on the data it receives."

Alexis leans back in his big leather seat, a puzzled look on his face. He looks from Gilbert to me and back. "That last bit, I didn't understand a word."

Gilbert turns to me, looking helpless.

"Explain it like you did to me. With the eggs."

Gilbert gives me a puzzled look. I can sense the cogs in his mind turning as he digs into his memory and retrieves the data. He smiles. "Right, the eggs." He nods and turns back to Alexis.

"Okay, imagine it like this: every transaction entered into the back-end system generates a payment. This bit of data, bits and bytes, zeros and ones, is one egg." Gilbert reaches for a piece of paper and a pencil and draws an oval-shaped circle: his egg. "It includes all data that the system needs, like payment recipient, invoice number, amount, and so forth. The more transactions there are, the more eggs are generated." He draws a lot more eggs. "Now, contrary to the popular saying never to put all your eggs in one basket, in IT, we do exactly that. We put all the eggs in one basket for processing." He draws some more eggs and something that's meant to be a basket but looks like a bucket. Alexis is smiling now, watching Gilbert.

"That's called batch processing. Okay, once we have put all the eggs in the basket, we proceed to the checkout, like in a supermarket." He tries to draw a supermarket checkout but gives up. Alexis is grinning, enjoying the effort Gilbert is making. "The checkout is the interface to the next system – in most cases, the accounting system – and then comes the interface with the banking software. At the checkout, you'd expect to have a cashier sitting and waiting—" Alexis interrupts him.

"A checkout *chick*," he says, proud of his little wordplay. We laugh politely.

"Okay, the checkout," Gilbert reverts to his narrative, "manned by your chick. Well, except here, there isn't one."

Alexis looks up, suitably surprised. "Why?"

That's what Gilbert has been waiting for. He smiles. "Quite simply because the software engineers didn't bother to install a checkout chick at this point because they anticipated that the details of the transactions are all checked when the data is entered, which is true. There is a four-eyes principle in place. One member of staff enters the data and another checks it and authorises the processing. So, at this point, the software programmers didn't foresee the need for any more checks and controls. The programmers designed the software just so that the cart with the baskets of eggs gets pushed through. No stop and no more checks. And on top, the programming is shoddy. There are bugs in the software. And that's where we plant our little seed."

Alexis nods. "Okay, but what does the seed do?"

"The seed takes the lid off the eggs," Gilbert replies, allowing himself a quick laugh. "No, seriously, the seed is a little program disguised as a security patch. You can imagine it as a little worm that unobtrusively makes its way through the IT network and attaches itself exactly at that spot. If you like, it emulates the checkout chick. It sits there, waiting for the command to execute its orders. And the orders are to take the lids off the eggs that pass through, extract the yolk there and put in our yolk. Once done, the eggs are passed through with that new configuration and voilà, as the French say."

Alexis nods. "Okay, that's the seed. And then you send another seed to trigger the one that's there."

"I wouldn't call the second one a seed. It's a trigger. I prefer to call it a beetle – my killer beetle. Or assassin bug, whatever. The seed is planted and waits to be triggered. The trigger doesn't do anything else apart from activate the seed to open up, and perform the instructions contained within."

"Right," Alexis replies. "And it all depends on someone getting an email and printing off a PDF."

"The printing off is how we get past the security software. Printers are vulnerable but not stringently monitored. Seed and trigger are split into two to avoid detection. They are sent on their way through the printer," he explains. "As long as they are embedded in the network," he adds.

"And what if the person that receives the email doesn't open the PDF? Surely there are procedures in place for that kind of thing?"

"All banks have procedures," Gilbert concedes, "but most employees will occasionally ignore these. How many employees send stuff from their private email accounts to their work email to print something or even look at something, like holiday photos?"

"I'd kill anybody who does that here..." Alexis says. But after a moment's thought, he adds, "But yes, can't be ruled out."

"Alternatively, one could plant the seed somewhere else, but it must get into the system some way. Unless one places it there directly via a terminal or interface, that means access to a terminal or computer on the premises, which is tricky. Like a castle, most systems are protected against direct entry from the outside. You have a moat and high and thick walls on the outside, but once you're in, there's not much to stop you. But you need to find a way in. Email is best unless you can physically get into the network. Once inside, security is a lot slacker and can be overcome." Gilbert thinks for a moment, then carries on. "The ideal entry point is a device like a multifunctional printer or copier that is embedded in the IT network infrastructure. Most personal computers have screening software installed. It is possible to make any attachment appear clean to screening software, and then activate it when it's sent to a printer or multifunctional device. But it would have to be a multifunctional printer where the document is parked and then opened to be printed. Most banks have these types of printers these days."

"Okay, and how would you select the appropriate bank?" Alexis asks.

Gilbert ploughs on. "First, we would need to identify banks or financial companies – not all asset finance companies are necessarily banks – that use this particular system, which is called Galileo. The system is the industry standard and has been for many years. It's become an expensive system to maintain over the years, and we would need to look out for medium-sized finance companies and banks that use the system and have not invested in the latest upgrades. Why medium sized? Because the big banks will undoubtedly have the latest upgrades. I would expect the software developers to have closed that gap in the system in the latest versions by now. But upgrades are very expensive, and many companies are still using versions that are not fully upgraded."

"And how would you find out which banks these are?" Alexis asks, stroking his beard once more.

"As I said, the system is the industry standard and used throughout Europe. I would start researching the Finance Association members. They are listed in the annual reports or even on the websites. And then break it down."

Alexis nods. "How long would that take?"

"Depends – days, weeks at the maximum, I would think," Gilbert replies.

"Got any plans for the next few weeks?" Alexis asks with a smile on his face.

50

We spend the next weeks researching, mostly in Alexis's offices in the marina. It feels like having a regular job. Alexis doesn't trust Gilbert; that much is obvious. But he's put him up in Camiro, in one of the many spare guest rooms. All the better to keep an eye on him, of course, but Gilbert doesn't realise that. We get up early, grab a coffee in the kitchen and set off into Limassol.

Alexis has arranged a small hire car for us so that we can come and go as we like. Gilbert likes it in town; he says Limassol reminds him of Cannes even if Limassol lacks the glamour. But it's a vibrant place, and here he can breathe freely. And he has a proper task, albeit a criminal one. Gilbert has made the most startling transition. He's positively come to life. The Gilbert I had got to know in Cannes was a quiet, reserved man with an aura of defeat, except for when he laughed. But now, and here, he's beaming, full of life and laughing all the time. That has as much to do with his new role as it has with Sakura.

Zuki and Sakura come into town most days and meet us for lunch. Sakura and Gilbert get on like a house on fire. They have the same reckless sense of fun and are constantly laughing. Zuki and I, we laugh with them and at them; they are a good comedy act, but it also leaves us to spend time together. The girls will easily take up two hours of our time at lunch and when we return to the office to resume our work, we often have to physically force ourselves to concentrate. In these moments, the surreality of it all hits me. Gilbert and I are sitting here in an office in Limassol, doing our research in order to plan and execute a major crime.

What are we looking for? The perfect fit. The ideal target.

We start with the major associations. The European Finance and Leasing Association, and the National Associations of England, France, Italy, and Germany. We read the associations' annual reports and go through their member lists. We check these individually, doing additional research on the web and looking for articles in industry magazines and newsletters. We start building profiles on banks and financing companies that catch our attention. We discard the big global banks and multinational financing companies which are too big. What we need is a bank or financing company that uses the Galileo software.

Whilst doing my research, I come across several articles on Hamlays. It's to be expected, but nonetheless it hits home and makes me uneasy. I've avoided reading anything to do with Hamlays and apart from that one article I'd stumbled across whilst on the train to Montpellier, I have steered well clear of the coverage about the Hamlays fraud.

As my mind lingers on the subject, the name Willem de Vries pops into my head. I enter his name into the search bar. There are many entries, mainly connected to the Hamlays fraud and his subsequent disappearance. There's mention of him having been potentially involved in many other schemes whilst at Hamlays, and one article puts forward the idea that major shareholders had protected de Vries. There's rot everywhere, apparently.

Scrolling through the articles and pictures of Willem de Vries, I spot a photo taken at a dinner party at one of the many associations' yearly functions. Willem de Vries, tall and elegant standing in the middle of several managers and CEO. Reading the caption beneath, and the names of the VIPs gathered for the photoshoot, I see a name that triggers a memory: Günther Borrell, Chief Executive Officer of *Bankhaus August Canarus AG*.

I remember a request from this German bank concerning financing of H.I. drilling equipment in Germany under the cover of a guarantee from H.I. head office in Horsham. They had asked us to provide an opinion on H.I.'s credit status, seeing that we were the major financing partner of H.I. in the UK. Such requests are not unusual, and the request had been passed on to me as the key account manager for the H.I. account. They politely asked our assessment of the equipment in terms of collateral value, remarketing experience, and so forth. I remember that I wrote an email saying that H.I. were top-notch and the equipment was great. Little did I know at the time. I also remember that somebody from the bank called me after I'd sent the email and asked a few questions. I can't remember his name, but the bank's name was *Bankhaus August Canarus AG*.

I look them up on the internet and spend the next hour collecting data: Canarus is an old family-owned, medium-sized bank. They originated in Belgium in the eighteenth century and spent their first decade financing Belgian coal exports and later steelworks. They expanded into Germany, setting up their German offices in Düsseldorf close to the growing coal extraction and steelworks industry of the Ruhr area. They grew rich financing these activities until the First World War. In the aftermath, their

323

fortunes dwindled until the rise of the German industrial output in the run-up to the Second World War. After the defeat of Germany, Canarus suffered serious setbacks, resulting in the sale of the bank to the Borrell family. When the German *Wirtschaftswunder*, the rapid economic growth period in the fifties, set in, they capitalised on this and soon their German business was bigger and stronger than the business in Belgium. According to their website, they closed the Belgium arm in the early seventies. Since then, they have focused exclusively on Germany whilst branching out to develop an asset finance and leasing business. The details they provide lets me draw the conclusion that they are a carbon copy of Hamlays but smaller.

I'm getting excited by the information and their presentation of the bank's activities on their website. My gut feeling tells me this is heading in the right direction. I continue reading.

One article, about ten years old, focuses on Canarus's implementation of their brand-new IT system and, most importantly, their assessment of suitable IT solutions for handling and processing finance contracts. It's written as a kind of best practice case study and their decision-making process in selecting the best software. The conclusion, which has me sitting upright, is their decision to purchase and implement the Galileo software solution. Bingo!

I call over to Gilbert, who's engrossed in his research but yawning expansively from too much wine at lunchtime. I show him what I have found.

"Look here, Gilbert," I say, pointing to the monitor.

"What am I not seeing?" he asks after a moment.

"Here," I say. "Look, in this interim statement – it's the most recent one – they write that they have experienced a downturn in business volume and margins, especially in their asset finance and leasing business. They have written off assets due to the collapse of Holden Industrial."

"So they do," he says, stifling a yawn. "This is too much business speak for me."

"Apparently, they had a significant portfolio of H.I. equipment on their books, and the collapse of H.I. has had a knock-on effect on their customers and subsequently on them." I feel a twinge of guilt as I read that but push the feeling aside. "Here, this is significant. They have implemented cost-cutting measures, including some downscaling of the workforce, and ambitious and rigorous measures to optimise operational expenditure. This is corporate language, meaning cost-cutting across the whole company."

"Great," he says. "Why is this good for us?"

"We need to find out if the cost-cutting has included their IT department and systems. If it does, it may mean that they have not invested in any upgrades so far."

"Right," he says, finally latching on to what I'm looking for.

51

That evening, as we drive back to Camiro up in the hills, I can't suppress the conflicting thoughts that have come streaming back into my mind after reading so much about Hamlays and their desperate measures to overcome the turmoil in the aftermath of the H.I. fraud.

"How do you feel about this, Gilbert?"

"Feel about what?" he asks, hands on the steering wheel and yawning non-stop.

"Well, you know, what we're doing? Our research into what is a target at the end of the day."

"It was your idea, buddy," he replies.

"Yeah, it was. But nonetheless, how do *you* feel about it?" I persist.

"I don't mate," he says. "It's your shot. You're the secret undercover agent."

"Christ, Gilbert," I say with some alarm, "don't mention that, ever." Despite having informed Alexis, I don't want Gilbert spouting any of that to Sakura. "And anyway, this is no longer part of the undercover activities."

"Hey, relax, man, I won't," he says in an appeasing tone. "But, if there's money in it for me, mate, I'm happy to go ahead with it." We drive on in silence for a few minutes, the lights of the town receding as we start climbing up into the hills. "In any case," he adds, "I have no idea if it'll work. It's a bloody long shot."

"Yes," I say, "that too. But the moral side of things, doesn't that worry you? Plus, what happens if we get caught?"

"Caught? Who's going to catch us? It's not as if we walk in there with a cry of 'stick 'em up'. It'll be remote. All we need to do is make sure we cover our tracks, and they don't trace us back to here. We go through fake IPs and a VPN and a server farm somewhere like Lithuania or, even better, Russia. The biggest challenge is to get in."

"That reminds me, how can we be sure the seed and the beetle work?" I ask.

"We can't. I mean, we can only test it up to a certain point. Once it's embedded, it either works or it doesn't. No way of saying for sure whether it will."

"And – don't get me wrong, Gilbert – where did you get it? The beetle, bug or whatever you call it?"

He gives me a long, sideways look before answering. "Man, you're spoiling my mood. Where did I get it? It's not as if I bought it from a dodgy-looking bloke in an alley, like."

Now it is my turn to give him a long, sideways glance.

"What?" he asks, noticing my expression.

"Oh, come on, Gilbert. It's a legitimate question, don't you think?"

"All right, calm down. If you want to know, I wrote it myself."

"You did?" I ask, startled by this revelation.

"Yeah, when I was working for the bank in Paris, I became what they call an application manager. For Galileo. Which means I really got stuck in, like, right into the belly of the system. I took courses, learnt all about programming and when I realised my so-called partners were ripping me off, I decided to do something for myself.

I learnt the code that was used to develop Galileo. And I wrote my little program for myself."

"Hang on, but you never tried it out, or what?"

"I did. I designed it to work the way I told you. I sent it to myself at work. When I opened the attachment, the screening software on the terminal I used blocked it. So, I adjusted the setup and split the thing into seed and beetle. That worked."

"Wow, cool. And what happened then?"

"I got the seed embedded into the system and it parked itself in the designated gap. When I sent the trigger to activate, it didn't respond."

"Great, now that is reassuring."

"Hold on, I worked out why it didn't and I corrected the fault. I was about to start the process fresh when they nabbed me." He falls silent. We're out of town now, climbing higher into the hills. "It's probably still sitting there," he says after a minute or two.

"What?" And then I have a thought. "Ha ha, we could trigger it and hey, bingo, double wham."

We laugh all the remaining way until we reach the gates of Camiro.

52

"Any feedback so far?" I ask.

"No," comes his reply from across the office. "Not yet. You?"

"Friend request still unanswered."

"This is tedious business," Gilbert says, letting out a long sigh of frustration.

Gilbert has set up accounts for himself and me in various web-based platforms. Facebook, Instagram, LinkedIn and a couple of platforms where companies are rated from employees' point of view. He has spent days making our accounts look real. Adding fake CVs, fake background and photos to our social media accounts.

We have also made a long list of people who work or have worked at Canarus and cross-linked these to the social media platforms. It's been a tiring job, but we have a number of promising candidates. We have termed them candidates, almost as if we're recruiters. I suppose it *is* a form of recruitment. These are candidates who we think will chat openly about Canarus and candidates currently working for Canarus who might be the ones to pull the trigger for us.

Gilbert has contacted a guy working in Canarus's IT department. A request to link up on a platform that exists to broaden one's professional network. I have identified a woman who works in Canarus's sales team. I found her profile on one of the social media platforms and after having scrutinised her social activities and interests have sent her a friend request. We have designed one of my accounts to match hers as much as possible. She has a cat. I have a cat. She's into cooking. I'm into cooking. She's mid-fifties and single. I'm sixty and a widower. Gilbert has given me the name Hermann Meyer and profile photo that is far too handsome. We have done the same with other potential candidates, and now we're waiting to see if any will take the bait.

Whilst we're waiting, Gilbert has stripped his seed and his killer bug and checked and checked again that they work. "As far as I can tell, they work. Nothing more I can do," he's stated on several occasions before checking them again. Gilbert is right; it's a tedious business.

"Here, look," he says.

I rush over to his desk. "What?"

"Look at this," he says, showing me a message he's received. It's from an ex-employee. A guy who used to work in the Canarus IT department but has moved on. His verdict on Canarus as an employer is devastatingly negative.

Gilbert reads out a passage. "I can only advise you not to work for Canarus. They have cut costs to such an extent that the IT systems are totally outdated. Security is a joke! It's a disaster waiting to happen. And the pay is crap. No pay rises due to cost-cutting. Thank God there's a good market out there for IT professionals. Good luck."

Bad news for Canarus, but good news for us. We share a grin.

I return to my desk and am delighted to see that I have a message on my smartphone. My friend request has been accepted.

My turn to say, "Look at this." Gilbert now rushes over to my desk, and I show him.

"Right, Hermann, you ladies' man, get started," he says, laughing and slapping me on my shoulder.

There's one thing we haven't quite done yet. And it's proving to be a bit of a hard nut. How do we handle the money? That's if we succeed. It's a question that Alexis has been reluctant to answer as it means he has to give us access to his most secret of secrets: the setup of his illicit banking network. But without access, we can't organise the route the money will need to take. I understand his reluctance, but it's his contribution to this mission.

"Alexis, we need access; otherwise, we don't know how to route the money," I say to him that same evening as we sit in his den up in Camiro.

"I don't trust him, Neil," he says for the hundredth time.

"Then just show me."

He scrutinises me almost as if I'm a total stranger to him.

"All right," he says after a long moment. "Come round and I'll show you."

We sit side by side, and he takes me through the intricate banking network.

"What we need is an account with a bank that won't ask any questions," I say, thinking out loud.

"The Russians are good for that," he replies, and then shows me.

53

"Bloody hell, Neil." Gilbert laughs out loud. "You are a right Casanova."

I smile, but I don't feel happy about it like Gilbert does. The woman I have befriended, a woman called Kerstin, has taken the bait – hook, line and sinker. She's texting me non-stop about wanting to meet me. I'm having to think of one excuse after another why I can't. She's desperate, and her loneliness is painful to see.

But I have to concede, she's perfect. I have sent her stuff, recipes mainly, and she's reporting back that she has printed them off at work to take home and try out. She's asking for more and seems to have no qualms about printing off PDF files at work. She's everything we need.

And we have more. Gilbert has been messaging back and forth with the IT guy at Canarus. IT nerds exchanging intimate details. The guy would be sacked on the spot if anyone read what he's sharing with us. The main insight is that Canarus is still using the old version of the Galileo software. There's no budget for the upgrade.

With what we have now, we're ready to strike. All we need to figure out is the timing.

We sit down with Alexis and discuss our thoughts. At the end of this process, we have our projections. Kerstin has been instrumental in enabling us to do this. She likes a moan, especially when it comes to her workload. *It's so busy*, she keeps writing. Exactly how busy is the tricky thing to get out of her.

But I've found out that business is up. She states that she hasn't experienced such a rush like this towards the year end for years: *All these customers wanting to get their finance contracts processed before the year ends. They have all year to do that. Why do they all have to come now?*

I have tried to get hard facts, but Kerstin doesn't have access to that data, apart from the info she picks up in team meetings. And this information suggests the best time to strike will be the last week in November when the year-end rush reaches its climax. Two weeks to go.

We set out the details of our schedule. We decide on the exact timing. We plan as if it's a country we're invading, and an incidental reference to D-Day seals it: Operation D-Day.

And then the phone rings, and the hospital informs us Michalis has died.

54

Despite the fact that it's been on the cards for weeks, it's a paralysing shock. Alexis is shattered by Michalis's passing, and his pain at losing his partner and friend is tangible. A heavy grief descends on the house and stays there for days. Gilbert and I are the only people moving about the house and it's a surreal atmosphere in which we tread silently. After a couple of days and prompted by Gilbert, I decide to speak to Alexis.

"Alexis," I say to him as I discover him sitting in the darkness of his den, "I'm so sorry, and I hate to have to approach you in a time like this. If you want, we can postpone the mission or even cancel it."

"No," he says, his voice for once small and weak. He sits there, shrunken and empty. My heart aches for him.

"I'm so sorry, Alexis, I really am."

"Ah, Neil, it's a nasty trick the mind plays," he says, looking up at me. "An hour is always sixty minutes, and sixty minutes are always the same everywhere. A day is twenty-four hours, always the same time. And a year is always twelve months. It never changes; it's always the same amount of time. And yet I sit here and I look back on the many years I had with Michalis, and it seems to me as if it went by in a flash. What can I say? One moment you're living life together and the next he's fading and then he's gone. I can't find the words to describe the loss."

All I can do is nod my agreement. I make to speak, but he puts up a hand to stop me.

"And now, Neil, just do it."

We move to a rundown office complex in an equally rundown industrial estate destined to be knocked down and developed. It's a dreadful place, but it serves us well. Any fingerprints or other signs that we have been here will be lost in the dust and the rubble once the wrecking ball takes over. Alexis doesn't want us to be in his shiny office building down on the marina despite Gilbert's assurances that our activities can't be traced. But Alexis is doubtful, and I agree with him. In my experience, everything can be traced. Gilbert rolls his eyes but goes along with Alexis's decision.

D-Day arrives and we sit in the dusty and cold building at our monitors waiting for Alexis to arrive. He wants to be here and watch us perform our digital hit-and-run. He arrives, dressed in black. Not just because he's in mourning but also because he feels it's the right disguise. Black trousers, black shirt, black overcoat, black scarf and black hat. He even has sunglasses on. We suppress our smiles whilst he takes a seat in a corner watching us.

I have no idea what he's expecting to see, and his disappointment is great when he realises that all we do on D-Day is send an email. We make a show of it, but that's it.

"Okay," Gilbert says as we both sit side by side at our computers, staring at the monitors.

For Alexis's benefit we go through a checklist. But it's nonsense. Everything is prepared.

Admittedly, we have spent many hours drafting the email I will be sending to Kerstin. It has to look innocent, but it will have the seed in one of its attachments. She has to send them to the network printer and print them off.

Only if she does that will the seed be activated and detach itself from the PDF file and worm its way into the system.

Kerstin has been moaning that she's feeling worn out. She thinks she has a cold coming. I have researched and selected recipes for soul food, full of vitamins and energy. Gilbert has made PDF files out of these and buried the seed in one of them. I have been sending her very sympathetic messages, urging her to try them out once I send them to her. *I will*, she texted me back. *I need all the energy I can get.*

We go through the email one more time:

Kerstin, dearest,

Attached are the superb recipes I have put together for you. Believe me, they are fantastic and work wonders. Print them off at once and on your way home, pop into the supermarket to buy the ingredients. You'll see, you will be fit as a fiddle in a couple of days. Oh, and remember the ginger has to be fresh!

I wish I could be there to prepare this all for you.

Take care, dearest.

Hermann.

"Do you think it's too much?" I ask.

"No, and I like the bit with the ginger." He smiles at me.

"Okay. What's the time?"

"Coming up to three p.m. local time, Düsseldorf," he says.

"Right, she leaves work at four p.m. So, here goes…" I press the send button.

The email is carried off through the VPN Gilbert has set up and via several countries renowned for their nasty practices on the internet. Hopefully no one will be able to trace the email back to us. If they do, we trust in the efficiency of the wrecking ball.

Done, we lean back and turn to look at Alexis, who is stirring in his chair. "That's it?" he asks. We nod in affirmation.

"That's step one," I say. "If she does as we hope, she'll receive the email, send the PDF files to the network printer and then print them. If she does that, the seed will detach itself and do its work. Then we move on to step two."

"Hmm." Alexis sounds disappointed and certainly not convinced.

We wait an hour. 4 p.m. German time. I send Kerstin a message. I write: *Have you received my email? Don't wait, dear, go and get the ingredients. Guten Appetit und gute Besserung. (Enjoy your meal and get well soon.)* Finished with a smiley face. A few minutes later, she sends a message back: *My dearest Hermann, you are so good to me. I have and I've written down what I need to buy. I'd love for you to be here and to prepare this soul food for me. Kisses K.*

Big grins all around. Alexis is laughing as he steps outside into the corridor, where Vincent is waiting for him, and all the way down to where his black Mercedes is parked three floors below.

We watch the big black car drive off. I turn to Gilbert. "Now we have to prepare to send the killer bug."

"Yes, and that is when I pray it works."

"Why shouldn't it?" I ask with sudden unease.

"Because this is like driving in the dark with no lights on. I designed the seed so that I could ping it. Like a destroyer uses sonar to ping a submarine. To get an echo. But we can't do that. I can only hope the seed is where it's supposed to be."

55

We wait a day. And then we decide to wait another day. It's nerve-wracking, but we don't want to be too pushy.

Gilbert can't stand the tension and takes Sakura out for a change of scenery and some fresh air.

I mooch around the house.

"Hey, darling." Startled, I jump up. Zuki has appeared for the first time in days.

"Hey, honey," I say, taking her into my arms.

"What are you doing?" she asks and for a moment, I'm at a loss what to say.

"Waiting for you to come to me," I answer, kissing her gently on her forehead.

She smiles a tired and sad little smile at me. "Shouldn't you be at work?"

In fact, I should. That's what Alexis and I have agreed on. I'm now a general manager in his holding company.

"Yes, but I want to be here for you," I say, and it's the truth too. She takes me by the hand and leads me upstairs to our bedroom.

I'm back in the kitchen, Zuki fast asleep, when Gilbert and Sakura come back. He joins me.

"Right, let's do it," I say.

He comes to stand next to me as I open the social media app through which we send our messages. I type out a message: *Hello, dearest. Wie geht es dir? (How are you?)* I send it and we wait.

Nothing.

After several hours, still nothing.

Like tigers in a cage, we walk back and forth, checking the screen every few seconds. God, where is she? I ask over and over again. We need her to be at work in order to send the second email. We can't just send it and hope she opens it. We need confirmation that she's at her desk and primed for Hermann's next load of recipes.

Another two agonising days pass by.

And then I hear a chime. A new message has arrived. I rush to the smartphone.

Lieber Hermann, I'm so sorry. I have been so ill, she writes.

I can't help but let out a massive sigh of relief.

Meine liebe Kerstin, I'm so sorry to hear this. I was worried, I type. After a moment's thought, I add: *I have the right thing for you. To get you back on your feet. I'll send to your work email.*

Back at work tomorrow, she writes back, adding a smiley face and a kiss.

The next morning sees Gilbert and me hurtling down the road into Limassol and to our office in the derelict building. We fire up the computers and bring up the email we have prepared. Hunched over my computer, we carefully redraft the email:

Kerstin, dear,

I'm so sorry the soul food didn't help to fend off your cold. But I have the right thing for you: power smoothies!

These will have you up and running again in no time! Smiley face, smiley face…

We attach the PDF files we have now prepared. Gilbert buries the killer bug deep inside the first PDF attachment. We check our watches. Too early.

We sit and drink coffee, wait for the right time to come up.

"Right," I say as I check my watch. "I think we can send it out now."

"Okay," he says. "Do it!"

And I click on send.

56

Shortly before Kerstin usually leaves work, I send her a text message: *Did you receive my email, dearest?*

No reply.

"Damn," I say out loud. Gilbert chews his nails. But there's nothing to be done. We have to wait.

"If she's printed them off, then the killer bug is in the system," he says. "Let's assume she has."

"And then?" I ask.

"Depends on when the files are processed. If they do a night run, we should see tonight or first thing in the morning."

We decide to spend the night here. No point driving back to Camiro. We call Alexis and explain our plan.

"Okay," he says. "I'll tell the girls you are working on an urgent project. They're off early tomorrow morning anyway."

It's a pinprick reminder. Beyond these walls and our mission, there's a different life going on and the arrangements being made are of a totally different nature.

"Damn again," I say as we end the call. Gilbert nods. We should be there for the girls.

We stay up all night and I send Kerstin a message via the app at a time when I assume she might still be up. Still no reply, though.

Sleep is impossible. We sit and wait. After a while, Gilbert pops out and buys some food and beers. At least that makes the waiting easier.

At some point, I must have dozed off in the chair, as I awake wondering for a moment where I am. I check my watch: 4 a.m. I yawn, rise from my chair, my back killing me, and make some coffee. It's the only little luxury we have brought along with us.

Gilbert stirs, stretching his limbs, the stiffness visible in his face. "Jeez, what time is it?" he asks.

"Four a.m.," I say, stirring powdered milk into the instant coffee.

I hand him his mug, sit down at the computer and enter my password to clear the screensaver.

"Bloody hell," he says, taking a sip.

I turn back to the monitor, accessing the online bank account of the Russian bank.

"Jeez." Gilbert winces in pain, and I turn to look at him. "My tooth," he says, holding a hand to cover his mouth.

I turn back to the computer and stop in my tracks. "Look," I say, pointing at the screen.

He comes over, his tooth all forgotten.

The screen shows a balance of EUR 10,624,897.49.

A moment's shocked paralysis and then we whoop and we dance, embracing and clapping each other on the shoulders. It's bloody well worked and it's double what we had expected.

"Quick," I say, "we have to activate the transfer."

My hands fly over the keyboard. I enter the details and transfer everything out to the first of our offshore accounts. I look to see what Gilbert is doing. He's on the phone, big grin on his face, waiting for Alexis to answer his call.

57

We clear everything away, pack up the computers and monitors and load the car. Trying hard not to exceed the speed limits, we drive as fast as we dare back up into the hills to Camiro.

Erasure's "Ship of Fools" is belting out on the speakers as we get there. Alexis's signature tune. We walk into the kitchen laughing and congratulating ourselves on our success. Alexis stands by the fridge, opening a bottle of champagne. He's singing along as loud as he can, once more his ebullient self. He fills three glasses, and I'm glad the girls are away today.

"Boys!" he exclaims, embracing us again in a one-armed bear hug, the other arm outstretched, glass in hand, the champagne spilling over. He gulps down what's left in his glass and refills it. "Never dreamt that would work!" he cries out.

Gilbert is grinning and laughing, gulping down his champagne, intoxicated by the success of a plan he never thought he'd be able to put into action. Alexis gives me a tremendous slap on the shoulder that almost knocks me flying.

I'm as intoxicated by our success as they are, but I have felt the vibrations of my phone in my pocket, indicating incoming messages. I take out my phone and look at them. As I expected, they are from Kerstin.

The first message is timestamped 7:30 a.m. local time that morning: *Hermann, you won't believe what is happening here.*

We have been the victim of a cyber-attack. How awful. The whole company is in panic.

The next message sent at 8:32 a.m. local time: *Police are here. Internal auditors are investigating. It is so dreadful.*

The third message was sent a few minutes ago: *Hermann, they are saying the cyber-attack was triggered through an email and infected documents. A virus in a PDF file. I am deeply worried.*

My mind is in turmoil. I feel bad. Very bad. I have a pain in my chest and I feel nauseous. I feel the blood drain from my face and grab the nearest solid object to steady myself. Gilbert is standing a couple of feet away from me, jumping from one foot to the other, totally intoxicated. I can sense he's already dreaming of what he can do with the money. We agreed a three-way split. One-third each: three and half million each.

Alexis stands, refilling his glass, but he's watching me. He's still grinning, but his eyes are not. He comes over to me, takes me by the arm and leads me out to the courtyard pool. He gently pushes me into a chair by the poolside table. Sitting down opposite, he looks at me intently. I just sit there, totally drained, feeling giddy with guilt.

"You have to think about yourself, Neil, and what makes you tick," he says in an almost fatherly tone of voice. "Are you cut out for this? This is nothing casual anymore. You left that behind when you came here." His tone becomes firmer. "You wanted this. You had the plan and you executed it."

For a long moment, I'm unable to put my thoughts into words. "I know," I say after a while.

I have nothing better to say. Inside, my emotions are in a tangle. I feel so guilty. Lives have been damaged; Kerstin's texts are just a prelude of what will happen to her once the facts become clear. I look up at him. His face is a mask. And I realise once more that he's capable of putting on masks at the snap of a finger. For all the jovial and benevolent appearances, inside, I know him now to be a ruthless man. Once again, I have that sensation of him being able to read my mind.

"If you don't want this kind of life, you will have to make a choice. You now have the means at your disposal to lead a different life, which is what you wanted. I will accept that and think no worse of you."

A new track comes thundering out of the speakers. Gilbert has gone through Alexis's collection of CDs in the kitchen and found something. ABBA's "Money, Money, Money" bounces off the walls. We sit listening to the beat and the lyrics. After a moment, I feel a smile spreading on my lips. Alexis breaks into a smile, too. And then we both laugh and start singing out loud: "*Money, money, money…*"

58

Zuki and I spend New Year's Eve in Limassol. We stay at one of the most expensive hotels – a gift from Alexis. I still wonder how much Zuki knows, and I expect her to broach the subject – perhaps today? Despite the diversion that Michalis's passing away created, Zuki can't have been that blind not to wonder what Gilbert and I were up to. That story about a miracle business deal, she can't have believed any of it. Gilbert is hardly being discrete either, splashing money about and buying Sakura everything she wants.

"Neil," she calls out to me as she comes through from the bathroom. Dressed in a fluffy bathrobe with a towel wrapped around her wet hair, she looks like a fluffy teddy. I grin at her as she comes to sit on the bed by my side.

"What?" I say, noticing that her expression is earnest and she's searching my face. I turn the volume down on the TV and face her. I reach for her hand, worried now.

She smiles at me, opens the top drawer of the bedside table and takes out a piece of paper. She looks at it intently for a moment before passing it over to me.

"What is it?" I ask. I look at the paper, which is a black and white printout. I don't know what it is. She laughs as she sees my look.

"Neil," she says, her eyes fixed on mine. "I'm pregnant."

I realise in that instant why she never mentioned or asked anything. I had it all wrong. She had a different priority. For a split second I'm shocked. But then I feel an elation growing inside me that becomes so powerful I hug her, tears welling up in my eyes now, too. "Oh, Zuki," I say. "Zuki, that's…just…amazing."

Alexis hugs us so hard when we get back that I´m worried he might cause Zuki some damage. But she just laughs when I tell Alexis to go easy on her. Isabelle leads her inside like a poor, ill woman. Alexis and I roll our eyes. We speak to Sakura and Gilbert in the US where they have now moved to via video chat.

We inform Naomi, Zuki's mum. After she drops the bomb, she passes the phone over. Naomi is delighted despite the fact she's only ever heard my name before. What an introduction, I think.

In a rush to call Ben, I grab my old smartphone and we ring him. He dashes round to my mum's house, ringing us back via video call on the mobile. Zuki and I sit huddled together so Mum can see us on the small display. She, too, is delighted, taking to Zuki immediately, even if she can't refrain from chiding me.

I'm sitting in a café waiting for Zuki after her doctor's appointment when a figure appears at my side, pulls out the chair opposite and sits down. I give a start when I look up and see it's Alice.

"I suppose congratulations are in order," she says, smiling at me.

"You what?" I say dumbfounded.

"It's the only time that app worked the way it was supposed to," she says.

"Sorry?" I say, not understanding a word.

"That app John installed, it can do more than you think, Neil."

"I don't understand."

"It can listen in on conversations," she explains. "That's how I know."

"Good lord," I mumble, trying to grasp just what this implies.

"Don't worry," she says, "your secret is safe with me. I made sure of that."

I sit studying her for a long moment. She just smiles at me.

"What happened?" I ask. "I never heard from you anymore."

"No," she concedes. Her coffee arrives and she takes a sip.

"Is this an official visit?" I sense something isn't quite right.

"I'm on my holidays," she says. "Cyprus seemed like a nice place."

"I still don't understand," I say, that feeling of panic still with me.

"Oh, Cannes wasn't just a game changer for you, Neil. It was for me, too."

I wait for her to go on.

"You know John and I had a fling," she says.

"Yes, well, you weren't too discreet about it," I reply. "Thin walls in that hotel," I add as she looks at me, searching her memory.

"Oh, okay." She laughs.

"What happened, Alice?"

"Well, that little fling, it's cost me my career," she says with a note of sadness she can't disguise. She sighs. "Long story, but the agency doesn't approve of company relationships. John killed it and, in the process, killed me, too. I'm out."

"I'm sorry to hear that, Alice," I say, meaning it. Despite her resigned appearance, I can sense the inner turmoil and anger underneath. "What are you going to do now?"

"Find a new job." She gives me a long look. "Or a new vocation, like you." She smiles at me again.

Nerves tingling, I just stare at her.

"You wouldn't have anything to do with the cyber-attack on that bank in Germany, would you?" she asks as a "by the way".

"Cyber-attack?" I ask, overdoing the innocence, I realise. She smiles. "No. But as you know, I'm working for Alexis. I sent you all those messages but never got a reply. Mission was successful," I say, thinking at the same time how to possibly spin this.

She puts a hand on my arm. "Don't bother, Neil. I'm good at my job." She then finishes her coffee and makes to get up.

"Alice," I say. She pauses, looking at me. "I'm sorry things turned out like that for you."

"Don't be," she says. "A bitter lesson learnt." She turns to leave, but stops. "And Neil, get rid of those phones. Bury them deep. And never forget Neil – you got away this one time."

"I don't know what you mean," I reply. "I returned the money to you and John."

She gives me a look and what one would call a knowing smile. I wonder just how she can know.

"They're out to get you, and Cyprus isn't a safe haven. Crime never pays. You'll be on the run forever."

Alice hands me a card. I look at it. Her name, telephone number and email address.

She puts on her sunglasses and shoulders her handbag. "As I say, a new vocation maybe. Give me a call if you need intelligence. I might just become a freelancer…like you," she says before walking over to the door and out into the sunshine.

The End

14326438R00208